THE
FALLEN
GATEKEEPERS

EXTENDED EDITION

C. R. Fladmark

THE
FALLEN
GATEKEEPERS

EXTENDED EDITION

A Novel

C. R. Fladmark

SHOKUNIN

The Fallen Gatekeepers is a work of fiction. Names, characters, places and
events portrayed in this book are the product of the author's imagination
or used fictitiously. Any resemblance to actual persons, living or dead,
events or locales is entirely coincidental and not intended by the author.

Fladmark, C.R.
The Fallen Gatekeepers / by C.R. Fladmark.
Second Edition – Extended Version
ISBN: 9780993777660 (eBook)
ISBN: 9780993777677 (trade paperback)

Edited by Shannon Roberts (www.editorialdepartment.com)
Support Services by Ryder Author Resources (www.ryderswriters.com)
Japanese Calligraphy by Yuriko Ho-sen

Printed in the U.S.A and internationally.

First Edition: February 2017
Second Edition – Extended Version: October 2018

10 9 8 7 6 5 4 3 2 1

For Alexis,
who makes my novels far better than I ever could on my own

CHAPTER

1

THE AIR SHIMMERED AS SHOKO MATERIALIZED, kneeling on the damp grass of the San Francisco Presidio grounds, not far from my house. She wore modern clothing today, a short, pleated skirt and a tight white T-shirt under a black leather jacket. She had a racquet case slung over her shoulder. Her *wakizashi*—a short curved Japanese sword—would be inside.

She stood up, hands on hips, and looked around.

I'd already made sure no one was nearby. I could sense things, what I called tapping into the *stream*. I could sense emotions and thoughts—sometimes more that I wanted to—and most importantly, danger.

I did a quick energy sweep again just in case. I picked up the happy energy of the kids in the nearby park and the darker, discontented energy of their parents. The only energy I recognized was distant. My dad was at home, which was the reason I'd met Shoko here. He didn't know about my other life.

"I am sorry to be late again, Junya," she said in Japanese, looking serious as usual. "The Elders think I require no sleep."

"I'm just glad you came," I replied in Japanese. While my dad was Caucasian, my mother—my *Okaasan*—was Japanese, so it was my first language.

She smiled up at me. "I have missed you." When she took my hands, I gasped as her energy, pure and sweet, flooded into me. We stared at each for a long moment.

"Me too," I said.

She pulled back and inspected me. "How are your wounds?"

I reached up to rub my left shoulder where the giant lizard had bitten me.

"Not bad. Only hurts sometimes." I lifted my arm, rotated my shoulder. "And it's stiff in the mornings."

"And your leg?"

"Almost as good as new." My limp was barely noticeable.

"And ... your blood?"

"It's still red." After I'd been bitten by Bartholomew, the leader of the Evil Ones, and infected with his poisonous blood, I pricked my finger every morning to check, though I hadn't done that in a while. If it hadn't turned black by now, it probably wouldn't.

She looked relieved. "Good."

I smiled. "So today, I really want to show you the Christmas decorations at Pier 39. You've got to see—"

She shook her head. "I have something better in mind. That is, if you will allow me to choose?" She made it sound like a question, but we both knew it wasn't.

I hesitated. "Sure, I guess so ..."

She grinned. "Good! I will be right back."

She dropped to one knee and slapped her left palm onto the grass. The rush of energy blew outward, sending the fallen leaves whirling in every direction as she vanished.

I stuffed my hands into my coat pockets and leaned against a tree, waiting for whatever surprise Shoko had in mind. I was curious, but a little disappointed. With Christmas only two weeks away, I wanted to show her the huge tree they'd put up at Pier 39.

When Shoko reappeared about ten minutes later, she wore a long thick skirt, a wool sweater and high boots, with a sheathed *katana*— a curved Japanese long sword—pushed through her waistband. She also carried a heavy-looking duffle-type bag.

"You look like you're dressed for the North Pole."

"We are going to the world's tallest mountains," she said, smiling brightly. "I want to visit a hot spring there."

"Which would require *traveling*..." Traveling was how Shoko and her people moved between our worlds, and to places within each. I hadn't traveled since I left the ancient shrine in Izumo last summer, bitten, bleeding, and with a death sentence on my head.

"I will do all the work," she said.

I eyed her with suspicion. "What are you up to?"

She looked down, as if she'd become quite interested in something on the ground. "I have found a new remedy."

"Shoko …"

"You will not have to eat anything bad this time, I promise." Her long lashes blinked at me. "These hot springs are said to heal skin afflictions."

I tapped my shoulder. "This is a bit more than a skin affliction." We both knew there was poison in there.

"Still, it may ease the pain." Then she stepped closer. "Would you rather we did not go to the hot springs, alone and far away from here?"

"Just us … alone?"

She nodded, smiling again. "And the remedy, of course."

I eyed her for a moment longer, then reached down and lifted the duffle bag. It was heavy. I took her hand and pulled her toward the ground. "Let's go!"

She slapped her hand on the grass and the world around me disappeared as we tumbled in swirling darkness. My stomach rose into my throat and my skull felt like it would crack open, just like it felt the first time I'd done this many months before. Only the feel of

Shoko's hand holding mine kept me from screaming out.

"Breathe deep, Junya," Shoko said, sounding far away. "Welcome to Tibet."

It took a few minutes before I managed to open one eye. I sat up. Knee-high grass surrounded us for miles in all directions. The landscape rippled in the wind like the surface of a lake, swirling over rolling hills until the land rose and the grass thinned out, replaced by desolate rock that climbed toward the sky—and the sky, my God! It was so blue, so close. Snow-capped mountains rose in the distance. Were those really the Himalayas?

The wind's bite made me shudder and I struggled into a thick coat Shoko pulled from her bag.

She smiled. "This is better than your plan, yes?"

"It's hard to compete with you."

Shoko pointed to a small stone building on the mountain slope above us. "That is the shrine to the god of these hills."

I eyed the tiny building. It was a humble home for a god—smaller than your average bathroom—but it was well built. The stones fit tightly together and the carvings on the freshly painted red door were intricate. Someone had recently swept the front steps.

"There is a gateway inside the shrine, a passageway *across* to the Other Side—my side," she said as we walked closer to it. "I am told their shaman still holds the ancient ceremony every twenty-four moons."

"Why every twenty-four moons ... months?"

"That is when the gateway opens."

There was a lot I still didn't know about the parallel world Shoko came from.

"Could I watch a ceremony sometime?"

She gave me a curt nod. "Yes, but I will take you to an important ceremony," she said. "This god has grown weak, a mere shadow of what it was when its people roamed proud and free in these mountains."

"What weakened it?"

4

"A god's power depends upon its number of worshipers."

I looked at the little shrine. "Maybe we should say hello then."

Shoko nodded her approval. "Yes, we should."

We held our hands in prayer position and clapped twice, to get the god's attention, I presumed. I didn't know what Shoko would say to it, or even what I should say, but I did my best.

So, hello there ... mountain god. I hear you don't have many worshipers anymore, but this place is awesome ... I think you're still needed here so maybe—

Shoko's double clap interrupted me. She was done.

"It is okay that he is weak now," Shoko said as we continued on our way. "I am told he was inclined toward war, far more than most other gods."

"You know a lot about this place," I said. "Have you been here before, or are you showing off how smart you are?"

She gave me a mischievous smile. "Both. I needed to test the hot springs myself, but I was on my side. There is no village there, as there is on this side."

"What village?"

She pointed to a narrow river that flowed through the valley below us. Trees grew beside it, following its twisting course, and beneath them was a scattering of square stone buildings. I didn't see any roads leading to the village, but in the distance, a line of pavement sliced through the grasslands and led to a modern-looking town.

We waded through the grass toward the buildings.

"Are the hot springs in the village?" I asked.

"No, but out of respect, I will ask permission to use the springs."

We were still some distance away when a young girl wearing a bright, colorful outfit ran toward us. When she got close, Shoko said something in a language I'd never heard before.

The girl stopped, her big brown eyes glued on Shoko. Then she motioned for us to follow and ran back to the village.

"What did you say to her?"

"That I wanted to see their shaman." Shoko frowned. "I know

they are not accustomed to visitors, but ..."

I glanced at her katana. "Well, you are kind of a scary visitor."

By the time we reached the edge of the village, three men were waiting. They were dark-skinned and sturdy-looking, dressed in leggings and layers of shirts that reached their knees. The girl stood a few yards behind them.

"Something's wrong," I whispered to Shoko. "Their energy is anxious ... and sad."

"Thank you for telling me." She smiled. "If you want to understand this language, tap into the *stream* and listen."

Why not? I began to build energy within myself and felt a small warm glow in my chest.

"Not energy, Junya. Just listen." Then she put her hands together and bowed to the men. I did the same.

"Welcome," the oldest man said as he returned the bow. It took me a second to process that I *had* understood him.

"Je-tsun ..." He indicated the girl behind him. "... said you wish to greet our shaman."

"I wish to extend greetings from Izumo."

The two older men didn't react, but the youngest one, a boy about our age, looked dumbfounded.

"Did you say... *Izumo?*" he said.

Shoko nodded. "Yes, and we seek permission to visit your sacred hot springs."

Before anyone could reply, the boy fell to his knees, his eyes locked on Shoko.

The oldest man stared down at the boy. "What is this about, Gyurmi?"

"She ... she is a Gatekeeper from the Grand Shrine of Izumo Oyashiro. They are the protectors and servants of the gods."

"How do you know what I am?" Shoko's energy changed. She suddenly looked regal and powerful.

He kept his head lowered. "I went *across* last time, to the gods' realm, with our shaman. Gatekeepers greeted us as we arrived on the

Other Side." He hesitated, then seemed almost relieved. "Did you come because of the killing?"

Shoko and I exchanged a look.

"Who was killed?" I was sure I'd butchered their language, but the old man seemed to understand me.

"Our shaman," he said. "His body was torn apart, as if by some wild animal."

Shoko pointed down at the boy. "Who is he?"

"This is Gyurmi. He is … was … our shaman's apprentice."

Shoko nodded slowly. "Are there wild animals near here?" I noticed her hands now rested on the hilt of her katana.

The man nodded. "Yes, but they are seldom seen anymore."

Gyurmi straightened but stayed on his knees. "Honorable Gatekeeper." He looked scared now. "Our old stories talk of a lizard, the Black Life-Stealing Fiend. There are those here who believe this beast came in the night and killed our shaman."

Shoko glanced at me. "May we see the body?" she asked.

The oldest man shook his head. "The death was reported to the Chinese. They came and took the body even as we were preparing for the funeral."

"Did something …" I struggled with the words, still unsure they'd understand me as easily as I understood them. "… something happen before he was killed?"

Gyurmi answered without hesitation. "Nothing. It is a quiet time for him."

"When does the gateway next open?" Shoko asked.

"Not until next year's winter solstice." The anxiety was plain in the old man's voice. "Do you think the Black Life-Stealing Fiend did this?"

"I do not know." Shoko turned to me and said in Japanese, "Do you?"

I hesitated, then turned to the men. "Can you show me the place it happened?"

They led us upstream, well beyond the last house in the village, where a humble stone house stood in a small clearing. It overlooked a deep pool of water. A good fishing spot, I decided. They all looked at me expectantly, even Shoko, so I closed my eyes and let my energy flow.

"Just listen!" she said in Japanese. "How many times must I say that?"

I shot her a look, not happy to get a scolding in front of the men. They may not have understood, but I was sure they *understood*. An irritated woman sounds the same in any language.

"I've never tried to sense Evil Ones after the fact," I said. Without waiting for a reply, I walked into the little house.

My shoulder started to ache. I froze, confused. When I squatted, the ache increased, and as I touched the floor, my shoulder exploded in pain.

I jerked my hand back. No question: Evil Ones had been here.

I'd been able to sense danger for a while now, like a cringing feeling in my neck. And I could feel the energy of people around me if I tried. But this ache, still radiating from the scar on my shoulder, was new and the worst thing I'd felt by far.

Shoko stood at the doorway. "What do you sense?" She asked in Japanese.

"Evil Ones were here. At least two."

Shoko's eyes narrowed. "As men or giant lizards?"

Komodo Dragon would be a better description of the shape-shifting creature that had bit my shoulder and arm. "I thought they couldn't transform on this side."

"As far as I know they cannot." She glanced outside at the group gathered there. "But they said his body was torn apart."

A shiver ran up my spine. When I'd first seen an Evil One, on a bright San Francisco street, he'd looked like a man. But it was his eyes—black holes in his face—that got my attention. When I'd cornered him, he'd hissed and flicked out a thin, forked tongue, which had freaked the hell out of me. But when I saw them shapeshift into giant lizards, I hadn't been *here*, in this world. It was some version of a place I recognized as Zion National Park in Utah, but in an alternate reality, so that's the name I used for it. But could they shapeshift here, in my world? I sure as hell hoped not.

I stood up. "I can't tell, but if they can have a lizard tongue here, why not the whole body?"

Shoko pursed her lips as she looked outside. "What should I tell them?"

I thought for a minute. "Probably not the whole truth," I said. "They're already pretty freaked out."

We stepped back outside.

"The sensation of evil lingers," she said in their language. "It was something with wicked intent, no doubt about that."

All three men took a step backward. The girl, who'd followed us here, did not.

"What should we do?" the old man said, his fear palpable. He looked at Gyurmi. "You're the shaman now, tell us!"

The boy's anxiety spiked. He wasn't ready for this.

"Do as your traditions dictate," Shoko said. "Perform your rituals to cleanse the village of this evil."

Fear showed in Gyurmi's eyes, and I heard the whisper of his thoughts: *What if they come for me?*

I passed it into Shoko's mind.

"I doubt they will come again." Shoko looked from me to him. "Not once you perform your rituals."

I nodded. "They were only men," I said, though I was positive they weren't. "Strong men like you can easily stop them."

The old man looked relieved and stood a bit taller. "We will see that no more cowards sneak into our village!"

The man who had remained silent until now bowed to us. "Thank you for visiting," he said. "Please enjoy the hot springs with our blessings."

As the men turned to go, the girl didn't move. Gyurmi touched her shoulder.

"Come Je-tsun, you should not be here."

She ignored him and looked at Shoko. "I want to be a Gatekeeper too."

Shoko smiled at her. "You are strong. Become stronger and we shall see."

Je-tsun stared at Shoko a moment longer, then grinned and ran after the men.

"Why would Evil Ones come here?" I asked Shoko after we were away from the village. I was following in the path she made in the long grass. "This isn't exactly a popular spot."

"I do not know," she said over her shoulder. "But I wonder if this is connected."

"To what?"

She slowed so I could come up beside her. "Since the last winter solstice, before I met you, our recordkeepers noticed a subtle change in the number of crossings. Sometimes gateways opened, but no one came across."

"Isn't that a good thing?"

"Not everything that crosses over is bad," she said, walking beside me now. "Spiritual leaders, those we refer to as shamans, cross over and commune with their deities, just as our own Elder, the *Kannushi,* does with ours. But the last five hundred years have been hard on the gods." She shook her head sadly. "So many religions wiped out in the name of another God. And without belief, without worship, the god's power withers away."

High above us, a huge bird—maybe an eagle—circled. Its high-pitched screech sent a shiver up my spine.

"What does all this have to do with the dead shaman back there?"

"Evil Ones have hunted shamans for as long as they have both existed," Shoko said as we walked on. "If they find a shaman performing a ceremony, there is usually an open gateway nearby, and the Evil Ones will try to get through to attack the land of the gods."

"But the guy back there said the gateway won't open until next year's winter solstice."

She looked at me. "Exactly, so why would an Evil One be here?"

We were quiet for a while. The only sound was the wind in the grass and the eagle's cry. Finally, Shoko turned back to me.

"Perhaps this is not the only shaman who has fallen victim." She looked troubled. "Perhaps they have not been crossing over because there is nobody left to cross."

CHAPTER

2

WE CAME TO A THICK STAND of bushes and trees, an odd thing in the endless sea of grass. As soon as we started along the thin trail between the trees, I heard falling water. Suddenly we were there. A steaming pool of jade green water about thirty feet across, fed by a half-round waterfall about ten feet high.

Shoko pulled a thick towel from her pack and handed it to me. "The falling water on the left is spring water," she said. "Very hot so stay away. The smaller falls carry cold water from a nearby stream. It is the perfect temperature at this end." As if to prove it, she knelt and dipped her hand in. She nodded her approval. "You may go first."

"Are you sure?" I said. "Aren't you cold?"

"The air is warmer here. Go ahead."

"Turn around then." When she did, I stripped to my boxers. I wasn't going in naked, even though that was the Japanese way. Not with her here.

The water stung, that moment when your body can't decide if

something's ice cold or boiling hot. I figured it was probably about 105 degrees, and I cringed as I sunk in.

I pushed through the water toward her. She was mashing something in her hands.

"What's that?" I asked.

"The remedy I spoke of."

"I thought the hot spring was the remedy."

"When combined with this." She showed me a ball of brown paste. "A *Miko*, one of our medicine women, gave me this."

A Miko willing to help me? "I thought I was public enemy number one in Izumo."

"You confused a lot of people, especially our spiritual Elder, the Kannushi," she said, her voice a bit strained as she continued working the paste. It looked pretty firm.

"He didn't seem confused when he sentenced me to die." Besides being a high priest in Shoko's world, the Kannushi was also a senior Elder, able to decree a death sentence, and he wasn't very happy with me that last time I'd seen him.

She sat down on a rock and continued mashing.

"You rescued me from an evil world—the place you call Zion—where no one with a pure heart can go, let alone come back from. Then you spoke to and received a reply from the gods of Izumo, something only the Kannushi has ever done."

"But—"

"And you were bitten by Bartholomew, the leader of the Evil Ones while in Zion, and infected with a poison that no one had ever survived." She held up the paste. "What did you expect? It was as if Bartholomew himself were standing before us."

The hot water did nothing to stop the cold lump that formed in my stomach.

"Is that what you thought?"

She didn't look up. "Of course not. You rescued me. I had no doubt of your pure heart." She tossed the paste to me. "Stand up and spread it onto your scars."

14

The paste was strangely warm. Was that from her hands, her energy, or something else?

"You will need to stay above the water for a while."

"But it's freezing out here!"

"Suffering promotes discipline."

It wasn't long before my teeth began to chatter. I wrapped my arms around my chest. "How l–l–long?" I was sure my lips were blue.

She shrugged. "The Miko did not say."

"Then w–w–why—?"

She started to laugh.

I dropped back into water. "Argh, you're so mean!" When she laughed harder, I splashed her.

After she made sure I wasn't going to splash her again, she said, "Does your shoulder feel different?"

"It's tingling." As to whether it felt *better*, I couldn't say, but she looked so hopeful I didn't want to disappoint her.

"Good!" Then her expression changed, and she stared at me. A smile flicked at the corners of her mouth.

"What?"

"I have never seen you with your shirt off."

"You did in the dojo." Oh shit, that hadn't been her. Bartholomew had sent a copy of Shoko to seduce me, and when that failed, it burned down our family training dojo with me inside. I got out just in time.

Shoko crossed her arms. "I do not like that my evil twin saw you naked."

I sank further into the water. "I only had my shirt off."

"It is rare I see any man with his shirt off, other than my father," she said, her smile returning. "But the ones I have seen look nothing like yours. Your body is … I like it."

"I do work out a lot" Then I gave her a mischievous smile. "Does your body look like your evil twin's?"

She made a face. "You will risk being cut down to find out?"

I laughed and felt good inside. The only part of her not covered by heavy clothing was her face, and it looked cute surrounded by the furry hat. She looked like a happy teenage girl, but I knew that in a second, her expression could be replaced by the face of a warrior.

Her eyes met mine and held them.

"Why do you like to kiss me?" she said.

I wasn't expecting that. I'd given her a peck on the cheek a few times but wasn't brave enough to try her lips.

"Because I like you," I said.

"You like Mack and you do not kiss him."

I rolled my eyes. "I like you in a different way." I studied her. She looked distracted. "Why, don't you like it?"

She brushed a strand of hair out of her face with a gloved hand. "For me it is just ..." A few seconds ticked by. "I do not know."

"Oh ..." was all I could manage at first. "I thought you liked it too." Something wasn't adding up. "And you said you wanted to come here so we could be alone."

"Why do you want to be alone with me?"

Good grief. "Ah ... because being alone gives us a chance to get to know each other better."

She tilted her head and looked at me. "What else is there to know?"

"Well, like ... what's your favorite color?

"And if I tell you this, you will be happy?"

"Yes ... well, no. If you learn things like that about each other, it makes you closer, you know?"

"That sounds stupid."

I ran my hand over my face to clear the sweat off.

"That's just an example. There's other stuff too." And that was just it. I did want to know her better, but how could I when she responded like that?

She stood up. "You have been in there long enough." She didn't sound happy anymore. "It is my turn now."

I got out and wrapped s towel from the duffel bag around myself. I couldn't feel the cold yet. I was still too hot from the steaming water. As I toweled off, she removed her jacket and began to untie her belt. More layers came off and she laid them next to her sword.

"Please hurry," she said, her back to me. "It is cold, and I cannot get undressed while you are here."

I struggled into my clothes and heavy jacket as quickly as I could. By then she was down to a thin inner layer, somewhat like a nightgown.

"Go up there while I get in." She pointed toward the trail. "And no peeking."

With a sigh, I tromped up the trail the way we'd come.

"Okay, you're safe now," I called over my shoulder when I thought I was far enough. Then I looked back to make sure. Too soon!

She was naked, barely up to her knees in the water, turned slightly away, her katana held above the water with her left hand. The afternoon sun touched her skin, lit the curves of her body. I held my breath until she sank into the water. Then I spun back around and faced up the trail. My heart raced. She was the first girl I'd seen naked. The first *real* girl I mean.

"Oooh, it is perfect!" she said. I didn't reply. After a few minutes, she called, "Junya?"

"Yeah?" I tried to sound innocent.

"You can come back now."

I walked extra slow. She was in up to her neck, her katana on a rock beside her, always within reach. I sat down and tried not to look at her in case the guilt showed on my face, but I couldn't get the image of her out of my head. Plus, she was still completely naked, with only the sheen on the water to hide it.

She looked up at me. "It is time you tried traveling again, on your own."

My eyes popped open. "Shoko—"

She held up a hand. "Your training is not complete, and you cannot move forward if you refuse to try." When I didn't reply, her eyes narrowed. "Are you still afraid you will summon Bartholomew's evil power?"

"I don't think *afraid* is the right word."

"It is the Mother Earth's energy that we use to travel." She let out a frustrated grunt. "You are always shooting out your energy like a dog peeing on a tree, here and there, everywhere. It is unnecessary. You let Bartholomew—"

"Why do you have to keep throwing that in my face?" I glared at her. "You have no idea what it's like having his energy inside."

She crossed her arms. "Do not be weak, Junya. I do not like that."

"Being *wary* of Bartholomew's energy doesn't make me weak. It means I'm smart."

She muttered something I couldn't hear and looked skyward. For a second, I considered traveling out and leaving her there. Of course, I knew I couldn't and that made me feel even worse.

After a few minutes, the splashing of water made me look at her. She was moving her hands back and forth, making small waves. When she saw me looking, her expression softened.

"I am sorry, Junya. You faced a dozen lizards to save me." Her body gave a little shudder, then her expression changed. "You are very strong ... and very brave."

I smiled and felt heat rise in my cheeks for the first time in months.

She sent me back up the trail again before she got out. I told myself to be a gentleman and not peek. I succeeded, but barely.

When she came up the trail a few minutes later, she looked at me with an odd expression.

"It is blue," she said.

I stared at her, confused.

"Like the color of the sky right before dawn," she said. "That is my favorite color."

CHAPTER

3

"THAT'S INTENSE," MY BEST FRIEND MACK SAID when I finished telling him about visiting Tibet with Shoko. We were walking up the hill from the bus stop, on our way to the last day of school before Christmas break, not that it mattered much to me. I'd been doing a computer-based distance-learning thing since September while I recovered from my injuries, but I still had to show up at school every few weeks for tests and assignments I couldn't do online.

"You think *they* killed him?" Mack said.

I smacked his arm. "Shut up, will ya?!"

"Who cares?" He waved a hand, dismissing everyone around us. "They're oblivious."

Mack's nonchalant attitude toward my new life had taken a while to develop. I'd started by telling him the *normal* stuff, like how the chief financial officer of my grandpa's company, Walter Roacks, had skimmed millions and dumped it in offshore accounts, nearly bankrupted the company.

Then there was the part Mack knew a bit more about, like how Walter had hired mercenaries to kill me after I became my grandfather's heir. Then when I hacked Walter's bank accounts and took all his money, he couldn't pay the mercenaries, so they came after me, and my family, to collect. Mack got caught up in that part.

"You still haven't explained what happened in the warehouse that day," he'd said when we talked about my confrontation with the mercenaries in a building owned by my grandfather. "When they dragged me out of the truck, you stood all alone in the middle of the warehouse with about a dozen soldiers facing you. Maybe you thought I was unconscious, but I saw the way you moved. You were like, in fast motion, zooming across the room."

"Yeah ... something happened to me in there," I said. "Sergeant Jackson had—"

"Who?"

"Sergeant Jackson, the mercenary leader," I said. "He's the one who kicked you when they dragged you out of the truck."

Mack nodded. "Ah, that asshole. I remember him."

"After I saw my mom—my Okaasan—had a gunshot wound and you were beat up, I kind of snapped. Then things got weird. When Sergeant Jackson ordered a bunch of his guys to take me down, time sort of slowed down, so kicking the crap out of them was easy."

"Easier than usual, you mean?" Mack knew how well I could fight.

"Right. Then Jackson got pissed and shot at me—"

"I remember that too," Mack said. "I think that's what woke me up again, the gunfire."

I nodded. "I don't really know what happened, but I raised my palm, and ..." I tried to find the right words. "... everything froze except the bullets, and they flew by me at a walking pace. Pretty easy to avoid. I walked over to Okaasan and gave her a *katana*, a Japanese long-sword, then I took Jackson out. After that, everything started moving full speed again."

"And your mom lopped that guy's head off and the police came storming in and shot all the bad guys."

I nodded. "And after that I went after Bartholomew." This was the hard part, because I first needed to explain about Shoko and the world she lived in. How the Gatekeepers, a bunch of female samurai-like warriors, kept the realm of the gods safe from invaders.

"When I got to Zion, Bartholomew's realm, he tried to convince me that everyone was against me, even Shoko."

"You believed that?"

"I still thought it was her who'd tried to kill me by burning down the dojo. Bartholomew gave me the opportunity to kill her as revenge."

Mack's eyes went wide. "He actually thought you'd kill Shoko?"

I needed to take a deep breath. "I was so mad at her, felt so betrayed ... but when I looked at her, really listened with my senses, I realized Bartholomew had tricked me and I ended up fighting a bunch of these shape-shifting lizards—"

"Hold up," he said. "Shape-shifting lizards?"

That's when I'd told him about the Evil Ones, how they could turn into lizards and how Bartholomew had nearly bitten my arm off.

He stared at me for a long moment. "A shape-shifting lizard-man bit you?" He started to laugh. "You're so full of shit!"

I grabbed the hem of my T-shirt and pulled it over my head. Eight ragged holes, now scarred over and pink, curved across my left shoulder onto my bicep in a wide semicircle.

His jaw nearly hit the ground.

I turned so he could see the matching scars on my back.

"I promised I wouldn't lie to you," I said.

He blew out his breath. "Shit, no wonder you couldn't see me all summer."

"I'm sorry, Mack." I had to look away. "I was really sick. The lizard's bite is poisonous, usually deadly." Then I pulled up my pant leg and let him get an eyeful of the long pink scar across my calf, a deep slice from a lizard's claw.

He gave my leg a quick glance then leaned forward and examined my chest.

"Must've been one hell of a big lizard."

"They look like those Komodo Dragons, you know, from Indonesia?" An involuntary shudder passed through me.

He nodded, still looking at my scars. "I've seen pictures."

"When they're in human form, you'd never know."

He looked thoughtful and remarkably calm. "So, these things are walking around us?"

"Yes, and I can sense them." I gave my shoulder a rub.

"That's probably a good thing."

"I'm not so sure."

He leaned back and looked at me. "So now what?"

I sat down on my desk chair. "My first goal is trying to make my life normal again."

"Your life's never been normal, bro."

—

"Are you working with my dad this weekend?" I asked Mack as we crossed the football field toward school. He'd pretty much taken over for me. Even if I had the time to help my dad, my leg and shoulder put me out of commission for a while. Besides, I didn't need the money and Mack did.

"Yup. We ripped out the walls last week so there's a ton to do. And I'm probably going out with Isabella Saturday night. You?"

"I dunno." I was really hoping to go on a date with Shoko, if she ever had the time.

I pulled open the door and we entered the busy hallway.

"Don't forget to limp," Mack whispered. "Or your little home-schooling scam will be over."

When we got to our lockers, I stopped dead. Christmas wrapping paper covered my locker door, and about a dozen girls had written little messages. Some even wrote their names. Someone else had scrawled crude messages about what each girl was willing to do to become the "Christmas present" for the heir to the Thompson empire.

I glanced around. A cute girl I remembered from English class last year gave me a big smile. I wondered if one of the messages was hers.

"Oh, to be you," Mack said with a laugh. "I never dreamed I'd say that." Then he turned toward the crowd surging past us. "Just want you girls to know," he said, "that I'll be personally prescreening all potential applicants."

"Oh you will, huh?"

Mack's eyes went wide and he spun around. Isabella laughed and socked him in the stomach.

"Ouch." *She* said it. Punching Mack was like hitting a wall.

"Hiya babe!"

They'd been dating for a few months, during which time Mack hadn't even looked at another girl. That had to be a record for him.

Isabella smiled at me. "How're you doing?" she said with the slightest Italian accent. "Good enough for basketball yet?"

I shook my head. "Maybe next season," I said. "My … leg's not ready for that."

She looked past me at my locker door. "Anne's nice," she said. Then she looked closer. "I'm not sure she'd do that, though. She's pretty shy."

I leaned in and my eyes widened. "It does sound interesting, though."

Isabella smacked my arm and laughed. "Boys are pigs."

"Not me," Mack said, his arms crossed on his wide chest. "I respect women far too much to ask for that."

"But if a girl offered?" Isabella said, looking up at him.

He smiled at her. "Depends on who it was."

I looked at Isabella and felt a twinge of jealousy. Her energy spoke how much she wanted to be with him, but there was also uncertainty. He'd been a player and she didn't want to be played. His thoughts were almost the same, only opposite. He didn't think he was worthy of her because of all the other girls he'd fooled around with.

"Hey, *Mr.* Thompson."

Before I turned, I knew it was Tyler, the little prick who'd been hassling me since the eighth grade. I'd never kicked his ass, though Mack suggested it many times.

"Piss off," Mack said.

"Hey Big Mack," Tyler said with a sneer. "I saw your mom outside the liquor store the other day, pissed drunk as usual."

Mack's face went red with anger, and maybe embarrassment.

"You're such an asshole!" Isabella yelled at him.

I pushed Mack back with one arm before he had a chance to move. I didn't plan it, but I felt fury and my energy begin to rise.

"You piece of shit." I glared into his eyes, into his mind. "Quack like a duck, Tyler." I said it through gritted teeth and just loud enough for him to hear.

Tyler let out a loud "quack," then another. A few kids started laughing as he put his hands over his mouth. No one noticed he wasn't kidding around.

I laughed as I watched him struggle to regain control of his body. I'd finally delivered the retribution I'd wanted to for years, and it felt damn good—until pain exploded in my shoulder.

From somewhere in the distance, I heard laughter.

Was it Bartholomew's, inside my head?!

"Oh no ..."

Only Mack heard me. Everyone else was laughing as Tyler stumbled backward, trying to get away from me. I tried to form words but couldn't.

Isabella peered around Mack. "Are you okay?"

Mack studied me intently. "What's wrong, bro?"

I took a deep breath and looked past them both.

"Stop it Tyler ... please."

He silently stared at me for a long moment, a look of horror on his face, then he turned and ran down the hallway, pushing kids aside as he went. I glanced around to see if anyone had noticed our exchange, but everyone was either still laughing or had moved on toward their classes.

I collapsed back against my locker, shoulders slumped.

Mack was in my face again. "What'd you do?"

"I used Bartholomew's power," I whispered so Isabella couldn't hear. "I didn't mean to, I just … I was so pissed. He shouldn't have said that about your mom."

"That's my battle to fight, not yours."

"What's going on?" Isabella said, moving closer.

"His leg gave out," Mack told her. "Nothing serious."

Isabella tugged on Mack's sleeve. "Then come on, we're late for class."

Mack didn't move, just stared down at me. "You gonna be okay?"

I knew my face was covered in sweat. I nodded. "Yeah, go ahead."

He studied me for a moment. "I'll see ya later then. Be careful." He let Isabella pull him away.

The second he was gone, I slammed my locker shut and pushed my way through the crowded hallway. I needed to find Tyler. As I rounded the next corner, I saw him heading toward the exit near the science labs. I started to run, but I only made it about fifty feet when someone shoved me into the lockers, hard.

I stumbled over a girl sitting on the floor and ended up on my knees next to the lockers. My attention was still focused down the hall though. I couldn't see Tyler anymore, but I could still feel his energy. His terror.

Someone nudged me with their foot and I looked up. A big guy, the football-player type, stared down at me with his arms crossed.

"You hit my girlfriend," he said, his expression showing the superiority I'm sure he was used to.

"Don't be a dick," his girlfriend said. "You caused it!"

"That's James Thompson!" a high female voice called out, as if the Beatles had just walked in.

"Hey, I'm sorry. You okay?" I asked the girl. She didn't look mad at all, just smiled and told me she was fine.

Her boyfriend was a different story.

"I don't give a shit who you are," he said. "I wanna hear an apology."

I stood up but still had to look up to see his face. "Don't you have something better to do, because I do."

He went to shove me into the lockers again. I sidestepped, pulled his arm and let his momentum carry him into the lockers. Then I pushed his elbow into his side, grabbed his fingers and cranked down and back. Foot sweep and he went down hard. I let go before his wrist and elbow snapped.

I looked down the hallway again. I reached out with my energy and tried to sense Tyler. There was nothing. He was gone.

For the first time since I'd left Zion, I'd used Bartholomew's energy. I put a hand on my shoulder. It still throbbed, but this time I welcomed the pain. I deserved it after what I'd done. I turned to go back to my locker, but found the hallway blocked.

"What that hell did you use on me?" It was the football player, on his knees now, brushing the dust off his butt.

I thought for a moment. "*Aikido.*"

One of his other equally large friends grinned down at me. "That's cool! Think you can take us both?"

I felt myself go cold. "I don't have time for this."

They exchanged looks, then stepped aside.

I'd used Bartholomew's power and he knew it. I could no longer deny that some part of him lived inside me.

The question was, would I be able to control it?

CHAPTER
4

"THE CLUB" WAS THE MOST EXCLUSIVE EXECUTIVE club in San Francisco, mostly because hardly anyone knew it existed. There were no signs outside the Pacific Heights mansion, only an imposing stone wall and a high steel gate. City records listed it as a private conference center owned by the sole shareholder of the Thompson Corporation, Edward Lawrence Thompson.

I called him Grandpa.

The steel gate slid open after I punched in a code and pressed my thumb against the panel. I walked toward the underground parking lot where a serious-looking man in a dark-blue suit stood waiting.

"Name?" the man said.

I rolled my eyes. "You know who I am." I'm sure I was the only member who walked through the gate, and definitely the only one who took the bus.

"Name."

"Do you ask the Chairman his name too?"

He stared down at his tablet and frowned. "Oh, I'm sorry, we're not expecting any smart-asses today. You'll have to leave."

I looked at his name tag. "You know, Jason, that thumb-print thingy outside's already making you redundant. Don't push it."

He pointed toward the elevator where another equally serious man stood.

"But it can't smack loudmouthed teenagers upside the head like I can."

I grinned. "Good point."

A woman wearing an elegant black cocktail dress greeted me as I stepped off the elevator into the lobby.

"Good afternoon, Junya," she said with a slight bow. "We've been expecting you."

I smiled. "Hi Kobe, is my grandpa here yet?" I hadn't seen his Bentley downstairs.

"He's on his way." Kobe led me past antique tables and dark-cherry woodwork toward a quiet area of the lounge. The Christmas decorations were a bit too perfect-looking for my taste—everything new and color-coordinated—but at least the place looked festive. The cheery traditional music helped too.

I scanned the room as I followed Kobe. Besides the usual negative thoughts and energy, the stream told me there was nothing out of the ordinary.

Two older men in suits looked up as we passed. I met the gaze of one. His energy reeked of confidence and he was curious, about me.

Kobe stopped by a pair of dark leather chairs, positioned to have the best view of the city.

"I'd be happy to keep you company until the Chairman arrives," she said.

When I nodded, she sat and smoothed her dress against her legs. She was beautiful, though not like Ms. Lin, Grandpa's executive assistant and now fiancé. I always enjoyed talking to her. Kobe was smart and had a wicked sense of humor.

"Don't you think this is all kind of sexist?" I said. "All these beautiful *hostesses* and stuff?"

She laughed. "Says the guy who's staring at my legs."

I made a point of looking her in the eye and grinned.

"None of these women are complaining," she said. "It's clean and safe and pays well, enough to cover rent and tuition, even for med school, which Sabrina over there is halfway through."

I checked out the girl she'd indicated. Her dress was even shorter than Kobe's.

"I bet she makes a lot of money here."

"There's none of *that* here and you know it."

I scrunched up my face. "Sorry."

She placed one graceful hand on top of her knee. "It's all right. We're supposed to be distracting. Just another one of the Chairman's business tactics."

"What?"

She smiled. "Men act different with beautiful women around." She lowered her voice. "And the guests often say things that interest the Chairman."

"You're spies?"

"Second oldest profession." She looked up and over my shoulder as she said it, so I wasn't startled when a man spoke behind me.

"Good afternoon, James." It was the club manager. "I trust Kobe is looking after you."

I looked up at him. "No complaints here."

He cleared his throat. "The Chairman just arrived and he nearly ripped the head off one of the valets. I thought you'd like a warning."

I shrugged. It had been a while since I'd been intimidated by my grandfather. I hadn't heard him yell in a while, though. Something must've riled him up.

Kobe stood and hurried toward the elevator.

The manager was right. Grandpa looked pissed when he stepped off the elevator flanked by John and Miles, his bodyguards. He looked good though, like he'd lost some weight. Having a fiancé thirty years younger was obviously keeping him busy.

They turned in the direction of the manager's office.

29

"Good afternoon, Chairman."

Grandpa stopped. "Ah, Kobe ..." He hesitated, then bowed slightly to her. "Good afternoon." I noticed Miles and John exchange smiles.

"I have your favorite place prepared," she cooed. "And James is waiting for you."

He glanced one last time in the direction of the manager's office before he followed her. I rolled my eyes.

"You're looking lovely as usual," Grandpa said from behind her. "How do you afford such beautiful dresses?"

"The Chairman is more generous than he realizes."

Grandpa paused beside the two men I'd noticed earlier. They spoke in lowered tones. At one point, Grandpa glanced over at me, along with the other two, before moving on.

My grandpa was the richest businessman in San Francisco, if you didn't count those Internet guys. He didn't consider them real 'businessmen' anyhow. He was old-school rich, as he called it. A quintessential self-made man who grew up poor and worked his butt off to get where he was. Now he owned hotels, banks, department stores and office towers. He even owned my favorite radio station. He was also a major player in international monetary funds. He and a group of like-minded billionaires got together every few months and made decisions that affected everything, from the price of corn to interest rates. As the Chairman of that Committee, he was not a man to be taken lightly.

As he dropped heavily into the chair opposite me, a waiter arrived with a glass of eighteen-year-old scotch for him and a cola for me.

I tilted my head toward the men. "Who're they?"

He glanced their way. "Long-time associates having a look at my heir." He looked up at Kobe. "Would you mind ordering us a snack?"

"Of course, Chairman," she said. "Something unhealthy, I presume?"

He smiled at me. "That would be perfect."

He watched her walk away.

"You're a kept man, remember?" I said.

He chuckled. "Women are my Kryptonite."

"And here I though Bartholomew was. How're things going with that?"

He grunted. "We're almost back to where we were before," he said. "But from now on, I'll be financing all new projects myself so no one can screw me over like that again."

I nodded my approval. Bartholomew, when he was in human form, was an elderly financier, one of the top money men in the world. He'd nearly bankrupted Grandpa by cutting off billions in financing right when Grandpa needed it the most.

Grandpa smiled and nodded toward the window. "Have you noticed we're working on the Bayview Complex again? Tower One is almost done."

The three towers were visible out the large windows, growing taller each week.

"They better not block the view."

He laughed. "They won't block mine."

I took a sip of my drink then asked. "What were you so mad about when you got here?"

He scowled. "I'm trying to demolish the dump I bought in the Marina District," he said. "But those pencil pushers at City Hall claim it's a heritage building!"

I knew the place he was talking about. It was a four-story building, an ugly duckling in a trendy shopping area, but I'd always had a soft spot for it. It had *potential*.

"What's your plan?"

"High-end retail on the main floor and luxury condos above," He grinned. "Eight or ten stories high."

"A condo tower on Hemlock Street?" I stared at him for a long moment. "That's a stupid idea."

He leaned back and regarded me over the rim of his glass. "Sometimes I don't like the new you."

"Yeah?" I leaned toward him. "And I don't like being part of a company infamous for tearing down heritage buildings for office towers and overpriced condos."

He harrumphed. "Where do you think your inheritance comes from?"

I pointed a finger at him. "You're not tearing it down!"

He didn't reply, just regarded me as he took a drink of the scotch.

"Tell you what," I said. "Why don't you give it to me?"

He wasn't expecting that, and he nearly choked on his drink. "What?!"

"You could make it a Christmas present." I puffed up my chest. "It'll give me a sense of responsibility and pride of ownership."

He rolled his eyes, but I could tell he was thinking about it.

I couldn't resist prodding him. "So?"

"I'll think about it," he said, then cleared his throat. "The guards told me you walked here again."

I knew when to back off. "Yup, from the bus stop."

"How many times do I need to tell you?" he said, loud enough for the sous-chefs in the kitchen to hear. "You should have a car and driver."

I made a face. "I'm not riding around in a blue four-door granny car."

He rolled his eyes. "Isn't it better than the bus?"

"No." Then I grinned. "But, if I got to pick the car ..."

I got his *over the eyeglasses* look.

"I'll even pay for it myself."

He grunted. "With the money you stole from Sergeant Jackson, I presume?"

My mouth dropped open. "You know about that?"

"There's not much I don't know." He fell silent for a long moment, then said, "I trust you haven't forget the golden rule of money? It applies especially to cars."

I recited it along with him. "'You only spend money on things that will make you more money.'"

"Yeah, yeah, I know but I need transportation to places where I can make money, like the building you just gave me."

He stared at me with that expression he got when he was thinking. It could go either way.

"Fine," he finally said. "Barrymore has to approve the driver, and you're paying for the car, but ... I don't see why you can't pick the car you want."

"Yes!" I pumped my fist.

—

I got a ride home from Mr. Barrymore, Grandpa's security chief. He was the only one available when my request for a ride came in.

"The Chairman said *any* car?" He looked skeptical.

"Yeah, and whoever you give me better be able to drive."

The car rolled to a gentle stop at a yellow light. "All my people—"

"I mean *drive*." I cranked an invisible steering wheel in my hands. "You ever see Ms. Lin behind the wheel?"

"Unfortunately. Her speeding tickets come out of my budget." He eased the car forward when the light went green. "I presume you're thinking about a sports car then?"

"Maybe."

He let out a deep sigh. "I'll think about it."

"And they need to have a sense of *humor*." I leaned forward and stared right at him.

"Keep that up and *I'll* be your new driver."

CHAPTER
5

SHOKO CAME TO SEE ME TWO days later, arriving in the Zen garden in my backyard. Both Okaasan and Dad were out, which of course Shoko knew. She could *see* my side from hers before she travelled.

She walked over and took my hand. After a quick glance around, she lifted onto her toes and kissed me, on the lips. A warm feeling passed between us that had nothing to do with magic or energy.

"Was that okay?" she asked when she pulled back.

I had to suck in a breath before I could answer. "Wow. Yeah, but … what was that for?"

Her brows came together. "You did not like it?"

"I *really* liked it. It was just a surprise."

She looked pleased. "I once saw a girl do that," she said. "Her boyfriend appeared to like it."

"I'll bet." I tried to get my mind to refocus. "So, um … I'd like to take you to Pier 39 today."

Her gaze dropped. "There is something I must do. I am sorry."

I let out a sigh. "Again?"

"Please do not be upset," she said. "I have my duty."

And for Shoko, duty would always come first.

"There is a gateway opening tonight, very ancient," she said. "This is a popular ceremony which occurs each year without fail. I am to observe the shaman and worshipers from this side of our worlds."

"On *this* side?" I was surprised. "That's unusual, isn't it?"

She smiled. "Because of my time with you, I am offered many interesting assignments."

I tried to smile back. "Glad I can be of *some* help. Is it because of the missing shamans?"

She hesitated. "I was not told the reason," she said. "But I believe so, yes."

I stuffed my hands in my pockets. "Well, that sounds pretty important."

"You said you wished to see a ceremony." She sounded excited. "Would you like to come with me?"

"Seriously?" When she nodded, I grinned. "I'm in!"

She smiled. "I am glad."

Then she stepped back and inspected me.

"What?"

"You will want to change into something cooler."

When I came back out a few minutes later in shorts and a t-shirt, she didn't say a work. She just held out her hand. I'd barely grasped it when she knelt and slapped her palm on the sand.

The world became a spinning blur and my backyard disappeared as the Mother Earth engulfed us in her swirling energy. This was even worse than the last time and when everything finally stopped spinning, I sagged forward, dizzy and disoriented.

"Steady Junya!" Shoko yanked me backward. "If you fall from here, you will die!"

I opened one eye and jerked backward. We were perched on the top step of a steep stone pyramid, nearly a hundred feet up.

"Where are we?!"

"A place called Chichén Itzá, an ancient Mayan city." She loosened her grip on my shirt but didn't let go. "This is El Castillo, the main pyramid."

"Why the hell did you travel us to the top?" If she hadn't grabbed me, I'd have broken my neck.

"I wanted you to see the view," she said.

Our perch on the largest and tallest structure on the site towered above dozens of other ancient stone buildings scattered across the acres of land below. One had a dome like a modern observatory, though it had crumbled in places. Another looked like some kind of temple, with hundreds of stone columns standing around it.

"It is an amazing sight, yes?"

A shudder ran up my spine. I tilted my head to listen to the energy around me.

She turned to me. "What do you sense?"

"There's a lot of dark energy here." I closed my eyes and tried to make the sensation go away. "Maybe it's because this place is so old," I said. "I don't know …"

The feeling passed when Shoko's hand covered mine and her pure energy flowed into me.

—

It grew darker and the park closed for the night and the security guards began their rounds, walking the perimeter trails looking for wayward tourists. Shoko and I faded into the sparse trees near a smaller pyramid as they passed, speaking Spanish.

A full moon bathed the closest ruin in an eerie blue light. Unlike El Castillo, this structure—the Ossario—had never become a full pyramid. Whether by design or fate, it ended about a third of the way up, leaving a flat surface. I assumed the Mayan builders had stopped when they realized the natural cave they'd built it over was a gateway to the Other Side.

The guards were barely out of sight when I felt the energy of

Mother Earth flex. I grabbed Shoko's arm, hard enough to spin her toward me.

"Why are Gatekeepers coming?"

She didn't pull away. "They are my apprentices. I thought this would be a good experience for them."

The earth's energy ruptured, and I looked toward the spot between the trees where I sensed they'd appear. It began with a shimmering above the ground, like heat waves in the desert. Then figures began to materialize: four young teenage girls down on one knee, their left palms pressed against the earth. They all had a katana and a wakizashi pushed through a wide fabric belt, and two carried bows. They wore the traditional uniform of the Gatekeepers, which was like a kimono but made of a thinner, lighter material, and was light green, like the color of the underside of a leaf. The long slits in the sides, designed for easy movement while fighting, fluttered open as they stood.

They looked anxious and disoriented. All of them squinted, obviously fighting the *noise* on my side, the result of so much inherent negative energy.

Suddenly, the oldest one grabbed her head and dropped back to her knees. "My senses are overcome!" she cried out in Japanese.

Shoko ran toward her. "Aya, close your mind!"

It took a minute before the girl regained control. "I feel lost … defenseless."

"It is always like that the first time," Shoko said in a kinder tone. "Junya is here, he will alert us to any danger."

Aya looked up at me and gasped.

"Junya, the one with the gaping mouth is named Aya," Shoko said. Then she pointed to another girl, perhaps the youngest. "That is Kyoko. The other two are Yukie and Rina."

I remembered those two. They'd been waiting near the San Francisco Japanese Gardens when Shoko first crossed back to see me after all the trouble in Izumo.

Kyoko, who looked far less impressed than the others, walked over and handed Shoko a sheathed katana. Then she gave me a *bokuto*, a curved wooden sword made of *shirakashi*, Japanese white oak blessed by the gods of Izumo. Shoko knew it was my favorite weapon, when I needed one.

I glanced at Shoko. "Are you expecting trouble?"

She didn't look at me as she fed the katana through her belt. "If you are prepared, you have no need to worry."

"The gateway will open soon," Rina said. She was soft-spoken and the shortest of the four.

"How can you tell?" I said to her.

"Because the *Controller* who is about to open it said so," Kyoko said. She sounded sarcastic.

I stared at Kyoko long enough that she looked away, then I turned back to Shoko.

"What's a *Controller?*"

"They are those who open and close the gateways." Shoko said. "Their energy is very strong."

"But I thought ... don't gateways open by themselves?" It had when I crossed over in the Mojave Desert.

"Some do," Yukie said. "That is what makes our duty so exciting!"

Shoko smiled at Yukie. "The Controllers open some gateways based on a schedule that is centuries old," she said. "Most, however, open on their own, at regular intervals."

"Like the one in Tibet?" I tried to remember. "Every ... twenty-four moons?"

Shoko looked pleased. "Exactly."

"If I may explain it, Shoko?" Rina said. Then she glanced at Kyoko. "Without interruption."

Shoko nodded. "If you do well, perhaps I will count this toward your grading."

Rina turned to me and bowed. "Honorable Junya, there are thousands of gateways all over your world that allow entry to the world of the gods. When one needs to be opened, based on the ancient records, it is a Controller who performs this task."

"How?" I asked.

Rina stared at me for a long moment. "I respectfully asked for no interruptions."

I cringed. "Right, sorry."

"When a gateway requires opening to allow shamans to cross, a Controller—with a Gatekeeper escort—travels to the gateway and uses her energy to open it. However, while most gateways open by themselves at regular intervals, as Shoko said, a few open at random, perhaps on the whim of some god or Mother Earth. We are only alerted to those openings if someone happens to come across. Those openings, as Yukie has said, are the most interesting."

"Because?"

Yukie laughed. "Because you never know what will come across!"

I glanced quickly at Rina, hoping the "no interruption" period was over.

"How are you *alerted?*" I was pretty sure Shoko had told me this once, but I still wasn't sure I really understood.

Rina took a deep breath. "There is a break in the energy field of the Mother Earth each time someone, or *something*, crosses. When that break is detected, whoever has crossed over is intercepted. Depending on their intentions, they are welcomed, returned, or killed."

That seemed simple enough.

"But only Gatekeepers can travel *without* using a gateway?"

"That is correct, Junya!" Yukie said, still sounding excited. I decided I liked her.

"The *only* exception there has ever been is you." It was Shoko who said that, and it stopped the conversation like a slammed door.

—

Darkness closed in and the night sounds began. There was a lot of energy here among the ancient ruins. Maybe the place was getting to me, but …

I took a step forward. "Something's out there."

Shoko squinted into the dark. "Is it the Mayans?"

"Yes, but there's something else too. It feels like Evil Ones." From the growing pain in my shoulder, it had to be.

I glanced at Shoko. She didn't look worried, but then, she never did.

Several minutes later, torches bobbed into view, revealing at least fifty people, all colorfully dressed. The shaman was easy to pick out by his headpiece and the long wooden staff he carried, though he looked younger than I expected.

The group stopped and formed a silent half circle as we eyed each other. The screech of unseen birds was the only sound. Then the shaman stepped forward.

"Be gone from here!" His energy was strong. I felt it leave him, felt the air ripple between us. Shoko winced as it hit us.

Without thinking, I exhaled. I only let a small amount of energy escape me—I hadn't even meant to—but it sent the shaman and the Gatekeepers to their knees. The others felt nothing, only saw the six people fall.

After a moment, Shoko stood up and shot me a homicidal glare. Then she brushed off her knees and looked to see if her apprentices were okay.

The shaman stood up, helped by two anxious older men. He bowed, his hands clasped in a prayer position.

"Please forgive me." He had trouble taking in a breath. "The legends speak of beautiful warriors in green robes, but it is said they wait for us on the Other Side." Then his eyes met mine. "And there are no tales of one like him."

"Where is Cebrián?" Shoko said it loud enough for everyone to hear.

The shaman looked at the ground. "Cebrián is dead."

Shoko looked confused. "How? And when?"

His gaze rose to meet hers. "He was killed by … something, two days ago."

"It was the *Dark-Man*," an old woman in the crowd called out. Several others murmured in agreement.

Shoko stared at the shaman for a long time, then turned to me. "Does he speak the truth?"

"His energy's sincere," I said. "And ... he's the rightful successor of the staff."

She nodded and turned back to the shaman. "The gateway will open soon," she said. "Begin your rituals. Your gods await you."

The group moved past us silently, keeping their distance. After they formed a circle around the Ossario, the shaman climbed the stairs, knelt, and began chanting.

Shoko and I stood side by side watching the ceremony until my shoulder began to ache again. I moved a few paces away, probing the darkness with my energy.

Shoko moved to my side.

"Evil Ones are coming," I said.

Her hand moved to the hilt of her katana. "How many?"

"Two, maybe more." I concentrated. My apprehension was growing. "Definitely more."

"The ancient rules do not permit us to—" She froze when she saw my body jerk.

My shoulder throbbed now. Somewhere in the dark, they moved closer. I walked a few paces in their direction, squinting into the darkness, trying to locate them.

Shoko saw them first. "There."

Between the trees, about twenty yards away, stood two men dressed in black, their long black hair shining in the moonlight. A shudder traveled up my spine.

From behind me came the whisper of a katana sliding from its sheath.

They broke into a run, heading toward us. Moonlight flashed on blue steel and gunfire erupted. Semiautomatic fire.

I dove off the pathway.

Shoko remained on the trail. She seemed disoriented ... or

reluctant to retreat. An Evil One, bearing down on her, raised his gun.

"No!" I lunged at him but stumbled when my leg gave out under me. I watched his finger squeeze the trigger.

He jerked backward as an arrow pierced the center of his chest. The second man faltered and swerved to avoid his fallen comrade.

I jumped onto the trail and swung. My bokuto sliced toward his head and connected with a dull crack.

"Apprentices, cease fire!" Shoko shouted. Then she grabbed my arm. "We are forbidden to fight Evil Ones on this side!"

Gunfire and screams came from behind the Ossario, shouts in Japanese and cries in Spanish. Rina, who was down on one knee on top of the Ossario, had her bowstring pulled back halfway, another arrow ready. She looked at us, anxious and expectant.

"It's too late now!" I pulled away from Shoko and ran toward the gunfire. "Fight back, Rina!" I shouted.

As I rounded the corner of the pyramid, I tripped over an apprentice who lay sprawled on the ground. I rolled onto my knees, eyes and energy searching, and saw three men among the trees. One down, two still firing their pistols.

"Rina, engage!" Shoko yelled above the noise.

Something hissed through the air beside me and an arrow thudded into one of the gunmen. A split second later another arrow lodged itself in the man beside him. They both fell to the ground.

I looked back. Rina, still atop the Ossario, had another arrow notched.

"Junya!" Shoko shouted. "Are there others?"

I sprinted to the top of the steps and spun around, concentrating. The world became a thermal image. Trees and shrubs were light blue, the ground a warmer yellow, not yet cooled from the daytime heat. I saw small orange shapes—birds and rodents—and one human-size shape lying about twenty yards away.

I spotted Shoko in the mayhem below. "There's still one out there, hurt, but the others are gone!"

I jumped back down the stairs, taking three at a time. As I hit the ground, I sent my energy out again, earning a curse from Shoko. The Evil One still hadn't moved, but its warmth had faded. A gun lay nearby, within his reach.

"Be careful," I whispered to Shoko.

But when I reached him, I knew I didn't need to worry about the gun. Two arrows protruded from his chest, both wounds seeping black blood.

I knelt next to him.

He rolled his head to look at me. "Cousin ...?"

"He is not your cousin!" Shoko tried to step past me, but I blocked her.

"I am dying, cousin." His voice was a choked whisper.

Mixed emotions surged inside me. I knew it wasn't human, knew it would kill me if it could, but ... it was dying.

"You would've died anyway," I said, "if you tried to cross."

He looked confused. "We were not ... trying ... to cross ..."

I looked back toward the Ossario. Rina was still on top, scanning the tree line. Kyoko sat beside Aya. The rest of the people were gathered in a circle, some kneeling, others standing. Many were crying.

"Who got hurt?" I asked Shoko.

"Aya was hit, Kyoko was grazed. A deep cut." Shoko sounded like a newscaster. "And the young shaman is dead."

The Evil One smiled. "Then we ... succeeded ..."

His eyes rolled back, and a moment later there was a burst of energy, like a balloon popping. He vanished, leaving behind a body-shaped cloud of dust.

I jumped up and stumbled back against Shoko. "What the ...?"

She grabbed my shoulders to steady me. "They vanish when they die," she said. "You did not know that?"

I sat leaning against her, heart pounding, and watched as the dust settled onto the dry ground. The cries of people started to register. I walked back toward the crowd and gently pushed my way through.

The shaman lay in a pool of blood, head tilted back, his feet pushed into the ground, as if he were still trying to run away. He had six small holes in his chest and stomach. No energy though. He was dead.

Shoko came up beside me and stared down at the young shaman. "That Evil One said they were not trying to go across."

Did it matter? "Is anyone else hurt?" I said to no one in particular.

"No," an old man said from beside me. "They only shot at him … and the girls in green."

I looked down at Aya. She'd been hit in the shoulder. Kyoko, bleeding from the arm, knelt over her. Rina, her bow still at the ready, remained on guard. I didn't see Yukie anywhere.

"Is there another to take his place?" Shoko asked the old man.

He shook his head. "His son chose to work at the resorts." The man ran a hand over his bare head. "I fear this is the end of our ways."

I heard something on top of the Ossario and looked up. Yukie had reappeared with a *Miko*, obvious in her red *hakama* pants and white *kimono* jacket.

Shoko let out a gasp. "That is Himiko," she whispered.

I knew the woman, but not her name. She'd bandaged my wounds on the staircase of the Izumo shrine when I brought Shoko back from Zion.

"Is that a big deal?"

"Yes," Shoko whispered. "She is a powerful priestess and healer, and Miko do not cross over. Ever."

Shoko bowed low as Himiko hurried down the steps toward us. "Why have you come, honorable Himiko?"

Himiko made a sour face. "An Elder was concerned," she said. "He suspected there would be trouble, especially if you were here." I couldn't tell if she meant Shoko or me.

Himiko knelt beside Aya and Kyoko and opened her black bag.

"That old Mayan woman said something about a 'Dark-Man' killing their shaman," I said to Shoko as we watched Himiko work. "And those villagers in Tibet called it the Black Life-Stealing Fiend.

They sound an awful lot alike."

"Many cultures speak of dark entities," Shoko said, but her thoughts were obviously elsewhere. "What do they gain by killing the shaman?" she said after a while. "It makes no sense."

I wondered about something else. "Did you know Evil Ones would be here?"

She finally looked at me, surprised. "None of this was expected. As I said, fighting on this side is forbidden." She let out a deep sigh. "I pray that what we have learned will make the Elders overlook our transgression."

CHAPTER

6

I DIDN'T HEAR ANYTHING FROM SHOKO until mid-morning the next day. She wanted me to meet her at the same small park on the Presidio grounds. She was usually late so I took my time, but I was surprised when I found her leaning against a tree, waiting for me. She was wearing her Gatekeeper uniform.

"The Elders want to see you."

A heavy feeling settled inside me. The last time I'd seen an Elder—the one called the Kannushi—I'd been on the other side, at Izumo, and he'd tried to have me killed.

"It will be safe," she said, noting my reluctance.

I stared at her a long moment, searching her face and her energy, for more information, but I couldn't sense anything.

Her eyes narrowed. "Do you think I would trick you?"

I looked away. "Duty always comes first, right?"

"Junya, look at me." When I did, she said, "You have *my* word."

I nodded, then smiled. "I'd probably feel better if you kissed me again."

She shook her head and held out her hand. "The Elders are waiting."

We arrived in the meadow not far from her little straw-roofed house, kneeling among the tall grass and wildflowers. This time there was no pain, no head rush, only the feeling of peace flooding into me. The air was alive with it, but I felt it most through Shoko's hand. Being back here seemed to triple her energy.

She smiled at me. "Welcome back."

I squeezed her hand and was surprised when she didn't let go.

"I can feel your energy," she said. "It is lighter now."

I sucked in a lung full of pure air. "It's so good to be back here," I whispered.

We walked side by side through the meadow to the wide road that led to the shrine. This was the home of the god of Izumo. It was he who had brought Shoko's ancestors here millennia ago to be the protectors of this place, a sanctuary he created for all the earth gods.

I gazed up at the shrine, towering above the trees at the top of the long wooden staircase, its X-shaped roof pointed like open scissors toward the clear blue sky. Halfway up the wide staircase, a man scrubbed the wooden steps, absorbed in his task.

"We will thank the gods for allowing us to be his servants and enjoy his splendor," Shoko said. Then she knelt at the bottom of the staircase and clapped four times.

I knelt beside her and followed her example. I silently offered my thanks for the help I received the last time I was here.

When I opened my eyes, Shoko was still praying so I sat and studied the staircase. It was truly amazing, both in its craftsmanship and its size. Rising at a low angle, the staircase climbed at least 150 feet above us, and the shrine itself was held aloft by massive red posts, each wider than any Redwood I'd ever seen.

Shoko stood. "Are you finished?"

"I guess so. I don't know much about this stuff."

"A servant of the gods must be familiar with *this stuff.*"

She was probably right. "How old is the shrine?"

"Since time here began. Thousands of your years."

"When was it last rebuilt?"

She screwed up her face. "Never."

"On my side, they rebuild the Izumo Shrine every sixty years."

She looked surprised. "Why?"

I shrugged. "Because wood doesn't last very long," I said. "It decays and rots or dries out and starts to fall apart."

She reached out and touched the velvet-smooth timber. "This is original."

I had to shake my head. "I wish I could show this to my dad."

She waved up at the man cleaning the staircase. When he noticed her, she bowed and called out, "Thank you, sir!"

"Who's he?" I said.

"The man who cleans the staircase."

"Okay ..."

She gave me a look. "He is doing a fine job. It is right to thank someone for that." Before I could reply, she pointed across the compound where a small delegation was gathering in front of another structure. It was far more elegant than the grand shrine, with a peaked straw roof and a huge braided festoon strung across the front that looked like it could easily weigh a couple of tons.

The Kannushi, who wore black robes and tall black headpiece, stood at the front of a group of older men and women who were all dressed in white. On either side of the group, at a discreet distance, stood several armed Gatekeepers.

Shoko nudged me from behind. "Bow low when you reach him," she whispered.

I stiffened. Bow to that jerk?

As if she knew my thoughts, she said, "Do it for the gods, if you cannot bring yourself to respect his place as a liaison to them."

I waited for her to walk with me, but she shook her head slightly.

"I must remain two paces behind."

I swallowed and started forward. I wasn't scared of the Kannushi, but I was uneasy at the sight of the crowd and the ceremony of it all.

When we reached them, I did as Shoko asked and kneeled and prostrated myself on the ground in front of him. The whole time my thoughts were of the gods sitting far above me. It was to them I paid my respect.

The Kannushi thumped his staff against the ground. "Rise!"

I'll admit I stood up far too casually. Okaasan would've smacked me if she'd seen me, probably Shoko too if she wasn't still on her knees behind me.

I folded my hands in front of me. "You wished to see me … sir."

His eyes narrowed to slits as he glared at me. "As Shoko was instructed to tell you, you have nothing to fear from us."

"Oh, I'm not worried."

"Junya!" Shoko hissed from behind me.

He cleared his throat. "We wish to speak to you about your presence outside the gateway in the Mayan lands," he said. "Shoko has reported that an Evil One called you *cousin*. I assume this is because you were bitten by the Lord of the Evil Ones and you now share common blood."

I looked skyward. "You asked me here to insult me?"

"Junya!" I don't know why Shoko bothered whispering, since everyone could hear her.

The Kannushi pointed at Shoko. "Come forward!"

She crawled forward and bowed at his feet.

"Engaging in combat with Evil Ones on the Other Side is a violation of our laws," he said. "You were instructed to observe. Explain your actions and those of the apprentices under your command."

"We did observe, honorable Elders," she said in a reverent but strong voice, addressing those behind the Kannushi as well. "But once the attack began, it was … difficult not to become involved."

"And any Gatekeeper," an elderly man behind the Kannushi said, "regardless of where she finds herself, has an inherent right to self-defense." Then, to my surprise, he winked at Shoko.

The Kannushi scowled. "And you brought this boy with you."

She glanced at me then nodded. "I ... I thought it would be good experience, just as it was for my apprentices."

The Kannushi considered that for a long moment, his gaze never leaving my face. When he spoke again, his tone was far different.

"Shoko has assured us of your positive contribution to the defense of the gateway. This means much to us."

I nodded, unable to hide my surprise. Was he actually saying something nice?

The Kannushi turned toward the old man behind him, the one who'd defended Shoko.

"Honorable Grand Elder, you wish to speak?"

I glanced down at Shoko. There was no way she could get closer to the ground without becoming part of the dirt.

The Grand Elder stepped in front of me. Up close, he looked really old. He was shorter than the Kannushi and far shorter than me, but he was definitely intimidating.

He leaned heavily on his staff as he stared up at me. "We understand the Evil One told you he had no intention to come *across*."

I nodded, showing genuine deference this time.

"Has this young Gatekeeper informed you that Cebrián, the Mayan shaman, is only one of many who have recently been killed?"

I nodded again. "Yes sir."

The Grand Elder rubbed his neck as he studied me. "The summer solstice is the largest celebration of the year. Millions gather to pay respects to the earth gods. This year, though ..." He shook his head. "There were far fewer crossings, far less worship than usual. The autumn equinox was the same." He glanced up toward the shrine. "The gods send out troubled energy. Many of the lesser gods need this worship to stay strong. Without it, they become lonesome and whither, which in turn lessens the strength of other gods. This is something we can no longer ignore."

I didn't know much about the gods, but that didn't sound good.

"Is there some way I can help, sir?"

"We ..." he swept his arm to take in the small group behind him, "were troubled by the events that previously brought you here. You are the son of a wayward Gatekeeper. You went to Zion, the place no one with a pure heart can go. You were bitten by an Evil One, but still managed to bring this young one back." He paused, and I felt his eyes probing me. "You survived what was believed impossible."

I nodded, unsure what he expected me to say.

"And you left here as a powerful and angry young man." He clicked his tongue. "None of this is good." He stared at me a long moment, then said, "Have you had any further contact with the Evil One, Bartholomew?"

"No sir, I haven't."

"Is he the source of your energy?"

He might be behind some of it, but I *knew* he wasn't behind all of it. "I don't believe so."

"His energy was already very strong before he was bitten," Shoko said from beside me. "I know this to be the truth."

"Let us see." The Grand Elder pointed at the ground. "Kneel!"

I dropped like a rock beside Shoko.

He put his hand on my head and his energy poured into me. I resisted—it didn't feel good—and he quickly drew his hand back.

"Your energy *is* strong ... but confused. Darkness and light." He looked up to the top of the shrine again and rubbed his chin.

"Grand Elder—"

The old man waved the Kannushi quiet. "He had the evil thrust upon him because *we* failed to protect him. He has a pure heart, but his blood runs thick with darkness. We should not have cast him out."

I tried to process all he was saying. The most important thing from my point of view seemed to be that they—or at least the Grand Elder—were admitting they'd been wrong, which was a step in the right direction.

The Grand Elder touched Shoko's head. "This one is quite persuasive in her defense of you, and quite familiar with the state of your heart." He gave Shoko a little smile, barely discernible. "And what we need done cannot be completed by those here. A different approached is called for."

I caught Shoko's eye. She looked as confused as I felt.

"Shoko," the Grand Elder said, causing her to drop her forehead back to the dirt. "You will further investigate the disappearance of these shamans. We must discover why the Evil Ones are targeting them before the effects become … irreversible."

"Certainly, Grand Elder. I shall do these duties as you command."

He looked pleased, even though I was sure there was no way Shoko could decline.

"Given the circumstances," he said, "you will have to work from his world, using whatever resources you deem necessary to accomplish this assignment. Furthermore, you have my authorization to use lethal force to prevent the death of any shaman or his followers. This I decree before those gathered here."

A stir went through the crowd, and from the size of Shoko's eyes, I'd say she was shocked too. She glanced around as if looking for someone to confirm what she'd heard.

"It shall be as you command, Grand Elder," she said.

"And you, Junya, son of Misako, were asked to come here because we need your assistance in this matter. Though others disagree, I believe your abilities are perfectly suited for the complexities of this mission."

My mouth dropped open. They needed *my* help?

The Grand Elder looked down at me. "Do you accept our request?"

"Yes sir." I bowed. "I will do my best to serve the gods."

"Then I hereby grant you access to this world, subject to all its privileges *and* obligations, as we all are. It is up to the Mother Earth to decide whether to grant you the energy to travel."

—

"That was unexpected," Shoko said as we stood outside the

Gatekeeper weapons-training area a while later. "To give us this task *and* allow us to fight Evil Ones on your side?" She shook her head in disbelief.

"You really didn't know about this when you came to get me?"

She shook her head again, still perplexed.

"What's with the old guy anyway?" I said, referring to the Grand Elder. "He seems to like you."

She laughed. "I am a favorite of his," she said. "I used to bring him his afternoon tea. I always put a drop of honey in it."

"Good to have friends in high places," I said with a laugh. "You're pretty important around here."

She stood a bit straighter. "I am the only Gatekeeper to have been across to the Evil Place and return alive." She grinned. "Many consider me the strongest Gatekeeper in all of Izumo."

"But I did all the work!"

"Perhaps, but I now outrank girls even in their twentieth year."

"Seriously?" I was about to demand a better explanation when Shoko suddenly dropped to the ground. It was no wonder Gatekeepers' knees were always bruised.

I looked up and saw a grey-haired woman in a dark-green kimono with a wide golden belt, standing on the far side of the compound, staring toward us. A group of Gatekeepers, all of them about my Okaasan's age, surrounded her.

I heard Shoko whispering, "Please do not come over, please ..."

After a long moment, the woman moved on, taking her entourage with her.

"Who was that?" I whispered to Shoko.

She peeked up. When she saw the woman was gone, she sat back on her heels and brushed herself off.

"That is Chiyoko," she said. "She is the highest-ranking Gatekeeper."

"So much for you being the strongest Gatekeeper around."

"My pride will be the death of me yet," she said, still staring in the direction the group had gone.

"Well, she left you alone, so I guess you're okay."

She scowled up at me. "I was noticed because of you."

"Why me?"

She stood up and brushed her knees off. "Because you are her grandson."

My mouth dropped as I tried to wrap my head around a bunch of things all at once. Okaasan's mother—my grandmother—was the highest-ranking Gatekeeper in Izumo?

"I ... I should've said hello or something, then. But why didn't she—?"

"Do not *ever* speak to her or seek her out!" Shoko stabbed a finger into my chest. "I have been warned, she does not wish to know you."

I nodded, feeling a bit overwhelmed. I suddenly realized how odd it was that I'd never thought about Okaasan's family before. *My family.*

"So, what do we do next?" I said, wanting a distraction.

"We should eat," she said. "I am hungry."

I had to laugh. "I meant about the assignment and working together and stuff. I can't believe—"

"Come on!" She grabbed my arm. "The men made red-bean cakes today. If we do not hurry, I will miss out."

"They make cake here?"

"And far better than anything I have tasted in your world, except maybe ice cream and hot chocolate."

"What about my mom's food?"

"Her food is good because she is from here."

She dragged me to the end of a long lineup outside what looked to be a dining hall. We'd barely staked out a spot when a young girl, maybe thirteen, knelt and bowed low in front of Shoko.

"Honorable Shoko, I wish to become your apprentice."

Shoko looked surprised. "Do you not already have a master?"

"I do," the girl said, her face still on the ground. "But her methods are tedious and unchallenging. She refuses to recognize that my gifts are much stronger than hers."

The whole line fell silent, followed by a wave of muttering and dark looks. Shoko looked like her eyes would pop out.

"Stand!" she yelled, and the girl sprang to her feet. "You insult your master in front of those gathered here?" Shoko reached out and smacked the girl across the head. Then one of Shoko's apprentices—Rina—strode up.

"Stupid girl!" Rina was small, but definitely scary. "You are not worthy to clean the excrement of dogs!" She grabbed the girl's arm and dragged her away.

"Who was that girl?"

Shoko let out a deep sigh. "Her name is Sakura, the young *Cherry Blossom*."

"I guess she really wants to be your apprentice."

She rolled her eyes. "As do a hundred other girls. They all know I need a new apprentice since Aya was hurt in Chichén Itzá, but no one has been as blatant as Sakura. Her master will surely punish her."

I winced. "I think the smack you gave her was punishment enough."

"Except that after her master finishes punishing her, she will dismiss her," she said. "And that is unfortunate, because Sakura *is* gifted." She looked unhappy. "Girls are fighting each other in hopes of impressing me. Even my own friends have become distant." Then she pushed past me and headed in the direction of her house. "I have lost my appetite."

Shoko trudged through the meadow with me hustling to keep up. She seemed to have forgotten I was even there.

"Are you taking me to your house?" I said when we were halfway across the meadow.

She stopped dead and turned around. "Of course not." She looked flustered. "You know, being *special* has many wonderful benefits, but scenes like that I can do without."

Then she knelt and held out her hand. "I will take you home," she said. "I have much to think about."

CHAPTER

7

I SLEPT IN THE NEXT MORNING, WHICH was a rare treat, but it *was* Sunday, after all. The *stream* told me my parents were up but not in the house. It had become second nature to know these things.

On the way to the bathroom, I stopped to pat Tama, our white tabby cat. She lay in the hall in her usual warm place and purred as I stroked her fur. Through the glass, past the Zen garden, I saw Okaasan in the old Japanese teahouse in our backyard. She was doing her *kata*, the repetitive routines used in martial arts.

After Shoko's evil twin had burned down the dojo, Dad replaced it with a small Japanese teahouse, half the size of the old building but still big enough to swing a sword. Okaasan said she wasn't going to use it as a training dojo. That lasted about a month.

Okaasan smiled when she saw me crossing the small bridge over the Koi pond.

"Good morning, Junya." She seemed awfully perky. "Come to get your butt kicked?"

"Just gonna do some *Iaijutsu*." We hadn't sparred in a long time.

She nodded her approval. "That's good. You need to keep your shoulder and arm muscles flexible." What she didn't say was that it was good for my mind, too. Iaijutsu, the ancient Samurai art of fast-drawing the sword, was a moving meditation, part of my regimen to keep my mind quiet.

I pulled my katana off the rack and knelt near the open *shoji*—the rice-paper sliding door—where I had a good view of the gardens.

"You want to join me?" I said.

She smiled and hurried to get her katana. "I don't get enough practice these days …"

I began, enjoying the feel of the katana in my hand as I went through the routines I'd practiced thousands of times.

Okaasan joined me. "How's your leg feeling?"

"It's okay, but it still gives out once in a while." I finished an overhand cut, the blade whistling through the air, then flicked off the 'blood' and sheathed the sword.

"I suppose you need to stay in the home-schooling program?" There was obvious sarcasm in her tone.

"Yeah, but that's not the only reason." I told her about the last day I went to school. "I don't want to be a celebrity." Then I added, "And look how much my grades have improved."

She couldn't argue with that.

We kept practicing, but after a few minutes, I noticed she'd stopped. When I turned to see why, she was watching me.

"What's on your mind?" she said.

I frowned. She could still read my thoughts a little too well for my liking.

"I need to tell you something … about Shoko." I took a deep breath. "She's been coming across again."

Her hand went to her mouth in mock surprise. "Gosh, have you been *lying* to me, Junya?"

I deserved that. "Yeah, I know." I released a deep sigh. "I'm sorry.

I didn't think you'd like it, after what happened over there."

"That wasn't her doing."

I let a few seconds go by. "You already knew, didn't you?"

She gave me her famous *do you think I'm stupid* look. "You've been a lot happier lately, like a weight came off your shoulders. Why did she come back?"

I shifted into a cross-legged position. Kneeling was hell on my knees these days.

"Well, at first she was hoping to find a cure for my shoulder, to try and stop the pain."

She smirked. "She's trying to heal you?"

I rolled my eyes as I told her about the potions Shoko had made me eat and our recent trip to Tibet. But when I mentioned that Shoko thought I should try traveling on my own, she flipped.

"What? No! You might use Bartholomew's power!"

"Calm down," I said. "I didn't say I was going to try."

"Good, because I'm sure Shoko doesn't have a clue how to stop you from using your dark energy."

I was getting annoyed. "She knows about as much as you."

She spun toward me. "When you get angry, you can access Bartholomew's power, and if you use it you may start to like it! Then what?"

"Why do you think I'm out here doing this meditation every goddamn morning?" I said. "And thank you *so much* for your faith in me!"

She began another kata, her katana swishing through the air with more force than necessary. When she finished, she sheathed the sword and looked at me.

"Okay, you're right," she said, although she didn't sound the least bit apologetic. "I'll shut up."

"I don't want you to shut up, Mom," I said. "But I don't need you yelling at me either. I use the same energy that's always been inside me." I hesitated before plunging on. "There was one time when I used his energy, but I was *very* aware of it and I stopped instantly." I still felt awful about Tyler.

"How do you know the difference?" She didn't sound mad any more, just curious.

I shrugged. "I don't think my energy *is* different. Before Bartholomew bit me, if I got mad, my energy got really strong and dark." I rubbed my face, becoming a bit overwhelmed. "I guess it's all about intention but ignoring it or freaking out won't help."

"Okay." She changed to a seated position and stretched her legs out. "You said there were a couple of things you needed to tell me."

Now was the tricky part. "Shoko took me *across* yesterday."

Okaasan's mouth gaped open. "Oh Junya, why?"

I told her everything, from Chichén Itzá right up to the Grand Elder's decree.

"They must be really worried," she said when I finished. "Allowing the Gatekeepers to fight on this side is unprecedented."

"Yeah, I'm getting that."

She reached up to tighten her ponytail, giving her time to organize her thoughts. "After all we've been through, I never dreamed I'd have to face this."

"Face what?"

She smiled, but her voice sounded sad. "I trained you as if you were an apprentice," she said. "So, I can't complain now that you've practically become a Gatekeeper, can I?"

"You think I'm a Gatekeeper?"

She nodded. "As close as a boy can get, I suppose." she said. "Protecting the gods is a very noble task. I'm proud they chose you."

I took a moment to process that.

"You know," I said. "I'd never heard of any of these religions or their gods before meeting Shoko. But all over the world, people are still worshiping them."

"The ceremonies are very important to those who still observe them."

"They must be if people are still doing them after all this time."

She nodded. "I think that is what makes it so special."

—

Okaasan had breakfast ready when I walked into the kitchen after my shower. After all our family had gone through, she'd done a great job of keeping things normal, at least around the house.

On the kitchen table, two plates waited with omelets, toast, and sliced fruit. She always had her breakfast before I did, but she'd have her tea with me while I ate.

She reached for the phone. "I'll call your dad from his workshop."

"Wait." I held up my hand. "I forgot to tell you I saw Chiyoko yesterday—your mom."

She didn't seem surprised. "How did she look?"

"Like a queen, all regal and stuff."

Another sad smile. "My mother always carried herself well."

"Are you … were you supposed to succeed her?"

She stared at the table. "Yes, it was likely," she said. "As Shoko once humbly mentioned, I was the best they'd ever seen until she came along."

"Is it hereditary?"

"No, but if a leader's daughter was extraordinary, it's possible the Elders would choose her." She smiled. "My mother worked very hard to see that it happened."

"But you gave it all up, just to marry Dad?"

She shot me a dirty look. "It was a good choice, both then and now."

"Shoko nearly died when Chiyoko looked at her," I said with a laugh. "How important is she anyway?"

"She carries the traditions of a thousand of years on her shoulders, and she is an Elder herself."

I stared past her, out toward the living room while I gathered my thoughts. This was all a little weird.

"So … wait! Is that why you didn't face a death sentence when you disobeyed the Elders?"

That made her smile. "No one kills the daughter of Chiyoko."

"And she let you go, never to see you again?"

"She gave me a way out and wore the shame herself," Okaasan said. "I didn't understand it until I became a mother myself, but we do things for our children ..." She sighed. "We try to do what we think is best, even if it ends up hurting us."

—

"Morning you two." My dad kicked off his work boots and bent to give Okaasan a kiss on the lips.

She smiled up at him. "Your coffee's ready."

"How're you this morning, James?" he said as he poured the coffee into a cheerful multi-colored mug, one I'd made years ago in art class.

"It's Christmas break," I said. "So, I'm great."

"I haven't seen your report card," he said. "How'd you do?"

I shrugged, so Okaasan jumped in. "It was *okay*, but I know he could do better."

"*Okay?* I made honor roll for god's sake!"

I waited until we'd finished eating to drop the bomb.

"I saw Grandpa the other day," I said, trying my best to act casual. "He's letting me buy a car."

Okaasan's teacup, on its way to her lips, froze. "Excuse me?"

Dad cleared his throat. "It's not his decision to make."

I held up a hand. "I won't drive it," I said. "I'll have a driver, one that Barrymore has to approve of. That way I won't have to take the bus everywhere or be chauffeured around in an ugly sedan like I am now."

Dad grunted and Okaasan glared. After an agonizing silence, she said, "What kind of car?"

I grinned. I knew I'd won. "Something sporty."

"I want your word that you won't drive it."

"I need your permission to get my license," I said. "So, I *can't* drive it."

I was just finishing the dishes and Dad was pulling on his work boots when Okaasan walked in wearing new athletic gear.

"I decided to start running," she said in response to my and Dad's shocked expressions. She knelt to tie her shiny neon-green running shoes. "Without Junya to train, I'm bored and need the exercise."

CHAPTER

8

IT WAS A BIT AFTER FOUR o'clock on Christmas Eve when the front doorbell rang. It was Mack.

"Yo," he said when I let him in. "Thought I'd come a bit early." Then he sniffed the air and frowned.

"Sorry, my mom decided not to make dinner tonight. You have to go."

I caught something in his expression, a look of rejection, followed by a message carried on the stream. I immediately regretted what I'd said.

I smacked his arm. "I'm kidding bro, the Tourtière is already in the oven," I said. "My mom will turn it on when she gets home." My other grandma—Dad's mom who'd died before I was born—was French Canadian, and Okaasan had gotten her recipe for meat pies, or *Tourtière* in French. They were a Christmas Eve tradition at our culturally mixed up house. "You can have some of her Christmas baking while we wait for dinner."

He immediately brightened and he kicked off his shoes. "Thanks. There's nothing being served at my house 'cept bullshit."

"Is that Mack?" Dad called from somewhere in the house. "I've got his paycheck here."

Mack grinned. "I love coming here."

—

Mack and I left my place at about six-thirty, both of us ready to burst from meat pie and mashed potatoes with gravy. I'd been eating a lot of odd stuff lately. Whenever Mack was there, Okaasan changed dinner plans from a Japanese-style dinner to something more familiar to him. We'd talked about it and agreed Mack was welcome anytime he showed up, even if it was late in the evening, which had happened more and more often lately. I never asked him about it, though. If he wanted to talk, I knew he would.

We'd decided to go to a movie, an action flick opening for the coveted Christmas release. Fog had settled over the city and I couldn't see much beyond a block or so, but I liked the way the Christmas lights glowed in the mist.

"Did you buy Isabella a Christmas present?" I asked Mack while we waited for the crosswalk light to change.

"Yup," he said. "But it wasn't easy. I want to show I care, but not go overboard either, like I'm trying too hard."

I laughed as the "walk" sign came on. "You guys have been going out for like ..." I counted off on my fingers. "Eight weeks. What's wrong with you anyway?"

"She's really great," he said with an odd tone in his voice. "We've been getting closer this past month, but I'm taking it slow."

"What do you mean by *slow*?"

"Slow as in I waited a long time for her to agree to go out with me again," he said. "I don't want to blow this."

"Okay, now define *close*," I said, though I already suspected the answer.

"Her parents went away last weekend—"

"Uh oh."

"She invited me over, made an authentic Italian dinner, ricotta-and-spinach something. It was amazing!"

"I'll bet."

He shrugged, looked a bit bashful. "She had candles and stuff, really nice, and we ended up, you know …"

My mouth dropped open. "You scored with Isabella Ricci?"

He stopped and glared down at me. "I didn't *score*, James. I like her, a lot."

I gave him a look. "You've liked a lot of girls *a lot*."

"Maybe, but this is different." He jammed his hands into his pockets and we walked in silence for about half a block before he turned to me. "You and Shoko do it yet?"

I hesitated. "No, but I've seen her naked … from a distance." I told him what she'd said about kissing, then how she'd kissed me a few days later. "I don't know where we're at."

"She's kinda giving you mixed signals." He sounded sympathetic. "Why don't you make a move, step things up a notch? The worst she can say is 'no.'"

"Or she could kill me."

He gave that some slow, serious thought, then nodded. "That's a risk, a definite risk. But if she's confused, I think that's a good thing."

"Why? She might be ready to back off."

He shook his head. "Confusion means *maybe*. Does she know you want more?"

I shrugged. "She knows I like her," I said. "But I'm not sure she knows what to do, and god knows I don't."

He thumped me on the back. "Don't worry, she'll let you know."

"How?"

He shrugged. "Isabella said she was giving me signals for weeks, but I never noticed. I think I was being too careful with her." He laughed. "I'm sure when Shoko's ready, she'll make it real clear for you. So pay attention."

"How did Isabella make it *clear*?"

He smiled. "When she pulled out the condom."

I started to laugh, but then ... that tingle in the back of my neck.

Mack laughed. "When she—"

I spun, on full alert, trying to *listen.*

Mack froze. "What?"

There was a flash of energy. I shoved Mack into a doorway and ran toward a thin alley about a half block away. I rounded the corner in time to see Shoko materialize, down on one knee, dressed in her traditional Gatekeeper's uniform. Yukie, Kyoko, and Rina appeared a moment later. All carried bows, along with their swords.

"Junya, catch!" Yukie tossed me a bokuto.

Mack ran around the corner and skidded to a stop beside me.

"Holy shit!" he said. "They're real ... I mean *really* real!"

"What's going on?" I said.

"There is a battle in the land of the Druids!" Shoko said, puffing as if she'd run here. "This is a chance to learn more, perhaps even save a shaman."

"This is going to be great!" Yukie yelled as she vanished.

Shoko reached out her hand to me. "Come on!"

—

The energy of Evil Ones hit me before we'd even materialized, but there was other energy too, and it was pretty damn strong. The grass was wet, the air cold and thick with fog, but the moon shone down on a rough circle of tall standing stones. Stonehenge? No, the rocks were too short, too thin and jagged. Plus, Stonehenge was in England not Scotland.

Suddenly a bright flash like lightning blasted from inside the stone circle, illuminating a small cluster of robed figures, all with beards down to their stomachs. Another group in kilts fought off a large cluster of men dressed in black.

I didn't need my senses, or my throbbing shoulder, to know the guys in black were Evil Ones.

One of the figures within the stone circle raised his staff. White light blasted out again, this time straight toward us. I didn't have time to think. I held up my palm and shoved out my breath.

The bolt of light bounced like a laser beam off a mirror and disappeared into the sky.

"What the hell was that?!" I shouted.

Shoko squinted into the dark. *"These shamans are strong!"* she said into my head.

The man fired again and I deflected it again, this time sending it right back over his head. The stone circle and everything near it lit up again. I noticed the Evil Ones and the kilted Scotsmen were fighting with swords and bows. It was like a scene from a Medieval movie.

"Why aren't they using guns?" I said to no one in particular.

"Are those seriously druids?"

I spun around to see Mack behind me, pointing to the group of men inside the circle.

"What the hell are *you* doing here?!" But I couldn't think about that right now because the same druid was squinting at us, his energy strong but confused.

We are friends! I sent the message straight to his mind.

The druid froze, but we'd caught the attention of several Evil Ones. A few started toward us.

One raised a crossbow and fired. Yukie fell. I thought she was hit, but a second later she released an arrow from the ground. It hit the Evil One in the throat and lifted him off his feet. I dropped to my knees as more arrows came our way.

"I think this was a bad idea!" I yelled at Shoko.

Her katana slid out as a dozen Evil Ones closed in. Kyoko and Rina joined Yukie and began picking off Evil Ones, one arrow at a time.

"Rina, look after Mack!" I yelled over my shoulder.

She responded by knocking Mack's feet out from under him, sending him to the ground. It was probably the safest place for him.

Shoko engaged a group, maybe five, and her dance began. Evil

Ones were dropping fast, their screams ripping through the mist.

A Scotsman appeared off to my left and attacked an Evil One closing in on us. The Scotsman was winning until he punched his opponent in the nose and black blood squirted out.

He faltered.

The Evil One pulled a knife and stabbed him in the stomach, then yanked the long blade out and aimed it toward the Scotsman's heart.

I lashed out, a wild spin-kick that knocked the Evil One backward.

As the Scotsman collapsed, the Evil One turned on me. I jumped back and the blade slashed though my jacket. Another Evil One jumped over the fallen Scotsman and suddenly I was fighting two of them.

Now Evil Ones aren't sissy-pants, as Grandpa would say, and one still had the knife. My energy rose and I let out a yell as I caught his wrist, took control of the blade, and shoved it into his throat. As that one fell, black blood spraying from his neck, I swung my bokuto and caught the other one in the side of the head. He dropped like a stone.

Someone shoved me from behind.

"Get down!"

I hit the ground as an arrow whistled overhead. An Evil One I hadn't even seen had a crossbow pointed straight at me. Shoko hit the ground, disappeared, then reappeared behind the shooter, katana raised high. Her blade caught the moonlight as it sliced downward, and there was a sickening sound as it cut into flesh. Then she leaped over him and rushed back toward me.

"Watch your back!" she yelled as she plunged her blade into another Evil One.

Just then, the Evil One I'd hit with my bokuto sprang off the ground, right beside me. Before I could even lift my weapon, Mack leaped forward and hit him in the chin so hard his feet came off the ground. The Evil One fell backward into the arc of Shoko's katana.

I ran over to the stabbed Scotsman. He was losing blood faster than I'd thought possible. Already there was a puddle underneath him.

"Oh shit …"

I looked up. It was Mack. He stared down at the man, whose stomach hung open like a piece of meat. Then he turned around and threw up.

"Medic!" I shouted, an automatic response learned from war movies.

Shoko and I stepped back as two women, who seemed to appear from nowhere, rushed over.

The clang of steel and the battle cries had lessened. The Evil Ones were retreating, leaving their wounded crawling across the ground, the dead already vanishing. As the Scotsmen and Shoko's apprentices chased down the rest, I did a quick inventory. The apprentices, Shoko and Mack were all accounted for.

Energy hit my back with enough power that it knocked me forward. I turned, my head buzzing, my hand coming up to block it—and froze.

Five bearded men holding long staffs stood glowering at us.

"You do not belong here," an ancient-looking druid said, his voice hollow like the wind. "You should return." He thumped the ground with his staff.

"One belongs," the short man beside him said. He stepped toward Mack, who towered above him. "Who be you, lad?"

Mack glanced sideways at me. "Mack … Anderson."

"Ah, MacGhilleAndrais," he said, the name rolling off his tongue. "You have heritage, boy. Seek it out."

They turned and walked slowly into the mist, then disappeared.

"You're welcome," I said, but quietly.

A heavy hand clasped my shoulder. "Well, I appreciate it, lad," said a deep voice thick with a Scottish accent.

I spun around. Why the hell was everyone sneaking up on me today?

"Your warriors are impressive."

"You were prepared for this attack?" Shoko asked in such a thick Scottish accent that I struggled to understand her.

He looked at her in surprise, then slowly nodded. "Aye lassie, they arrived yesterday on a private jet. Our gods don't lack followers, so we don't lack information."

"They missed the solstice by a few days."

"There was a big crowd here that day," he said. "And the druids only come out when it's quiet. Can't say I blame them. Surprised these evil fellows know that."

"Why don't you guys use guns?" Mack said.

"The energy's so strong it makes the bullets explode." He held up his broadsword. "Besides, this is the way real men should fight—and women too." He looked at Shoko and the three girls standing behind her. They were dirty and disheveled but stood straight and proud. "The old druids don't speak much about their practices, but we know they live in the Underworld, and they've spoken of the warrior-women dressed in green. You be them?"

"Aye, we be," Shoko said. I choked back a laugh.

He bowed deeply. "I am honored." Then he looked at Mack. "Mr. Anderson, should you ever want to visit Scotland, look me up. I know a bit about what your heritage might be."

Mack looked surprised. "I ... that's really kind of you ..."

The man held out his hand. "William McLeod, of the village of Stornoway."

"I just might do that one day," Mack said after pumping the man's hand firmly. "Thank you."

As he walked away, I turned to Shoko and grinned. "You speak like a wee Scottish lassie."

She put her hand on my chest. "Aye."

"What do you think he meant?" Mack said, still looking in the direction the druids had gone.

"I don't know," I said, looking around Shoko at him. "Are you Scottish?"

"My great grandfather came from there ... here."

"Then do as he suggested," Shoko said. "Perhaps you are more than you seem."

"After that, I'm almost afraid to," he said. "Do you think they were really druids?"

"I don't know, but it was awesome!" I said, waving my bokuto like one of their staffs. "The way they zapped the Evil Ones was crazy!"

Shoko nodded. "I have never seen such power on this side," she said.

I gave her an exaggerated frown. "Not even from me?"

"Hah!" She smacked my arm. "How many times did I save you tonight?" She turned suddenly serious. "Must I assign an apprentice to watch your back every minute?"

Yukie grinned. "I will protect him!"

"Did you see the thumping I gave that guy?" Mack smacked his palm.

I nodded. "You laid him out pretty good."

"That was not *pretty*," Shoko said. "But what you lack in skill you made up for in brute strength."

Mack grinned. "Technique is overrated."

Which reminded me. "I guess I should make formal introductions."

I introduced the three apprentices first, saving Shoko for last, which turned into an awkward mixture of attempted bows and handshakes.

"Yeah, wow," Mack said. "It's really awesome to finally meet you! You guys are amazing!" He gave Shoko a lopsided grin. "I kind of thought James was going crazy for a while." He looked around for a moment. The moors, the mist, the battlefield. He shook his head. "Or maybe it's me who's gone crazy."

"I have heard much about you, Mack," Shoko said, looking up at him. "Junya speaks highly of you, but you are much larger than I imagined."

I poked him in the ribs. "And what the hell are you doing here anyway?"

Mack pointed at Rina "She brought me."

I gave Rina the evil eye. "And you're okay?"

He shrugged. "That *traveling* thing was weird, felt like falling into a hole, but it was cool. No problem."

Rina laughed.

"He screamed like a little girl," she said.

CHAPTER
9

AFTER SHOKO AND RINA TRAVELED US back to where they'd found us, I stood for a long moment, taking in the surroundings and *listening*, before I stepped out from between the buildings onto the sidewalk. Nothing had changed since we'd left, but I felt different and I was damn sure Mack felt different too.

"I will come back shortly," Shoko said as she knelt to travel away. "We have much to talk about."

Once Mack had recovered from the traveling, we walked toward a coffee house a few blocks away. I ordered an eggnog latte and a slice of pumpkin pie. Mack had only tea, which was unheard of.

"You sure you're okay?" I asked him after he took a sip of tea.

He looked up at the ceiling. "Good question," he said. "Honestly, it was like a 3D movie. Amazingly lifelike but not *real*. And now we're sitting here sipping our drinks, all nice and safe." He leaned toward me, elbows on the table. "But if it was real, then I saw *real* people die." He lowered his eyes, his skin ashen. "I've never seen anything like that before."

"I'm getting a bit too used to blood," I said, adding a laugh to ease my own tension. When I went to take a bite of pie a moment later, I found I had no appetite.

Mack traced his finger on the ring left by his mug. "Those guys, the ones with black blood … they're Evil Ones, right?"

I nodded.

"They disappear when you kill them?" He looked up at me. "Poof …?"

I closed my eyes. I hadn't planned to bring him into this no matter how *cool* he thought it was. When I opened my eyes, he was staring at the wall behind me.

"This is crazy." He was struggling, I heard it in his voice.

"I'm sorry, Mack. I don't know why Rina brought you."

"What was she supposed to do, leave me in the street?" There was an edge to his voice now. "No matter what, that was the most amazing experience of my life."

I managed a half smile, but I was still worried.

"Do the Evil Ones all look like that?"

"Their faces are different," I said, "but they seem to wear the same clothing and stuff."

"All the time?" he said.

"I don't know." Even Evil Ones must get a day off now and then.

"Are there female Evil Ones?"

I thought of Shoko's evil twin. "I think so."

He took a sip of his tea. "What if that guy …" He indicated a tall man waiting for his drink. "… was an Evil One?"

"I'd sense it."

"But I can't. Shoko can't." He glanced around. "Can your mom?"

I thought for a moment. "Probably." Okaasan had mentioned that once. "But I don't think you need to worry about Evil Ones."

"Maybe not, but …" He looked like he was onto something. "I'm just thinking, this Bartholomew guy is a powerful world banker, right?"

I nodded.

"Well, a guy like that has way more power than a president or a king. Nowadays, anyway." His face creased as he concentrated. "So that means there are tons of people out there who work for him, not just these Evil Ones."

"I guess so. What are you getting at?"

"The regular people who serve Bartholomew, they could be all around us right now, like that guy."

I waved a hand. "I'm pretty good at sensing evil intention toward me—"

"What if they don't have evil intentions?" he said. "What if they think what they're doing is right?"

I didn't reply. I'd never thought of it like that before.

"I'm just saying." He glanced around the coffee shop one last time. "If this Bartholomew dude wanted to kill shamans, or even you or me, he doesn't need an Evil One. And you might not see it coming."

Shoko arrived about fifteen minutes later, dressed in a short skirt over black leggings, a dark blouse, and flower-patterned sneakers. She wore her leather jacket too, which was a good thing. It was getting cool outside.

She pushed past two guys on their way out and stopped beside our table.

"Hello," she said. She looked quite pleased about something.

Mack stood up before I even had a chance to reply. "Can I get you a coffee or something?"

"That is most kind, but no thank you." She bowed. "It made me feel jittery the last time I had some."

"And trust me, we don't want her feeling jittery," I muttered.

"Um, they have green tea?" Mack said.

She nodded as she sat down beside me. "Thank you."

I waited until Mack was out of earshot, then put my hand on top of hers.

"Hi. What are you so happy about?"

"The Elders are pleased with us."

"Us?"

Shoko broke off a corner of my pie crust and popped it into her mouth.

"Three more shamans have failed to cross over," she said. "The Elders believe they were killed before, or as, the gateway opened. They are happy to see we are taking action."

"Why do you think they wait for an opening?" I thought about what Mack had said earlier. "The Evil Ones could kill them anytime."

"Why waste time searching for and identifying a shaman when it is so easily done at an opening ceremony?" Shoko picked up my fork. "May I?" Before I could answer, she took a bite of my pie.

"But how do the Evil Ones even know the schedule?"

"They have had centuries to figure it out," she mumbled while chewing. "That is why we always must be vigilant." She took another forkful.

I gazed at my disappearing pie. "None of that explains why they're killing shamans, though."

She nodded, her mouth full.

Mack placed a steaming cup of tea in front of Shoko, then dropped heavily onto the chair. "What did I miss?"

"More shamans are disappearing," I said.

He looked thoughtful. "So, during the attack tonight, even though they didn't kill any druids, they still interrupted the ceremony. Can they count that as a success?"

Shoko sipped her tea and made a face. "Perhaps, since it is worship that makes the gods strong."

"That's gotta make a difference," I said.

Shoko nodded. "And the Elders are wondering how that might affect *us*."

"As in the Gatekeepers?"

"Yes," she said after she'd cleaned off another forkful. "This is delicious!"

"I wouldn't know." I grabbed the fork. "I haven't had any yet."

"I am not stopping you."

After I swallowed a big bite, I said, "How could it affect you guys?"

"All our powers are gifts from the gods," she said. "If they are weakened, we may be weakened as well."

I thought about my last trip to Izumo. I hadn't noticed anything different, but how would I know what to look for?

"It is only a theory, of course," she said while eyeballing my pie. "No such thing has ever happened before."

I sighed and slid the plate and fork toward her.

"Why didn't the Mayan shaman put up a fight like those druids?" Mack said. "They could've kicked their evil asses."

"The Mayan gods are not strong anymore, so neither are their shamans," Shoko said. Then to my surprise, she fed me the last piece of pie. "The Celtic gods are *very* popular again, being worshiped by people all over the world now, and that makes them powerful. Those druids benefit from that power, as you saw tonight."

"So, worshipers power their god, who then gives the power back to their shamans, *and* to you guys?" I said after my mouth was empty.

Shoko shook her head. "We benefit from the power of all the gods, because we defend all the gods," she said. "Not only our own."

"If you're right," I said, "then maybe all Bartholomew has to do is kill *enough* shamans. It might be a while, but it could weaken the Gatekeepers eventually."

Mack frowned. "Maybe that's why he's doing it."

We were all quiet after that, each of us thinking about this puzzle. Mack broke the silence several minutes later.

"Is Bartholomew the devil?" he said. "Because that Zion place sure doesn't sound like hell."

Shoko tried another sip of the tea and looked less disturbed than before. "Zion is not hell, just as Izumo is not heaven." She pointed at her chest. "Heaven and hell are in here."

"Yeah, but—"

"The only thing evil about Zion is those who can travel there or come back."

I think Mack realized what she'd said a few seconds before she did. The conversation stopped dead, both of them suddenly quite interested in the table top.

I broke the awkward silence.

"Yes, I did, and I probably still can go to both places," I said. "It seems I'm—"

"Special." Shoko took my hand. "That is what you are." She smiled at me in a way that made my heart flutter.

Mack's eyebrows came together when he saw that.

"But when we were in Zion, Bartholomew said he'd use me to get into Izumo." I looked at Shoko. "And you and Okaasan are worried about my energy too."

"I am not concerned," she said, "other than about the way you blast it around."

Mack didn't seem to be listening to us. "Do the Elders think you might go bad and bring a bunch of Evil Ones into Izumo?" he said.

My stomach went cold. He'd spoken my worst nightmare so casually.

"How do you propose Junya would let these Evil Ones in?" Shoko asked, her tone displaying her displeasure.

I let out a sigh. "Rina said the Controllers open gateways using really strong energy," I said. "Maybe I can open gateways too."

A slight frown crossed Shoko's face.

Mack nodded. "Yeah, then you could cross over and bring an evil army with you."

Shoko *really* didn't like that comment.

"But since you're not evil," he said, unaware of our mood change, "you could as easily bring a bunch of Gatekeepers over here." He broke into a grin. "Hell, your army could wipe out the Evil Ones."

Shoko and I looked at one another. My mouth had dropped half open. Her eyes looked about ready to pop. We both looked at Mack.

He looked nervous. "What?"

"An army of Gatekeepers." Shoko said.

I smiled. "That's a really good idea."

Shoko stared at the ceiling. "Perhaps if it were a special group ..."

I nodded. "They'd need to be able to fight on this side, with the noise, like you and your apprentices."

Shoko bit her lip. "But the Elders would never approve."

"They said to do whatever it takes to stop the killings, right?"

Mack looked back and forth between us. "I was only thinking out loud. I didn't mean to—"

"I know," I said with a grin. "But it was an awesome idea!" My heart felt light for the first time in weeks, though it was probably because of the way Shoko still held my hand. "We could stop them *before* they kill any more shamans."

Shoko nodded her approval. "Yes. Learning why they are killing shamans is less important than stopping them, I believe."

Mack looked disappointed. "I want to kick ass too!"

Shoko shot him a look. "Technique is *not* overrated," she said. "Rina, my smallest apprentice, could kill you like that." She snapped her fingers. "Brute strength means nothing."

Mack frowned. "She'd be out cold if I punched her in the jaw," he said. "Not that I would, of course."

"You would be dead before your punch connected," Shoko said.

I held up a hand. "Since you practically live at my house," I said to Mack. "Why don't you ask my mom to train you? She's bored and misses beating people up."

That made Shoko laugh.

"Since my fists are *worthless*," he said, glowering at Shoko. "What do you think I should learn?"

I thought for a minute. "*Aikido, kenjutsu* and *iaijutsu, jujutsu* ..." I counted on my fingers. "And *bujutsu* and *ninjutsu*."

"And *shurikenjutsu*," Shoko added.

He looked doubtful for a long moment, then brightened. "Hey, maybe she'll stop jogging and dinner will be ready on time."

I laughed.

Shoko looked at me. "How come I never get invited to dinner?"

She pointed toward Mack with her chin. "Am I less important than him?"

"Ah …"

Mack pushed himself back from the table. "I'd love to hear you get out of that one bro, but I should go home and join the Christmas Eve celebrations."

"Are you sure?" I said. "You can hang out. It's been a rough night."

"Rough, but *very* interesting," he said as he stood up. "And I talked to an honest-to-god druid!"

"True." I searched his face. "You sure you're okay?"

He nodded as he backed away. "I need to get used to things," he said, then winked. "You keep your eyes open tonight."

I raised a brow at him, confused.

He smiled at me. "Look for signs, bro."

CHAPTER
10

AFTER SHOKO AND I WATCHED MACK leave, she lightly squeezed my hand. When I turned to look at her, she gave me an amused grin.

"Look, about dinner—"

"I was teasing you," she said, leaning closer to me. "But I am not unhappy he left."

I smiled at her. "Can you stay for a while?"

She smiled back. "I am yours for the evening."

I liked the sound of that. "Well, how about we go to Pier 39," I said. "The Christmas tree—"

She bounced off her chair. "Yes please!"

I glanced at my watch as she dragged me out the door. "Damn, it's later than I thought. By the time we get there—"

She pulled me into the shadows beside the café. "We can travel," she said and slapped our hands onto the ground before I could answer.

We materialized a moment later in a bunch of scruffy bushes about fifty feet away from the cable car turntable at Aquatic Park. I fell backward onto a shrub with a crash. Several people in the long line for the cable car turned to look in our direction. There was enough light from the streetlights for them to see us.

"What the hell are you doing?" I hissed at Shoko.

She stood up and brushed a few leaves off her leggings. "Even if anyone saw us appear, do you think they would believe what their own eyes were telling them?"

I stood up too.

Everyone had already drifted back into their usual daze, except a few kids who still looked. Maybe they still believed in magic.

Shoko headed toward the turntable where the workers were spinning one of the cable cars, readying it for its trip back up Hyde Street. She glanced back at me. "If there is not enough time for us to *ride* the cable cars, I want to at least see them—" Shoko froze, her mouth dropped open.

They'd decked out the cable car for Christmas with a sparkly blue wreath on the front, colorful lights around the windows, and plastic icicles across the back. I thought it looked great.

"This is part of your winter celebration?"

"Yup, it's the biggest holiday of the year."

She nodded her head several times. "It is quite extravagant." She pointed at a large sign. "Is this *Santa* a god? He seems to be an important part of the rituals."

I stood staring at the picture, thinking about how to answer that.

"Santa didn't use to be part of it. It's a Christian holiday meant to celebrate the birth of Jesus."

She puzzled over that for a moment. "Ah yes, I remember this from my schooling," she said. "The Roman Church used this celebration to replace winter solstice celebrations among the old religions. Many earth gods withered because of this."

"Yeah well, Santa did the same thing to Christianity." I laughed at the irony of it. "Now it's all about buying stuff you don't need. I guess the real god now is materialism."

"Is this *Materialism* a good god or bad god?"

"Everyone says it's bad, but they keep worshiping it," I said, "and my grandpa wouldn't be rich without it."

"Materialism is very powerful then."

"If a god's strength is based on how much people worship it, then I'd say materialism is the most powerful god there is."

—

Shoko's eyes nearly popped when she saw the sixty-foot Christmas tree at Pier 39. I have to admit, it was spectacular, but for her, that tree was probably as amazing as it was for me to look up at the Grand Shrine at Izumo. Maybe more.

Shoko was in a great mood, bouncing and laughing, pulling me into all the shops on the Pier and she rode the carousel three times before I grabbed her by the waist and lifted her down.

We got some fish and chips for takeout and ate it overlooking the noisy crowd of sea lions on the docks below us. I kept glancing at her as we ate. I really liked being with her. Okay, I was crazy about her. She was so ... *alive*. I wondered if it was because so much of her duty involved death and this was so opposite, or because she was a teenager out having a good time.

She didn't notice me watching her. She was too busy laughing at the sea lions. The more I looked at her and thought about her, the more I wished she could really be my girlfriend. Maybe Mack was right. I had nothing to lose by making a move.

When we were done eating, we walked back west on Jefferson Street. The sidewalks were packed with couples, tour groups, and families walking together. We took our time, looking at the restaurants, the shops, Fisherman's Wharf. As we passed the red-and-white checked tables outside Castagnola's, I put my arm around her waist. The first thing she did was look around. I felt a spike of frustration.

"Nobody here knows you, Shoko."

"Perhaps, but—"

I let my arm drop as we continued walking. "Why can't you relax and act natural?"

"Natural?"

"Look around," I said, spreading my hands. All around us couples were holding hands, cuddling, and laughing. Over by the railing, two people were doing some heavy making out.

She stared at them for a long moment before she turned away.

"I just want ..." I looked down. "I really like you and I want to be with you, like a normal couple." I stuffed my hands in my coat pockets.

She turned to look at me.

"Be like a couple?" She looked confused. "I am sorry Junya, but this is not easy for me." She pointed at a billboard advertisement for some trendy brand of jeans—a Thompson Media sign. The two young models were both topless, their bodies entwined with only his well-placed hand keeping her nipples from showing. "Do you think that is *natural* for me? In my world, people do not touch with affection, ever."

"Your parents must've touched a few times," I said. "Otherwise you and Taro—"

She hit my arm. "Do not be stupid! You know that is not what I meant."

"Sorry, but ..." I was getting frustrated. "... they might not walk around holding hands, but there's got to be some people messing around."

"What is *messing around?*"

"You know, sneaking off to be alone together, kissing, cuddling ..." I felt my cheeks getting a little warm. "... maybe more."

"Such liaisons are forbidden by the Elders."

I stopped. "You're telling me there are hundreds of teenage girls walking around Izumo and not one of them is making out with the village boys?"

"We do not train all our lives to dishonor ourselves that way."

"So, it *never* happens?"

She sighed, exasperated. "Of course it does. We are all curious about the changes in our bodies and theirs, so it is not as if we do not think about it. I know some girls 'mess around' with boys, but they do not usually have intercourse."

"Has anyone ever gotten pregnant?"

"More than the Elders want to admit."

"What happens to them?" I asked.

We started walking again, no longer holding hands. "They are dismissed from the Gatekeepers, partnered with the father, and become a mother."

"No second chances?"

She shrugged. "If they succumb, this shows their destiny was never to be a Gatekeeper. They must leave."

"That's a bit harsh."

"Why, do you consider motherhood punishment?"

"No but—"

"Do not misunderstand me. They are not dismissed in disgrace. By saying destiny, I mean that by becoming pregnant, their destiny changes. Their destiny is motherhood, at least for now."

"Does the boy get punished?"

She smiled. "That depends on whether you consider becoming a father and husband at a young age a punishment. Many would." Her smile turned into a grin. "Cooking, cleaning… these are men's tasks over there."

I laughed. "That should be a pretty good deterrent!"

"We all know the power of nature, especially in boys. It appears to be a powerful force, and it affects their judgment. Like when they try to peek at us when we bathe. We have the authority to beat them senseless for that or for any form of unwanted conduct, but that is rare. After all, he may be the one we are destined to be coupled with."

"Coupled?"

She nodded. "All Gatekeepers are assigned a life partner at twenty-five years."

"Jeez, even that's assigned? And why twenty-five?"

"The Elders need women when their reactions are the fastest, when they are the most *obedient*." She said that word as if it tasted sour. "They cannot have girls becoming mothers too soon, otherwise who would fight?" She glanced suspiciously at a group of homeless men sitting on a low concrete wall, their belongings scattered at their feet.

"But this partnering," she said after a while. "It is not like I see with Misako and your father, or others on this side. They obviously *love* each other."

"But your parents loved each other enough to create a family."

"Love does not make babies," she said. "Partnering is based on compatibility. That is the most important thing for any couple. My parents get along very well, but they have no expectations of anything more."

"That's kind of sad."

"Yes, but expectations are the root of turmoil." She looked up at me. "Like with my mother, Tomi, and your grandfather. When he crossed over by accident and was met by her, it changed them both. She discovered love, then lost him three days later. What chance would my father have competing with that memory?"

I didn't know what to say to that.

She looked away, toward the brick building across the street. Somehow, we'd made it all the way to the Argonaut Hotel.

"I like that," she said. "What is it?"

"Ah, it's a hotel, a place where you stay when you're away from home." It was a century-old red brick building a city block long with thin arched windows and doorways spread across its red brick face. I think it used to be fruit-packing plant or something. "We ran through it when we were running from my Grandpa's bodyguards, remember?"

Shoko and I were riding the cable cars and I'd noticed some men following us. I assumed my grandpa had decided to put a discreet protection team on me because he'd just named me his heir. For fun, Shoko and I took off running and cut through alleys, hotels and stores until we lost them.

She nodded. "Yes, that was our first real day together." She kicked a rock toward the gutter.

"That feels like a long time ago."

"And nothing has become easier," she said. "*This* is not easy."

"I'm sorry, Shoko." I stopped, turned, and faced her. "I ... I guess I keep expecting you to act like a girl from here." Without thinking about it, I moved a bit further away from her. "I'm forcing you to be something you're not and that's wrong. I'll stop."

She looked down. "I have done nothing against my will, Junya," she said. "And I want to hold your hand."

With our fingers interlocked, we continued walking west along the road below the cable car roundabout and onto the pathway by the marina. The crunch of our feet on the gravel was the only sound besides the lap of small waves.

She stopped in the shadows under a large oak tree and turned to me.

"Did you peek at me at the hot springs, while I was undressing?"

I looked skyward and tried not to smile. "Not on purpose, but ..."

She punched me softly in the stomach. "And did you like what you saw?"

Now I had to smile. "I'm not sure I saw enough to tell."

I looked down and found her staring straight at me.

"On that day, we spoke of kissing and being alone." She looked sad now. "I felt funny inside and became angry at you because I felt confused."

"Yeah, I really wasn't sure what I did wrong."

She gave me a half smile. "You did nothing. It was because ... when you were unclothed in the pool and I saw your body, something changed inside me. I felt *drawn* to you and I did not know how to deal with that."

"You liked seeing me?"

Her head bobbed up and down several times. "The rules of the Elders do not feel natural to me anymore. I want to follow my desires. I want to be with you."

She put her fingers through the belt loops of my jeans and pulled me close until our bodies touched. Excitement roared through my body as our lips met. Hers were warm, soft, wonderful, passionate, and I lost myself in the moment. Our mouths moved together, tongues touched. It was the sexiest thing I'd ever experienced.

When she pulled back, I could hardly breathe.

"That was ... wow!" she said, breathing hard. "Why did you not show me this sooner?"

I shrugged, a bit timid. "I don't really know what I'm doing."

"You do know, believe me." She fanned her face with her hand and blew out a long breath. "My body is very warm and," she glanced down at herself, "excited."

Our bodies were still pressed together, so I'm sure she could tell I was excited too.

"I feel that way a lot."

She let out a small laugh. "Yes, this is not the first time I have felt your excitement." She looked over my shoulder. "And lately, my body responds in new ways when I think about you. It is far better in reality though."

I grinned. "That's for sure." Then I glanced around us. A few couples walked by, hand in hand, but didn't pay us any attention. "I guess you're not worried about being seen anymore."

"It is private enough here," she whispered. Her lips were so close to mine. "And I feel safe when I am with you."

I put my hands on her hips and they found warm, soft bare skin under her blouse. She sucked in a quick breath and we kissed again. It could have lasted two minutes or an hour. A hundred Evil Ones could've walked by and I wouldn't have noticed.

When our lips finally separated, she let out a sigh. At that moment I felt closer to her than I'd ever felt with anyone.

She rested her head on my chest. After a while she said, "I can hear your heart speaking."

I laughed. "What's it saying?"

"It says you are happy."

CHAPTER
11

CHRISTMAS MORNING AT THE THOMPSON HOUSE was always exciting. Okaasan had fully embraced the holiday and learned how to make everything from eggnog and fruitcake to the full turkey dinner. She also made sure Dad had the outdoor lights up and the tree decorated no later than December first. So, it was her who dragged me out of bed to show me all the presents *Santa* had brought me. I ended up with the usual clothing, plus some games and software I'd hinted at.

I'd already received my Christmas present from Grandpa. I had the deed to the property on Hemlock Street in my safety deposit box. I'd asked him not to tell my parents. I told him I wanted it to be a surprise when it was done.

Around noon, I made the mistake of walking into the kitchen to grab a couple of mincemeat tarts and ended up helping Okaasan wrestle a giant turkey into the roasting pan. Then she handed me a vegetable peeler and a pile of yams and sweet potatoes. As I peeled, I told her what had happened in Scotland and our idea to organize a special group of Gatekeepers to fight on this side.

"What do you think?" I said as I crammed a few yams into the pan beside the turkey.

"Good lord Junya, which part?" She glanced over at me. "This whole business, the killing of shamans, is odd."

I nodded. "Yeah, I thought invading Izumo was Bartholomew's goal. I mean, isn't that why the Gatekeepers exist?"

"He isn't the only threat facing Izumo." She leaned against the stove. "He's one of the most imaginative, which makes him very dangerous. And we know he has a personal interest in you."

I finished the last yam and started to scoop the peels into the recycling bin. "Do you think fighting them on this side will work?"

"The Gatekeeper's skills are far superior to the Evil Ones'," she said. "The biggest dangers will be their lack of senses and the possibility of guns."

"Do you think it's weird the Elders asked me to help with this?"

She slid the huge roasting pan into the oven. "They have nothing to lose, and they have Shoko watching you. Never forget that's part of her duty."

I sat down at the table. I *had* forgotten about that, though I was positive what was happening between us had nothing to do with duty. Unless the Elders tasked Shoko to get close to me, like Okaasan was with my dad … no, that wasn't it. That couldn't be it.

"Well, I'll try not to disappoint them," I finally said. "Maybe once we start attacking the Evil Ones, they'll realize it's me who's keeping Bartholomew out."

That got her attention. "I want you to promise me you'll always have Shoko with you."

"I think you've taught me well enough. And I've got my senses."

"Fighting them is too easy for you and you may get careless. I want Shoko covering your back."

I thought of Shoko's arms around my back, kissing me. "I promise I won't let her leave my side."

Her eyes narrowed as she folded her arms. "Are you and Shoko getting close?"

I looked away. "We spend a lot of time together," I said. "The Elders said we had to, remember?"

She tried a different tack. "Is she your girlfriend?"

I hesitated. "I'm not sure she'd call it that, but we *like* each other."

"That's not good."

"We're just having fun." I shrugged. "What's wrong with that?"

"If she got pregnant—"

"We're not doing that!"

She still didn't look happy. "Shoko's destined for greatness. I wouldn't be surprised if she's a candidate to succeed Chiyoko someday, so don't get too attached to her."

The two of us were silent for a while. Okaasan fussed with the table settings and I helped by lifting my elbows so she could put down a placemat.

"Do all Gatekeepers get partnered or do some get to choose? You know, if they actually fall in love with someone?"

She tilted her head. "Shoko told you about partnering too?"

"Yeah."

"There's no time to fall in love. It's like here. You try to keep your teenagers so busy with sports and school that they have no time for relationships." Then she glared at me. "Obviously I haven't kept you busy enough."

I smiled.

"Anyhow, a Gatekeeper only learns who her partner will be a few days before they're joined. The Elders of old discovered that if the girls—and especially the boys—found out sooner, the girls were pregnant within a few months."

I laughed, but something dropped in my gut. Someday Shoko would belong to someone else. But who was to say? That was still years away and a lot could change by then. A lot had already changed.

"What was the hardest part about living on this side?"

"How about everything?" She laughed. "The only thing that came easy was fighting, but my new family got tired of me hurting everyone." She pulled the plates out of the cupboard. "No, the hardest part was being without my senses. I was as vulnerable as anyone here and that took some getting used to."

"When did your senses come back?" Because obviously, they had.

"That took a while, a couple of years."

"Before or after you met Dad?"

She glanced away. "After."

———

"Why don't we go do something fun tonight?" Dad said after Christmas dinner. "It's been a while and I need some fresh air after that feast." He patted his stomach, which was as flat as mine was.

"Like what?" I asked.

"How about a drive?" Okaasan said, looking excited. "We could go to the coast, maybe Ocean Beach?"

"A *drive?*" I groaned. "Do you have any idea how much I hate *drives?*"

"I've never been on one," Mack said, "but I imagine it's more about the journey than the destination?"

Dad grinned. "Well said, Mack." Then he looked at me. "Any objections to a *journey?*"

I sighed, knowing I wouldn't win this one and no longer sure I cared.

"A *journey* it is then."

Half an hour later, after Mack and I rushed through cleaning the pots and pans, we were cruising down Ocean Highway with the wide stretch of beach beside us. Mack had his nose pressed against the window like an excited dog.

After Dad parked the Audi, he and Okaasan walked toward the water, holding hands. Mack and I sat on the sand and watched the surfers. There was at least a dozen of them out in wetsuits, sitting on their boards outside the break zone, spread out in a line, waiting. West Coast surfers were a die-hard bunch. If you waited for warm water, you'd never get to surf.

There was a good swell, though, and a nice right-hand break that a few surfers were trying to catch. Two guys bailed, but a girl with bright golden hair was up, riding the face, doing bottom turns and getting air almost every time she hit the lip. I was even more impressed when she did a dignified kick-out, riding up the face and over the top to wait for the next wave.

"You're not that good," Mack said.

"Not even close."

My parents were sitting on the sand now, well out of range of rogue waves. Dad stared out at the water while Okaasan did yoga. It reminded me of all the times the three of us had come here over the years, at first with my bucket and shovels, later with a boogie board, and finally to surf. It had been a lot of fun.

We hadn't done anything like that in a long time.

"Mind if I go talk to your mom?" Mack said. "I'm going to ask if she'll train me."

"Go ahead. It's your funeral."

He laughed and walked away.

After a few minutes, I stood up and headed toward the surf. The breeze carried the smell of salt and the ocean, something I'd always loved.

"Hey, wait up!" Dad jogged up beside me.

I glanced back. Okaasan was in some crazy yoga pose, a handstand with her toes pointed toward the sky. Mack was sitting nearby, talking to her.

"It's been a long time, hasn't it?" Dad said.

"I was just thinking about that."

"Life gets so busy, and then you forget." He lightly punched my arm. "And you went and grew up too fast."

"That's because you work too much."

He shrugged. "I need to make a living."

"No, you don't." I looked out at the ocean. "You don't *need* to do anything."

He was quiet for a while, the only sound the rush of water up the beach.

"I want to be my own man, and I want to provide the best for you and your mother." He bent down and examined a shell, then tossed it toward the water. "Your mom had a hard childhood. I've always tried to make up for that."

"What makes you think Mom had a hard childhood?"

He grunted. "You've seen her hands. They were in worse shape when I met her. All she did was work for her family."

I decided to go with it. "They were merchants, right? Business people?"

He nodded a few times. "Right. Plus, they were pretty famous for maintaining Zen gardens and *Niwaki*, stuff like that."

"What's Niwaki?"

"Like bonsai, but on large trees."

I smiled. I knew the ninja had often disguised themselves as gardeners.

We walked in silence after that, both of us watching the surfers. An offshore wind had picked up and the waves were curling nicely.

"What was Mom like when you first met her?"

He laughed. "She was a very cute, sweet girl, and shy." He thought for a moment. "Actually, naïve is a better word. She had a damn strong personality and a ton of confidence. But I'd had a few girlfriends and I was your mom's first boyfriend, and she was awkward. It was kind of sweet actually."

"Were things weird with her parents?"

He laughed again but it sounded less pleasant. "They were actually pretty happy, considering I was a foreigner and all."

"Did you and Mom have trouble?"

He smiled. "We had our share of misunderstandings, and love can only get you so far. A lot of times it's compatibility that gets you through."

We'd stopped again, both of us watching the big waves.

"We lived in Japan until you were five," Dad said a few minutes later. "But even there she had trouble. She made a lot of people uncomfortable. She was very formal—almost regal—but not snobby, and she had amazing inner strength, this incredible peace like no one I'd ever met. And it was obvious she was no regular merchant's daughter."

"What do you mean?"

We started walking again. "One night when I was walking her home beside the Matsue Castle's moat, a group of bikers went roaring past. They aren't like bikers here though. They're more like immature dropouts who ride noisy little speed bikes and annoy the hell out of everyone. Anyhow, they came back and started yelling at us, about me being a foreigner, and they said some rather rude things about your mother. Man, did she get mad! She beat the crap out of them. Kicked some right off their bikes." He shook his head. "It was brutal. There were ten guys on the ground not moving when we walked away."

"Now you know why I had so many injuries over the years."

Like a message from the stream, Mack's yell carried across the sand. I grabbed Dad's arm and pointed. Mack was on his way to the ground after a rather impressive flip. Then he was back up, faster than I'd ever been, only to be taken out again.

Dad laughed. "I hope she doesn't maim him. I need him to work next weekend."

I knew my questioning was starting to sound a bit too pointed, but I kept going. There were too many things I'd never understood, too many things we hadn't talked about.

"Is there any other reason you think she wasn't a 'regular merchant's daughter'?"

He stopped and stared at me. "Because your mom didn't have a clue about merchandising and as you know, she couldn't keep a plant alive to save her life."

I swallowed. "Yeah, that is kinda weird …"

"Your mother radiates positivity like nothing I'd ever felt, especially considering her fondness for the deadly martial arts."

"Deadly?"

"All the arts you practice end in *jutsu* and not *do*. That means you're always studying for combat, not sport."

That was why I'd broken a bully's arm in grade school, and why I'd never used it at school again. Okaasan had issued a severe punishment when she found out. It was only recently that I came to understand how deadly the skills she'd taught me could be.

Dad shot me a sideways glance. "Lin's the same way."

I stared at him. "Why would you say that?"

He shrugged. "Lin's related to your mother, so I'd expect she can fight too."

"You know they're related?" I said then immediately regretted it.

He didn't say anything for a long moment. "Matsue's not that big a city," he said quietly. "I know who she is."

I struggled to get my thoughts together. "So, her being with Grandpa and stuff ..."

He nodded. "Quite the coincidence wouldn't you say? And quite odd that she pretended she didn't know your mom."

Although I kept trying, but I couldn't tell anything from his energy. It was as if he was blocking it.

"I barely recognize you anymore," Dad said, just loud enough to hear over the wind. "You're strong inside now, just like your mother ... so much like your mother." He looked out toward the ocean at the setting sun. He looked so sad.

"Dad?"

"Did you know your mom almost left me once?" He didn't wait for a reply before he continued. "We'd only been in San Francisco for a year—you were six—when she told me she wanted to go back to Japan. She said she couldn't find herself here." He glanced over at me. "That was the only time I've ever seen her mentally collapse, and I was terrified she'd leave. That's when I built her the dojo, the Japanese tub, the Zen garden. I worked my ass off to recreate her world, but she still was having trouble so I did the only other thing I could think of."

"What?"

"I told her she should teach you everything she learned as a kid, and I would never ask any questions. She's been content ever since."

I looked up at him. "You know a lot more than you let on."

"Maybe." He rubbed his chin. "That's why I've never asked about how you got injured. I was horrified when I saw you, but when your mom says to back off, I do." He sighed. "As long as it doesn't change our family or our life, I'll look the other way as best as I can."

"That's a crappy way to live."

"Is it?" he said. "Any relationship is about compromise. I've asked so much of her, and in return she's given me a wonderful life of peace and happiness. She's my perfect partner, she loves me, gave me an awesome son and she saved me."

"From what?"

"From myself." He looked deep into my eyes. "If that means I have to overlook a few peculiarities, I will."

CHAPTER
12

WE GOT BACK FROM THE BEACH in the evening and mom invited Mack to stay overnight. We spent hours checking automotive websites, reading reviews, and watching videos of awesome sports cars, customized 4x4s, even electric vehicles. It was well after midnight when we made our decision. We knew what I should buy, but we definitely watched too many Porsche videos. We needed to go for a test drive in a Porsche 911 Turbo S.

I wasn't impressed when a blue Lincoln Town Car pulled up to the curb outside my house, several long minutes after ten o'clock, to take us to the Porsche dealership. It got even worse when the driver stepped out: it was Jason, the guard who'd hassled me at The Club.

He leaned on the car and gazed at me through dark sunglasses. He looked about as impressed as I did.

"I hear we're doing a little Boxing Day shopping," he said.

Mack laughed. "Yeah, I guess you could call it that."

"Well, let's get going then."

"Don't you need to check my ID first?" I yanked the front door open as Mack hopped in the back.

"Whoa, nice car!" Mack said as Jason got back in.

"Yup, pretty snazzy." He held out his hand to me. "I'm Jason, in case you don't remember."

I shook it. "That's my bro, Mack." I jerked a thumb toward the backseat.

Mack shook his hand. "Nice to meet you."

"So, why'd Barrymore pick you?" I asked as Jason eased away from the curb. "Did he hear you'd like to smack me upside the head?"

Jason laughed. "I've been begging to get off the Club gig for weeks. Talk about boring." Then he reached for the two-way radio microphone. "Control from Delta six," he said into the mic. "I've got Sprout and Maxwell Anderson on board."

"Copy Delta six," came the immediate reply.

Mack laughed. "Sprout?"

I leveled my gaze at Jason. "I better not *ever* hear you call me that again." I guess my voice had taken on a different tone because when he turned to me, he looked surprised.

We rode in silence for the next couple of blocks.

Finally, Jason spoke. "Where do you want to go?"

I handed him a piece of paper with the address of the Porsche dealership.

"That's way down in Redwood City," he said.

"They're the only ones who've got what I want to see," I said. "And you're paid by the hour, right?"

Mack and I started chatting back and forth until we hit the 101, when Jason cleared his throat.

"Listen James, I was told to use the code-name thing, all right? I wasn't trying to be a jerk."

Mack laughed. "I think it's perfect."

"Don't sweat it," I said, relaxing a bit. "But I want it changed. In fact, I don't want one at all."

The salesman at the dealership—his tag said Jerry—looked

skeptical when we walked in, but having Jason there helped a lot. The dark blue suit, the curly clear wire leading to his ear, and the way he kept his back toward the wall were enough to convince the salesman I was important.

"You call earlier?" Jerry said.

I held out my hand. "Yup, James Thompson."

He shook it. "Right, 911 Turbo S. We have one in a dark-blue metallic that I think you'll like." He led us across the showroom, and there it was, sitting on a slowly spinning turntable.

"Sweet!" Mack was already behind the wheel, but I stayed where I was, squatting to see every part of it as it turned. What an amazing piece of machinery.

Jason came up beside me. "Wow."

"Yeah." I hopped into the passenger seat, which would be my official spot on this ride. Jason wanted to see the engine.

"She has 560 horsepower, top speed 198 miles per hour. Zero to 60 miles per hour in 2.9 seconds." I tuned out while Jerry rattled off the rest of the stats.

"We gotta go for that test drive!" Mack said.

I climbed out. "Yup, let's do it!"

Jerry's enthusiasm lowered. "That's not possible, guys," he said. "This thing's worth almost a quarter million dollars."

I pulled out my wallet and handed him a credit card. It was platinum, from the private 'Wealth Management' service of a well-known, high-end bank.

"Take whatever deposit makes you feel comfortable."

Jerry's eyes flickered from the card to my face. "I'll need to speak to my manager."

About two minutes later, Jerry was back with the manager and a set of keys.

The manager pumped my hand. "Pleased to meet you, Mr. Thompson," he said, far too enthusiastically. He tried to hand me the keys, but Jason grabbed them.

"I'll be doing the driving," he said.

Jerry had slid the glass showroom doors open and the car sat pointed toward the narrow opening.

"I'll need to come with you," he said.

"Fine, but you're riding in the back," I told him as I held the door open.

"It's pretty tight back here." Mack was already crammed in the small back seat.

When Jason got behind the wheel, he looked uncomfortable. "A quarter million dollars," he said under his breath. Slowly, he eased the car out the doors and through the lot.

"Can you drive, I mean *really* drive?" I asked.

"I've got my driver's license, which is more than you can say."

We drove around for a while until Jason was getting the feel of it.

"Turn here," Jerry said. "You really need to try it out on the freeway."

Jason took the cut toward the Highway 101 southbound on-ramp. Jerry was in the middle of spewing more facts about something called "launch control" when Jason suddenly stopped the car.

"What are you doing?" Jerry's voice kicked up a notch. "This is an on-ramp!"

"Goodness, you're right!" Jason punched the pedal.

I slammed back into my seat as the Porsche rocketed onto the freeway, blasting past sixty and climbing steadily.

"Wahoo!" I yelled. I'm sure I heard some swearing coming from the backseat.

"I think that was faster than 2.9 seconds," Jason yelled as he wove through traffic, moving so fast it felt like the other cars had stopped. We blasted under Highway 114, and I was sure we were still doing about ninety when we went into the clover leaf at the Palo Alto exit.

A few minutes later, Jason pulled into the parking lot of a fast-food restaurant, tires squealing, and parked in a spot far away from any other cars.

He killed the engine. "Well, I'm sold."

I let several seconds go by for my heartbeat to slow down. "Does

... does Barrymore know you drive like that?"

He shrugged. "My résumé says I'm into racing. Just as a hobby of course."

Jerry was mumbling in the backseat. "That was ... you can't be driving ... that was—"

Jason and I got out so the other two could untangle themselves from the cramped backseat. He leaned on the roof of the car and looked at me.

"You're going to spend more on this car than most people make in five years."

"And?"

"I guess if you got it, flaunt it."

I leveled my gaze on him. "I don't recall asking your opinion."

"Yeah, well, I'm the type who likes to offer it."

"Which reminds me, I don't need a bodyguard," I said. "And I'll be making sure Barrymore knows that."

Mack and the salesman managed to pry themselves out of the back.

"That was awesome!" Mack slapped Jason on the back. "You da man!"

"Yeah," Jerry said, starting to look happy. "You certainly gave her a good test run."

Mack looked longingly toward the restaurant.

I laughed. It had only been about two hours since he ate breakfast. "Who wants a burger?" I said. "My treat."

I think the salesman thought he had a sale, so he was all in for a burger. As him and Mack walked away, I stopped Jason and lowered my voice. "Sorry to break it to you, but you better enjoy the ride back to the dealership because that's the last you'll see of this baby."

He raised his eyebrows. "What, you're firing me already?"

"No, I actually want a Jeep. This was just for fun."

He grinned. "Yes, it was certainly fun," he said. "A Jeep huh?"

"Yup. Rubicon, four door, bright Orange."

Then I patted the hood of the Porsche. Someday.

CHAPTER
13

MY CELL PHONE RANG A FEW HOURS LATER, while Mack and I were still talking excitedly about my new Jeep.

"Hi Junya," It was Lin, and she was whispering.

"Hi." I lowered my voice. "Why are you whispering?"

"Your Grandpa's going to call you in a few minutes," she said. "He's going to ask you to come to the Committee meeting this evening."

"Are you kidding me?" I said, no longer bothering to keep my voice down.

"I said he was going to *ask*."

"Well, he's dreaming."

"Just keep an open mind." She hung up.

Mack was staring at me. "What was that all—?"

The phone rang again. "Hi Grandpa." I said.

"Hello James." He was so loud I had to pull the phone about a foot away from my ear. "I want you to come with me to the Committee meeting today," he said. "And before you refuse, I want you to hear why."

"Okay." But despite Lin's request, I didn't really have an open mind.

"These are colleagues of mine. I've known them all for years and having contacts like these are important," he said, a bit quieter now. "Someday, somehow, you might need these men."

"Didn't they screw you over when you needed them?"

"That was business. They couldn't defy Bartholomew. I probably would have done the same in their shoes."

At the very mention of his name, pain shot through my shoulder and I winced.

"Is he going to be there?"

Grandpa made a snorting sound. "Of course not. Mr. Müller always represents him." He paused for a moment. "I want you there. You're my heir, and this is important."

I was about to refuse, but then I realized something. Maybe Müller could tell me what was going on with the shamans. He was Bartholomew's right-hand-man, after all.

"Okay," I said.

"*Okay?*" he said. "Just like that?"

"Yup," I said, trying to sound innocent. "It'll be interesting to see how you tycoons ruin ... I mean *rule* the world." I was only half-joking.

I got a harrumph in response.

I changed into the new suit Lin had tailored for me after Grandpa announced I was his heir, and at precisely three o'clock, Grandpa's Bentley pulled up in front of my house. Two black SUVs, one in front and another behind, escorted us the whole way and when we stopped beside the red awning in front of the Saint Francis Hotel, it was John, Grandpa's principal bodyguard, who opened the door to let us out, not the doorman in the long blue coat.

We took a glass elevator to the thirty-second floor. Its name— the Imperial floor—became obvious when we stepped off the elevator. Tall windows, maybe fifteen feet high and draped with heavy curtains, carpet almost too lush to walk on, and chandeliers so big I wasn't sure how the ceiling stayed up.

Ms. Lin was already there, dressed in a conservative dark-blue business suit, the skirt ending at her knees, her heels lower than usual. There were about forty people in the room, mostly men, all dressed in expensive suits. The women were dressed similarly to Lin.

I tugged my lapels and grinned at Lin when I caught her eye. I'd bitched when she'd made me endure a tailor measuring every part of my body, but I was damn grateful now. Too bad it was getting a bit tight in the chest and arms.

Grandpa moved toward the head of the table, Lin a step behind him. John and Miles took up positions against the wall, not far away, and two more of his security guys stood near the elevators. I'd just sat down beside Lin when the back of my neck starting tingling, followed by a sharp pain in my shoulder.

Two men in long black coats, hair past their shoulders, walked off the elevator and took up strategic locations nearby. There were plenty of serious-looking men in the room, obviously bodyguards, but none were as creepy as those two.

Mr. Müller stepped out of the elevator a moment later. He sat on the opposite side of the table, several seats to my left, looking as starched as usual. Two aides sat behind him, looking only slightly less severe than his bodyguards.

As if he felt me looking at him, he turned and our eyes met. His expression was completely neutral. Then a slight smile curled his thin lips, again with no emotion behind it. Just there.

I didn't smile back.

After a few hours of back and forth formal speeches about interest rates and falling commodity prices, I was certain I would die of boredom. I nodded off a few times, and each time was jolted awake by a well-placed nudge from Lin's elbow.

It wasn't until an older man with a tight English accent started talking about "the little people" that I snapped to attention.

"There's too much talk about financial inequality and I don't like it," the man said. "History has proven that at some point, they *will* stop acting like cattle."

Grandpa—the Chairman, I reminded myself—held up his hands. "I see your point, Francis, but as long as people have enough money, they'll spend it and that makes them, and us, happy."

"Agreed," said several voices around the table.

"And we always have a new cell phone app ready to go if needed," another man said, his accent distinctly Eastern American. "That usually buys us a few months."

Someone else laughed. "Yes, that *candy* game was quite impressive."

"And we made a fortune," a woman beside him said.

I elbowed Lin and gave her a look, but all she did was raise an eyebrow and shake her head slightly.

Before I even thought about it, I was on my feet.

"Ah, excuse me," I said. "If keeping people happy is the goal, then why not give everyone a fair share? Then you wouldn't need to make apps to keep *the little people* from rising up." I could barely disguise my disgust. "I mean, how much money do you guys need?"

A low chuckle came from down the table. It was Mr. Müller.

"May I introduce James Thompson," Mr. Müller said. "The heir in waiting, as it were."

Grandpa crossed his arms. "It's not your place to make introductions, Mr. Müller."

"True," Mr. Müller said. "But one cannot address a new member without introduction, and thus it is done." He steepled his fingers. "Now James, contrary to appearances, there is a finite amount of money in the world. If everyone had a more *equitable* portion of the pie, then we ..." he spread his hands. "... would no longer hold the reins of power."

"The good old one percent?"

"Actually," Mr. Müller said, "we represent the point-zero-zero-one percent."

Despite Lin tugging on my pants, I stayed standing. "Don't you think they should at least be able to live above the poverty line? You know, afford little things like food?"

The Englishman chuckled. "One day you'll have the power to change that, assuming you still feel the same."

I held his gaze for a long moment before I sat down. "Maybe I will," I muttered.

Mr. Müller cleared his throat. "If we can move on, my employer has stated he wants to create downward pressure in the oil and gas sector."

—

I tuned out after that. By the time they took a late dinner break, I decided I'd talk to Müller, then slip out.

Lin cornered me near the buffet table looking as serious as I'd ever seen her.

"Not a great first impression."

I picked up a butter tart, one of my Christmastime favorites. "I don't give a shit what these old cronies think about me."

"What about your grandfather?" she said, hands on hips. "Do you give a *shit* about him?"

I sighed. "I'll apologize to him if I need to, but honestly, these guys are assholes." I popped a second tart into my mouth.

Her eyes narrowed. "Junya—"

"Don't worry." I pushed her away gently. "I'm not going to—" My shoulder began to ache.

Look behind you.

When I turned around, Mr. Müller was right behind me, with two long-haired men on either side.

Lin took a step back and faced them. She'd definitely switched into combat mode.

"Just the guy I was looking for," I said, but I was watching his *men.*

Mr. Müller looked at Lin. "We would like a little privacy, if you please."

111

"Tell your male models to back off and I'll do the same."

Mr. Müller regarded her. "Or you will fight them?" He tilted his head as if thinking. "Go ahead, if you don't mind Edward learning what you really are."

Her eyes narrowed to slits, but she didn't reply. Her energy was mixed: hate and fear.

Mr. Müller led the way to two armchairs in front of an ornate fireplace in a quiet part of the floor.

"It's a pleasure to see you again, James," he said. "You look healthy and strong."

"Yes, I haven't turned into a lizard yet."

Mr. Müller gave me an odd look.

"And my grandpa's still alive."

He frowned. "Edward's heart attack was unfortunate," he said, "although the results of a stressful, unhealthy life are predictable. And with such a young mistress—"

"Whatever." I felt the anger start to grow in my belly. "Bartholomew's not leaving us alone like I told him to."

His face returned to deadpan. "No one *tells* my employer to do anything," Mr. Müller said. "He cancelled Edward's financial annihilation. Isn't that enough?"

"I want to know why he's killing all those shamans."

Mr. Müller looked surprised, the first genuine emotion I'd seen him display.

"The shamans have nothing to do with you."

I leaned forward, gripping the arms of my chair.

"It does when you kill them right in front to me," I said. "Does he think I'll plead to make him stop, or maybe let him into Izumo?" I gave him a tight smile. "It won't happen."

He stared at me. "You actually think his initiative against indigenous religions is all about little James Thompson?" His face changed, like a brick wall collapsing, and then he started laughing. He needed to wipe his eyes before he could continue.

"You've chosen to become involved, all because of that girl you want so badly to impress," he said from behind the linen handkerchief. "In any case, it is the Gatekeepers who threaten the balance by bringing the fight to this side. They're breaking the rules."

"You stop killing shamans and they'll stop killing your boys. It's as easy as that."

"Nothing is ever *easy*," Mr. Müller said. "I suggest you leave it alone."

"If he keeps this up I'll—"

"You'll what?" Mr. Müller's placid demeanor vanished. "Make me quack like a duck?"

A cold chill shot up my spine. How did he know that? I thought about what Mack had said: maybe Bartholomew really did have people everywhere.

He tented his hands in front of him, fingertips touching.

"It's curious," he said, "that the Elders still allow you to enter the world of the gods." He stared at me a long moment. "My employer was quite excited when he learned that. It could lead to unexpected ... opportunities."

"He's not getting into Izumo, or into me!" I said through gritted teeth. "So, screw you."

He stood up and looked down at me. "I assure you, if he decides to use you to enter Izumo, there won't be a thing you can do to stop him."

I watched him walk away, my mind working hard to process everything. Finally, as the meeting was about to resume, I managed to stand. I glanced at Lin as I walked toward the elevator, but she didn't look like she planned to stop me.

I'd just pressed the elevator down button when pain stabbed my left shoulder again. I turned and found myself face to face with one of Mr. Müller's bodyguards. He was tall and as he gazed down at me, a thick strand of black hair fell across his face, the contrast making his skin look even more pale.

"Hello cousin," he said, almost sounding friendly. "I am called Sébastien."

"He actually gives you names?"

He smiled. "One day, not so long from now, perhaps you and I will feast upon human flesh together." Then his pupils changed, from round to slits, from deep brown to yellow. "I would like that."

I jumped back into the open elevator and stood gaping at him until the doors slid closed.

CHAPTER
14

NO ONE WAS HOME WHEN SHOKO appeared in our backyard the next morning, arriving on the small bridge that arched over the pond. Wearing her Gatekeeper uniform, she looked beautiful against the backdrop of our Zen garden.

"Come here."

I raised an eyebrow. "Giving orders now?" But I did, of course.

She grabbed my shirt. For a second I thought she was going to attack me, until her lips met mine. I knew our days of little pecks on the lips were long gone.

When she finally broke away, she said, "I am *very* happy to see you!"

"Likewise," I said, breathless.

"Practice makes better, yes?" Then she kissed me again, longer but softer this time. I tried to concentrate, but after a moment, I needed to push her away.

She looked confused. "Did I do something wrong?"

I let out a laugh. "No way, it's only that ... I saw Müller and some

Evil Ones yesterday, so it feels weird." I looked toward the teahouse, where the training dojo once stood.

"Ah," she said softly, "because of that girl, my *evil* twin."

I nodded.

"There is one big difference, of course," she said softly. "I am real."

I smiled. "Yes, you are."

She gave me a curt nod. "We must work hard to resolve this issue." Then she rose onto her toes and kissed me again. It didn't take long until the only thought in my mind was her. The *real* her.

When we finally broke apart, I grinned at her. "I'm cured!"

"Good!" Now she looked excited about something else. "Now that you are permitted on my side, I will take you across to Izumo and give you a real tour."

We materialized in the meadow. I raised my face as peace and calm flowed toward me, overtook me, relaxed me. It was like negative energy didn't exist here, and my fears of Bartholomew's power dissolved. I let out a deep sigh.

"Sometimes I wish I could live here," I said to Shoko. "Being this close to the gods is amazing."

"It is a blessing I never fail to acknowledge, especially after I return from your world."

As I whispered a silent prayer of thanks, I faltered. Maybe I was getting used to being here, but the energy of the gods seemed a little less than usual.

———

I'd never been into the village that stood a short walk away from the Grand Shrine. There was one main road, about a regular city block long, lined with shops made of wood with steep straw roofs. Some offered day-to-day household items, others fruits and vegetables. They had a better variety of produce than any store I'd seen in San Francisco.

"This place is awesome!"

Shoko smiled at me. "After seeing the beauty of your home, and Edward's, I thought you would find this primitive."

"No way, my dad would freak if he saw this!" I pointed up to the complicated joints used to connect the beams. "Let me guess, they didn't use any nails, right?"

"A true craftsman, a *shokunin*, can join the wood pieces together so perfectly it is as if they become one, never to separate again." She looked behind her. "Do you think nails could hold the Grand Shrine together?"

To be honest, I couldn't imagine how they'd built the thing in the first place.

As we walked, everything seemed odd to me. The buildings looked old, yet at the same time so fresh I'd swear they'd built them yesterday. It looked like a movie set, a perfect re-creation of a five-hundred-year-old Japanese village, complete with a cast of actors dressed in period costumes. I didn't see anyone carrying purses, though.

"What kind of money do you use here?"

She looked at me. "Money is not required," she said. "One takes only what they need, and everyone contributes in some way."

"And I suppose the weather is always like this too?" The sky was clear blue, only a few puffy clouds drifting across.

She smiled. "Yes, it is always pleasant during the daytime, and a light wrap is all that is needed after dark."

Like Hawaii in the wintertime.

"Does it ever rain?"

She shrugged. "Whenever the earth needs water."

"Sounds like Utopia."

Shoko pursed her lips. "The earth here is also well nourished with the bodies of Gatekeepers," she said. "There is no 'perfect' place."

She stopped under the wide overhang at the front of a shop and pulled a tiny outfit down from a hook.

I laughed. "What's that?"

"This is the first uniform a Gatekeeper wears when she begins her schooling," she said. "I still remember the day I got mine. I was so excited!"

"I bet you were really cute."

A slight pink rose in her cheeks. "How do I look in this one?" she said, indicating the uniform she was wearing.

"Not cute," I said. "You look beautiful." And really, I thought she looked better in it than modern clothing. It was elegant yet functional and accentuated her confidence and authority.

The shop next door had racks full of all different size swords inside.

"Is this where you got your katana?"

"One does not *get* swords," she said, looking quite offended. "This is the shop of the Master Sharpener."

"Oh, I—"

"My blade took weeks to create and was made especially for *me*. There is none other like it in all of Izumo."

"Wow."

She nodded. "Creating a blade is a sacred art, accompanied by many Shinto rituals, and many Master Craftsmen are involved in the process." She reached down and touched the hilt of her Katana, which had red inlays in the handle. "I chose this design myself."

I nodded, impressed. "So, men build the swords, but do any of them learn to fight?"

She stared at me a long moment. "Imagine how different your world would be if men could not fight or dominate women," she said. "The god of Izumo, in his wisdom, decided the life-givers should also be the life-takers. Men lack discretion in such things."

We continued past a few small places that served food or tea, and a shop with tools for farming and construction. That was it for the village. Everything you needed to live.

The people we met were friendly and surprisingly good-looking, and I'm not only talking about the younger ones either. Everyone looked fit, clean, and healthy, but I didn't think it was just genetics. They worked hard and led a healthy lifestyle in a clean environment.

There was no missing how highly people respected Shoko, despite her age. It was also obvious that every person we met knew about me. They gave me respectful greetings and a wide berth.

Shoko denied it, but as far as I could see, this *was* Utopia.

⁓

We were leaving the village when I noticed the girl who'd asked to be Shoko's apprentice, the one from the lineup for red-bean cake. She was walking up the street alone, wearing regular clothes. Well, regular for here.

I nodded. "There's that girl."

Shoko grunted. "Ah, Sakura ..."

"Was she punished, like you figured?"

"Her master dismissed her." Shoko shrugged. "It was an obvious consequence."

"What happens to her now?"

"Her apprenticeship is incomplete," Shoko said. "And it is unlikely another master will accept her now. She is disloyal."

"She just threw it all away?" I watched her draw closer. "That was stupid."

"And that is what I cannot understand. She knew I could not accept her request, even if I wanted to, because she already had a master." Shoko let out a deep sigh. "One who had no interest in Sakura's gift."

"What's her gift anyway?"

"She can *see* across to the Other Side."

"I thought all Gatekeepers could."

"We can all *see* directly across from where we stand," she said. "To see further into your world is a rare gift. Besides myself, there are few who can do it." Shoko looked at me. "I hear your mother could."

Somehow, that didn't surprise me.

"Which is why I wanted Sakura as my apprentice," she said. "However, while I was recovering from my ordeal in Zion, another master selected her."

"Did Sakura know that?"

"I made no secret of my interest," she said. "But there was nothing either of us could do."

Sakura was close now, eyes still on the ground.

"Maybe that's why she did it."

Shoko gave me a strange look. "Why?"

"So you *could* accept her."

Shoko looked puzzled, then she stepped into Sakura's path.

"Shoko!" Sakura bowed low.

"Good afternoon, *Cherry Blossom*," Shoko said after returning Sakura's bow. "Are you happy with your circumstances?"

Sakura kept her head down. "It is the outcome I expected."

Shoko studied her for a moment, then poked at something in Sakura's belt. "What is that?"

The girl's face was a deep red as she pulled the small wooden sword from her belt and handed it to Shoko.

"It is unfortunate you did not complete your apprenticeship," Shoko said as she turned the little sword with her hands. "You would have been a fine Gatekeeper."

"I am a stupid girl."

Shoko was silent for a moment. "Have you ever crossed to the Other Side?"

Sakura's mouth dropped open. "I … it is forbidden without permission."

Shoko handed back the wooden sword. "I apologize for stopping you."

As she walked away, I whispered to Shoko, "Why did you ask her that?"

A small smile curled her lips. "I know she has been across," she said. "She is a liar, a good one."

I grinned. "Like you?"

She nodded and seemed to be thinking. "Perhaps."

Shoko and I sat cross-legged in the shade of a black pine, watching several groups of students training on the grass-covered compound. It was a wide-open space, about half the size of a football field, with several rectangular straw-roofed buildings along one side.

One group of what looked to be the oldest girls were practicing with katana against multiple straw-man attackers. They were better than I was, but then, multiple attackers with swords had never been the focus of Okaasan's training, and I didn't practice nearly as much as those girls did. Luckily, I'd never been in a real sword fight.

I mentioned how good they were to Shoko. They were perfect for our new force.

She shrugged. "They are in their final year of study before being assigned a master," she said. "They still have a long way to go yet."

"Oh."

"Mack's idea would require Gatekeepers of full rank, with real combat experience," she said. "And they must be able to last against me for at least a minute."

I tried not to smile. "And they'll need the right personality," I said. "You know, a little proud and a little reckless, like you."

She gave me a look.

"You know what I'm saying," I said. "They need to think on their own, not wait for someone to give them orders. And they'll probably need some extra training, like how to deal with guns, how to fight inside buildings and without their senses."

She considered that. "If we do this, how many would we need?"

"Maybe two or three dozen?" I said. "And what do you mean *if?* This is a great plan."

'It is an unauthorized *idea*," she said. "I will not do this without the Elders' approval."

My enthusiasm dropped. "But you've obviously been thinking about it."

She nodded. "I have started a list of candidates, but I must be careful where I draw them from. I cannot leave any group short or without proper balance."

"What do you mean, *balance?*"

She picked up a stick and began to draw in the dirt. "There are six commanders under Chiyoko, each with about sixty Gatekeepers in their group who range in age from fifteen to twenty-five. These groups are broken into sections, which are led by those with the most skill and experience. It is not only about age." She smiled at me. "I was already a section leader when I met you."

"When you were fifteen?"

She nodded. "Then the sections are broken into units, which depending on the tasking, could be anywhere from twenty Gatekeepers down to teams of two or three. So, the commanders try to keep experience, age, and skill somewhat balanced throughout the six groups. This is what I must consider when I make selections."

I'd been doing the math while she spoke. "There're only three hundred and sixty Gatekeepers protecting your whole world?"

"It has been enough so far."

In the compound, a girl, far smaller and younger than her opponent, was taking a serious beating. Her movements were awkward; it was obvious she wasn't a good fighter.

"You grew up training like that?"

Shoko nodded. "It is a hard life. We fight every day, with fists, bokuto, and eventually katana, and always against girls older, larger, and stronger."

"Did you beat up smaller girls like that one?"

She frowned. "Never with that large of an age difference," she said, watching the fight.

"So, no matter what, you got beat up?"

"It is a blessing to have the opportunity to fight one stronger than yourself. How else does one get better?"

"How many don't *get better?*"

"Some die trying," she said. "And some are dismissed, like Sakura but that is a great dishonor."

"It shouldn't be." I looked at that girl again. "That girl should be kicked out. She's a crappy fighter."

"She will get better the more she fights."

"She's not fighting. She's getting beaten up."

Blood ran down the smaller girl's face, spilling onto her shirt.

"You need to stop them."

As the little girl rolled onto her knees and tried to crawl away, her opponent kicked her in the stomach so hard it lifted her off her feet. The other girl laughed. Even Shoko scowled at that.

"Do something!"

She gave her head a quick shake. "It would be an affront to the instructor."

"I don't see any instructors," I said, getting angry.

"She is the one doing the beating."

Something snapped inside me. Before I realized I'd made the decision, I was striding across the grounds toward them.

"Get back here, Junya!"

I ignored Shoko's warning and stepped between the fallen girl and her attacker. She was almost as tall as I was and a bit older. I shoved her hard, knocking her backward.

"You're real tough, beating up a girl half your size!" I shoved her again, my anger growing.

She stepped back, bowing in submission.

"Junya." Shoko had moved closer.

"Fight me, you bully!" I jerked the girl upright and shoved her again. Then I threw a kick at her, a slow side-kick she easily avoided. At first, she only blocked, retreating with each of my blows, but after a few more kicks she began to move onto the offensive. I blocked her first few strikes—they were harder than I'd imagined—then landed three direct blows and a kick that sent her to her knees.

But I stumbled as I landed. My leg was hurting.

She came back up fast, hitting with full power. I deflected a kick, took two more strikes to the body, then flipped her, dumping her onto the ground. I let out a satisfied growl.

As I moved back, pain stabbed through my leg again. She paused, then came at me with an odd gleam in her eyes. I knew why a second later, when she faked a fall, then spun and kicked my injured calf.

I let out a yelp of pain as it collapsed under me.

Now she was coming at me full bore, and any chance she got, she targeted my leg. I pushed some of the energy into my leg and the pain eased.

"You are no better than her!" Shoko shouted. "You are using your energy!"

"Damn right," I said as I took another hit. I blocked the next then struck out. This time I connected and she faltered. She came at me and the next two blows hit my leg. With a roar of pain, I caught her fist and exhaled. She winced and stumbled backward, her hands on her head.

"Enough!" It was Shoko.

The girl shook her head, as if to clear her mind, then she charged at me.

Shoko kicked her in the head. "I said enough!" Shoko shouted. This time, the girl didn't get up. I wasn't sure she could—I hadn't ever kicked anyone that hard.

Shoko spun toward me.

"Do not use your energy here!" Then she kicked me with enough force to send *me* to my knees.

I started to get up, my anger simmering just below the surface, but the look in Shoko's eyes stopped me. We stared at each other a long moment, then she held out her hand.

As I reached my feet, I looked down at the instructor. Two of her students leaned over her unconscious form. Then I turned to see the little girl she'd beaten.

She lay curled up in a fetal position, clutching her stomach. I started limping toward her, but Shoko caught my arm.

"You will only make her life worse."

"How could her life be any worse?" It was loud enough for her to hear, but I didn't care. Then I held out my hand to the little girl.

After a long moment, she took it. In that moment, all her pain and thoughts poured into me.

It hurts ... my stomach hurts so much ... I do not want to do this anymore ... why did the ogre choose me?

A flood of thoughts followed, enough to bring tears to my eyes. More than her pain had.

I looked up at Shoko again and spoke a message into her head.

She doesn't want to be a Gatekeeper. She'll never be good enough, and that shouldn't be a dishonor.

I gently let the girl back down, then knelt and put my hand on her stomach. The energy that came from the area below her ribs screamed out its destruction. I looked around, hoping for some help. Himiko, the Miko, hurried toward us with a black lacquer box under her arm.

"There's something broken in her stomach," I said to her. "She's bleeding inside. A lot."

"You know this?" Himiko knelt and touched the girl gently, feeling around under her ribs. The girl let out a deep moan, but in her mind she screamed. I winced.

Himiko looked at me. "You can hear that too?"

I nodded. "What's wrong with her?"

"A rib is broken," she said. "It has penetrated an organ."

"Can you fix her, with a potion or something?"

Himiko took the girl's wrist to feel her pulse. "She grows weak. By the time I cut her open and find the problem, she will be gone."

No, please!

I clenched my teeth. "You're not giving up."

"Junya," Shoko said quietly from beside me. "There are some things that cannot be fixed."

I felt the presence of the people gathering around us. I looked up at Shoko.

"Get them away from here!"

Within a few seconds of Shoko's command, we were alone with Himiko.

I put my hand over the girl again. Her energy had already weakened. If I could use my energy to help with my pain, maybe it could help keep her alive.

I exhaled and focused my energy, ever so gently, into her stomach. The girl let out a deep sigh.

Himiko looked at me, eyebrows together. "What are you doing?"

I didn't reply. I had my eyes locked on the shrine as I concentrated harder. A warm breeze floated down over us, tussling the little girl's hair.

Suddenly, I was seeing her insides: there, where the broken rib poked into a purplish thing. I tried to remember what I'd learned in anatomy class. Was that her *spleen*? I exhaled again, let my energy flow, then looked at Himiko.

"You cut her open here and get the rib out," I said, my finger over the exact spot. "Then use the healing potion on the punctured organ."

Himiko shook her head. "There will be too much blood—"

"I'm holding her blood in so hurry up," I said through gritted teeth.

Himiko stared at me a moment longer, then dug into her bag. She poured some liquid over her hands that I hoped was some kind of antiseptic before she slid a thin knife from its sheath.

I closed my eyes and focused, kept the image of the girl's insides. I saw the blade cut in.

She let out a small whimper.

"To the left," I said.

Himiko inhaled sharply. "There is no blood."

I felt the little girl's body twitch, but she didn't cry out and her mind was quiet, even as Himiko's fingers probed inside her.

"The blue bottle please, Shoko."

A moment later, the girl sighed and I studied her face, worried she was dying, but instead, she wore a look of relief.

"The wound is closing!" Shoko said.

"Can you keep doing that Junya?" Himiko said, her voice strained. "I need to move this rib and it is going to hurt."

Sweat poured down my face from the effort, but I wasn't giving up. A long moment passed.

"There," Himiko said. "The rib is back in place." She looked at me with satisfaction.

"There's a lot of blood inside her. Is that okay?"

Himiko looked thoughtful. "No, we need to drain that out, but that is an easy task. The worst is over. Release your energy."

I let it go slowly, my eyes on the girl's face. When nothing bad happened, I slumped back on the grass, exhausted.

"Thank you," a weak voice said.

"It was my pleasure," I whispered.

Shoko knelt beside the girl. "What is your name, little one?"

"Nene."

"I am sorry to tell you this Nene, but because of this injury, you will need to give up your dream to become a Gatekeeper."

Nene looked about as shocked as I felt.

Himiko looked confused. "This injury will not—"

"Tell Nene the truth, Himiko," Shoko said, looking the older woman in the eyes. "She will need to find another calling, perhaps as a Miko's apprentice? If you speak those words, there will be no dishonor in this for her."

Himiko nodded slowly. "The truth," she said, "is that Shoko speaks with wisdom beyond her years. It shall be as you suggest." Then she looked at me. "And you should be a Miko, young man. We need a strong one like you."

I shook my head. "I'm not usually good at helping people."

"Yes, your energy is confusing," she said. "However, from a first time, there can easily be a second time." With that, she helped the girl up, and with a sharp command to two students, hurried her off to the infirmary.

"She is right about your energy," Shoko said, still kneeling where she'd been. "One moment you call up dark energy to fight, and then the next you bring pure energy to do something like this." She looked up toward the top of the staircase and shook her head. "How can this be? Why do the gods allow you to use dark energy here in

Izumo?"

"You and Okaasan say it's dark, but it feels the same to me. Who decides whether it's good or bad?" But there was one difference, I now realized. When I fought, the energy came unbidden. When I'd helped the girl, I'd summoned it myself.

Shoko turned to look at me, her face questioning. "That is an interesting thought." She looked away, toward the meadow. "I hope it is true, because I do not want to lose you."

Then she took my hand and traveled me home.

CHAPTER
15

WE ARRIVED IN MY LIVING ROOM, which nearly gave me a heart attack. It was the first time she'd taken us right inside my house. Of course, Shoko knew no one was home before we left Izumo. I just wished she'd warned me.

"Do you want something to eat?" I asked her as we walked into the kitchen.

She shook her head. "Some tea perhaps?"

"That I can do."

She sat at the kitchen table and looked around. "Your house is so beautiful."

"Did I tell you I helped build it?"

"You did not."

I pointed to the doorway leading outside. "I installed all that wood when I was twelve. Pretty good, huh?"

She looked impressed. Then for some reason, as she looked at her own hands on the table top, she frowned. "It is good to have skilled hands, I think."

"You have skilled hands," I said from where I still stood by the stove. "You're an amazing fighter."

"Mine are only skilled at destroying."

"Considering your duty, it's a good thing."

"Yes, but you can fight *and* save a little girl's life."

I leaned against the stove, thinking about what I'd done. "It just came instinctively."

She nodded slowly. "When you choose, good energy comes from your hands," she said as she stood up. "I liked the way your hands touched my skin the other night."

Something jumped inside me. I glanced at the kettle. It was starting to boil.

"Forget the tea, Junya."

She pulled me to her. We kissed, gentle at first, but firmer when she laced her fingers through my hair and pulled me closer. I pushed her against the cabinets as my excitement grew.

After several minutes, she broke away. "This is not comfortable."

"Um ... we could go to my room?"

When she nodded, I swept her off her feet and started down the hall. She laughed in surprise and pretended to struggle, only to hold on tighter. Tama rolled on her back to get a better view as we went past and Shoko waved to her, looking happier than I'd ever seen her.

I kicked my door open and looked around. The only tidy place was my bed. Thank god Okaasan insisted I made it every day. I lowered Shoko gently onto the edge then sat down beside her.

"Is this okay?"

She bounced a few times. "It is soft."

I touched her arm. "So are you."

She smiled and stared at the floor, suddenly timid. I felt odd too, as if the bed had made things too ... official. She turned and kissed me and her touch sent electricity through my body, first through her lips, then her hands. We started to tip, her sliding backward until we were on our sides, facing each other. Our kissing became more urgent and everything else faded away until nothing existed but her. Like a magnet to iron, my hands slid inside her blouse and found her breasts. She let out a small noise when I touched them.

She reached inside her blouse and released her bra. I was enthralled with her breasts. They felt odd but wonderful. Something I'd imagined so much but had no idea what they would really be like. She let out more moans and her hands caressed my chest, feeling my muscles, roaming as she discovered something new as well.

Her blouse came off, then my T-shirt, then pants, socks, and eventually, our underwear. Everything about her body fascinated me. Around every curve was another revelation; her body was so different from mine. My hands explored places I'd never touched, while she touched me.

She took my hand. "Here," she whispered. "It feels good when you touch there." She became lost in another world as I continued. She eventually let out a deep sigh, then drew back and smiled.

"What do you like?" she said between breaths.

I showed her, and it wasn't long until I let out my own deep sigh.

"It seems," she whispered into my ear, "that my touch does not always calm you."

"Apparently not."

"Have you had intercourse before?"

I hesitated, remembered what Mack said: she'd figure it out pretty quick if I lied. "No."

"Me neither." She giggled, and her cheeks reddened. "But that is obvious, I suppose."

"Actually" I smiled, not feeling any embarrassment. "I've never even touched a girl's body before, not like this I mean. It's pretty cool."

"Cool?"

I shrugged, searching for a better word. "You know, interesting." I ran my hand over her stomach, taut with muscle yet still soft.

She thumped her small fist against my chest. "And your muscles are solid and you are hairy!" She paused. "Your body is cool too." She ran a finger up the center line of my stomach muscles. "Does it feel good when I touch you here?"

"It's nice to be touched, but it doesn't feel *good*."

"Only when I touch you there?"

"Pretty much."

She looked puzzled. "It seems that anywhere you touch me feels amazing."

I ran my hand down her side, first dipping at her waist, then curving up and over her hip, down the outside of her thigh. A woman's body was so magical.

"Do you pleasure yourself?"

I laughed, embarrassed. "Of course, I'm a guy." Then I looked at her. "Do you?"

"Of course, I am a girl. My body is very interesting."

"Yes, yes it is."

"Does Mack have sex with Isabella?"

I hesitated. "Yeah."

"Are you not curious?"

I licked my lips. "Of course I am."

She snuggled closer so our faces were inches apart. Her breathing was quick, her body tight against mine. "I have this hunger … it is as if I cannot stop myself." She kissed me then pulled back. "I would like to try intercourse too."

I was pretty excited, but … "Ah…" I blew out my breath. "Me too … but we shouldn't."

"But this is a perfect opportunity." She drew back so she could see my face. "A moment alone like this is so rare."

I thought about what Okaasan had said. "You could get pregnant."

That got her attention. She rolled away, onto her back.

"I see why the Elders keep boys and girls apart. Nature is too powerful."

I flopped on my back beside her, interlocked her fingers in mine and let out a sigh. Why did I always have to be so damn responsible?

"There are things we can use so you won't get pregnant," I said. "But I don't have anything here."

She rolled up on her elbow. "There is such a thing?"

I laughed. "Lots of things. We have these pills a girl can take every day and you won't get pregnant, no matter how much you do it."

"What is in these pills?"

"It's medicine." I thought about it. "Or maybe more like a chemical."

She made a face. "I will not be doing that."

I nodded. "And then there are condoms." I gave her a brief demonstration of how it went on.

"Hmmm." She tilted her head and looked thoughtful.

"Those are probably ... shit!" I sat up. "Okaasan's coming home, get dressed!"

We both jumped up and tried to find our clothes.

"Your shirt is on backward," Shoko said as she pulled on her panties.

"And your hair is a mess."

The back door opened with a clunk followed by the rustle of paper grocery bags.

"Junya, are you home?"

I hopped on one foot trying to get my jeans on. "Yeah, Mom, do you need help?"

"Why did you not sense her earlier?" Shoko whispered while struggling with her bra.

"I was a little distracted," I whispered.

"That would be nice," Okaasan called.

Shoko gazed at me. "If we were about to be attacked, you would not sense it?"

"Coming," I yelled, then lowered my voice. "That's a different sensation. I would notice." *Probably.*

"I hope so," she said as she walked into my bathroom.

"Junya!"

I ran down the hall. As usual, Okaasan was trying to carry more bags than she could manage.

"Why don't you make two trips?" I said as I relieved her of most of her load.

"Why didn't you come faster?" Then she looked at me with an odd expression.

"What?" I tried to keep my thoughts on anything but what I'd just been doing.

"Your T-shirt is inside out."

I glanced down. "You're right." Then I started digging through the bags, looking for a snack, which was my normal thing to do. As I searched, I wondered where Shoko was. I hadn't felt her travel away.

I came across a sirloin steak and pulled it out. "What the heck is this?" We never ate steak at home.

"That's for Mack. He needs more protein in his diet," she said, taking it from me. "That boy's nutritional needs are not being met at home."

"And that's your problem?"

"It is now that he's in training."

I grunted. "Bet that's a challenge."

"Yes, he's big and slow, so I—" She turned suddenly as Shoko walked into the kitchen, braiding her hair. "Shoko, I didn't know you were here."

Shoko bowed. "Hello, Misako. It is a pleasure to see you again." She looked absolutely normal, as if nothing happened a few minutes ago. "Did Junya tell you what he just did?"

My eyes nearly popped out.

To my relief, Shoko told her how I'd saved Nene's life.

"His energy was amazing," she said.

Okaasan looked at me, her face glowing with pride. "Maybe I should take back what I said about your energy."

"You see? It's not all bad."

Shoko smiled slightly as she nodded in agreement. "Please excuse me, but it grows late and my other students are waiting." She bowed again to Okaasan, who returned it. Then she looked at me. "You will see me off?"

As soon as we were outside, I grabbed her arm and pulled her toward me, arms around her waist. "You're good at pretending nothing happened."

"We did nothing wrong." She glanced once toward the kitchen, then kissed me lightly on the lips. "I will see you again soon." Then she knelt and was gone.

CHAPTER
16

I SEE SHOKO'S LITTLE STRAW-ROOFED HOUSE across the meadow. She waves at me from the shaded doorway. It looks quiet and peaceful as I walk toward it. The grand Izumo Shrine towers over my left shoulder, lit bright by the mid-afternoon sun. A light breeze moves the grass and rustles the leaves of the trees beyond the meadow, and somewhere in the distance comes the sound of children playing.

I can hear Gatekeepers shouting as they practice in the courtyard beneath the shrine. Some shouts are commands, other cries of exertion. There are no cries of pain. That would be a dishonor.

Then there's a change in the energy of the Mother Earth. The children are silent.

I laugh.

The ground begins to shudder. A moment later, the trees collapse under the pounding feet of a hundred lizards and men—soldiers. Shots ring out, machine-gun fire. I dive to the ground and the lizards thunder past, ignoring me.

There were more shots and screams now. Sounds of pain and death, human and lizard. Evil Ones move up the staircase to the shrine, a long line of them, steady as an escalator. They trample Gatekeepers beneath their feet.

Smoke pours from the shrine compound. More screams and gunshots. Where is Shoko? She'll be fighting, but I need to get her away. I hear a scream, feel sudden heat, and spin around. Shoko's house is ablaze; its dry straw and wood burn as fast as our training dojo had.

In the doorway, two lizards are crouched over a figure lying still in a pool of blood.

"Shoko?" This wasn't part of the deal I made with Bartholomew.

I start forward. The lizards raise their heads, jaws dripping with bright red blood. They leap toward me. I turn and run. They're so fast! I feel their breath, smell the putrid stench of rotten flesh. I stumble. A lizard looms over me, and two more pin my legs to the ground. Behind them is Bartholomew, dressed in his Hawaiian shirt.

He smiles as he aims a gun at my chest. "There's no such thing as a fair deal."

———

"Wake up, Junya!" Okaasan said. "I'm not coming anywhere near you until I know you're wide awake."

I cracked one eye open. I was soaked in sweat, my sheets twisted around me.

She walked toward me, looking wary. "Bartholomew?"

I rubbed a hand over my face. "Yeah, but different this time."

Okaasan bent to pick up my clothes off the floor. "I wish you'd have a nightmare about being attacked by laundry."

I sat up. "Have Evil Ones ever invaded Izumo, right to the shrine compound, I mean?"

Her eyes widened. "Good lord no! Not once in the thousands of years we've been protecting the gods."

"But they've gotten across?"

"All the time." She hefted my laundry basket and headed for the door. "Now come on," she said. "I made waffles."

They were whole wheat waffles, but she made up for that with blueberries, whipped cream, and real maple syrup.

"So what's new?" she said as she filled her tea cup.

"Oh, there's never a dull day in Junya-land," I said around a mouthful of waffle. I told her about the Committee meeting, and what Mr. Müller had said.

"Do you think it'll really throw things off balance if the Gatekeepers fight on this side?" I said.

She looked thoughtful. "Our Elders forbid Gatekeepers to cross over to fight, but the Evil Ones breach gateways any time they like," she said. "Where's the balance in that? It sounds like he's trying discourage you, which means the clashes you've had must be making a difference." She raised her tea cup to her lips then put it back down without taking a sip. "Is Mr. Müller human?"

"Yeah, I'd sense it if he wasn't." I shrugged. "Maybe he's like a publicist for Bartholomew and says what he's told to say."

She nodded. "Whenever a celebrity's publicist denies someone's having an affair, it always turns out to be true," she said, a bit too enthusiastically. "I mean, what's with that actor who—"

"Seriously?" I let out a laugh. "You've been reading the celebrity rags again?"

"I just got my hair cut." She looked guilty. "That's all there is to read while I wait."

I grinned at her and went back to my waffles. After a few bites, I put down my fork.

"What exactly is Bartholomew?" I said. "I mean, I know he's this powerful financial leader with huge influence, and I know he's not human and can shape-shift into other forms, but what *is* he?"

Okaasan let out a deep breath. "There are so many theories." She shrugged. "But I don't think anyone knows the truth."

"Okay, but what does he want? I thought it was getting into Izumo, but now that seems more like a hobby or something."

"His priority is controlling the world, which he and his kind are very successful at," she said after taking a sip of tea. "But for whatever reason, he has a deep-seated hatred against the gods, going back more than a thousand years."

"He's a thousand years old?!"

She nodded. "That's why he needs to shape-shift into different bodies," she said. "He can't keep getting older and not die, right?"

I'm sure my eyes went wide at that.

"They use a body, aging normally, until it's elderly. Then they let the body die, people hold memorials, and he gets his place in history, like any other important person."

"*They?*"

"I just told you," she said. "There are others."

"Like who?"

She put her finger to her lips, thinking. "The leader of a huge Japanese business consortium died last year," she said. "I read that he was replaced by some man most people had never heard of before. That fits the pattern perfectly."

I was trying to get a grip on that when I had a horrible thought. "Do they take over someone's body?" Like mine, for instance.

She smiled. "No, they're not using a real body. They only take the shape of one."

"Anyone?"

"It's always someone important, not usually kings or world leaders though, because that's too hard to maintain. They'd have to shape-shift into a baby and grow up." She tapped her nail against the rim of her cup. "No, they're usually in the background, quietly but strongly influencing others."

"For what purpose?"

She shrugged. "Power, of course."

"That's actually too scary to think about."

She shook her head. "No," she said, "The most frightening thing is, we'll have no idea what the next persona will look like."

"What if he came back looking like someone we know?" I said.

"I'm told that they can never perfectly imitate another person," she said. "You could tell with *other* Shoko, right?"

An image of Shoko's evil twin came to mind. She was amazingly similar, but her mole was on the wrong side.

"If I wasn't being distracted ..." Then I blushed, the first time in months. "And I can sense them now, so that won't happen again."

She smirked at me. "Then I guess you don't need to worry, do you?"

I drained the last of the milk. "Speaking of worrying," I said, jumping at the chance for a change in topic, "How much do you really know about Dad?"

She looked at me with a confused but defensive glare. "Everything I need to, thank you. Why would you ask that?"

"He knows way more that he lets on."

Her eyebrows came together. "Whatever do you mean?"

"He knows about you and Lin," I said, leaning forward as if someone might overhear. "He said you were both trained in martial arts meant to kill and he doesn't buy the whole merchant-gardener family thing."

Her eyebrows narrowed. "He said that?" Her tone sounded more apprehensive than surprised. "When?"

"On Christmas night, at the beach," I said. "And he said he let you train me so you wouldn't run back to Japan, but he's starting to wonder if I'm like you now."

Okaasan folded her arms on her chest. "That little ..." She shook her head. "There're too many damn secrets in this family."

"According to him, he's happy to keep it that way."

—

After breakfast, Okaasan left to vacuum while I cleaned up the dishes. As I washed the hot plate, my thoughts kept returning to Shoko. Making out with her had changed everything between us.

As I hung up the dish towel, I made a decision. Shoko wanted me to start traveling, and I really wanted to see her. I could travel straight across, to this exact place in her world. I figured that was the safest way to start.

I left home and walked a short distance into the Presidio grounds. Safely among the trees, I knelt and bowed with my head on the ground.

"Please, Mother Earth," I whispered. "Let me cross."

The earth gave a little shudder and warm energy set my palms tingling. The sensation grew stronger as the warm energy of the Mother Earth moved through my body. I sat up and thought of the world I'd seen with Shoko, directly across from here, then I slapped my palm against the ground.

It was odd this time: the swirling was faster, but the journey felt far longer. Finally, the spinning stopped and I steadied myself.

When I opened my eyes, everything looked the same as the last time I'd come here with Shoko. Beneath me, a thick carpet of needles covered the ground, massive ferns pointed up toward the giant redwoods that towered above me. It was daytime here too, but under the canopy, it was cool and dark. The breeze carried the scent of the ocean.

At first, I just sat on the ground and let the pure, clean air into my lungs, one deep breath after another. I felt calm and relaxed. I wasn't sure it was possible to be stressed out here.

Shoko said she could see her destination and hear me call her from the other side—my side. I closed my eyes to send out my energy, then I started to laugh, remembering how Shoko had compared me to a peeing dog. I only needed to listen.

I stood and listened, waited for the stream to speak.

Nothing came. The only sound was the wind in the trees. It was blowing harder now, enough to move my hair and ruffle my shirt, and it had an odd feeling to it, like it didn't want me there.

I knelt back down. "Mother Earth, please take me to Shoko."

A moment later, the air began to blur.

When the swirling stopped, I was on a smooth stone floor—a wet stone floor. I'd arrived in a small, rustic room with wooden walls, a high peaked ceiling, and a large wooden tub. A cloud of steam rose from it.

A small face peered at me over the rim.

"Junya!" It was Shoko's little brother, Taro, grinning down at me.

When I stood up, Shoko, her mother Tomi, and Taro were all up to their necks in hot water, white cloths laid flat on their heads, their eyes wide with surprise.

"What are you doing here?!" Shoko yelled. I couldn't tell if she was angry or just shocked.

I averted my eyes. "I'm sorry," I said, truly embarrassed. "I traveled on my own and wanted to surprise you." I hadn't thought this through very well.

"I would say you accomplished that," Tomi said, almost sounding amused. "Honestly Shoko, I do not know whether to cut him down or invite him into the bath."

"He is hard to kill," Shoko said as she sank lower into the water. "But I am sure he would enjoy the tub."

"You can travel now!" Taro said. "Will you take me across?"

"Junya will *not* take you anywhere!" Tomi's eyes met mine and I nodded. I wouldn't risk crossing that woman. Imagine if she knew what I was doing with her daughter—

My eyes widened. Had I kept my mind closed? I must have, because Tomi didn't jump out of the tub and kill me.

As I waited outside the front door, where I should've traveled to in the first place, thoughts of my dream came back, of the lizards feasting right on this doorstep, climbing up the staircase to the shrine. A shudder went through me.

I gazed up at the shrine. It overshadowed everything, like standing under the Golden Gate Bridge. I waited for the flow of energy to reassure me, to fill me with peace. The quiet calm I so desperately sought.

I was still waiting when Shoko came outside a while later.

I grinned at her. "I traveled to see you!"

When she didn't respond I said, "I guess I won't be getting a—

ouch!" She'd kicked my shin.

While I rubbed my leg, she stared at me.

"That is why you came?" she said, louder than she needed to. "To show me something I already know you to be capable of?"

"Jeez, what's with you?"

We moved a dozen yards away from her house before she spoke again, this time in a whisper.

"What if Tomi had heard you?"

It took a second to process that. "Oh sorry! I was so happy to see you I didn't think."

Shoko didn't say anything more until we were well away from house, walking along a worn pathway in the meadow.

"I am happy to see you too, Junya," she said, "but we must *never* show affection here, not in our words or even share a smile." She glanced back at her house. "One mistake is all it will take to end this."

Reluctantly, I nodded. Then I told her about the dream.

"It is only a dream," she said, but she didn't sound convinced, and she didn't look at me. "Men with guns have come across before, many times."

"Seriously?"

"Every once in a while, some adventurer in the rain forests or some desert land stumbles through a gateway, and often they carry guns. If they try to use them, they die. But most often, they are so spellbound by the young Gatekeepers that sending them back unharmed is easy."

"Have Evil Ones ever brought guns across?"

She gave me a look. "How can a lizard hold a gun?"

"But when they're men—"

"Everything and everyone that crosses must do so in its true form."

Now that was interesting. "Okay, but what if men, like the soldiers who attacked me, crossed with machine guns and stuff?"

"Machine gun?"

"A gun that can fire lots of bullets really fast."

"Ah, those," she said, not looking the least bit concerned. "Men with those have crossed too."

"And you fight them with swords and arrows?"

"Do you remember the Evil One who shot the arrow at me in Scotland?"

I frowned, then the realization hit me. "You disappeared!"

"Yes," she said. "How hard is it for an archer to appear, bow already taut, and release an arrow? But it is easiest to just appear behind the man and cut him down. Even a dozen men will be dead in minutes."

"Wow, you really keep up with the times."

"Your dream is silly because it can never happen."

"I guess, but how many men have gotten through at once?"

"Before we closed the gateway?" She looked thoughtful. "I believe twenty-two was the most, but many years ago. Long before Tomi was born."

"What if you couldn't close the gateway?

"We can always close them."

"But what if you couldn't? What if Bartholomew found a way to jam them?"

"He does not possess the power to do that." She was starting to sound annoyed.

"Okay, what if there were simultaneous attacks through a dozen gateways at once?"

"It has never happened, Junya!" Her hands went to her hips. "With the power of the gods, we have all the strength we need."

We walked beside a small stream that trickled through a clearing in the birch trees. Shoko was quiet, and the only other sound was the wind in the leaves. It was beautiful, but I couldn't help thinking: What if what I felt, or didn't feel, was a decrease in the gods' energy?

I turned to her. "What would happen if the gods did get weak?"

She stared at me a long moment. "That is not something I wish to think about."

We came to a clearing and Shoko flumped onto her back and

stared at the sky. After a few minutes, I did the same. We lay side by side, our shoulders touching, watching the fluffy white clouds drift over us.

She pointed at a cloud. "That one looks like a horse."

I tried to follow where she was pointing. "It looks like mashed potatoes to me," I said. Then I pointed to another batch. "Now that totally looks like a train."

She laughed. "I suppose, if trains were fluffy white blobs." She folded her hands on her stomach.

An odd gloomy energy, so out of place here, seemed to drift in on the breeze and settle over me. I looked over at Shoko.

"I feel like something's wrong here."

She turned to look at me. "Like what?"

"I'm not sure exactly, but ... the Elders are worried for a reason, enough to let you break a lot of rules. We need to get the new force ready right away."

"I have finished selecting the girls and have spoken to each of them."

"So, what's the next step?"

"We take them across and test them," she said. "After that, I will seek the Elders' blessing."

I was about to answer when a faint gong sounded in the distance.

She bolted upright. "Ah, the men made cake today!" She jumped up. "Come on, I will race you to the kitchen." Then she was off, running flat out in bare feet.

That girl sure did like cake.

—

We got some odd stares as we arrived at the back of the line, both of us sweating and panting. As Shoko moved away to put more space between us, I noticed an older girl, about eighteen, wearing a scarf around her neck.

I elbowed Shoko. "That scarf looks modern."

Her eyes widened. "She is one of the potentials for the special force." Shoko pushed her way out of line toward the girl.

"What is this?" Shoko said as she pointed at the scarf.

"Shoko!" the girl said. "Is it not beautiful?"

"Where did you get it?"

"I crossed over and bought this myself!" The girl looked really proud. "Rina gave me … money."

Shoko's eyes shifted between the scarf and the girl's face.

"It is good to practice crossing, is it not?" the girl asked, her tone sounding doubtful under Shoko's stare. "I wish to be prepared."

I came up beside Shoko. "Did you have trouble?"

The girl shook her head, her excitement obvious. "I watched other customers, saw how they paid. The shopkeeper had to count my money though. I had barely enough."

I looked sideways at Shoko. "This is perfect," I whispered. "She's exactly what we need."

Several girls had gathered around, the cake forgotten, to admire the scarf. The girl looked like she would burst with delight.

Off to my left, I heard a girl say, "Why does she get to break the rules?"

"Because if you are favored by Shoko, you can do anything." I turned toward them and they both looked down. Luckily Shoko hadn't heard them. She'd already gone back to her place in line.

"You think this is a good thing?" Shoko asked me later as we sat eating cake.

"The easier they can operate on my side, the better," I said. "Besides, it's only a scarf." Still, those other girls' comments stayed with me. Jealousy wasn't an emotion I expected over here.

I took another bite of cake and nearly choked. That same odd feeling I'd had while we were staring up at the clouds hit me, harder this time. Something was wrong.

A moment later, bells rang out.

"What is it?" I said.

"There are intruders." Shoko squinted toward the shrine, listening. "In the place you call Africa. Three men have come through." She scowled, concentrating hard. "One is a shaman and he is dying."

I grabbed Shoko's arm. I don't remember whose palm hit the ground first.

CHAPTER
17

WE ARRIVED TO GROWLS THAT SHOKO and I instantly recognized. Then came the pain. It ripped through my shoulder, made me cry out, but I pushed it down as we scrambled to our feet. We'd arrived near the top edge of a round pit in the earth, maybe eight feet deep and twenty feet wide. A mutilated tribesman lay sprawled on the grass-covered bottom with a broken spear nearby. Two other men sat huddled against the stone wall of the pit, both bleeding from deep wounds, both terrified.

"There it is." Shoko sounded calm as she pointed toward the giant lizard. So far, only its scaled head and neck were though the vertical shimmering surface of the gateway. Two Gatekeepers fought it, stabbing and hacking with their katana as it thrashed its head, snapping its jaw at them. Three other Gatekeepers stood behind them. A second line of defense, I guessed.

Strong energy hit me. An older woman, dressed different from the Gatekeepers, knelt not far from me, hands pressed together in prayer. If she was a Controller trying to close the gateway, it didn't seem to be working.

The Gatekeepers fighting the lizard were cutting it, but slowly, like axes hitting a tree. Behind it, barely visible through the glimmer of the gateway, I saw a second figure.

Then another Gatekeeper jumped down and joined them. Shit, it was Shoko!

"Joining, right side!" She called out. Then she struck the lizard on the head with her katana. Blood spurted. She'd done more damage than the other Gatekeepers, but it still wasn't enough. The second lizard was now trying to get past the first, as if frenzied by the blood of its companion.

Three more Gatekeepers appeared above the pit beside me, two with bows.

"Archers, stand ready!" someone yelled.

I borrowed a katana from the archer nearest me and leaped in to help Shoko. The lizard had clamped its jaw into her katana and was flipping her back and forth like a rag doll.

I shoved a Gatekeeper aside and thrust the katana between the lizards rotting teeth, driving it into its mouth. The lizard screeched as black blood squirted out of the wound, and it let go of Shoko's katana.

She jumped back. The lizard was still coming through, its shoulders now visible.

"It is breaching!" Shoko yelled.

The lizard got its foreleg through and gouged the Gatekeeper beside Shoko. I swung the katana into its face. Its screech nearly drowned out the scream of the injured Gatekeeper.

"Shoko, get her out of here!"

As another Gatekeeper moved in to take her place, Shoko shoved the injured girl up the wall. When she turned back, the girl's blood covered the front of her clothes.

"Get him out of the way!" someone yelled.

Shoko grabbed my arm and yanked me backward.

"Release!" The order came from outside the pit.

Something whistled past my ear and the lizard grunted. An arrow protruded from its eye. Another arrow followed the first, barely a second apart, into the same eye, but it still surged ahead, both front legs through the gateway now.

Shoko swung her katana and sliced deep into its head. With a wild yell, she spun and cut its neck from below, then jumped back as black blood gushed out.

I started to move in again, but Shoko shoved me back.

"Again!" she yelled.

Two more arrows pierced its other eye, and with a shriek of pain, the second lizard's head came through.

"Another one!" Shoko yelled over her shoulder. "Be ready!"

I grabbed Shoko's arm. "We can cross over and attack them from behind!"

She hesitated, then nodded. As we sank to the ground, the second lizard let out a horrible screech of pain and jerked backward into the gateway.

We crossed.

The pit was identical, but now we were staring at the back end of the lizards. Except they weren't lizards on this side. One pair of human-looking legs, from the knees down, anyway, protruded from the shimmering surface, black boots digging into the dirt. A second man was backing out toward us, clawing at two arrows sticking out of his butt.

Two men lay nearby, their painted bodies covered in blood, both dead. But who shot the arrows?

The Evil One pulled his head out of the shimmering surface and staggered to his feet—in fully human form now. He wrapped his hand around the arrow shaft and yanked. It didn't come out. He noticed me when I started to laugh.

He lunged and caught me off-guard. I grunted as his foot hit my ribs, then he swept my feet out from under me and my katana went flying. He dove and I rolled, not fast enough. He grabbed my throat, his yellow eyes crazed, and slammed my head into the ground.

I hip-thrust, sending him up and off me. Then I flipped up and got my feet under me. He came at me, moving more like a lizard than a man now. I kneed him in the face and his head snapped back but he managed to grab my ankle. I went down again.

"Junya!"

I kicked out, rolled away and caught the katana she tossed. As he lunged toward me again, I swung the katana and sunk it deep into his arm. He pulled away screaming, black blood flowing. I heard another screech, this one muffled and I looked toward the sound. Shoko had sliced the legs off the Evil One that was still half-way inside the gateway.

I rolled onto my knees. The Evil One came at me again, his forked tongue flicking out, his arm spewing black blood and dove straight into my swinging blade.

I rolled out of the way as his body fell toward me. His head landed on the far side of the pit with a thud.

I staggered to my feet, lungs heaving, searching for the next threat. Shoko was already halfway up a shaky wooden ladder out of the pit. I sprang toward the rock wall, kicked off, and cleared the lip of the pit just as she climbed out.

An Evil One lay face down on the grass with Shoko's knife buried to the hilt in his neck. A widening pool of black expanded into the dry grass around him. Even as we watched, it turned to dust and vanished.

I glanced at Shoko. Her expression gave nothing away.

"Do not move!" The strong female voice came from behind us.

Of course we both spun.

A young African woman stood before us in traditional ceremonial dress. On her head she wore a colorful woven headpiece with braided tassels that dangled down to the sarong tied around her waist. A group of men stood behind her, all similarly clothed but without the headpiece. Some of the men carried spears, and one carried a bow with an arrow notched and aimed at us. That explained the arrows in the Evil One's butt. Three men had rifles, currently pointed at the ground. Beyond them, several bodies lay on the grass. Another woman was yelling into a cellphone, telling someone to come, quickly.

"Who are you?" said a tall, muscular man next to the woman, his spear pointed at me.

"We are Gatekeepers from the Other Side." Shoko stared at the woman curiously. That's when I noticed Shoko's arm was bleeding, her sleeve nearly soaked.

As I moved toward Shoko, the man cocked his arm to throw the spear. I didn't see him do it, I just *knew*. I exhaled my breath toward him.

I reached Shoko's side, but she wasn't moving. Nothing was moving except the spear, which had left the man's grip and was drifting slowly toward us. I batted it aside with the katana and released my energy.

They responded with shouts of surprise. Like magic, the spear had snapped in two on its way toward us.

I stood facing them, hand raised, palm out.

"You could've at least tried your guns," I said, glaring at them. "That *might've* been a challenge."

"They are empty," the man muttered.

"You are not Evil Ones?" the woman said.

"We came to help," I said.

The woman's shoulders seemed to sag. "Where is our shaman?"

Shoko pointed into the pit. "Are either of them him?"

The woman peered in. Her eyes betrayed her shock, but her voice didn't falter.

"No, he made it through after they attacked."

"There are three men on the other side of this gateway," I said. "One is dead. Two are badly hurt." Somehow, I knew the dead man was the shaman.

"We will bring them across so you may perform your death ceremonies," Shoko said, sounding less stern. "Now tell me, when did these men arrive?"

"As the ceremony began," the woman said, her voice shaking now. She was younger than I'd originally thought and was starting to break down. She pointed to a new Land Rover parked some distance away, engine still running, doors wide open. "They drove up and started shooting. We were surprised. We ... our shaman crossed, but he was wounded. Not long after, we heard shouts from the Other Side."

Shoko and I exchanged looks.

"Why did this happen ... why?" the woman said, tears streaming down her face now. A few of the others started to back away.

"This place is cursed," one said.

A man dressed in Western clothing looked close to hysterical. "Is this ... a sick joke? It must be, must be," he stammered. "I drove all the way here ..." He began backing toward the half dozen small trucks parked not far away.

"We must stay away from here!" an old woman cried out before she collapsed into a sobbing mess. The expressions on the others' faces said the same thing.

Shoko held up her hand. "Your god is still there!" she said. "We will open the Gateway so you can continue your worship."

"With who?" the muscular man said, anger in his voice. "Our shaman is dead!"

"We will help you!"

But it was too late. All of them had turned and run away.

Shoko knelt and reached for my hand. "This is bad," she whispered, "very bad."

"So is your arm." The hand she'd offered was slippery with blood.

She glanced at it, then kneeled and slammed her palm into the grass.

Nothing happened.

She tried again, then her eyes, wide with shock, met mine. "I cannot!"

I looked around us. We were in the middle of Africa ... somewhere.

"You try!" Something like alarm was in her voice.

I did as I had earlier. I thought of the other side of this gate, pictured it. She still had her palm against the grass, and when I touched it we crossed back.

—

The lizard without its legs lay in the pit in a pool of black blood, not yet dead. The three tribesmen were still down there, all dead now.

Off to one side, well away from the wounded, lay the body of a Gatekeeper, an older woman, perhaps forty and probably a master. The lizard had bitten off her arm and it lay beside her body, swollen, black, and grotesque. Her skin had a gray tinge to it. A girl, maybe thirteen, sat cross-legged beside the body, trying hard not to cry.

Two Mikos, distinctive in their white tops and long red skirts, tended the injured Gatekeepers. The one who'd taken a claw to the leg was doing okay because only the teeth carried the poison.

Remembering Shoko, I gently took her arm and examined the cut. She needed some of that potion, but then, maybe I could do something.

I focused my energy on her, let it flow from my hand. The bleeding stopped, but it didn't heal. The cut looked as ugly as before. I borrowed a cloth bandage from one of the Miko's bags.

"That will keep it clean until you can get some potion," I said as I wrapped the bandage around Shoko's arm.

Shoko watched me work. "You learn quickly," she said. "The pain is gone too. Thank you."

If this were our army, they'd call this a "mop-up operation." Several Gatekeepers stood guard over the now sealed gateway and the lizard. They must have arrived with the Mikos.

"What'll they do with it?" I asked Shoko, indicating the lizard.

"When it finally dies, it will disappear, just as the men did in Chichén Itzá."

"Even from here?"

"Yes, thankfully. It is one less thing to deal with."

There were men here now too, equipped with blankets, rope, and shovels.

"Are they ... like undertakers?" I couldn't think of a better word.

"Undertakers' assistants," she said. "Undertakers are women, those deemed too kind to be Gatekeepers."

Two women knelt beside the dead Gatekeeper and began to clean her, reverently.

"It is the highest honor to prepare a fallen Gatekeeper for the final ceremony." Shoko spoke softly. "One must be ready to greet the gods."

Two young Gatekeepers arrived. They hurried over to where the undertakers worked and sat with young girl, held her as she began to sob.

"I know it is selfish," Shoko whispered. "But sometimes I wish I was not the daughter of Tomi."

"Why?"

"Then I would have nothing to live up to, no family line to dishonor." Shoko indicated toward the girls. "Do you think I could ever cry like that, or receive such comfort?"

Without thinking, I went to put my arm around her. She shoved me away.

"No!"

A few heads turned in our direction and a stir went through the group. They had noticed, or forgotten, that we were there. Then, as if someone threw a switch, the mood changed and the whispers started. Some looked at us with admiration, others with hatred or at least envy, although that last one seemed to be directed at Shoko, not me.

"Wow," I whispered to her. "What's with that?"

"Many girls dislike me because of my superior skill."

I let out a laugh. "You sure it's got nothing to do with you being an arrogant snob?"

She stood a bit straighter. "How can it be arrogance when I am stating a fact?"

A commotion near the pit interrupted my reply, which was probably a good thing. The lizard was gone, leaving only pools of black and red blood.

Shoko stood staring at the scene. "That was a hard-won battle," she said with a sigh. "It is often better to let them through and then kill them. I doubt the master would have died up here on the open ground, even against two of them. Fighting them from the front is dangerous."

"Well, I think we just proved there's a better way," I said.

"What do you mean?"

"Who actually ended the attack?"

She thought about that. "We did, from the Other Side."

"Exactly. Fighting a man, even if he has guns, is way easier than fighting those monsters, right?" I looked toward the dead woman. She was on a stretcher now, ready for transport. "Three or four Gatekeepers, trained to cross over and attack from the rear, could've ended this in seconds."

Shoko stared at me for a long moment, then slowly nodded. "You are correct. I need to convince the—"

"I mean, trying to fight in that pit was crazy," I said. "I'm surprised we didn't end up hurting each other."

Now she frowned. "Besides the lizard, the greatest danger in there was you! And you would have a few arrows in your head had I not pulled you down."

"Well, I didn't know—"

"Exactly," she said, sounding annoyed. "It was not 'crazy' in the pit. We have a system, with strict but fluid rules for defense and attack. You were jumping around, interrupting others ..." She jabbed her forefinger into my chest. "... and you *never* shove someone out of the way as you did with that Gatekeeper!"

I cringed. All right, she was definitely annoyed. "It didn't look organized," I muttered. "Sorry."

"We have been doing this for a while, you know."

"Shoko, do you sense that?!"

Shoko turned toward the Controller who'd called her. "I am sorry." She moved toward the woman. "I was not paying attention."

I could feel it now too. "What is that?" I asked, coming up behind them.

The Controller looked at me. "That is the cry of the god of the grasslands," she said. "He has sensed his worshipers flee and is saddened."

I tilted my head to listen. It was easier now because a hush had fallen over everyone. The sound was like the wind whistling through trees, but higher pitched, almost like a scream.

The Controller shook her head. "Something was wrong," she said. "I should have been able to slam that gateway closed before they got in, but ... I did not have enough energy."

I turned to Shoko. "You see? The killing of shamans has got to stop."

Just then, I felt another disturbance in the surrounding energy.

Shoko looked confused. "The Kannushi is coming," she said. Then she shouted: "The Kannushi is coming!"

By the time he appeared, surrounded by his honor guard of eight older Gatekeepers, everyone including me was kneeling. Unlike the others, I only went to one knee.

The Kannushi looked around and spotted Shoko. "Shoko," he shouted, striding toward her. "A cry from the gods was heard all the way to Izumo! Report!"

From her position on the ground, Shoko told him everything, noting the significance of the weakened Controller. She concluded by explaining how we'd stopped the Evil Ones from my side.

He looked down at us. "It is not only this god who is weakening," he said. "Even the gods in Izumo appeared subdued."

I glanced at Shoko. She hadn't been able to travel. I knew it was my energy that brought us back.

"These are dire times, Shoko." The Kannushi lowered his voice. "We have heard of the force you are gathering. The Grand Elder wishes you to proceed with your plan."

She glanced at me, then bowed again. "We will begin assembling the new force immediately."

———

Everyone eventually traveled away, leaving only the Gatekeepers who'd actually fought plus a girl of about ten. I had no idea when she'd arrived. She was in similar attire to a Miko, except her long skirt was a deep burgundy, not red.

She knelt and placed a glazed earthen bowl on the ground and rotated it until it was in the perfect position. In relation to what I couldn't tell, but I knew this wasn't the time to ask. Then with equal care, she poured what looked like water into the bowl from a beautifully carved wooden bottle. Her movements were slow but deliberate, like a skilled dancer.

By this time, the Gatekeepers had gathered on their knees in a tight circle around her, hands held in prayer position in front of their chests, watching her. Not knowing what else to do, I got on my knees beside Shoko.

The girl seemed to be in a trance as she set the bottle on the ground. I squinted to get a better look at it. I'd seen a lot of amazing woodcarvings in Dad's high-end carpentry magazines, but I'd never seen anything as exquisite as that.

She pulled up her sleeves and tied them back, then placed her palms flat on the earth. After a long moment of silence, she methodically washed her hands in the clear water, though I couldn't see any dirt there. Without warning, she flung her arms toward the sky, palms coming together and sending water droplets into the air, where they vanished. She sat frozen like that for several seconds before her small hands slowly descended, hovering just above the bowl.

Suddenly the girl and every Gatekeeper in the circle simultaneously clapped twice. Fire exploded from between her palms as the liquid in the bowl burst into flames. With a puff of breath, she extinguished it.

Without a word, everyone leaned forward, knees touching, and cleansed their hands in the clear liquid. Shoko indicated I should join them.

After all the Gatekeepers thanked the young girl for her work, Shoko turned to me.

"Earth, water, wind, and fire," she said solemnly. "And thus we are cleansed of this ordeal."

CHAPTER

18

I DIDN'T GET A LOT OF SLEEP that night. Dreams of dead shamans and Gatekeepers didn't make for a good pillow, and by the time I crawled out of bed the next morning, I was in a foul mood.

We needed to stop Bartholomew.

No, not *we*: me. I needed to do everything I could to stop him. He was my responsibility.

Shoko was busy with final selections for the special force and apparently didn't need me, so I decided it was about time I went for a ride in my new Jeep. I didn't know what hours Jason worked, but when I called the security office, they said he'd be there in an hour.

They were wrong. It was an hour and fifteen minutes before it arrived.

"Where to?" Jason said as I walked out the gate. He was dressed casually. No blue suit or radio earpieces today. That was good.

"I want to go cruising. I haven't ridden in this baby once since I bought it."

He frowned. "Okay, anywhere in particular?"

"Down the coast to the Number One. I'll figure out the rest once we get there."

"Yes sir, boss man." The engine roared to life.

I glanced sideways at him. "I don't need any shit today, okay? And keep to the speed limit this time."

He raised an eyebrow but concentrated on driving after that.

I stared out the side window, lost in thought about what had happened the day before. I couldn't get the lonely cry of that god out of my mind.

It wasn't until we were merging onto Highway 35 and an old minivan passed us that Jason said something.

"Can I do a little more than the limit here?" He glanced in his rearview mirror. "I've got a tanker truck climbing up our back bumper."

I let out a frustrated sigh. "You're the driver. Can't you figure that out?"

He nodded slowly. "So, disregard your first order?" There was definitely sarcasm in his voice.

I rolled my head on the headrest and looked at him over my sunglasses.

"Look James," he said, annoyed. "If you insist on giving me *orders*, don't get pissed when I follow them."

I realized I was being a jerk. "Do whatever you need to," I said, turning back to the window. He hit the gas and the Jeep's engine responded with a satisfying roar.

"I'm sorry," I said after a few minutes had passed. "I had a crappy day yesterday."

"Looks like someone else did too."

I looked over at him. "What do you mean?"

"You've got some heavy bruising on your hands and elbows," he said, eyes back on the road. "Those aren't from training."

I let that go unanswered.

"So, how does it handle?" I said after a while. I was trying to be friendly, but I was also trying to change the subject.

He grinned. "It's got lots of power. The turbo's real smooth."

"Well enjoy."

He chuckled. "Too bad it looks like a giant pumpkin."

—

We were southbound on the Number One near Pacifica when he slowed the Jeep by a pullout.

"Mind if I stop and stretch my leg?"

The spot he picked had a nice ocean view. I got out and checked out the Jeep while he paced and did some stretches; he looked pretty mobile to me. I also noticed he checked out every car that passed us, and when a car pulled in with a couple and two kids, he stopped and leaned against the guardrail, arms crossed, until they finished their picture-taking and drove off. This guy was wired, way more than Grandpa's usual security guys. I wondered if he was armed. I had a feeling he was, and I wasn't sure I liked that.

"So how did you get this great job?" I said.

He looked over at me. "Lin hired me a few months ago."

"Where do you know her from?"

"We've got some history."

For some reason I didn't like the way he said that. "History?"

He smiled. "I met her when she was flying with Singapore Airlines. Mind you, she wasn't flying at the time."

I shot him a look.

"I meant she was in a hotel bar, not on a flight." He got a wistful look in his eyes. "After she left the airline, we kept in touch, so when she heard I got an honorary discharge because of this ..." He pointed at his knee. "... she offered me a job."

I stuffed my hands into my jean pockets "The Chairman might not like hearing about your *history*." And even though it was none of my business, I didn't like it either.

He shrugged. "We were both unattached at the time. You might be a little young to appreciate this, but the person you're sleeping with today probably isn't your first and won't be your last, or theirs.

Nothing lasts forever."

I thought of Shoko. She was the first person I'd been with—well, almost been with—and I wanted her to be the last. What was wrong with that?

I took a deep breath. "The last time we talked, you said Barrymore had nothing to do with you getting this driving gig."

"Lin again."

"Why?"

He watched a black SUV speed past before he replied. "She knew I was dying of boredom at the Club, and she said you were interesting."

"Lin told you about me?" What was she thinking?

"She said you're fond of martial arts, and good at it, which is damn high praise coming from her." He sized me up. "And you've been training since you were a little kid?"

I nodded. "It gave my mom something to do for the last twelve years."

"Your mom taught you?" He considered that for a minute. "Well, she is Lin's cousin."

I studied him. "You know an awful lot, Jason."

"Lin trusts me."

"Since you know my story, what's yours?"

"Actually, I don't know your story." His mouth twisted into a half grin. "I've heard a few versions of what happened to Sergeant Jackson in the warehouse. I do know it was a police bullet that killed him, and I'm open-minded enough to believe some of the other stuff that happened there." When it was obvious I didn't intend to comment, he said, "You're pretty mature for your age." Then he grinned. "But you can be a bit of an ass sometimes."

I smiled. I was starting to like this guy.

"I've hung around The Chairman since I was five, and my mom and dad never treated me like a kid." That was an understatement.

"Lin said you're solid." He glanced around. "The information I'm about to give you is for your ears only. It's not on my application

164

form. If you talk, you answer to Lin because she backed you, understand?"

I nodded, curious now. "I presume that works both ways?"

"Deal." And I knew from the look in his eyes, and his energy, that this guy was someone I could trust.

"When I met Lin, I was in Singapore winding down after an op in Southeast Asia," he said. "I was an operator in the Combined Applications Group back then."

"You were in Delta Force?" I said. "That's a tier-one special forces unit, right up there with the SEALS, JTF2, and the SAS."

He looked impressed. "You know your stuff."

"Actually, I just read it on the Internet last night."

"Most of that stuff is bullshit." He stood back up and walked to the driver's door. We got in, the engine roared to life, and he pulled out into traffic.

"What happened to your knee?"

He waited until he passed a semitrailer carrying steel beams before he answered.

"I was doing a HALO jump and landed the wrong way."

"What's that?"

"Stands for High Altitude Low Opening. You bail out of a plane at thirty thousand feet, usually over a friendly neighboring country, then you free fall with about two hundred pounds of gear. You only open the parachute when you get real low. It wasn't a bad injury, but we were stuck out in the boonies in Afghanistan for five days. The team medic did what he could, but it wasn't enough. By the time I got medevaced, I knew I was done." He let out a sigh. "A least I didn't do it stumbling pissed drunk outside a bar."

"And they made you quit?"

He glanced at his mirror before he said, "Couldn't be in Delta anymore." He didn't sound happy about that. "And I sure as hell wasn't going back to regular army, so I left. I had lots of buddies on the outside, so once I was up and about, I did some consulting in the Middle East and Africa. I made enough off that to live the easy life for a while, a long while, if I'm careful."

"They paid a lot?"

"Twenty grand a week."

I grinned. "So why are you driving around a pain in the ass like me?"

He shrugged. "I was having ideological issues about who I was training," he said. "I needed something else to do."

"So, what makes Special Forces guys so good?"

He took a moment to answer. "It's kind of Darwinian, you know, survival of the fittest. You draw the best of the best from other fighting units, then test the shit out of them. Not only physical strength and endurance, but also intelligence, psychological strength, and mental stability. They can't be afraid of anything. Not heights, snakes, aliens, *anything*. If it's in there, it'll come out at the worst possible time. And you gotta have a never-give-up attitude. I've seen the strongest, smartest, most capable guys just give up. It's all up here." he tapped his forehead.

"What do you mean?"

"Imagine you're been humping a two-hundred-pound pack for three days in the pouring rain, day and night. Then you see trucks waiting up ahead. A hot meal, dry clothes. You know you've made it but just when you get close enough to smell the bacon, they drive off and leave you there. You'd be surprised how many guys give up right there."

"That's harsh."

"Yeah, only about one percent make it. You take those guys and train the shit out of them. Navigation, first aid, hand-to-hand combat escape and evasion, diving, parachuting, and precision shooting with every kind of weapon there is. We'd burn through two or three thousand rounds of ammunition a week during training. And you never stop training. You can always be better. And then, you apply that training in every environment on earth, from the arctic, to tropical jungles, deserts and everywhere in between."

I realized a lot of this could apply to the Gatekeepers. They were already amazing fighters, and Shoko was picking out the best. They wouldn't need most of the other stuff he mentioned because they could travel, but then I remembered Shoko's arm. It made a lot of sense to give them some first-aid training. We couldn't have a Miko with us.

"How many guys did you work with, as a team I mean?"

He downshifted and roared around a tight curve before answering. "Usually four guys, sometimes more depending on the job."

"That's not a lot."

"It is when you're highly trained and you work together as a unit. You plan, plan, plan, figure out your *what ifs*, then execute. And you always have three backup plans in case things go south, which they usually did."

"Sounds like you liked it though."

"Nothing better," he said. "The Special Forces are the perfect place for soldiers who hate the army."

"Why's that?"

"Because we pick our own gear, wear what we want, grow our hair and beards, and plan our own ops. We still respected rank, but Special Forces men are judged by their skills and experience. Plus, there're no drill sergeants barking about discipline and rules, so basically there's no bullshit."

I considered that. This was sounding better and better. Shoko and I needed to organize and train Gatekeepers to work in small teams, both on their side and ours. But having no rules or orders would be a problem. Even Shoko, who was pretty rebellious, had trouble with that.

"If I wanted to organize an elite combat team, what would I need to do?"

He grunted. "Hypothetically?"

I smiled. "Of course."

"You get some good guys and some very good trainers, then go at it."

I nodded. "Are you interested in doing some consulting again? I can pay as well as the Saudis."

He glanced sideways at me. "I never said I worked for the Saudis, and I don't have the patience to train your high-school buddies."

"Actually, I was thinking about teenage girls."

CHAPTER

19

THE NEXT MORNING, I TOLD OKAASAN the Grand Elder had approved our plan for the special group of Gatekeepers. She was wearing her *gi*, just tying her worn black belt in place. Mack was in the guest room getting into his new uniform. He was here so often I was starting to think of it as *his* room.

"The Elders are that concerned?"

"Yeah, the Kannushi said it was *dire*."

She frowned. "But there are thousands of cultures that still worship Mother Earth, in one form or another," she said. "I can't imagine how killing even a hundred shamans could do this much damage."

"The problem is, we don't actually know how many have been killed, but if it's becoming noticeable in Izumo, it's got to be a lot," I said. "Even I can feel a difference."

"What do you mean?"

"I'm not sure, but the energy isn't the same." I tried to find the right words. "It's not as peaceful." Then I told her about how Shoko hadn't been able to travel.

"That's probably because she was hurt," she said.

"Maybe, but hearing that god cry out was scary."

She looked thoughtful. "I suppose there are a lot of reasons why people are forgetting about the old gods," she said. "Western technology and culture are far more interesting than worshiping some old-fashioned god."

"Sure, but how can you ignore a gateway to another world?"

"Pretty easy when you're sitting in a dark room zoned out with cable TV or the Internet, wouldn't you say?"

I frowned. "My room isn't dark."

Mack walked into the living room, all decked out in a fresh white *gi*.

"Hey, did you guys see the news?" he said. "A bunch of people were killed at that Inca site in Peru. I think it's called Machu Picchu." He looked worried. "Do you think it was Evil Ones?"

"A massacre in South America isn't exactly rare, Mack." Okaasan walked over and tightened his belt. They looked hilarious standing side by side; he was a full foot taller than she was and twice as heavy, not that it would make any difference. Mack was in for it.

There was a disturbance in the earth's energy and I turned toward the window in time to see Shoko materialize in the Zen garden. She was wearing her school uniform, but she didn't have her backpack, only a small purse-like pouch. Which meant she was unarmed and that was odd.

I slid open the glass door. "Hi Shoko."

She smiled but didn't appear happy to see Okaasan and Mack. Still, she bowed toward Okaasan, who returned the gesture.

"I came to tell you the final candidates are ready," she said to me. "Only twenty-eight proved capable of enduring the *noise* on this side. The rest were dismissed."

I grinned. "Twenty-eight is great! I'll get my stuff together and—"

She held up a hand. "Not yet, Junya. There are things we must discuss first."

"I'm surprised the Elders approved this," Okaasan said. "It flies in the face of a thousand years of tradition and it breaks our—your—laws."

Shoko nodded. "It seems they are now willing to risk the experiment."

"Did you hear about the bloodbath in Peru?" Mack said.

Shoko nodded. "There was a report of trouble in your South America. A Gatekeeper there was able to look *across*, and it was decided not to open the gateway."

"She saw people getting killed and didn't do anything?"

"Mack," Okaasan said gently. "Like you, the Gatekeepers aren't ready yet. And we don't fight when we're not prepared, without some advantage."

"Yes," Shoko said. "Once the new force is trained, we will take action."

"Speaking of which," I said. "My new driver is—" I stopped myself. I told Jason I'd keep the specifics of his past to myself. "He's an ex-combat trainer for the army. I invited him over today to check out the dojo and stuff. He'd be perfect to train the new force."

Shoko looked concerned. "He will be here soon?"

I glanced at my watch. "In about an hour, probably more. He's always late."

She turned to Okaasan. "Do not let me interfere with your training, Misako. I have more I wish to speak with Junya about."

They weren't even in the teahouse before she reached for me.

"I'm glad you—" was all I managed to say before she kissed me, with a hunger I hadn't expected. When we finally pulled apart, she reached into her handbag and produced a small box.

"I got some."

I took it and read the front: Twelve ultra-thin condoms.

"Do you have any idea how many kinds there are?" she said, not noticing the surprised look on my face. "I would have been there a week had I not sought advice from other women."

I handed the box back. "You asked for help?"

She nodded. "Several women gathered. They suggested we use something simple for my first time."

I pictured her in the Family Planning aisle, surrounded by housewives, and felt my face flush.

"Doesn't anything embarrass you?"

"When they heard it was to be your first time as well, they laughed and said I probably would not even get the condom on before you were done."

"Who says?" But to be fair, I was already getting excited, and nervous. "Anyway." I swallowed hard. "When do you want to try them out?"

She glanced toward the teahouse. "Now."

Dad wasn't home and Okaasan was busy beating up Mack. I could hear him yelping already. She wouldn't notice a bomb go off.

"Okay ..."

Shoko was already on the way to my bedroom, her short skirt swishing above her bare legs.

We sat side by side on my bed, thighs and arms touching. As usual, the energy between us was electric, but I'd never been so nervous. She wasn't looking very confident either, which was so unusual it made me even more anxious.

"You are uneasy?" she whispered.

"A little. You?"

She tilted her head to one side then back, as if thinking about it. "I am eager, which leads to anxiety."

"Why don't we see what happens?"

We started slowly, sitting side by side, only kissing, but it wasn't long before we were breathing hard and our hands started roaming. We undressed and slipped under the covers, and the magic feeling of hands on bare skin returned. I'd learned last time to listen to the little noises that escaped her lips. They told me where to touch, and when I did, the sounds grew louder. She had her hand on me and my own excitement grew. It wasn't long before her body shuddered, and she cried out. Of course, I'd lost it long before that.

She let out a deep sigh and lay still, panting. "It is so much better when you do that," she whispered a long moment later. "Gods, that was amazing!"

I collapsed beside her, breathing hard. "Yeah, wow."

We lay together, holding hands, while our breathing slowed. I listened to Okaasan's energy. She was still preoccupied so Shoko and I stayed in bed, talking and touching, and after about fifteen minutes, we were making out again.

She touched me. "You are hard again." She sounded surprised. "Does that mean we can?"

"Yeah." Hunger stirred inside me. "I'm ready."

"I feel ready too," she whispered. "Do you want to?"

I kissed her, then she rolled away and reached for the box.

She was ready, but I had trouble getting inside her. "Is this the right place?" I asked, feeling confused and stupid.

She bit her lip and tensed up. "Yes, but ..."

I froze. "I'm hurting you?"

"No, just go slow."

I'd watched enough videos on the Internet to know how sex was supposed to work. Well, the going-in part, anyway. They never showed the girl looking uncomfortable like this.

I started to pull out. "I don't want to hurt you."

Her hands on my butt stopped me. "No, I am okay," she whispered. "Keep trying."

I did, but I watched her face the whole time. She had her eyes closed, teeth against her lower lip, letting out heavy even breaths.

Finally, I was all the way in. I kissed her gently on the lips and her eyes opened.

She gave me a single, quick nod. "It is getting better."

"We don't have to." I searched her face for the truth.

"We have come this far," she whispered with a weak smile. "Keep going."

I began to move slowly, my eyes on hers. I knew I'd have more stamina this time and that actually worried me.

"It feels good," she whispered. "Keep going, Junya."

My movements grew faster. I stared into her eyes until it got too intense, and I had to close mine. I stopped and let out a deep breath.

She was breathing hard too. "You are finished?"

I nodded, eyes still closed.

"Then could you please get out?"

I moved back so I could see her better. "Are you okay?"

She screwed up her face. "I do not know." She was quiet after that and stared at the ceiling.

I brushed the hair off her face. "I'm sorry. I don't really know what I'm doing."

She rolled her head to look at me. "I do not think you did anything wrong," she said. "I was not relaxed. I was eager like you, but ..." She closed her eyes. "It is disappointing. What we did together earlier felt better."

We stayed like that, only our shoulders touching, both of us lost in our own thoughts. Of course, mine were about what I must've done wrong. When I slid my arm under her neck and turned to face her, she snuggled against me and we lay like that for a long time, legs intertwined and stomachs touching.

"It was such an odd feeling, having something inside my body," she said. "Did it feel good for you, even with that thing on?"

"Uh, I was worried about you, but yeah, it felt good."

She squeezed herself even closer to me. "Junya?"

"Yes?"

She paused, and I heard a sniff. "I have never felt so close to anyone before. It is an amazing feeling, like my heart will burst." Her voice was muffled. "I could stay like this forever."

I held her head close to my chest. I knew exactly what she meant.

CHAPTER
20

JASON SHOWED UP AFTER ME AND Shoko had showered together, another awesome first for both of us. But even with her beside me, water cascading off her body, I managed to keep a part of my mind focused on *the stream*. If Okaasan walked in on us, we were dead, or at least I was.

The doorbell rang while Shoko was still dressing. When I let Jason in the front door, I looked past him to see if he'd driven my Jeep, but I couldn't see the road because of our high concrete wall.

"I only drove it in case you wanted to go out after this," he said.

"Feeling guilty?"

"Nope, I'm on the clock right now."

I took him out back, across the bridge over the Koi pond.

"Man." He shook his head. "From the road this place looks like nothing, but this is amazing."

When we reached the teahouse, Okaasan was staring down at us, holding an oak bokuto. Mack was behind her, looking winded and bright red.

Jason nodded his head to Okaasan.

"May I come up, ma'am?" When she nodded, he heaved himself onto the deck and faced her. "I'm Jason," he said. "Pleased to meet you, ma'am."

Okaasan bowed. "I am Misako. It is my pleasure."

He looked past her at Mack. "How's the training going?"

Mack laughed, a labored, huffy sort of noise. "She's killing me."

"Now you understand how I've suffered my entire life!" I said.

"How long's Mack been training, ma'am?"

"Just a few weeks," Okaasan said with a mischievous smile. "He's still learning to sweep the floor correctly."

"Mrs. Thompson, I've been trying …"

Jason kicked off his shoes before stepping inside. Okaasan looked pleased.

"This is quite the setup," he said.

"Do you study the Arts, Jason?" Okaasan said, giving him the once-over. It didn't look like he was carrying any extra weight.

He shook his head. "We didn't have time for that in the Special Forces. We learned how to neutralize the opponent as quickly as possible."

"What other way is there to fight?"

Heads turned. It was Shoko, standing outside in her school uniform, looking up at us.

"True," Jason said, studying her. "But most martial artists can't fight worth a damn."

"There is a great difference between an artist and a warrior."

"Shoko, this is Jason," I said. "Jason, Shoko."

"Ah, you're James's girlfriend," Jason said. "Nice to meet you."

Shoko glanced at me, a slight smile curling her lips. Then she turned her attention to him.

"You are the soldier Junya spoke of."

"I guess so. I've heard you can fight."

"I can." She was still on the ground. "Can you?"

"I can take care of myself," he said, smiling down at her as if she was the cutest thing, which I thought she was.

She swung effortlessly onto the deck, pulled off her shoes and socks, and stepped onto the tatami. "Show me."

Jason glanced at me, then back at Shoko. "You want to spar?" He looked uncomfortable.

"Ah, Shoko," I said, worried she might still be feeling sore. "Are you feeling up to that?"

I winced when Okaasan looked at her with concern.

Shoko was staring at Jason, but she nodded. "I need to judge his worth."

Jason made a face. "My *worth*?"

"Shoko, he's one of the most elite soldiers in the world."

"Then he should have no problem impressing me." When Jason didn't move, she walked up and kicked him in the shin.

"Ouch." Jason looked more surprised than hurt.

Then she did a basic side kick which hit his upper arm with a solid smack.

He grimaced and looked at me. "That's a pretty good kick. She's good, I'm impressed, okay?"

Shoko's next side kick hit the same arm, higher and harder than the first.

He stepped back while rubbing his arm. "I didn't come here to spar."

"I think you had better at least defend yourself," Okaasan said.

He turned back in time to block an easy front kick. She repeated the kick and he batted it aside and sent her to the floor.

Shoko winked at me as he bent over to help her up.

"I'm sorry—"

Shoko back-kicked him in the chest and he staggered backward. Then she was up and hit him twice in the gut before he could recover. He managed to deflect a roundhouse kick and the next few strikes but I knew she was still playing. She went at him again, three or four times, with elbows and fists. He responded, although only with blocks, but he was definitely warming up. He handled her next barrage easily, blocking her blows and absorbing the ones he couldn't but when Shoko went through and hit him in the jaw, something in his eyes changed.

He put his palm into Shoko's face and shoved, hard enough to send her sprawling to the matt several feet away. He wasn't angry, or even agitated, like he should've been during a fight. He looked calm ... too damn calm as he stared down at her.

"I've had enough of this."

Anyone with half a brain would've backed down right then, but Shoko stood up, brushed herself off, and ran at him. She twisted into a butterfly kick, spinning three times so fast she was a blur and I doubt he even saw which foot hit him. He went down to one knee but managed to get his hands up to block another kick. As she spun away, he slammed into her, using speed and body size to send her to the mats again.

She stood up a little slower this time.

He held up his palms to her. "Come on, stop. I'm going to end up hurting you."

"I doubt that," she said. Then she looked over at me. "I am done now."

"Good," Jason muttered, but I think he thought she meant she was done fighting. I knew she meant she was done playing. He started to turn away.

"Jason!" I called out the warning.

He turned back in time to see her jump into a beautiful—but slow—spin-kick. Bait.

He reacted, faster than I expected he could. He grabbed her right foot as it flew past and he hauled her into the air, leaving her dangling upside down by one leg, her skirt flipped inside out.

"Kicking's useless in a fight!" He looked smug for about half a second.

Shoko's free foot landed on his chest and she kicked off for momentum, then slammed her heel under his chin. As his head snapped back, she flipped in the air and her feet barely touched the ground before she'd slammed three double roundhouse kicks into him that made his eyes bulge.

He started to defend, but Shoko was going all out now—almost. She drove him back across the dojo, using every type of kick I could imagine, in crazy, lightning combinations that he had no hope to block. As he banged in the far wall, she kicked him in the ribs, then finished him off with a spinning leg sweep that took his feet out from under him.

As he hit the ground, head and shoulders before his torso, she drove her knee into his chest while her right hand descended toward his throat, her fingers pointed like a knife. She froze with her fingernails on his wind pipe.

"You are dead, warrior Jason." Then she stood up. "Do you still believe kicking is *useless?*"

Jason rolled onto his side and let out a groan.

"That was amazing!" I said. "You're awesome!"

She smiled at me, the cute teenage girl again. "That was nothing."

Jason slowly sat up, one hand wiping at the blood from his lips, the other clutching his ribs. "Why the hell did you do this to me?" He didn't seem to be addressing anyone in particular.

Shoko's smile left her face as she turned to look down at him. "You claim to be a warrior, and I see you are skilled, and yet you would not fight me."

"I'm an ex-soldier who doesn't hit girls."

They held each other's gaze for a long moment. "I fight those who do not only *hit* girls, they invade our lands and *kill* them every day," Shoko said. "I am a warrior, as is Misako and if you will be with us, there is no holding back—not even with a *girl.*"

"Be with you?"

Okaasan knelt and handed him a tissue. "Do you need ice?"

He nodded. "I think she broke a rib."

Okaasan did a quick check. "It's not broken, but you better take it easy for a few days."

Shoko harrumphed. "I did not even hit him that hard."

I sighed. "I presume you're not impressed?"

She didn't reply. She walked toward Jason, then knelt and bowed low in front of him.

Jason glanced at me, unsure of how to react.

When she came back up she turned to me. "He is honorable, and in his eyes I see a true warrior, one who knows *The Way*. You are worthy to teach us, Jason-sensei."

Jason had his face screwed up. "Teach who, what?"

"Ah, Jason," I said, squatting in front of him with a box of tissue. His nose was still bleeding. "Do you remember those teenage girls I talked about?"

He stared at me. "I thought you were kidding."

"They know how to fight, like Shoko, but they need to learn some new tactics, like you used in the Special Forces."

Jason looked around. Everyone stared back.

"I'm not interested in teaching a bunch of ninja-wannabes."

Okaasan's eyes narrowed. "What do you know of the ninja?"

"He's a friend of Lin's," I said.

No one said a word after that.

Jason finally stood up. "You want me to train teenage-girl warriors some Special Forces skills?"

"How does twenty-five grand a week sound?"

He licked his lips. "I don't know ..." Then he looked at each of us before replying. "This is a really screwed-up family."

Mack held up a hand. "I'm not related."

"You said you know how to keep your mouth shut so I'm holding you to that," I said. "Whether you're in or out, this doesn't leave here." I paused and tuned in to the stream. He was intrigued, that was obvious, but unsettled, too.

He hesitated a long moment. "I won't tolerate any action against the US or anything supporting terrorism. I'll report your asses to the FBI in a heartbeat."

I laughed. "Believe me, this has nothing to do with America," I said. "So, what's it gonna be?"

"I'll listen to what you have to say."

Mack nudged Okaasan. "I want to learn that spin-kick next."

—

Jason, Shoko, and I sat at our dining-room table, a load of snacks and drinks in front of us. I also had a notepad.

"I guess you'll need some background." I glanced at Shoko. "We haven't really talked about this too much yet."

"I am sure our ideas are united," she said, which started my mind on a tangent I had to cut off quick.

I turned to Jason. "Okay, for starters." I tried to organize my thoughts. "Shoko and other warriors like her guard the gates of … let's call it a kingdom."

Jason looked skeptical. "And it's only teenage girls that guard this *kingdom*?"

I nodded. "It progresses from trainees in their early teens to full-ranking women in their twenties."

"Why only females?"

"Because that is the way it is," Shoko said with a note of finality in her tone.

"Anyway," I said, "there are gateways that are the only way in, but—"

"Not by air or water?"

I hesitated, thinking. "No, that's not possible."

He was looking even more cynical. "So, a *kingdom* without air or water access."

"The place isn't important," I said, realizing this all sounded rather far-fetched. "What matters is these girls are used to fighting together, in groups and small squads, I guess you'd call them, but they could use some new tactics."

"For combat?"

"Well yeah, but it's more like being bodyguards." I glanced at Shoko. "They escort people to a location and if there's trouble, they fight."

He nodded, looking more interested. "Okay, Close Protection is something we did a lot overseas," he said. "And women are damn effective in urban environments."

"Well it's not exactly urban—"

Shoko sighed. "May I?"

I nodded, feeling a bit stupid. "That's probably best."

"As Junya said, my fellow warriors and I defend gateways," she said. "And by doing so, we keep our … Important Ones safe. Most times when a gateway opens, the people who enter are expected and welcomed. But sometimes, bad people come through and we need to kill them."

Jason's eyebrows went up at that. "You *need* to kill them?"

She gave him a curt nod. "If the warriors present cannot stop the threat on their own, more are called until it is stopped."

He nodded as if he understood her. "You get in trouble, you call in the cavalry."

Shoko looked at me. "The *what?*"

I waved a hand. "Never mind." I looked back to Jason. "The thing is, they're elite fighters already. One-on-one or in a group, they're good—I mean, really good."

Jason rubbed his face where Shoko had kicked him. "If they're anything like her …"

"And what they've been doing is they wait for the intruders to get inside before they fight them, which means they're always in for a brutal, close-up and defensive fight. The intruders are always killed, but too many warriors die in the process."

Jason opened his mouth, ready to interrupt, but I held up a hand.

"What they need," I said, "is to learn how to operate in small teams and attack the enemy while they're still outside the gates."

Jason nodded slowly. "Well, that's what Special Operations Groups are for. What type of weapons are we talking about?"

"Swords and bows only," I said. "Plus hand to hand, but they don't need help with any of that."

There was a long pause while Jason looked us over. Then he

leaned back in his chair and crossed his arms.

"Swords and bows, huh?" He looked irritated. "You almost had me going there."

"No, it's—"

"Because I'm pretty sure even ninja use guns these days, silenced of course," he said. "You guys gotta keep up with the times."

Shoko didn't like that. "The ninja are like trained monkeys, but easier to cut down!"

"Just for your info," I whispered to Jason. "Shoko doesn't think much of the ninja."

He scowled. "Look, I don't even believe in ninjas, or dragons, or some mythical kingdom with female warriors and ancient gods and all that shit. The real world is scary enough." He made to stand up. "You kids have fun playing assassin without me."

Shoko laid her small hands flat on the table and glared at him. "We have *never*, not in millennia, taken a life except in the defense of our lands, our people, or our Important Ones," she said. Then her eyes narrowed. "But if you *ever* again refer to my sacred world or our gods as *shit*, I will make an exception and cut you down."

Jason's mouth sagged open. She'd said it quietly, in an even tone, but her words even sent a chill up my spine.

"Jason," I said quietly. "This isn't a game. Real people are dying all over the world, and her Important Ones are in trouble. Please, try to keep an open mind. We need you."

He stared at Shoko a long moment, as if trying to see into her head through her eyes, then he looked at me.

"You're serious about this?"

"Dead serious."

He nodded slowly. "Well, I'll have to modify my training a bit, but I'll do my best."

"So, you'll help?"

He nodded. "Oh, I'm in, and I don't need your money. Seeing this will be payment enough."

Shoko continued to gaze at him, unmoving, like a cat deciding whether to pounce.

"I've been to places … out in the desert and stuff … saw some weird things," Jason said. "I'll keep an open, and respectful, mind." Then he looked at Shoko. "I apologize. I truly am sorry for the disrespect."

She relaxed. "Apology accepted."

After that, we got to work. Jason came up with the curriculum, which we decided would take about a week.

"They need to learn first aid too," I said. "I think girls are dying when they shouldn't be."

Jason shook his head. "I can't teach that in a week."

"What is 'first aid'?" Shoko asked.

Jason did a better job of explaining it than I could, and as I expected, his training was practically at a paramedic level.

"That is what the Mikos are for," Shoko said.

"What's a *Miko*?" Jason asked.

"Their doctors," I said. "But they won't have a Miko with them, and besides, what's wrong with more people having practical skills? The Mikos are experts at the more magical healing methods anyway, but we should have a few who know modern stuff."

"Magical?" Jason said.

"Open mind, remember?"

Shoko looked thoughtful. "What about Nene?"

"The little girl I helped?"

Shoko nodded. "She has enough combat training to defend herself, if need be," she said. "Perhaps she could learn this … first aid."

"If you want, I can ask Barrymore if he'll teach her," Jason said. "He's a certified paramedic, and he's really bored these days."

When Shoko was ready to leave, she asked to see me behind the teahouse. I'm sure Okaasan and Mack thought it was because we didn't want Jason to see her travel home.

"How're you feeling?" I said, embarrassed and concerned.

"I am okay," she said. "It was uncomfortable, but I enjoyed the skin-ship."

"Skin-ship?"

"The sharing of the contact of our skin." She beamed at me. "That was wonderful."

I nodded. "Yeah, I liked that too."

Then she put her hands on my arms, leaned in, and gave me a kiss that made my toes curl.

"Come to Izumo tomorrow morning," she said. "I wish to show you the Festival of the Ogres. After that we will finalize the members of the new force."

Then she knelt and traveled away, leaving me standing there with a stupid grin on my face.

CHAPTER
21

OKAASAN HAD TAKEN ME TO THE Festival of the Ogres in Japan
when I was about four, and I vaguely remembered it. Basically, a
bunch of guys dressed as monsters and ogres and stuff go to a big
ceremony at the Izumo shrine. The ogres are blessed, then head out
where people line the streets waiting for them, just like an American
parade, except instead of floats and marching bands, the ogres scare
the crap out of little kids. To make things worse, parents push the
kids toward the monsters. If the kid could endure the horrible ogre
growling in their face, supposedly it'll be impressed and bless that
child with good health for a year.

I wasn't brave. I screamed my head off and wouldn't go near the
thing. I never did get sick though.

The ceremony in Shoko's world was similar, except only the little
girls had to endure it. Shoko and I had a good vantage point, sitting
on top of a high wall and looking down on the main road. We could
hear screams, but the ogres were still out of sight from us.

"Were you scared of the ogres?" I asked Shoko.

She harrumphed. "I kicked one so hard its mask fell off."

I gave her a skeptical look.

"I am the daughter of Tomi, the granddaughter of Saaya. Do you think I could do otherwise?"

"You didn't answer the question."

She didn't say anything for a moment. The screams had grown louder.

"Yes, I was afraid," she said. "But my fear was of dishonoring my family, not of the ogre."

They finally came into view: five big guys with horrible masks. Two of them were dressed as lizards. The little girls cried and screamed as the ogres approached. A girl directly below us sobbed, tears streaming down her chubby cheeks, but she stood still, her shoulders shaking as the ogre approached her, growling ferociously.

After what seem like the longest time, the ogre reached out and patted her head.

"You will be a strong Gatekeeper," it said. "Bless you and your family." Then it moved on to terrorize another girl.

Shoko nodded her approval as the girl's family hugged and congratulated her.

"That family is not known for producing Gatekeepers," Shoko said. "It is good to see."

Across the street, two girls cried out in fear as an ogre growled at them. The youngest one spun away, right into the arms of her slightly older sister who hugged her and said something. As the ogre got closer, the older girl wrapped her little sister in her arms and yelled at the ogre to go away. Surprisingly, it did.

"I guess she'll make a good Gatekeeper too."

Shoko shook her head. "No," she said. "They both failed the test."

"But the older one stood up to the ogre."

"Perhaps, but only to protect her sister," she said. "A Gatekeeper must think only of fighting."

I noticed the family still looked very pleased with both the girls. I asked Shoko about that.

"Because the older sister cares for others above herself. She is destined to help others, perhaps as a Miko."

"And the younger one?"

"We will see," Shoko said. "There are none without value."

The crowd began to cheer as several Gatekeepers appeared, walking up the street behind the ogres. The younger ones, apprentices judging by their uniforms, talked to the children and gave out sweets as they passed. Older Gatekeepers, women in their later twenties, gave out small wooden swords to a few girls.

"They are chosen now," Shoko whispered as the little girl below us, the one who stood up to the ogre, received her sword. "Their lives will never be the same."

Suddenly I remembered. "That's the same sword Sakura carried."

Shoko didn't answer. She was staring up the street.

I followed her gaze and saw Chiyoko bringing up the rear, nodding at the little girls with the wooden swords and looking regal as a queen. When she drew level with us, she stopped and looked up.

Shoko's head dropped as far as it could without her falling off the wall. I met Chiyoko's dark eyes.

"Hello grandmother," I said.

Shoko made a tiny squeaking sound.

"You look like her," Chiyoko said.

I nodded. I didn't know what to say.

"Is she content with her choice?"

"Yes, and she understands what you did for her."

She stared at me for a long moment, then turned and followed the small troupe on its way.

"What did I tell you?!" Shoko hissed at me when Chiyoko was gone. "You should have stayed silent."

"You told me not to go looking for her," I said. "She came to me."

⁓

"There have been a dozen more incursions since you were last here," Shoko said as we headed toward the training area.

"Lizards?"

"And a few men," she said. "Five Gatekeepers died."

"Five? That's crazy!"

"The Controller could not close the gateway." She lowered her voice, though no one was close by. "And I could not cross that day in the grasslands." She looked worried. "Maybe the gods really are losing their power."

"Okaasan said you probably couldn't cross because you were hurt."

"Do you truly believe that?"

I looked away, in the direction of the shrine. Being in Izumo no longer provided the serenity it once had. Did that mean their power really *was* failing?

"The event Mack spoke of truly was a massacre," she said, startling me back to reality. "Five shamans and dozens of worshipers were killed."

"I thought they were only killing shamans?"

"It appears they have added slaughter to their goals."

We'd reached the training grounds, where twenty-nine women had gathered in four perfect lines. Shoko explained why she'd chosen them and I was a bit surprised by her criteria. Most looked to be in their late teens and early twenties, and their confidence showed in their poise and energy. The silver rings on their right middle fingers meant they were all full-ranking Gatekeepers, except for one girl: Sakura stood at the end of the last line, the odd person out.

Shoko stood, arms crossed, glowering at women four or five years older than her.

"You have all passed the most important test," she said, loud enough for all of them to hear, "and have proven you can endure being on the Other Side. As you can see ..." she swept her hand over the group, "... over half of your colleagues did not. However, you still need to impress me, and Junya, with your skills, endurance, and most of all, your strength of mind."

Twenty-eight pairs of eyes turned to look at me. Sakura's gaze stayed fixed on the ground at her feet.

Shoko turned to me. "Would you like to address them?"

That caught me off guard, but I didn't hesitate. "Do you know why you were chosen?" When no one replied, I crossed my arms. "What are you, a flock of sheep? Answer me!"

"Because of our skill," a girl near the back answered. She was a bit taller than the rest and wore a smirk on her face.

"We have all completed our assignments and graduated," another said.

"We are not useless little apprentices," another girl said. It was a bitchy remark, but I couldn't complain. We needed girls with attitudes like hers. Still, I glanced over to where Shoko's apprentices were sitting. They didn't seem at all offended by her statement.

I turned back to the group. "I was actually referring to your records of bad behavior."

This time no one answered. Their energy was embarrassed and belligerent.

"From what Shoko tells me, some of you acted like undisciplined wolves when you were younger." A murmur rose so I spoke louder. "The Elders want us to stop the killing of shamans, and we think we can do that better from my side. For that, we need wolves." I said. "Gatekeepers who can think on their own, who can handle a new environment without freezing up. Gatekeepers who can hunt, not just wait for the enemy to come. You'll learn new skills, and in time you'll fight the Evil Ones in a different way. In short, we're going to kick some evil ass!"

There were collective sounds of approval that stopped when Shoko cleared her throat. Their discipline had obviously improved.

I looked at her. "I'm done."

"Very inspiring," she said as she stepped forward again. "But before we begin, there is one here who does not wear the ring, and is not worthy to stand among you," Shoko said.

Everyone looked around, and it didn't take long until all eyes were on Sakura.

"Sakura!" Shoko yelled. "Come here!"

Sakura ran over and skidded to her knees in front of Shoko. She pressed her forehead firmly onto the dirt.

"Sit up, Sakura!"

Sakura bolted upright, her face a mask of confusion and fear.

"I ordered you to come today, but you were never meant to be in this group." Shoko's tone softened. "Do you know why?"

"Because I am an unworthy, stupid girl," she whispered.

Shoko squatted and gently wiped the dirt off Sakura's forehead. "Do not insult me, Sakura."

Sakura's eyes widened. "I did not—"

"Because if I chose a stupid girl as my apprentice, would that not make me stupid as well?" Before Sakura could respond, Shoko knelt down in front of her. "Sakura Kiguchi, in front of those gathered here, I ask you to be my fourth apprentice. Will you honor me by accepting?"

Sakura couldn't speak. Tears streamed down her face, but she managed to nod.

A little girl, who had been waiting off to the side, walked up to Shoko carrying a flask and one small cup, and Shoko poured what I assumed was sake into the cup. Then, as we'd done with the apple juice on the beach in San Francisco months ago, Shoko took a sip and passed the cup to a still stunned Sakura. She took a sip and that was that.

Shoko stood and faced the group. "Change into these modern clothes." She pointed to several baskets piled high with clothing. "They will feel strange at first, but it is necessary for our work. Seek advice from my apprentices so you do not look silly. They have been across many times." The girls started to move, but Shoko stopped them. "You must choose clothes that will conceal as many weapons as possible. You are going to need them."

Shoko walked over to me. "Were you surprised about Sakura?"

she asked with a smile.

I smiled back. "Pleasantly. What happened?"

"When Sakura came to me that day in the lineup, I was dismayed. She was throwing her life away. It was a rash, stupid thing to do. By that action, she was no longer a Gatekeeper."

"You smacked her pretty hard for it too."

"But when we met her on the street that day, she was carrying her ogre-day sword, and I knew she still wanted to be a Gatekeeper." She pushed her braids over her shoulders. "And I realized you were right."

"About what?"

"The only person who could change the situation was Sakura herself. She needed to somehow make herself available to me, so she dishonored herself and forced her master to dismiss her."

"If you're right, she took a huge risk."

"Is that not better than a lifetime of regret?" She turned to watch as her apprentices walked toward Sakura, who still knelt where Shoko had left her, looking very happy. "And it was her who looked *across* and sensed the Evil Ones in Peru."

"Why was she—"

"She was granted permission by the Master Controller to observe the process," she said. "Sakura was already moving her life forward. I like that."

Now Rina, Yukie, and Kyoko stood staring down at Sakura, not looking at all impressed.

"You do not deserve to be here," Yukie said, her usual smile gone.

"You will need to prove yourself to us," Kyoko said. "And we will not make life easy for you."

"And if you ever show disrespect to Shoko or are disloyal to us," Rina added, "that last beating I gave you will seem like a kiss."

Sakura looked up at them with an expression of absolute delight.

"Thank you!" she said. "I do not deserve such kindness."

"That's *kindness?*" I whispered to Shoko.

Shoko leaned toward me. "To be ignored is the most horrible

punishment imaginable."

Then, to my surprise, the three apprentices knelt and bowed as low to Sakura as Shoko did to the Elders.

"Welcome to Shoko's family, little sister," Rina said.

I decided right then that being a Gatekeeper was far more complicated than I'd thought.

CHAPTER
22

"THERE ARE TWO GATEWAYS DUE TO open before noon, but in different parts of the world," Shoko said as we watched the Gatekeepers get themselves ready to cross. They looked excited, like a school group before a field trip. "Both gateways have been abandoned for centuries, but as always, Gatekeepers will be waiting on this side in case something stumbles through."

"So, the chances of Evil Ones being there is—"

"Unlikely. Which is why this is a good first exercise."

When the Gatekeepers were finally ready to go, looking fairly normal in their modern clothing, they divided into two groups. Shoko nodded her head toward a group of Gatekeepers closest to me.

"You take the apprentices and these twelve youngest Gatekeepers to the first site." She indicated the second group. "I will lead the older ones to the other."

"Wouldn't it be better if you took the less experienced ones?"

She shook her head. "The younger girls will be more forgiving of any ignorance you might show."

"*Ignorance?*" I said, hands on hips. "I'm the most experienced one here, remember?"

She ignored my comment and turned to address my group.

"Gatekeepers!" she said. "This will not be easy without your senses, so be wary. Junya is with you. Trust his senses and do not use force unless he authorizes it."

"Shoko," a girl of about seventeen said. "Junya will lead us?"

Shoko nodded. "Junya is your commander." The slightest smile curled the edges of her mouth. "He will provide instructions after he visits the Master Controller's village."

I leaned toward her and whispered, "Ah ... where's that?"

She motioned to Yukie. "Please accompany your *experienced* leader to the Master Controller and make the proper introductions."

"Certainly, Shoko." Yukie bowed. "I would be honored to assist our new commander!"

Shoko looked me in the eye. Her humor was gone. "Be careful, Junya."

As Shoko walked away, I looked at my team of Gatekeepers. I saw self-assurance, competence, and trust in me.

"You might as well all come along," I said to them. Then I turned to Yukie. "Lead the way."

Yukie held out her hand and we traveled across the valley to a cluster of buildings grouped in a half circle, near the top of a low mountain. These buildings were nothing like the others I'd seen here. While the village was mostly made of wood and thatch, these buildings were made of stone, long and low like World War II bunkers.

A middle-aged woman came out and looked at our group with curiosity. Her eyes finally settled on me.

"What brings the son of Misako to our doorstep?"

Rina bowed low. "He wishes to learn which gateway will open next, Master Controller."

"He will be with you?"

Yukie grinned. "He is our new leader!"

The woman sucked in a long, slow breath. "The next gateway will open by itself soon," she said, "but nothing has come through for many generations. I believe something blocks it on the other side."

I glanced sideways at Rina. "Something could still be waiting outside it, right?"

The Controller's eyes met mine. "You hope to find Evil Ones?"

"That's the plan."

She stared at me a long moment, then turned toward the low-roofed structure and gestured for us to follow. I glanced at the Gatekeepers. They seemed happy to wait outside, unlike the apprentices who crowded in behind me.

It was the perfect temperature inside the large room, not hot or cold, not humid or dry. A table ran the length of the room against the back wall and on it, unfurled from end to end, lay a scroll. A young woman stood near the middle, bent over the table, an ink brush in hand.

The master Controller said something to her.

"This is the gateway," the woman said, her fingernail on a line of characters on the scroll. "But no one has crossed through in over two centuries." She glanced at me. "I am told a stone building rests upon it on your side."

"In what part of the world?" I asked.

She clicked her tongue, then walked to the far end of the room. Without knowing what to do, we followed. She stopped near a row of tall wooden racks, similar to the type my dad used to stack and separate different types of plywood in his shop, except these held hundreds, maybe thousands, of thin flat boards.

The woman pointed to a section about three feet from the bottom of one row. Two boys, one about my age and the other twelve or thirteen, pulled a wide board from the slot and placed it carefully on a low table. It was a map, carved into the wood surface with an impressive amount of detail and color. I recognized the outline of the land and the Mediterranean Sea. It was Spain.

The woman leaned over it and after a long moment, placed her finger on a spot near the bottom of the map beside the sharp curve of a winding river. She called out a series of numbers to the boys. After a short conversation, the boys slid two boards from a different rack and placed them on the table in front of us. It was obvious the younger boy was a trainee.

This map depicted the same river, enlarged, along with a city, though vague. The second map also showed a more detailed view of what must've been the area around the gateway.

"Sakura, will you honor us with your Gift?" the Master Controller said.

There was a short silence before Sakura stepped forward.

"I will." She sounded like a different person, and a quiet, powerful confidence showed in her eyes. She held her hand over the map, eyes closed.

"There is a city, both old and new called ... Córdoba." She nodded. "The gateway is not far from the Templo Romano de Córdoba." The words rolled off her tongue in perfectly accented Spanish.

"Templo Romano, that's a ..." I thought for a moment. "A Roman Temple?"

"The gateway sits beneath a beautiful building made of red brick," Sakura continued, sounding as if she were within a trance. Then she held out her hand to me. "Come."

A moment later, I found myself standing in the middle of the intersection of four narrow streets. A silver motorcycle buzzed straight toward us, then through us as it headed up a steep street. Its small engine whined as it passed a gray-brown wall of stacked stone that lined the sidewalk. Above that, eleven Roman columns pointed toward the blue sky.

Everything seemed a little fuzzy, and I realized Sakura was doing what I could do on my side. She'd transported herself there in her mind and she'd brought me along. The difference was that her view was in full color, and mine tended to be a thermal image.

She turned and pointed down another narrow, curving street lined with three- and four-story cream-colored buildings, their balconies edged with ornate steel railings. Behind a long row of parked scooters was a three-story brick building with glass-fronted shops on the bottom floor. The top two floors had tall rectangular windows, each with bright flower pots behind black steel railings. The corner of the building had a rounded tower, topped with a golden dome, like the roof of a mosque.

"The gateway lies somewhere near that building." Sakura hesitated. "Or perhaps under it. I cannot be sure exactly."

I squinted up the street. "Do you sense that?" I asked her. At her questioning look, I said, "I feel Evil Ones here."

That surprised her, and me too. I hadn't realized I could sense Evil Ones from this side, this far away.

I spun in a slow circle, still holding Sakura's hand. Across the street from the temple ruins stood an old yellow three-story building with a modern sign in front advertising hamburgers. The building connected to the next by a plastered wall, maybe ten feet tall, with a black sliding gate wide enough for a car to pass. As I stared at it, the gate became translucent. The yard inside was lush with plants and a massive orange tree. A red Renault coupe sat parked against the wall.

"We'll arrive behind there," I told Sakura, pointing to the garden.

She nodded and let go of my hand. A second later I was standing beside the Controller again.

"Go dress in your modern clothes," I told the other apprentices. "And carry whatever weapons you can conceal."

"I ... I do not have modern clothing," Sakura said.

Rina sized her up. "You can borrow some of mine, little sister."

I stood outside with the other Gatekeepers, growing impatient as I waited for the apprentices to return. The other Gatekeepers didn't seem to mind, though. They used the time to check each other's outfits, making little adjustments and swaps here and there.

The apprentices reappeared after about twenty minutes, dressed in fashionable but casual clothing. Without anyone actually discussing it, we traveled with Sakura leading us, and ended up right under the orange tree. The garden was beautiful, but smaller than I thought. We were quite a crowd in there.

"Are you all okay?" I looked from one to the next. The apprentices looked all right, but some of the others looked uneasy.

"You can actually sense things here, Junya?" One of the older Gatekeepers—I think her name was Hana—looked dumbfounded. "It is like the roar of a waterfall, endless noise."

I nodded. "Which is why you need to shut off your senses and trust mine," I said. "And I sensed Evil Ones here earlier, so pay attention."

Somehow, the thought of that excited me.

I slid the metal gate open a foot or so and stepped out. Only the apprentices had made it out before a man started yelling at us in Spanish. I didn't understand him, but I bowed and said in Japanese, "Good day, sir." Without looking at the girls, I said, "Pretend we're lost."

"I think we *are* lost," Kyoko muttered.

"He demands to know why we were in his yard," Rina said in Japanese.

Now the man looked confused. We probably didn't look that threatening now, just five young teenage tourists, but we still had no reason to be in there. Thank god the others had the sense to hang back.

I glanced around, trying to decide how to take this guy out discreetly.

Then Yukie bowed deeply and held up an orange. She said how sorry she was—in Japanese, of course—and tried to give it to the man. She nattered excitedly about how fresh and ripe it looked, and how she wished she could eat it.

I sensed his anger begin to drop.

When I dug into my pocket and pulled out a few American bills, he smiled and waved away both the money and orange.

I peeked inside at the Gatekeepers before I slid the gate closed.

Travel to me when I call you.

They all winced. Only one managed a nod.

The man stood watching as we crossed the street toward the Roman ruin.

"Can you walk more casually," I said to the apprentices. "You look ridiculous."

They moved closer together and tried to walk less aggressively.

"It is difficult to be here," Rina said. "Without the senses we have had since children, in this strange environment."

"I told you, if there's anything to worry about, I'll tell you."

"You did not sense the angry man outside the gate," Kyoko said as we reached the brown foundation walls of the temple.

"That's because he wasn't angry until he saw us."

She let out a grunt but didn't pursue it.

We made our way into the temple. Standing among the ancient ruins, I sent out the message, and a moment later all twelve Gatekeepers materialized inside the temple wall. Some looked at the ruins in awe, while the others remained in combat mode.

I couldn't rein in my enthusiasm, though. The Romans were the greatest engineers ever and amazing architects too. I was explaining that when Kyoko interrupted.

"If they are so great, then why is it broken?"

I rolled my eyes. They obviously weren't interested, and anyway, we didn't come here for a history lesson.

"Okay, gather around," I said, feeling a bit like a tour guide. "The Controller said this gateway's blocked, that a building sits on top of it, but I'm pretty sure I felt Evil Ones when Sakura brought me here earlier."

"Excuse me, Junya." Her name was Mekie, I think. "If the gateway is blocked, there should not be shamans here, and therefore, no Evil Ones."

I nodded. "Right, so we need to find out why they're here."

"Do you still sense them?" Rina asked.

I hesitated. I didn't feel anything. "Let's get closer."

I led my little troupe toward the intersection. As we were about to turn the corner toward the brick building, my neck seized up. A second later, my shoulder followed. I froze.

"They're here," I said over my shoulder.

"Where?" a girl behind me whispered.

I suddenly felt completely unprepared. I'd never actually gone looking for Evil Ones, and even though I had a squad of elite soldiers with me, I didn't have a clue what to do with them. Whatever we did, we couldn't keep standing there on the sidewalk.

"Perhaps we should travel home?" Kyoko said.

"No, we need to see what they're up to."

Sixteen pairs of brown eyes stared at me.

I peeked back around the corner. There were a couple dozen scooters parked in a row along the curved narrow street in front of the brick building. A wide pedestrian lane ran perpendicular to the street. There were plenty of people, some sitting at tables drinking coffee, others gathered around the scooters. I couldn't see anyone who looked like an Evil One, but my shoulder was aching so much it made me twitch.

Hana moved around the corner beside me and leaned against the wall, all casual-like.

"Where is the energy coming from?" she asked.

"Definitely the brick building."

"Do you want them identified, or dead?"

"There are too many people here," I said. "Identified is good enough, unless they try something."

She nodded. "We will respond to your command," she said, sounding more official than her demeanor showed. She was good at this undercover thing. "However, unless there is an army of Evil Ones, you do not need all of us. Perhaps you and the apprentices can approach the building while the rest of us observe?"

Relief washed through me. This was supposed to be a training exercise, after all.

"Some of us could stay here and observe your tactics," she said.

"The rest can watch from further down this …" She turned to look down the narrow street. "… road."

I followed her gaze. "This must be pretty strange for you."

"To me, it looks like a canyon." She was silent for a long moment, then she whispered, "This is a most wonderful place …"

"Yeah." I took a deep breath. "Let's tell the others."

We moved back around the corner.

"Okay," I said, loud enough for all of them to hear. "Me and the apprentices will go have a look." Then I told them where to wait for us.

"And if you find Evil Ones?" Mekie asked.

I hadn't thought that far ahead. "I'll decide when I see what they're up to."

"*Decide*?" Kyoko made a face. "We must kill them, without hesitation."

I looked back toward the building. "There are too many people."

Kyoko's hands went to her hips. "So, you would have us stand here and *observe* Evil Ones?"

There was a muttering of agreement.

"I did not join this special force to observe," another girl said.

I crossed my arms. "No one fights unless I say so," I said, my own irritation growing. Part of me agreed with them, but that was beside the point. I was supposed to be commanding them, not arguing. "Once we check things out, I want you all to travel home. We'll meet you there later."

I counted to fifty after Hana's disgruntled group walked down the curved street, then led my little band toward the building. There was a café on the bottom floor, its large modern windows an odd contrast with the older façade above. I caught our reflection in the glass as we weaved our way between the parked scooters. We sure didn't look like we belonged, and neither did the four men in black that pushed through the café doors as we approached.

We all stopped dead, staring at each other. They looked confused, knew we were a threat, but it took a moment to figure it out.

"Here?" the one in front said.

I grinned. "Get used to it, lizard breath."

His eyes turned black and he came at me.

I kicked him in the head so hard he crashed backward over a nearby table. A woman screamed as dishes crashed to the ground.

The apprentices hadn't moved.

"Fight, but don't use weapons unless they do!" I yelled. Then it was chaos with people running and shouting, some toward us, others away as we engaged the Evil Ones in hand-to-hand combat. I think we all wanted to get the hell out of there, but neither group was willing to be the first to retreat, so it became a running battle down the steps of the lane toward the street behind.

More yelling came from the café and I glanced back. An Evil One argued heatedly with several customers and a waiter.

I crashed into a stack of plastic crates and went down, along with the dozens of beer bottles inside. I hit the cobblestones with a crash and lay stunned beside a widening pool of beer. As I stumbled to my feet, an Evil One crashed through a pile of empty beer kegs, knocking me back down.

I scrambled up and got in a few good punches before he lunged toward me. I batted his arms away, hit him three times in the gut, and sent him sprawling with a kick to the head.

I spun in a circle, trying to get oriented. Rina and Yukie were about a half block away, down a narrow cobblestone street lined with old buildings, windows covered with ornate iron bars. They disappeared through an opening as I sprinted toward them.

Rina was pulling her wakizashi out of an Evil One's chest when I skidded to a stop. She had him cornered against an iron gate inside the alcove of a little hotel, black blood gushing from the wound. Two women in the garden courtyard beyond were screaming.

Rina looked guilty. "I thought he had a knife."

We needed to get the hell out of there. "Where are Sakura and Kyoko?"

Sakura came crashing onto the alcove, answering part of the

question.

"Where's Kyoko?"

"I do not know," Sakura said, panting.

Sirens blared in the distance, but within the maze of narrow streets, it was impossible to tell what direction they came from.

I pointed at Rina and Yukie. "You two travel back and see if Kyoko's already there."

Rina frowned. "What about the other Gatekeepers?"

I stopped and listened, but I couldn't feel their energy. "They're already gone," I said, though I wasn't totally sure about that. "Now go."

As Rina and Yukie disappeared, I turned to Sakura. "I'm going to try and find Kyoko." Then I closed my eyes and listened with all my energy, but I couldn't sense Kyoko's energy anywhere nearby.

A moment later, Rina's message came to me.

She has not returned.

In a panic, I grabbed Sakura's hand and pulled her down to the stone floor of the alcove. Only a pool of black blood remained of the Evil One.

"When did you last see her?"

"Not since we first encountered the Evil Ones," she said. "You feel no energy, at all?"

"Nothing."

"How far can you sense someone?"

"A few blocks, maybe more," I said. "She's not close by."

"We could travel to her directly," Sakura said.

"Yeah, but we might appear in the middle of a crowd."

Sakura took my hand. It was sweaty. "There is a risk either way."

I nodded. She was right.

"Mother Earth," I whispered, "Take us to Kyoko."

—

We found her in an alley, huddled in the dark behind a row of yellow garbage cans. Other than a skinned knee, she didn't look hurt. She stared up Sakura and me with wild, wide eyes. She clutched a knife in both hands.

I glanced around again, searching for some danger I must be missing. There were a lot of sirens now, and they sounded close. Sakura kept an eye on the other end of the alley.

I knelt in front of Kyoko. "What happened?"

"I ... I cannot." Kyoko mumbled. The knife shook.

Sakura squatted beside me. "There is trouble, I think."

I leaned out from behind the garbage cans. A little police car had blocked the alley, its red and blue lights flashing, and two officers got out.

Sakura patted Kyoko's arm. "It is okay now, Kyoko," she whispered. "We will go home."

I took Sakura's other hand. "Yeah, let's get out of here."

We arrived back in Izumo, out of breath and scared. Thankfully, Sakura had the sense to travel us right outside the Miko's quarters. As a Miko knelt beside a dazed-looking Kyoko, Rina and Yukie came rushing over.

Yukie knelt in front of Kyoko. "You are okay!" Then she took Kyoko's shoulders and moved her face close. "Was it the city that scared you or the *noise?*"

Kyoko put her forehead against Yukie's. "I got lost and people were following me," she whispered. "I tried to travel home, but ... I could not." She started to tremble. "I could not travel."

"Probably because you were scared," Yukie said. "I was too. We must promise to stay together next time."

Then Yukie reached up and pulled Sakura and Rina down. Before long, the four of them were crying and laughing together. They really did look like sisters, and it looked like Sakura was *in*.

I felt pretty lousy though. That had been a major screwup, but considering it was our first outing, I guessed I hadn't done too badly. We just needed to organize better. I remembered what Jason said about urban environments. We'd have to incorporate that into our training.

My other Gatekeepers had traveled back as planned, though they were disappointed they'd missed the action. Shoko's group returned not long after that. They hadn't found any Evil Ones, so Shoko had let them explore. They couldn't stop talking about what they'd seen.

I was baffled by some of the stuff the girls brought back. Things I would've considered valueless, like a train schedule with pictures of the different cars, and magazines showing the newest fashions. One had an empty soda can.

A group of young Gatekeepers gathered around, fascinated by the stories, both the scary ones and the funny. A small group of girls near me whispered among themselves, close enough for me to hear them.

"She just became Shoko's apprentice and look at her!" One pointed at Sakura.

"I would like to wear such clothing," another said.

"Go across and get some, if you are brave enough."

"Maybe you will meet a boy like Junya," the first girl said.

I let out a sigh and they finally noticed me. They hurried away, giggling the whole time. Shoko was right, we needed to be careful.

I didn't hang around waiting for Shoko. I knew she wouldn't be happy with me, and I was dead tired, so I asked Sakura to travel me home. Yukie insisted on coming along. She obviously meant it when she said they'd stick together from now on.

We said our good-byes then I waited a few minutes, listening to the energy around my house. Okaasan and Dad were home, already in their room. Good. One less thing for me to deal with.

I went in, showered, and fell asleep within minutes.

CHAPTER
23

OKAASAN WAS TYING ON HER RUNNING shoes when I walked into the kitchen early the next morning. The table was empty, the stove clean. I didn't want to sound useless, but where the heck was breakfast?

"Isn't Sunday supposed to be a day of rest or something?" I asked her.

"Why don't you come for a run with me?" she said. "If your leg can handle it."

I shrugged. Why not? The training with Jason wouldn't start for a few hours, and I could talk to her on the road as easily as at the table. I'd just be hungry.

"If your leg can handle it, mine can."

We were only two blocks from our house, with the Arbutus Street hill behind us, when I turned to her.

"Guess what happened yesterday?"

"I thought you didn't … want me to read your mind." She was breathing a bit heavy already.

I rolled my eyes, then told her about our excursion to Spain.

Her pace slowed. "You promised you'd always be with Shoko."

"It was only a field trip," I said, slowing to let her catch up. "Besides, I had a dozen full-ranks with me."

"Do you think they were waiting for a shaman to show up?"

"I guess, but they sure were surprised to see us."

"I bet." She pulled in a deep breath. "Maybe they didn't know the gateway was blocked." She paused. "You looked pretty stupid when you crashed through the beer bottles, by the way."

I skidded to a stop. "How'd you see that?"

She stopped too but kept jogging on the spot. "Lin e-mailed me a link this morning. Someone caught the whole thing on their phone. It's already gone viral." She motioned for me to get going. "It shows men in black fighting some teenage girls in front of a café."

"Shit."

We waited until three cars sped by, then angled across the street.

"I hope you know how stupid that was," she said as we reached the curb. "Everyone has a camera now. If they'd gotten a better angle they'd have seen your face."

"Trust me, we won't be doing anything that public again," I said. Then I remembered. "Kyoko said she couldn't travel home."

Okaasan turned to me. "*Couldn't?*"

"That's what she said." I wiped my forehead with the back of my hand. "And I don't think it's because she was scared."

She shoulder-checked before crossing through an intersection. "By the way, why would Jason think Shoko's your girlfriend?"

"I think that's what Lin told him. I sure didn't."

"You and Shoko aren't doing a good job of hiding it. You were practically giving each other goo-goo eyes in the dojo."

"*Goo-goo* eyes?" We stopped at a traffic light and I leaned heavily on the lamppost.

She glanced at me. "I told you not to get too close to her."

"There hasn't been a lot of time for romance."

"You're too young for romance." She paused a moment, her eyes on the traffic light. "You asked me a while ago how I got my senses back. I'm wondering ... have Shoko's begun to work?"

"No, but it doesn't bother her as much as before. Why?"

She smiled as the light turned green. Then she was off, and I never caught up the entire way home.

—

Mack was sitting at the kitchen table, looking gloomy, when we got home. Even in her sweaty state, Okaasan stopped to fix him some breakfast before she hit the shower.

We yakked about a bunch of stuff while we ate, mundane small talk mostly. I was hesitating, trying to think of a way to ask Mack about Shoko and me.

Finally, as I finished smearing a thick layer of peanut butter on my toast, I decided to just say it.

"So, Shoko and I ... we did it."

He looked up from his plate. "*It?*"

When I nodded, he grinned. "Congratulations, bro!" He reached across for a high five. "You see what you've been missing?"

I looked down. "Well ..."

"Oh, don't tell me," he said, sounding disappointed. "You came the second you got inside?"

"No! But she didn't enjoy herself. She said it hurt." I took a bite of the toast. "I don't know what I did wrong."

"Were you in the right place?"

I gave him a look. "We'd made out a few times before that. I know where stuff is."

"Made out how far?" Mack seemed quite interested.

I was getting embarrassed. "Enough that we both got off, okay?"

He looked surprised. "Okay, that's good! Way-to-go-bro, making out with Sho-ko!"

"Shut up!" I paused to listen. Thankfully I could still hear Okaasan's shower running.

"Right," he said, almost in a whisper. "It was her first time?"

211

I rolled my eyes. "Obviously."

"Not necessarily." He smirked. "I knew a girl who 'lost her virginity' several times."

"She told me, and I believe her, okay?"

He waited until he'd swallowed a big bite of omelet before he continued. "Were you all hot and heavy when you did it, or was it a bit *technical?*"

"Technical is a good word."

He leaned back and waved a hand at me. "Give yourself a break," he said. "You're both first-timers, you're nervous, you're fumbling. What did you expect, a little movie magic?"

"Kinda."

Now he rolled his eyes. "It probably won't hurt next time, and you'll both be more relaxed. You'll get into it, you'll see." He picked up his fork. "Crazy kids. Gotta teach you everything." Then his eyes narrowed. "You use protection, boy?"

"Yes, sir."

"Good, because I don't think I can handle a bunch of little sword-wielding "yous" running around."

—

Shoko looked skeptical as she eyed the Jeep. Jason had parked it outside my house, sparkling clean and gleaming in the morning light, and now he stood at the passenger door, waiting for her to get in. Mack was already in the backseat. I'd be riding back there with him. We just had to convince Shoko to get in.

"It's like a train or a cable car," I said, ignoring Jason's raised brow. "There's nothing to be scared about."

"I am not *scared.*" She gave me a look, then climbed in.

Jason and I climbed in and the engine roared to life. Shoko folded her hands on her lap, but they soon turned white from squeezing them too hard. As Jason started to pull away, I tapped his shoulder.

"Go easy on her," I said. Then I frowned. I smelled a familiar scent in the car, but I couldn't put my finger on it.

"Shoko." Jason looked over at her. "How come you've never been in a car?"

"I thought I said no questions," I said, still thinking about that scent.

"There are no cars where I live."

"Fair enough," Jason said, though I wasn't sure who he was replying to.

The Jeep had a powerful engine and Jason had a heavy foot—both on the brake and accelerator—so it wasn't a smooth, leisurely ride. Every curve and corner, each moment of acceleration, got a reaction out of Shoko, and by the time Jason pulled into the small lot outside Grandpa's old warehouse on the Presidio grounds, she was so excited she could barely talk.

"That thing is awesome!" she yelled, with a grin as wide as her face. "And it is yours?"

I nodded, feeling pretty damn proud. "All mine."

She tilted her head. "Then why can you not drive it?"

My smile faded. "I ah …" I looked at Jason. "It's about time I learned isn't it?"

He frowned. "One thing at a time."

It felt strange coming back to the warehouse. In my mind I could still see Okaasan and Mack lying on the floor, her leg covered in blood, him unconscious from getting the crap beaten out of him, all because of me.

Mack came up beside me and plopped a heavy hand on my shoulder.

"I don't have a lot of good memories of this place either," he said. "And don't start apologizing again or I'll smack ya."

Just then, there was a strong knock on the side door. When it swung open, Lin walked in, looking amazing in a form-fitting white dress that ended several inches above her knees. I'd asked her if we could use the place, but I'd had no idea she'd show up.

Jason looked happy to see her. "Hi Lin," he said, walking to meet her. "You look great!"

They gave each other a quick hug.

Then she walked over to me. "I thought I'd stop by in case he freaks out on you," she said. "Although I may freak out too."

I looked her up and down. "Nice dress."

She frowned. "I have plans after this."

Fair enough. "You've never seen Gatekeepers?"

"Never." Then she leaned closer to me. "Does he know anything?"

"Enough to do the job."

As she nodded and moved away, I realized how I knew that scent in the car. It was hers, the perfume she always wore.

"I got everything set up," Jason said, his voice echoing in the high-ceilinged room. He'd had carpenters build six sections of wall, each about twelve feet long, with a single doorway in each. I'd told him to leave the walls unfinished and without a door, only upright two by fours every twenty-four inches apart, like a new house under construction. We also had the carpenters put wooden floors under where the girls would practice. They'd need to touch the Mother Earth to do this right.

Jason pulled an orange out of his jacket pocket and shifted it from hand to hand.

"So, where are my new trainees?"

I turned to Shoko. "Are they ready?"

"They have been ready for hours."

"You ready?" I asked Jason.

"Oh, I can't wait." He tossed the orange up, then caught it.

I walked toward the large overhead door. Shoko closed her eyes, put her hands in a prayer position, and concentrated.

"What's she—"

I winced as the combined energy of more than two dozen Gatekeepers crossing over slammed into me.

"You okay?" Jason asked. Apparently, he hadn't felt a thing. By the look of Mack and Lin, they hadn't either.

"Yeah." I forced a smile and hit the button, and the overhead door began to rise. "They're here."

Bare feet in sandals came into view first, then muscular legs showing through the long slits in the sides of the green kimono-like traditional Gatekeeper's uniform. Last was the peaked hats, made of bamboo, which shadowed their faces. Each woman carried a practice bokuto as well as their katana. Many also carried bows and quivers of arrows. None of them smiled as they strode into the warehouse.

Jason's mouth dropped open. "Good lord ... you gotta be shitting me."

"Form up!" Shoko shouted in English.

Their straggled entrance turned into military precision as the girls marched into three rows of eight—perfectly spaced of course—and faced us, feet apart, hands together in front of their skirts.

I turned to Shoko. "We lost four more?"

She nodded. "For some, the change was too much."

Rina, Kyoko, Yukie, and Sakura walked in, but they kept well away from the other Gatekeepers.

Jason took a few steps toward us. "Where the hell are these girls from?"

"Jason," Lin said from where she stood off to the side, near Mack. "Do you remember the need-to-know rule in the army?" When he nodded, she smiled. "Then shut up."

He looked the girls over. They hadn't moved a muscle since they marched in.

"Well, they have excellent discipline."

Shoko snatched the orange from Jason and threw it underhand, high in the air, almost hitting the thick beams far above. As it reached the apex of its flight, she called out.

"Mekie!"

As the orange fell, an arrow pierced it and it hit the concrete floor with a thud, knocking the arrow loose. I walked over and picked up the orange. I was impressed. I hadn't even seen her draw. I pointed to a cute girl in the front row and threw the orange toward her. Her katana cleared the sheath and four slices of orange hit the floor at her feet. She sheathed the blade and smiled.

"Shall I peel it for you, Junya?" she said, in what I thought a rather sexy tone. Shoko's eyebrows came together.

Jason came up beside me and looked down at the pieces. "That was my breakfast ..."

"This is Jason-sensei, your instructor," I said to the group. "He is a soldier, one of the most skilled and highly trained we have over here. He's going to teach you how to work in teams of four. You'll need to think independently but work together as a unit. You will learn to *look,* then cross over and attack. With these new skills, you'll become a special force among the Gatekeepers. It will be you who fend off the attackers *before* they get inside, the first on scene, the best!"

The girls exchanged glances of surprise.

"The doorways behind me simulate a gateway you're defending." I pointed to them. "How many of you ever look across when you're fighting the invaders?"

Not one hand went up. I pointed at Hana, who was in the second row. "Why not?"

She stepped forward. "We would only look if we intended to cross, which we would never do."

"Until now."

She nodded. "I suppose."

I called over Jason and Mack. "Can one of you stand in the doorway and the other behind the wall?" When they did, I turned back to Hana. "You can see the immediate threat, the one you normally attack. Is he easy to kill?"

"Not if he *changes.*"

"Right, but now if you look *across,* you can see the second one waiting to come through. Is that one easy to kill?"

"Of course," she said. "He is a man. He will die quickly."

"Right," I said. "So instead of the four of you attacking the first one, two of you could travel ..." I glanced at Jason. "I mean, go through the wall and attack the man there. If you can also kill the one in the doorway, before he has fully changed, then the threat is neutralized without needing to fight the liz—" I shot a sideways look at Jason again. "Questions?"

A hand went up near the back. "Do we still need a Controller?"

"It is their duty to open the gate so the shaman can enter," Shoko said. "Your duty is separate from theirs and that of their Gatekeeper escort."

"And if the ... *tokage* still manages to get through?" The girl had the wherewithal to say *lizard* in Japanese.

"Then you're in for your usual fight." I stood staring at them for a long moment. "If you're going to make this work, you need to arrive, instantly assess the situation on *both* sides, then attack. Killing them before they get inside is the key to this working."

—

"Pretty awesome, huh?" I said to Lin as we watched them train.

"Wow, they're young."

"Don't the ninja start training young too?"

She nodded. "But it's different," she said, watching Jason as he guided a Gatekeeper into a better position after she "crossed" through the wall. "They go out on missions, but not every day, and they only fight as a last resort. These girls are in actual combat, all the time by the sound of it."

"Did you know the Gatekeepers just stand inside a gateway and wait for a lizard to come through?" I shook my head and laughed. "I can't believe no one thought of this before. Hopefully once Jason's done with them, they'll be ready for what I have planned."

"Well, he's a real pro," she said, her eyes following him as he moved among the trainees. "You couldn't ask for a better trainer."

I glanced sideways at her. "What's with you and him anyhow?"

Her dark-brown eyes met mine. "He's an old friend—"

"Don't you mean *boyfriend*?" I cracked a half smile. "He told me, you know."

She looked shocked. "What did he tell you?"

"Oh, you know, guy talk." I tried to keep a smile off my face. "About how he picked you up in some shady bar in Singapore for a night of wild sex." Her eyes looked wide enough to pop, so I held up my hands. "I'm kidding. He was quite the gentleman about your little fling." Then I laughed.

She switched to Japanese. "I don't think this is funny."

"Actually, I don't think so either," I said, humor gone. "You two still seem awfully close."

"I told you, we're just friends," she said. "And our history is none of your business."

"When he's giving you rides in my car, it is."

Her expression darkened. "You're awfully high and mighty now, aren't you?" She put her hands on her hips. "If you're such hot shit, why do you even need Shoko and Jason to carry out your Master Plan?"

"I know what needs to be done, that's all."

"How nice," she said in a tone so cold it startled me. "Before you start throwing your attitude in my face, remember who loaned you this building." She pointed a manicured nail at my face. "Keep it up and you can find somewhere else to train your little army."

I looked back at her in surprise. A long, uncomfortable silence descended.

"I'm going to join them," I said. "See you later."

CHAPTER
24

JASON DRILLED THE GIRLS ALL DAY on approach, assessment, and attack. He taught them what positions they should take after they "crossed," depending on where the attacker or attackers were.

"They learn fast," he said as we watched a team of four take out six attackers waiting on the other side of the wall. Then he leaned closer. "But how exactly do they get through the wall?"

"It's a bit hard to explain," I said. "And you don't need to know, remember?"

"Fine," he said. "So, they *somehow* get through the wall. How do they get back? It's a lot easier to get yourself into trouble than it is to get out. They should have a back-up plan, probably more than one."

I thought about Córdoba. I barely had a plan, let alone a back-up plan.

"You can't always have one though, right?" I said. "I mean, sometimes things must just happen while you're out there."

"If I'm on a mission, I have a plan. There's no other way to think about it."

"Even if you're only going out to have a look at something?""

He raised his voice. "It's called a reconnaissance mission, and if you're on a mission, you *need a plan*!""

"Okay, I hear you." I'd have to talk to Shoko about this. What would they do if they couldn't travel back? For a Gatekeeper, that was the only way back to safety.

A message came into my head: *It is time for him to go for today.*

I nodded to Shoko. "Ah Jason, I'm gonna have to ask you to hit the road. You can take the Jeep home tonight if you want." I got raised eyebrows for that. "Be back at eight o'clock tomorrow?"

"Sure." Then his brow furrowed. "But it's Monday. Don't you have school?"

"I do it from home, remember?"

"Right."

After he was gone, Shoko stepped in front of the girls. "Take what Jason-sensei taught you, but remember you are Gatekeepers." She looked around. "Mack, would you please step behind the wall for a demonstration?"

He looked skeptical. When Shoko picked up the bokuto he looked downright unhappy, but he walked over and stood behind the wall.

"Even though our senses do not work on this side, we can access the information we need by crossing back." With that, she crouched on the wooden platform and a second later she was gone, only to reappear right behind Mack. She smacked him lightly on the shoulder with the bokuto and he spun, shocked. He barely had time to move before Shoko crouched and traveled back to this side of the wall. Then she traveled again, appearing behind him. She didn't hit him that time.

"Remember, the Evil Ones have guns," she said. "Travel back as much as needed to regain your senses and readjust to their position."

After a murmur of agreement, one girl stepped forward.

"Shoko," she said. "To travel across is more shocking and takes longer than traveling within one side. Is that action possible?"

Shoko pointed to Mack. "Try it. Cross to our side, *see*, then return and attack Mack."

Mack rolled his eyes. "Aw jeez …"

The girl walked toward the wooden deck, dropped, and disappeared. A long moment later, she appeared behind Mack. Unlike Shoko, she didn't hit him. She did, however, squint for a second or two.

"I understand," the girl said, then returned to her place.

"Do not worry, Mizuki," Shoko said. "The *noise* will grow less in time."

"Shoko?" I stepped forward and said in a whisper, "We need to consider what they'll do if they *can't* cross back."

Shoko's eyes met mine. She didn't look happy.

"I'll get Jason to talk about stuff like that tomorrow," I said to her. "If we're prepared, we don't have to worry, right?"

She couldn't argue with that.

―

Because I suggested it, Jason spent the whole next morning covering tactical planning. As it turned out, the Gatekeepers typically didn't do much planning. I didn't mean that in a bad way. They were well trained, disciplined, and always on their own turf, so they got along fine with lightning-fast reaction. But now that we'd be taking them behind enemy lines, without their senses, having some kind of plan made a lot of sense to everyone.

After that, Jason moved on to the subject of combat in confined spaces.

He took a bokuto from one of the girls. "This is a narrow space," he said, standing behind the open wall with the bokuto held in front of him. "You can see it's hard to swing a sword here and you should be engaging the enemy at a distance anyway."

"Honorable Jason-sensei," Hana said. "You are not holding it correctly."

Jason scowled, then pointed to a girl holding a bow. "Riku, let's trade." He positioned her in front of him, then crouched with the bow drawn back. "You can't see your enemy but if he's there, he's ahead of you, so Riku moves forward slowly, back to the wall. Me and my teammates come up behind her, bows ready and pointed in the same direction because chances are, when she engages the surprise threat, another one will also be waiting to attack." He let go of the bow string with a twang. "And I just took it out."

He stood up. "However, when you're patrolling—moving in the forest or a city street in four-man teams ... four-*person* teams—each of you should be covering a different *arc*. In your case, I'd suggest you do that with bows. This means, no two people should be aiming their weapons in the same direction. Think of yourselves as the four points of a compass."

He got a room full of blank stares. He looked at me and Shoko. "They don't use compasses?"

Shoko shook her head. "But they understand the four directions."

"Okay, so when moving together one behind the other, each girl covers a direction." He took three girls and set them up behind Riku, each facing a different direction. "That is your arc—that's where you watch as you move forward. That's where you shoot when the bad guy pops up."

"I must walk backward?" the fourth Gatekeeper in line asked.

"Yup." Then he tapped Riku on the shoulder. "You're covering west. When you hear one of your teammates start shooting to the east, north, or south, don't turn to help out—"

Several girls started to protest, but he held up a hand.

"This is where amateurs screw up," he said. "Ambushes usually come from several directions at once. If you cover your arc, no one sneaks up on you."

This concept was obviously new for them. They weren't used to someone sneaking up on them. Enemies came from one direction: the gateway.

Jason walked over to me while the groups practiced.

"This would be so much easier with guns," he said. "I get that they're dead shots." He jerked a thumb back toward the girls. "But at some point, bows and swords aren't going to be enough."

I remembered the weapons Sergeant Jackson's men had when they kidnapped Okaasan and Mack.

"If you ever want to try out guns," he said. "I can show you a thing or two. Then maybe you can persuade them."

I turned to look at him. "You'd teach me?"

"Anytime." He shook his head. "Because if this shit's for real, you need to be ready."

On Thursday night, we moved the girls to the only unfinished tower left at Grandpa's Bayview Project. Tower One was due to open in a few weeks and there was a big celebration planned, but Tower Three still had large empty floors.

Jason pushed them past their comfort zones, especially when he killed the lights and made them sneak around and fight with nothing more than dim city lights to guide them. Later that night, after Jason went home, Shoko called them together.

"This is a scenario Junya and I once faced, in the apartment of a man named Walter." She stomped her foot on the concrete floor. "We could not travel. One day you may find that you cannot find anything that still holds the memory of the Mother Earth, and you will not be able to travel away."

"Could we not carry something with us, Shoko?" Sakura said. "A piece of wood, perhaps our ogre swords? Then we are not ever out of the reach of the Mother."

Shoko stared at her with an odd expression on her face. "That, Sakura, is an excellent idea."

I knew Jason planned to teach us some basic first aid and CPR on Friday morning, but I was surprised and a little unhappy when Mr. Barrymore showed up with a box full of first-aid supplies.

"Look," Shoko said, pointing. "There is Nene!"

I hadn't noticed her come in.

Shoko smiled as she bowed to Nene and asked in English, "How is the training progressing?"

"She's unbelievable," Mr. Barrymore said as he walked over to us. "When I agreed to train her, I didn't have any expectations. I mean, she's only ten, right?"

Shoko and I both nodded.

"But she works hard, studies every night, and learns damn fast," he said, practically beaming. "I taught her more in one day than I can teach those army types ..." He jerked a thumb in Jason's direction. "... in a week."

I smiled at Nene. "So, you're like a Miko now."

She shook her head, which sent her braids spinning. "Barrymore-sensei says I am a *paramedic*."

He nodded in agreement. "Definitely the youngest one I've ever certified."

Mack stopped by after school and we watched the Gatekeepers show off their stuff. Shoko sat next to me with what looked like a katana wrapped in red cloth, but when I asked about it, she just shook her head.

"You will see later," she said.

When it was over, I walked up to Jason and shook his hand.

"You did an awesome job!" I said to him. "We really appreciate your help, and the fact you're going to keep this a secret."

He snorted. "How can I talk about something I don't understand?"

"Well, maybe someday—"

Shoko yelled a command in Japanese.

As a unit, all twenty-four girls dropped to one knee, their sheathed katana pointed at the ground. Off to one side, her four apprentices knelt as well.

Shoko walked over to us, carrying the cloth-covered item. She knelt in front of Jason, then carefully removed the cloth. I drew in a sharp breath.

The katana was beautiful, the handle's black cord interwoven with what looked like silver. Shoko placed it on the ground in front of her, then bowed low to Jason.

"We are the Gatekeepers of Izumo Oyashiro, the protectors and servants of the gods of Izumo, creators of Japan and all things under heaven." She sat back on her heels and held the katana up to Jason, just as she'd done when she presented me with my bokuto all those months ago. "Please accept this with our gratitude, and that of the gods we serve."

Jason's mouth dropped open. At first he didn't move, but after a quick glance at me, he reached out and received the sword reverently. The ceiling lights reflected off the polished curved blade as he slid it out halfway.

He let out a low whistle. He looked dumbfounded, but he was a soldier above all else. With the katana in one hand, he snapped to attention and saluted.

When Shoko stood up, I smiled at her. Nice touch.

I had a surprise too. I'd had thick silver bracelets made, modeled after the girls' hammered Gatekeeper graduation rings. I went around to each girl, bowing to her before slipping the bracelet onto her left wrist.

"These bracelets are made with silver from your sacred Iwami–Ginzan mines." My voice echoed in the large room. "They symbolize that you belong to an elite force. You can go places and do things other Gatekeepers can't. You will stop the killing of shamans and stop the gods from growing weaker!"

When we were done, no one moved and Jason began to look uncomfortable.

"Let me guess," he said. "I need to leave."

The door had barely closed behind him when Shoko called out, "Gatekeepers, return to Izumo! Eat, drink sake, and rest well tonight, for tomorrow we shall begin!"

I had to squint as the group traveled away. Mack couldn't feel anything, but he was still impressed.

"Un-freaking believable!"

After that, the three of us hung out in the warehouse. Shoko was able to run across the top of the six sections of training walls like a tightrope walker. I performed my own show of running up the wall and backflipping to the ground. Mack had Shoko hang off his wrists while he curled his bicep. He had no trouble keeping her feet off the ground.

"It is my turn again!" She handed Mack a leftover piece of wood. "Hold it at shoulder height." When he did, she executed a beautiful double spin-kick and knocked it out of his hand.

"Higher!"

"Ouch," Mack groaned when she hit it again. "Okay, Supergirl, let's see you hit this." He held the wood as high as he could, probably eight or nine feet off the ground.

She gazed up at it. "Can I have a running start?"

Without waiting for an answer, she raced toward him, landed her left foot on his hip and her right foot on his shoulder, then a spin-kick sent the wood flying. To all our surprise, Mack caught her on her way to the ground.

We finally sat down, tired and sweaty, with Shoko on one side of me and Mack on the other side, telling us a joke. Having my best friend and my girlfriend together felt awesome. Maybe one day, we could invite Isabella and go on a double date. I could finally take Shoko for pizza.

I felt happier than I'd been in a long time.

CHAPTER
25

I SENSED THAT OKAASAN AND DAD were home, so we arrived behind the shop. Though Mack managed not to scream this time, he was still bug-eyed when we materialized.

I patted his arm. "You okay, buddy?"

He nodded slowly. "I'm not sure I'll ever get used to that."

As Mack walked unsteadily toward my house, Shoko touched my arm. "Are you okay?" she asked softly.

"Yeah, why?"

"I feel as if you did most of the work traveling. It worries me."

I smiled at her. "It's probably because we were lugging Mack with us," I said. "He weighs a ton."

Dad saw us come in from the garden.

"Hey guys." He smiled at Shoko. "It's nice to see you again. Are you enjoying San Francisco?"

She bowed. "Yes, thank you sir," she said in heavily accented English.

"Good to hear. Listen James, your mom and I are heading out

for dinner so you'll have to fend for yourself tonight. Are you ready yet, Misako?" he called toward the kitchen. "I have no idea what's keeping her."

Okaasan came out of the kitchen. Her hair was up, and she wore an apron over an elegant blue dress.

Dad frowned. "What are——?"

"I'm just throwing together a quick meal for them," she answered. "Give me five more minutes."

"Jeez Mom. I can make something, you know. Get going."

"I'm not worried about you," she said as she disappeared back into the kitchen. "Mack needs something nutritious."

"Seriously?" I looked at Mack. "It's almost like you and me have switched places."

He stuck out his tongue. "I told you she likes me more."

A few minutes later Okaasan rushed out of the kitchen holding a basket.

"I made it picnic-style, so you can eat in the living room if you want." She handed the basket to Shoko, then slipped on her high heels and looked at Dad. "You're not even ready to go."

Dad rolled his eyes as he bent to tie his shoes. "Have fun, kids."

When Shoko took the basket into the living room, I pulled on Mack's elbow.

"Do you mind taking off after we eat?" I whispered. "You know …" I nodded my head toward Shoko.

He grinned. "Ready for round two?" Then he raised his voice. "I want to see Isabella so I'm going to eat and run."

"You haven't told Isabella anything, right?"

"I won't and you know that." His brow wrinkled. "I don't like to lie, but I don't want her to think I'm nuts either."

I nodded, my good mood suddenly dropping. Now my best friend had to lie, like my mom and I lied to my dad.

Okaasan had made burritos. Mack grabbed two.

"Adiós," he said as he headed for the front door. When Shoko answered him in perfect Spanish, he shook his head and let the door slam behind him.

As we ate burritos and drank lemonade, we talked about Jason, the training, and what we'd do next.

"I believe the Special Forces should remain on my side until the gateways open," Shoko said after taking a long swig of lemonade. "When their mission is complete, they should return immediately to Izumo."

"But they're supposed to hunt down the Evil Ones on this side."

"They can do that as part of a gateway opening. They kill any Evil Ones they find in the area, but I do not want them crossing over whenever and wherever they please," she said. "We will use my apprentices, working alongside you and I, to hunt down the Evil Ones on this side. To me, they are far more *special* than those others can ever be. Because of this extra experience and their time with me, they will rise to powerful positions. This I know."

"What about me?"

She smiled and touched my face. "You are far more special than any of them."

"That wasn't what I meant, but thanks." I leaned over and gave her a long kiss.

When I drew back, she said, "Would you mind if I had a bath?"

"Ah sure ... modern or traditional?"

"I would be most comfortable in the traditional." Then she looked down at herself. "I am sorry. I feel sweaty and dirty, and my clothes are filthy."

I grinned. "Kicking ass is dirty work," I said, standing up. "I can wash your clothes if you want."

"That will take too long."

"I don't use a creek, remember? They can be done in less than two hours."

She considered, then nodded.

Dad had created a traditional Japanese bathhouse, right down to the stone floor and deep wooden tub. But unlike the tub in Shoko's house, where the water trickled in from a nearby hot spring, ours had a gas burst heater on a one-inch waterline that could fill the tub with steaming hot water in less than five minutes.

As I adjusted the temperature, she turned to me. "I will not have anything to wear."

I moved toward her. "That's okay."

"No, it is not."

I put my arms down. "Okay, I'll find something."

"Thank you," she said, then closed the door behind me.

I headed for my room. What do you give a girl to wear? Whatever it was, I knew it had better be clean. I ended up picking out a pair of basketball shorts and a T-shirt. Certainly not what I'd like to see her in, but I didn't know what else to lend her. I left them outside the door, threw her dirty clothes in the machine, and hit the shower myself.

It was at least forty-five minutes later when she finally appeared in the living room. I was on the sofa, wearing a pair of jeans and a T-shirt and reading a sports magazine when she walked in, her bare feet padding softly on the smooth concrete floor.

I started laughing when I saw her. The shorts came down past her knees and the T-shirt drooped down her arms. She looked hilarious, and damn cute.

She scowled at me, one hand on the waistband. "These short pants will not stay up."

I did my best to stop laughing. "Don't worry, your clothes are already in the dryer."

She sat down on the sofa, one leg up, facing me. "That tub is wonderful!"

I put my arm around her and pulled her closer. "My dad will take that as a major compliment."

She snuggled in and sighed. "This feels like heaven to me, and that makes me feel guilty."

"Why?"

"Because I do not deserve this." She put her hand on my chest and looked into my eyes. "There are so many others who suffer, and here I am—"

I kissed her on the nose. "I don't know if anyone *deserves* anything, good or bad," I said. "But I think if something wonderful happens, you should hold on to it, really tight."

Her eyebrows pulled together. "Why?"

"Because it might not happen again."

She looked thoughtful, maybe even a bit sad. "To you, am I this 'something wonderful'?"

I nodded, and suddenly I felt sad too. Somewhere in Izumo was a guy the Elders would one day select to be her partner. I clenched my teeth and pulled her closer to me. She *was* my something wonderful, and there was no way any other man would be with her. It didn't matter how *compatible* the Elders thought some other guy might be, what we had was better. Somehow, I knew we were meant to be together.

As if she was thinking the same thing, she crawled up onto my lap and hugged me tight. We began to kiss and the warmth of her energy filled me. I closed my eyes and melted into her.

We weren't in a hurry. Our lips and hands moved slowly, enjoying the feel of each other's bodies. Soon her chest was bare against mine, our legs entwined. Things were definitely heating up.

She gently bit my earlobe, then whispered, "Your parents will not come home soon?"

I glanced at the clock. "Not for at least three hours." Okaasan didn't spend that much time with hair and makeup for a quick dinner out.

"Can we go to your room then?"

In the bedroom, we enjoyed each other. Nothing rushed, no awkward moments. It was like being in a dream or the perfect Zen state. I don't remember when the rest of our clothes came off, or even when the condom went on.

When I entered her, the sounds that escaped her mouth spoke of her pleasure—*our* pleasure—and the energy between us was magical. We moved as one, breathed as one, right up until her back arched and we cried out together.

We lay side by side, holding hands until our breathing returned to normal and even then we didn't speak. I think I may have dozed off, because when she finally spoke, it startled me.

"Junya ...?" She had the oddest expression on her face.

"What's wrong?"

She sat up, looked like she was concentrating hard on something. I sat up too and listened, first with my ears, then to the stream. I didn't sense anything. Certainly not Evil Ones or my parents.

She slid to the end of the bed and stood up.

"Shoko, what's the matter?"

She looked back at me with an expression of pure delight.

"I can hear!"

She walked into the hallway. I pulled on my boxers, grabbed my bathrobe, and ran after her. She'd opened the sliding door and was standing near the pond, her naked body bathed in a soft orange glow from the garden lights.

I put the robe over her shoulders. "Hear *what?*"

She turned to me again with a wide grin. "It's not like at home, but ... I can sense things!"

"Seriously?"

She pushed her arms into the sleeves of my robe, tied the belt, then walked further into the Zen garden. Her bare feet crunched on the gravel. She spun in slow circles, arms out.

"I lost myself, like I never have before," she said. "It was like a deep, mindless meditation. As we joined and moved together, every part of my body came alive. The energy between us was astonishing and now the noise is gone!"

"You mean ...?"

"Yes, it is quiet." She stood very still. Then she flashed me another excited smile, like a kid at Christmas. "I can hear the voice of the Mother Earth!" She leaped toward me and hugged me tight. "It is because of what we did. It awakened me! *You* awakened me!"

I stared at her a long moment. I was thinking about Okaasan. "Oh jeez," I muttered. "Okaasan said her senses came back after she met my dad."

"Because they had sex?"

I shrugged. "The first time we had sex, nothing happened. What we did tonight was different." I brushed a strand of hair off her face. "It was the most magical thing I've ever experienced." Then I laughed. "And I've seen the gods!"

She nodded, looked excited. "And I felt your energy, like never before," she said. "It was pure and powerful ... wonderful."

I pulled her close again. "Welcome to my world, Shoko," I whispered.

—

We were in the living room, staring out at the garden, when my parents came home a little after midnight. Of course, we were dressed but even with clothes on, only holding hands, our energy felt as connected as it had when we were in bed together.

"Junya, what are—" It was my dad. "Oh, hi Shoko, I didn't see you there."

Shoko waved.

He walked to the glass door, hands in his pant pockets, and looked up. There were a few stars visible. "Beautiful night," he said.

"I should go." Shoko whispered. She tried to let go of my hand.

"Don't." I didn't want this night to end.

Okaasan came in a few minutes later. "Oh, this is where you—" Then she saw Shoko. "Hello Shoko," she said. "You two look very content."

"You guys have a nice date?" I said, hoping to steer her thoughts in a different direction.

Okaasan nodded. "Your dad took me dancing! It was fun."

We chatted for a while. Shoko mostly stayed quiet, only joining the conversation when necessary. I think she was enjoying the peace of this place. The only problem was, every now and then, some energy escaped her. No thoughts spilled out for Okaasan or me to hear, but it was obvious she liked not needing to keep her mind clamped shut.

After about twenty minutes, they left us alone. "Make sure you get her home soon, Junya," Okaasan said from the doorway.

Shoko and I held each other for a long time in the Zen garden.

"I'll come to Izumo tomorrow," I said as she knelt.

She shook her head. "There is much organizing to do and I am afraid you will be in the way." She smiled up at me. "Come the day after." Then she placed her palm against the earth and traveled away.

When I went inside a few minutes later, Okaasan was sitting in the kitchen, her head resting on her hands.

"What are you still doing up?" I said.

She didn't lift her head, just pointed at my chair.

"Sit."

I sat and looked at her, expecting the worse.

"I hope to god you used a condom."

"Yes Mother," I said, more annoyed than embarrassed. "Was it that obvious?"

"To me, yes."

I let out a sigh. "Well, big news flash here mom. We're not the only teenagers having sex."

She looked up. "Shoko's not just another *teenager*! This could ruin her!"

"Like it ruined you?" As soon as I said that, I regretted it. "She wanted to. We both wanted to. It was pure, natural."

She sat there, tapping her fingertips on the table. "She wouldn't have awakened to the Mother Earth if it hadn't been."

"You could tell that too?"

"The energy between you two … she was practically glowing with it. That girl's soul was wide open."

"So is that … you know … why you can hear?"

She looked up and nodded. "It took a while for me—months, actually. Sex has great power. It connects with our deepest emotions, creates strong feelings, amazing energy. Enough to open your mind if you want it."

I nodded. That sounded about right.

"You have so much energy," she said. "I'm scared for you."

"You're scared of everything."

"Your energy changes people," she said. "To have that happen to Shoko in one night?"

My voice lowered. "Shoko balances me. I'm good for her too."

"But you don't belong there," she said. "And I won't let you keep her here. It's wrong."

I pushed back my chair and stood. "It's too late for that."

CHAPTER
26

"WHAT ARE YOU DOING TODAY?" It was Jason's voice on the phone.

I squinted at the clock: seven-thirty. Far too loud and way too early for a Saturday. "What'd you want?" I mumbled.

"I told you I'd teach you to shoot," he said. "So up and at 'em."

"You've got to be kidding me."

He wasn't. He was waiting impatiently in one of the security team's black SUVs when I ran out of the house at a quarter to eight with a piece of half-eaten toast in hand.

"I borrowed a few things from Barrymore's arsenal," he said as we drove away from my place. "He's got quite a collection."

"Yeah, I've seen the MP5s." Grandpa's bodyguards used to pack those, but not anymore, at least, not that I knew of.

He glanced over at me at the next traffic light. "You shoot one?"

I shook my head. "Never. I don't really like guns."

"I'm not really into them either."

"You were in Delta Force. All they do is shoot guns."

"Guns are tools," he said. "And I'm well trained to use them and know which is best for each application." He shrugged. "I'm just not fascinated with them like some people are."

About thirty minutes later, he pulled the SUV onto a side road and stopped at a chain-link gate. He hopped out and opened it, then drove through. I closed it behind us.

We drove along a dirt road through the dry rolling hills for about ten minutes before we came to a cluster of buildings.

"It's a private range, about a hundred acres," Jason said as he stopped near a concrete building. "One of my buddies from the Force owns it. He does a lot of training here for bodyguards, close-protection officers heading overseas, and quite a few actors. He works as a weapons specialist for the movies too, does pretty well for himself."

I waited until the dust cloud we'd stirred up settled, then opened my door. "You ever help?"

He nodded. "That's why I can use the place when I want."

"Meet anyone famous?"

"A few." He hauled a large plastic case from the back of the SUV and pointed to the other one. He set his case down on a table inside a low-roofed cabana, then watched while I struggled to lift the other one.

"You know, I did some research online," he said. "That god Shoko mentioned is like the head of all the other gods of Japan."

"That's how the legend goes."

He looked past me, out toward the hills. "I don't know what to make of all this. *Traveling* and *other sides*, gods and shamans."

"You don't need to know more, right?" Then I laughed. "Are you sure you don't want the money I offered? You did an amazing job teaching them."

"Why not? You've obviously got more money than you know what to do with."

"I'll have Lin make out a check." I hesitated, then decided to just come out and ask. "By the way, have you ever given her a ride in my Jeep?"

He eyed me for a moment, then nodded. "Yeah, the day before we started training at the warehouse. Hope you don't mind."

"Why?" I listened to his energy. There was definitely a subtle shift.

"Her car was in the shop." Then he folded his arms on his chest. "You got a problem with me, I'd rather you say it straight out."

I wasn't expecting that, and for a few seconds I stood there at a loss for words.

"Lin told me what you said to her," he said. "I don't appreciate it and neither does she. There's nothing going on between us."

"Then how about you stop giving me reasons to think it?" I said, more than a little annoyed. "Stop talking about her all the time, or hugging her, or taking her out in my car. It's disrespectful to my grandfather."

He looked amused.

"What?"

"You're very possessive of her."

I rolled my eyes. "Whatever."

His face turned dead serious. "Say whatever you want to me, but lay off Lin. You're crossing a line here, James."

"What *line*?"

"A whole bunch of them." His expression hardened. "And even if we were sleeping together, it's none of your goddamn business."

"Yeah, it is. She's my Grandpa's fiancé, and if something's going on, then—"

"Then what, you'll step in and put a stop to it?"

I hesitated. "Well—"

"You know, I didn't bring you out here just because I'm your employee," he said. "If you mess with my private life, ever again, you and I are done."

I stood there, stunned.

"Isn't Lin supposed to be your friend?"

I managed a nod.

"Then start acting like it."

A few long seconds slipped past. "Okay, I'm sorry. I'll give it a rest."

"Enough said, then." He hopped down from the table. "Now, I realize those girls are good—damn good—but it's dangerous going up against armed men with nothing but swords and bows."

I had to do a mental gear change. "You'd be surprised what they can do," I said. "Guns aren't a problem."

"Maybe not for them," he said. "But right now I'm thinking of you, so I'm going to show you my way of dealing with bad guys. Then at least you have choices. Okay?"

I nodded.

He pulled the latches on a case. There were three guns inside and he picked up the first one.

"Heckler and Koch MP5, German-made submachine gun, 9mm ammo, fifteen- or thirty-round magazine, shoots semiautomatic, two or three bursts or full auto, although only an idiot would shoot on full auto." He gave a quick demo of its functions, then picked up a handgun. "Sig Sauer P226 9mm, semiauto, fifteen-round magazines. Very nice gun." He put it down and picked up an assault rifle. "This is an M4A2 assault rifle, one of the most popular military weapons out there. Shoots 5.56mm ammo in semiauto, or two- or three-round bursts. Good up to five hundred meters if everything is perfect, which it never is."

I made a face. "I'm not shooting that."

"Why?"

"Too many school shootings, I guess."

He pointed at the Sig. "Are you more comfortable with that one?" When I didn't reply, he continued. "They're all designed to kill, James. But do I think any civilian should be able to buy a military weapon like this? It was designed to kill the enemies of America, by soldiers, not fellow Americans by wackos. I've been shot at with this type of weapon overseas but now I'm protecting people like your grandpa and instead of worrying about a wacko with a revolver or shotgun, I've gotta be prepared for this."

He put it back down and picked up the Sig. "How about we start with this."

He made me strip and reassemble the Sig about fifty times before I even loaded it, and over the next three hours, we burned through about three hundred rounds. Right around the time I felt like my arms would fall off, we had a quick lunch he'd brought for us, and after that he picked up the M4.

"I brought out the MP5 to get you familiar with it," he said. "Your grandpa's bodyguards carry them, so you might as well see how it works."

We spent about fifteen minutes going over it, but I didn't shoot it. When we were done he picked up the M4 and pulled back the charging handle "This is what I wanted to teach you to shoot. This and the P226 are all you'll ever need.

I shook my head. "I'm never going to need one of those."

"What if the bad guys start using them on you? With what you're up against, I don't consider you a civilian."

I looked at the weapon. Was I a civilian or a warrior?

By the time the sun was going down, I'd stripped that rifle, loaded and unloaded it about a hundred times, and shot it while standing, kneeling, sitting, lying down, running, and from the door of the moving SUV. I was half asleep when he finally pulled up in front of my house around nine o'clock.

"You ought to sleep well tonight," he said with a laugh.

I held out my hand. "That was great," I said. "I learned a lot."

We shook. "Anytime you want to practice, you let me know."

I swung the door open. "I think I learned enough today to last a lifetime."

"You can always be better." Then he pointed a finger at me. "You have an unhealthy disregard for firearms. You'd better revisit that attitude, because if you don't, you or someone you care about is going to die. You get me?"

I nodded as I stepped out of the SUV. "Thanks again. And sorry about what happened before."

"That's behind us now." He waved. "See you later."

I stood and watched him drive away. It was good advice, but he didn't understand about the Gatekeepers, or me.

Still, I'd try to keep it in mind.

CHAPTER
27

THE NEXT DAY WHEN I MET Shoko in Izumo, I decided not to mention the firing range, or the conversation I'd had with Okaasan the night before. I also did my best not to take her in my arms and kiss her the second I saw her. Instead, I stood, hands in pockets, and waited for her from a distance.

"Hello Junya," Shoko stood in the doorway of her house, wearing her Gatekeeper uniform.

"Hi," I said, still several feet away. God only knew who might be watching. "How'd it go with the Special Forces yesterday?"

"It took a while to get organized," she said as she walked toward me. "However, six teams attended over a dozen gateways."

"Wow," I said. "That's a good start." Still, I was disappointed I'd missed it.

"Yes, we decided they would arrive at each gateway a few hours ahead of the Controllers and their escorts." She grinned. "Evil Ones were present at four and were killed before they came anywhere near the shamans!"

"Yes!" I held up my hand for a high five, but she just stared up at it, looking confused. The time it took to explain it took most of the fun out of it.

Then her cheeks reddened. "That my senses work on your side helped too."

I glanced around. Now I really wanted to hold her. Instead I said, "Are any gateways opening today?"

"Several," she replied. "Our Special Forces are already preparing."

"Can we go out with them?"

She thought a moment. "My apprentices are expecting rigorous sword training today, but ..." She glanced back toward her house. "... I heard from a Controller that a gateway on the Island of Stone Labyrinths opens today. I myself am most curious to see that."

"Sounds like something from a movie," I said, repeating the name in a deep voice. "Where is it?"

"Far to the north, in the White Sea," she said. "The Russian people call it Bolshoy Zayatski Island. It is an ancient site, more than four thousand years old."

"A labyrinth is a type of maze, right?"

She squatted and drew a quick sketch with a stick. "A maze is a puzzle with many paths and dead ends. A labyrinth has only one path that leads in a circular pattern to the center." She tapped the middle of her second sketch with her finger. "And there is a gateway there."

I sat down, cross-legged. "I want to go there with you."

Her eyes met mine. "I would go anywhere with you, Junya," she said in a low voice. She looked toward her house again. Tomi stood in the doorway.

"I will call my apprentices," Shoko said, her tone all business again. "We will travel to the island together."

I nodded to Tomi, almost a bow, then asked Shoko, "Has anyone else had trouble traveling?"

She rubbed out her sketches with the edge of the stick.

"There have been a few reports," she said. "It seems girls are reluctant to admit to such difficulty. There is always some excuse, such as fatigue or injury."

"It happened to you in Africa."

"Yes, and the Controllers have also begun traveling in pairs. They do not want a repeat of that experience." Then she stood and bowed to her mother. "I will take Junya and the apprentices to the Island of Stone Labyrinths."

A smile raised the corners of Tomi's lips and I realized, perhaps for the first time, that she was truly a beautiful woman.

"I remember going there as a young girl," she said. "It is a special place."

Shoko nodded. "Then I look forward to sharing my experiences with you when I return."

—

We arrived on the small island on Shoko's side. It was fairly flat, maybe a mile wide, and there were no trees. Only clumps of small bushes not much taller than me. In some places, small red flowers grew.

A group had already gathered there: two Controllers, half a dozen regular Gatekeepers, and four members of our Special Forces.

"We have already performed our reconnaissance," one of our Special Forces, Ikumi, told us. "Thirty-two people have gathered. They have been here for many days and set up tents."

"No Evil Ones?" I asked, somewhat disappointed.

Ikumi shook her head. "Not yet."

Yukie tapped my arm and grinned at me.

"We can walk the labyrinth, Junya."

I hadn't been paying attention, but the labyrinth was right in front of us. Rows of rocks about the size of soccer balls marked the circular path, but it wasn't only one path spiraling toward the center. There were two spirals set one into another, interlinked, which led to a small pile of rocks in the center.

"Shall we?" Yukie said, starting toward the opening. "You take that one and I will take this one. Let us see who gets there first."

"Can I run?"

"No!"

I laughed.

"You see?" Yukie smiled back. "Doing this is far better than killing Evil Ones."

"Yeah, but—"

I felt a shift in the earth's energy. "Evil Ones have arrived, I think," I overheard one of the Special Forces say.

"Shoko, come see if you wish." It was Sakura. She was kneeling on the other side of the labyrinth with her hands pressed together in a prayer position.

Shoko and I both ran over to her.

"There are some buildings, and a boat." Sakura pointed toward the south point of the island. There was nothing there until she took our hands and transported us across in her mind.

Three buildings stood near the shore, two made of stone with peaked roofs. The other one looked like an old church, its wooden walls grey from the salt and wind. The dome on top of it reminded me of the ones on the Kremlin.

A small dock jutted out into the water, and a boat had just pulled up. It wasn't a big boat, maybe thirty feet long, and it looked like it had seen better days.

Eight men disembarked, all carrying long black duffle bags.

"They do not look like worshipers." Shoko's voice sounded far away.

The sudden pain in my shoulder confirmed that. "They're Evil Ones," I said. Then I smiled. "Perfect."

Sakura released our hand and we were back. Our Special Forces were huddled, discussing their plan, just as Jason taught them. Before I could offer them advice, they were off, two of them notching arrows as they ran. The other two drew their katana and moved out to where the road was on the Other Side.

"It is time," a Controller said.

Her six Gatekeepers spread out across the labyrinth, facing the center as the ground began to shimmer.

"They should wait," I said.

Shoko looked over at me. "Why?" Then she nodded toward the regular Gatekeepers. "They are prepared."

Yeah, but were they prepared to face eight lizards? Because if our Special Forces weren't here, that's what they'd be up against, and they had no clue.

"The shaman is preparing to cross!" a Gatekeeper called out.

Through the haze of the gateway, the shape of a man appeared, followed by the sound of gunfire.

Without thinking, I grabbed Shoko's arm and we crossed.

The gunfire continued, accompanied by screams and shouts in a language I didn't recognize. The Evil Ones had spread out, marching up the dirt road toward the worshipers and firing wildly.

Suddenly, two of our Special Forces appeared behind the Evil Ones and began cutting them down like bamboo. A moment later, the only Evil One still shooting in our direction took an arrow in the neck and collapsed beside his fallen comrades.

In less than fifteen seconds, it was over.

The worshipers stared at us, horrified and shocked. The Evil Ones had already begun to disappear.

"Is anyone hurt?" Shoko asked the worshipers in what must've been Russian. No one answered, but judging the distance, I'd say the Evil Ones had been too far away to make any accurate hits.

"When your shaman returns, they will explain who we are," Shoko said. "Carry on with your worship." She pointed to the spots where the Evil Ones had fallen. "Pretend we, and they, were never here."

Then Shoko turned to me. This time, her high five met mine.

"Yes!" I yelled toward the sky. "I knew this would work!"

"Okay," Yukie said from behind me. "Maybe that is more fun than walking a labyrinth."

CHAPTER
28

THAT WAS HOW IT WENT. There weren't always Evil Ones waiting, but when they were, they died quickly. Not one Gatekeeper or shaman had died since we'd begun patrolling the gateways. After a while, the Evil Ones seemed to disappear altogether, and the Special Forces were the toast of Izumo.

"The Elders are very pleased with us," Shoko told me as we snuggled in my bed, relaxing after another passionate encounter. Our energy levels peaked when we were together, and it became an addiction neither of us could resist. And with her senses back, now as strong and complete as they were in Izumo, we were truly equals in both our worlds.

"With me too?"

Yes," she said as she played with the few hairs on my chest. "Even the Kannushi. He told me himself."

I smiled. "Well, I guess they finally appreciate how useful I am."

"We are only useful if someone believes we are." Then she smiled at me. "For example, I am *very* pleased with you."

I linked my fingers behind my head and grinned at the ceiling. My parents were away on a road trip to Carmel for a few days so Shoko had stayed over the entire time, only traveling back occasionally to let Tomi know she was still alive.

Shoko sat up and grabbed my robe. "I would like to make breakfast today."

"Getting tired of my cooking?"

She smiled. "I want to practice being a good girlfriend."

"You don't need any practice at that." I got up and followed her to the kitchen. We were halfway there when the front door swung open. It was Mack.

"Thank god you lovebirds are up," he said as he kicked off his shoes. "Walking in on you once was more than enough."

"But you still don't use the doorbell?"

"Your mom gave me a key." He held it up for us to see.

Shoko smiled at him. "You are lucky I recognize your energy now."

"Yeah, lucky ..." He rubbed his left shoulder where Shoko had given him a *gentle* strike from the bokuto I kept near my bed.

"She barely hit you, ya big baby."

He sniffed the air. "When does your mom get back anyway? I miss her."

Shoko managed not to burn breakfast, which I didn't mean as an insult. Between modern gas appliances and a lack of cooking experience, she did pretty good. Scrambled eggs and toast was one of my favorite breakfasts.

After I cleaned up, the plan was to take her and Mack to see my new place on Chestnut Street. Grandpa had high expectations because I'd done so well renovating a bookstore the previous year. It was another heritage building he wanted to take down for an office building. I persuaded him to let me restore it instead. Grandpa was surprised when we made a good profit on it.

I'd called the same architect and contractor we'd used to restore the bookstore and they'd come running. It'd be stupid to turn down a call from a Thompson.

As planned, Jason pulled up in my Jeep just after ten. Mack rode shotgun and Shoko and I sat in the back, holding hands.

"How's everything going back in your … kingdom?" Jason asked.

"Your tactics are saving many lives, Jason-sensei," Shoko said. "Thank you again for your help."

"Good to hear and no thanks needed. It was my pleasure."

After Jason dropped us off, Mack, Shoko, and I stood on the opposite side of the street looking at the building. It had once been quite the classic Victorian building, and with my help, it would be again.

The first time I'd shown it to Mack, I'd been a bit embarrassed, but he was excited.

"You're a land baron, bro!" he'd said. "I mean, it's a dump, but hell, you *own* it!"

The little shop on the ground floor was still open, barely visible under the scaffolding that covered the entire front of the building. The builder decided they'd gut the upper floors to the bare boards and redo everything—a blank slate—but that was fine with me. The place would look original but have the latest technology inside the walls. They'd already finished most of the outside.

"And is the *crash pad* done yet?" Shoko asked.

"I thought you were calling it the *Love Nest*," Mack said over his shoulder as he jaywalked across the street.

I glanced sideways at Shoko. She was smiling.

My parents still didn't know about this place and I decided to keep it that way.

A thin layer of sawdust covered the top floor where my apartment would be. The walls inside were still bare, the wiring just going in, but the basic shape was evident. I'd designed it warehouse-loft-style, with exposed brick on the walls and the original fir floors. Not exactly a Victorian-style interior, but who cared?

We headed up to the roof where the new deck would be. Since it was the highest building on the street, it would be nice and private. Plus, I could see the Bay from there.

"You know bro, you're cool," Mack said as he cracked open a soda from his brief stop at the store downstairs. "Know why?"

I grinned. "I think it's obvious but tell me anyway."

He chugged the soda then threw the empty can at me. "Because you're always *you*," he said as he grabbed another one from his snack bag. "Even when your grandpa made you heir, you didn't change, not toward me anyway."

"I was too busy running for my friggin' life." I laughed. "But don't get used to it. I may still become a snob. I'm starting to like this business stuff."

"Yeah?"

"Sure." I spread my arms. "This is only the beginning, bro."

"Please don't tell me you're going to switch your university major to business."

I motioned for him to toss me two sodas. I passed one to Shoko. She looked at it skeptically.

"You don't want it?" I said, stifling a laugh. The first time she'd had one—and the last—she'd burped like a construction worker and blew pop out her nose.

She shook her head and handed it back.

"I don't know about university," I said after taking a long pull. "The whole point of going to school is so you can get a good job, and I don't need a job, right?"

Mack made a face. "I thought you wanted to be an architect?"

"Yeah, but do I need to? I mean, I can just hire architects and designers and stuff." I pointed at the building underneath us. "They'll bring my visions to life."

"Yeah, well, I at least gotta go to a trade school, because I *need* to get a decent job." He let out a bitter laugh. "Not that my parents have put away any money for it."

I waved a hand at him. "Don't worry bro, I'll give you a job."

He gave me a strange look. "Doing what?"

"I'll pay you big bucks just for being you!"

He managed a thin smile. "Getting paid to be your buddy?" he said slowly. "No thanks. I need to learn to do something."

"Grandpa says school kills kids' creativity by making them memorize stuff and repeat it. You don't become a millionaire by doing what everyone else is doing, but if you don't follow the rules at school, they fail you."

Mack laughed. "Remember my science experiment in grade eight?"

"You mean the water-powered engine?"

He nodded. "I still think it was brilliant."

"It didn't work!"

"There was a minor design flaw."

Shoko had walked to the edge of the roof to look at the water, but now she turned back.

"I must strongly disagree with you, Junya. Did not Edward go to college?"

"Yeah, but—"

"Schooling is what made his life possible." She held out her hands. "No one, not your employees or these designers you speak of, wants to follow a fool. Doing so makes them fools as well."

"I'm not a fool!"

"Learning ensures you will not become one."

"You didn't go to college and you're an awesome leader."

Her eyes narrowed. "Do you consider me stupid?"

I glanced at Mack. "Of course not."

He laughed. "Leave me out of this, man."

"I have studied my trade since age four," she said, arms crossed on her chest. "Do you think Chiyoko does not know the history of our people? Does your Okaasan not know how to count or write? Education is a privilege and a necessity for leadership."

I stared at my shoes.

"And do you think Bartholomew or Edward could manipulate the people here if they were highly educated?"

Mack nodded in agreement. "It's true bro," he said. "The uneducated scrape along, scared shitless of losing their minimum-wage jobs. And that sucks."

I looked at Shoko. "Sorry. I've never thought you were uneducated."

"Every child in Izumo attends school," she said. "Becoming a farmer or undertaker is not because of a lack of education. It is based on choice and callings."

Mack finished off his second soda. "If you're lucky, I *may* choose to work for you some day, but if I'm better educated than you? I'm gonna be laughing at you, bro. You'll be my rich-loser buddy."

I held up my hands in surrender. "Okay, okay," I said. "Jeez, you two really know how to gang up on a guy."

"Good," Mack said. "Then you'll have a chance to be king of the world, but if you ever get stuck up," he held up his sizable fist, "I'll bust you one."

Shoko held up her small fist. "And I will *bust you one* anytime I choose," she said with a smile. "Even if you become the king of my world."

Something jumped inside my chest. "The king of *your* world, or Izumo?"

She walked toward me and put her hands on my shoulders. "The way you are progressing, perhaps you will become king of both."

Mack made a gagging sound.

CHAPTER
29

THERE'D BEEN SOME RESISTANCE WHEN SHOKO and I traveled back to Izumo, like running into a strong wind, and there was an odd feeling in the air when we arrived. I looked toward the top of the grand shrine and listened. The energy was there, but something was off. Shoko sensed it too.

"What is happening?" Shoko asked the first girl we saw. She sat in the shade beneath the grand staircase, absorbed in a book.

The girl didn't look up. "With what?"

I leaned closer. She was reading a *manga* comic.

"Where did you get that book?" Shoko said.

"You are rude," the girl said, still not looking up. "Can you not see I am busy?"

She let out a squeal as Shoko hauled her to her feet with one arm. The manga tumbled to the dirt.

"You will answer my questions!"

"Shoko!" the girl gasped. "I am so sorry. If I had known it was you—"

"I asked where you got that book!" Shoko hadn't released her grip on the girl's shirt, and the material bunched and twisted in her fingers.

"I ... I crossed over and went to a ... store," she said, gasping for breath.

Shoko lowered the girl back down. "Why did you do that?"

"To prove that I am good enough to join the Special Forces one day."

Shoko's mouth dropped open. "The negative energy does not bother you?"

The girl blushed. "I can handle it long enough to get what I want."

"And what do you want?"

"To get things, like this book," the girl said, growing bolder. "The shops are amazing! *Everything* is amazing there!"

Something was bothering me. "How do you pay for stuff?"

She finally noticed me. Her eyes went even wider.

"I ... what is *pay*?"

"You're stealing things?"

"Stealing?" She said the word as if it was new to her. "I do as we do here and take what I need ... what I want." She began to look uncomfortable. "Many girls are doing it now."

"Crossing so they can join the Special Forces?"

The girl shook her head. "At first, but now I think they are more interested in what they find there." Then her tone changed. She actually sounded annoyed. "Why have the Elders kept this from us? If I could, I would live there my—"

"Stop." Shoko held up her hands. "Where is your master?"

"She has gone to the other side too. She wants a handbag like yours." She looked back and forth between the two of us. "If you are done with me?"

Shoko nodded, almost absentmindedly. Over near a small supply house, a group of young girls had gathered around two more girls dressed in Western clothing. Everyone was talking excitedly.

Shoko turned to me.

"This is bad," she said. "They are crossing over because of me, because of us?"

"Well, it's a bit more than I expected."

"And they are crossing over to shop!"

"Maybe it's not so bad," I said. "The ones who want to be warriors can join the Special Forces, and the rest can be normal kids and go back and forth between our worlds. Growing up in life without war will be amazing. We've liberated them!"

Shoko frowned. "Liberated them from a life serving the gods?"

"If we defeat all the Evil Ones, they won't need to protect the gods."

"There will always be war, Junya. Always more Evil Ones."

"Don't you get it?" I couldn't believe I hadn't thought of this before. "You'll always need a small Special Forces group, but the rest of society can do other things."

She looked incredulous. "No. That is impossible, unthinkable!" She turned away from me and looked toward the training area. "Oh gods, now what?"

She strode over to a group of girls in the training area with me hustling to keep up. The girls were dressed in their Gatekeeper uniforms, fully armed, obviously on duty, but they looked downright dejected.

"Are there no gateways opening today?" Shoko said.

The group leader bowed low. "Yes Shoko. There were two, but we have returned early because our presence was not required." At Shoko's disbelieving expression, the leader added, "The Special Forces were operating in the area."

"They told you to go?"

The girl looked down. "They said we are not needed anymore."

"So what?" A woman, maybe twenty, strolled over from where she and a few other older girls had been lounging in the shade. "You have more time to see *his* world." She looked at me then smiled at Shoko, though there was no friendliness in it. "Perhaps you can get a *boyfriend* too."

Another girl giggled. "A boyfriend?"

"Young Shoko has one, a handsome one," the woman said, gazing at me with what looked like lust. "You should see them together, on his side only of course." Her eyes narrowed. "Have you lain with him yet, little Shoko?"

Shoko's eyes widened and she stepped forward, her face within inches of the woman.

"Repeat those words."

She sneered down at Shoko. "You would fight me to avoid answering?"

A second later, the woman lay sprawled on the dirt, more shocked than hurt. Shoko's hand moved to the hilt of her katana.

"You speak such disrespect to me again and you will die! No one will question my right to do so!" She turned to the other Gatekeepers her gaze moving from one to the next. "Do any of you wish to speak as she did?"

All the girls held their gaze firmly on the ground. After a long moment, Shoko spun on her heels and strode past me. I hurried to follow.

"You say this is good?" she said.

Behind us, someone said, "She never answered the question."

Shoko went rigid and stopped.

"Ignore her," I said with a gentle nudge. "She's just a jealous bitch. It's not a big—"

She whirled on me.

"Are you stupid?" she said. "The Elders select very few to cross over. Your Okaasan was one. They only officially allowed me after I awakened you. Now it is suddenly okay for everyone to do it?"

"You sound jealous."

"Why would I be?" she said, hands on hips.

"Because you used to be special and now everyone's doing it."

"The whole point of our Special Forces was that they could cross over to fight, not buy handbags and get boyfriends!"

I was about to respond when Sakura came jogging across the

compound toward us.

"Sakura," Shoko said, sounding relieved. "At least you are here."

Sakura nodded. "The Elders wish to see you." Her gaze shifted to me. "Both of you."

"Oh shit," Shoko muttered.

—

Shoko led the way to a large building beyond the west wall of the shrine compound. It was the largest building I'd seen in Izumo, strongly built, with a low sloped roof. The Gatekeepers who stood guard outside were older, in their thirties, and didn't look at all impressed by us.

Sakura walked three steps behind us, her head down. As we passed through the entrance, I noticed she carried a red leather agenda book, definitely modern, and it looked expensive.

"Remember to be respectful," Shoko whispered after we'd bowed low to more Gatekeepers inside the main doors.

The seven Elders sat on pillows behind a wide, low table inside the large, dimly lit room. There were two thin pillows on the smooth wood floor in front, for us I presumed. After the required bows of respect, Chiyoko spoke.

"Report on your forces' activities." Her tone was harsh.

Shoko nodded then turned to Sakura, who remained prostrate on the floor. Shoko took the agenda from her and began to read off the number of attempted intrusions and locations, the number of Evil casualties, shamans killed versus shamans saved. The lack of Gatekeeper casualties didn't go unnoticed.

"You accomplished all this with only six of your special teams?" the Kannushi asked.

"Yes, honorable Elders."

Chiyoko glared at Shoko. "Who is responsible for my Gatekeepers wearing strange clothing?"

I let out a nervous laugh. "It was kind of my idea," I said, though Shoko had been wearing modern clothing long before the Special

Forces started. "They have to fit in when—"

"To *fit in* on the grounds of the Grand Shrine of Izumo?!" she said. "I will not deny your unprecedented victories, but your girls are a bad influence. They are too confident, too arrogant. They no longer fit in with the others."

"In my world, elite soldiers train constantly and see more combat than regular forces," I said. "They can't help but be better."

"Is that so?" Chiyoko said, turning her withering gaze on me. "Now they are not only *special*, they are also *elite*?"

"I'd say the results speak for themselves."

Shoko shushed me. "These girls are all experienced fighters, honorable Chiyoko," she said. "And I chose the best recruits. It is because of that, combined with the new tactics we have given them, that they are successful."

"Then I expect all Gatekeepers will receive this training."

"Yes, of course," Shoko said with her head bowed. "I will see to this immediately."

"You don't need to train them all," I said. "Just create a few more special teams and you can let the rest of the Gatekeepers live normal lives."

"Normal lives?!" Chiyoko's voice was icy. "And what do you suggest I do with hundreds of irrelevant Gatekeepers?"

"A lot of them don't want to be Gatekeepers anyhow," I said.

Just as Chiyoko looked like she might explode, the elderly woman beside her chuckled.

"I see your blood runs strong in his veins."

Chiyoko choked on whatever words were in her mouth and said nothing.

"We will not change anything," the Grand Elder said. "Our ancestors created this army to guard the gateways, and they will continue to protect us as they always have when Evil Ones or others attempt to invade this sanctuary."

"Sure, but our Special Forces can—"

"Engaging the enemy on the other side is still forbidden by our laws," Chiyoko said. "Is that not so, Grand Elder?"

"Indeed you are correct, Chiyoko." He sounded calm, though I could see red seeping into his face. "However, we ordered the young one to use whatever resources she deemed necessary, and her solution was the creation of the Special Forces. As you will no doubt recall, I authorized their actions because of the unprecedented situation in which we find ourselves." He looked at Shoko, then at me. His gaze seemed to probe into the far corners of my mind. I cut off my thoughts and a long moment later he stopped, his expression unreadable. I didn't dare probe back.

"However," he finally said, "finding favor only in those strong enough to cross has created instability. I am told many girls are crossing now, even those who have no reason to."

Shoko nodded, several quick jerks of her head. "Yes Grand Elder. I have only now heard about this."

"And?"

She swallowed. "I too am concerned. This was never our intention when we chose—"

"The consequences of our choices," said an older woman sitting to the left of the Kannushi, "seldom show regard to our intentions."

The Grand Elder tapped his fan on the table. "Your so-called Special Forces may continue to cross and strike against the enemy. This I declare before those gathered here. Your successes against the enemies of Izumo are too great to do otherwise."

A low murmur came from the others at the table.

"However," he said, somewhat louder, "let me remind you that there is nothing *special* about your forces. They serve the same gods and will not belittle or disregard the other Gatekeepers who perform their duties faithfully and honorably."

Shoko bowed low. "Yes, Grand Elder, Elders." Her voice was shaking slightly. "This shall be communicated immediately."

"It shall be *demonstrated* immediately," Chiyoko said.

"Furthermore," the Grand Elder continued, "I hereby decree that the wearing and possession of foreign items in this world is forbidden, from this moment onward."

There was a commotion at the side of the room. A man's brush worked feverously on the scroll in front of him. A moment later, he rolled it up and handed it a young boy who hurried toward the door.

The Grand Elder looked suddenly exhausted. "Your teams will wear the honorable uniform of the Gatekeepers while in this world. If they need foreign clothing to operate on your side, then keep them there."

CHAPTER
30

SHOKO CAME OUT OF HER HOUSE in her Gatekeeper uniform and carrying a large sack. Tomi and Taro followed her.

"Hi Junya," Taro said with a big grin. "The Elders have praised you and big sister!"

I smiled. "Yup, your big sister is a great leader."

"Do you have it all, Shoko?" Tomi said, not sounding impressed. "Nothing left hidden anywhere?"

Shoko turned to look at her mother. "I would never disobey a decree from the mouth of the Grand Elder."

Tomi's hands went to her hips. "You have no trouble disobeying everything else."

Shoko smiled. "The Grand Elder's decree leaves no room for interpretation as other rules do."

Tomi looked at me. "I do not like the things I am hearing in the training halls about you two," she said. "The Elders tasked you to train and work with my daughter. I trust there is nothing else going on."

I shook my head, hoping to hell she couldn't read my thoughts.

"Because your father did not understand our rules either," Tomi said, "and your mother did nothing to stop him from corrupting her. This will *not* happen with Shoko."

"I wouldn't worry," I said with barely a hint of a smile. "Shoko's just as strong as you were."

Tomi's eyes narrowed.

Shoko handed me the sack and thrust her feet into her sandals. Then she slid her wakizashi and katana through her belt and pushed past me without another word.

I walked through the meadow beside her. "Why does Tomi always have to get a dig in against my mom?"

"Regret is a terrible thing."

It was mid-afternoon and cloudy when we arrived behind the dojo. I sensed Okaasan's energy inside the house. Dad wasn't around but someone else was.

"Lin's here," I said. She and Okaasan had gotten closer since Lin and Grandpa got engaged. "Let's stay out here."

We climbed into the deck of the teahouse and I dropped Shoko's sack onto the tatami. "You can keep this stuff out here," I said. "Okaasan won't mind."

"And my apprentices' things as well?"

"Shouldn't be a problem."

"Thank you," she said. "I will have the Special ... our forces find their own hiding places."

We sat facing the garden. Shoko hugged her knees and rested her chin on them. I sat cross-legged beside her, my hand on her back.

"Are meetings with the Elders always that intense?"

She kept her eyes on the garden. "I have never been summoned to one."

"Not even when they tasked you to train me or after we came back from Zion?"

"No."

"Well, at least they see the plan is working." I laughed. "Even

Chiyoko admitted that. Boy, is she tough!"

"Now you see why I fear her."

After that, she was quiet and gave one-word answers when I talked.

"Are you okay?" I finally asked.

"I do not feel good."

"You're sick?"

"No, but in here," she pointed to her stomach, "I feel anxiety building." She finally looked at me. "I was excited about these new tactics, but now I fear we have created something bad."

"It's not bad, Shoko."

"Are your thoughts on Izumo and the shamans, or on the Evil Ones and Bartholomew?"

I hesitated. "I have to keep Bartholomew out of Izumo."

"He *is* out of Izumo." Her gaze returned to the garden.

"He's up to something," I said. "You know he plans to use me to get in."

"You only assume that."

"Does it matter? This is a good plan. We're keeping out the Evil Ones and saving Gatekeeper's lives *and* the lives of the shamans."

When she didn't reply, I tickled her. She squirmed and giggled, then twisted my wrist into a gentle lock.

I didn't try to escape. "Come on, we should be celebrating!"

She let go of my wrist. "I do not feel that way," she said. "Girls are crossing over and stealing. And that woman spoke to me with such disrespect. She *knows* we are being intimate!" She shook her head. "No, this is not good at all."

"Well I didn't think they'd start shoplifting, but focus on the success, not the failures. Those girls are just jealous."

"You do not understand at all."

"The only thing I don't understand is you! The Elders are happy, more or less, so why aren't you?"

She let out a frustrated grunt. "Do you not realize how incredible your world is?" She ran her fingers through her hair. "You have shiny cars and fast trains, things that fly, tall glass buildings, sweets and soda, and hot chocolate. Your houses are like palaces, grander than the shrine of Izumo, and your women dress like gods. What person could resist this? And now girls are standing around Izumo in jeans and miniskirts, reading manga and talking back to their superiors. They have forgotten their purpose, their duty. How can you not see how wrong this is?"

"Well, when you say it like that ..."

"And you are right," she said, as if she didn't hear me. "I *am* jealous that other girls are crossing over." She squeezed her eyes shut. "I was arrogant. I crossed over and wore modern clothes. I stole Edward's journal. I was bad, but no one ever punished me. The Elders let me come back here and work with you. I became famous and I loved it, even if I nearly died in Zion. Now I have a boyfriend and we have sex."

I grinned. "Now that's definitely not a bad thing."

"But it is forbidden! It is a decree and why do I break it? Because I *want* to, and conveniently, I do not need to worry about getting pregnant."

"You know that's the only reason they have that rule."

"Should I start passing out condoms in Izumo then?" she said, her frustration growing. "It is still a rule, written to protect me! Should I disregard it when it becomes inconvenient?"

"I ... I don't know," I said, beginning to feel bad. Nothing I said was helping.

She pointed at me. "You and I have changed the rules but left nothing to replace them except chaos!"

"Whoa, whoa Shoko," I said, pulling her toward me. "You're kind of freaking out here."

At first she resisted, but she finally relaxed and let me hold her. When she spoke, her voice was softer.

"I just ... I am agitated by everything that happened today. Besides Chiyoko, the Elders support us, but they do not know everything." She lightly banged her head against my chest. "The attitude of those girls is not good. It scares me."

I stroked her hair. "I think it's the start of something big, something good. Change is always hard at first. They'll adjust."

She broke from my embrace. "I am so frustrated by all this!" Then she leaned over and gave me a long, hard kiss. "I want to have sex."

Whoa, what? "Right here, right now?"

"Do you have a condom?"

I pulled one out of my wallet.

"Pull your jeans down."

I did as she said and lay back on the tatami mats. Even with her abruptness, I had no problem getting ready for her.

She hiked up her uniform and mounted me. She moved slowly at first, her eyes closed, face skyward, lost in her own place. I stared up at her and felt suddenly alone. We weren't doing this together as we always had. She'd left me behind.

Then she sped up, her eyes squeezed shut, her nails digging into my chest. It wasn't long before I couldn't take it anymore.

Shoko kept going for another couple of minutes before she let out a deep sigh and lay down against my chest. When I wrapped my arms around her, she started to cry.

"Shoko, it's okay," I whispered into her hair. "Everything will work out, you'll see."

After a while, her sobbing stopped and she lifted off me. We were both silent. She was in some other place and I was afraid of where she was. Then she crawled across the tatami, back to where she'd been sitting before, hugging her knees.

"Um," I said after a while. "That was different."

"You are not satisfied?"

"Sure, it was just … different."

"Change is good, remember?" Then she tilted her head. "Sakura is calling us."

I hadn't heard a thing.

CHAPTER
31

SAKURA WAS BLUSHING WHEN WE TRAVELED to her. With her gift, she could look across anytime she liked, and I suddenly wondered if Shoko and I had really been alone in the dojo.

"Excuse my interruption, Shoko, Junya," Sakura said, eyes still downcast. "But we cannot locate some of the teams. They are unaware of the new decree and must be informed."

Shoko groaned. "Please do not tell me they went shopping."

Sakura glanced at me. "They went on patrol this morning and have not returned."

"And what of the regular Gatekeepers?" Shoko paused. "I mean, the *other* Gatekeepers."

Sakura shook her head. "They came back with the Controllers. They know nothing."

Yukie, Kyoko, and Rina ran up. "We just heard teams are missing," Kyoko said, sounding scared.

Shoko gave a curt nod. "We will go see the Master Controller to learn their last location."

"I told her to expect your arrival," Sakura said. "She awaits you."

We found the Master Controller inside her bunker, with several maps laid out on the large table.

"The last gateway to open was here." She tapped her finger on the thin board.

"We heard the Controller returned," Shoko said.

"Yes, she is here." The Master called to her.

A woman of about forty came into the room, her graying hair tied back in a single braid.

"The special team came and looked across," Mikuni told us. "There were Evil Ones waiting, so they crossed to attack. They have not come back, nor did anything come through, so we left."

"You did not wait for them to return?"

Mikuni looked suddenly angry. "Your *special* teams often lack the courtesy to cross back and report in," she said. "Then I see them in the village, showing off their latest foreign items!"

Shoko looked at me. "This is all going wrong."

"Let's get going," I said. "I have a bad feeling about this."

Nothing looked out of place at the gateway when we arrived, still on Shoko's side.

"Are you sure this is the right place?"

"Sakura, look across," Shoko said.

Sakura knelt and put her left hand on the ground. A moment later, she gasped.

"They are all dead!"

"The Evil Ones?"

"No …" A sob choked Sakura's words. "Our Gatekeepers."

"What?" I couldn't get a breath in.

Shoko drew her katana. "Cross!"

"Wait!" I yelled as Shoko and her apprentices dropped to the ground. They all looked up at me, expectant. "What if whatever killed them is still there?"

"Sakura!" Shoko shouted. "See if there is further danger!"

Sakura knelt once more. Her expression turned vacant, then twisted in anger. Her eyes snapped open.

"Men," she whispered. "They are far away but waiting, with long guns."

"Waiting for what?" Rina asked.

I looked at Shoko. "Probably for more Gatekeepers to cross."

"Show me," Shoko said.

"I'm coming too." I knelt beside them. For once, I felt helpless. They could see and I couldn't.

Shoko looked up at her other apprentices. "Please call for reinforcements, and a Miko." Then her gaze dropped. "And the undertakers."

We held Sakura's hands, and again the process was weird. It wasn't like we traveled, but a moment later we stood together on the sand, holding hands like schoolkids. It was as if we were ghosts.

I looked down.

The four Gatekeepers lay where they'd fallen, covered in dried blood. They'd been dead for a while. Not far away, two piles of black dust, already scattering in the breeze, were all that remained of the Evil Ones. There were no guns, though. Someone else had shot them.

"Where are the men you spoke of?" Shoko's voice was flat, devoid of emotion.

Sakura nodded to a distant mesa, the rock face turned ruddy orange in the afternoon sunlight.

A moment later, we were standing beside a soldier lying prone on the sand, concealed by a desert-colored camouflage net. He had a damn-scary-looking rifle mounted on a bipod, with a huge sight on top, pointed toward where the dead girls lay. Not far away was another man with a similar setup.

I jumped on him, furious, but he vanished and I found myself on the ground with about a dozen Gatekeepers staring down at me while I pounded the grass with my fists.

"You let go of Sakura's hand," Shoko said to me. "And you

cannot harm an image of a man."

I rolled to my knees and glared at her. "Ya think?"

"Young man, your energy is unpleasant," an older Miko said. "Stop now!"

I took a deep breath. "Let's travel to those trees in the wash below the mesa. We'll assess from there and go kill those assholes."

"Are they Evil Ones?"

Were they? "No, I didn't feel anything"

Shoko regarded me. "Then you will be killing *men*, not Evil Ones."

"I don't care!"

Shoko and I joined hands and bent to touch Mother Earth, and after a frustratingly long wait in the churning darkness, we materialized under a group of scraggy mesquite trees. The heat hit us like an oven door flung open and we gasped as hot air seared our lungs.

A second later, we both dove onto the hot sand as a deafening thumping sound and a powerful wind hit us. I rolled onto my back, threw an arm over my eyes, and squinted toward the sky. The unmistakable shape of a Blackhawk helicopter, painted a desert tan, passed over us and disappeared beyond the edge of the mesa.

"What is that thing?!" Shoko screamed.

The noise and wind diminished, though we could still hear the Blackhawk. It sounded like it was powering down, its loud whine lowering by octaves every second.

I started to run up the gully, with only sorry-looking dried-out bushes for cover, to the bottom of the mesa where the wall went almost straight up. I looked back. Shoko was still where I'd left her, looking disoriented. I was about to go back for her when I heard the helicopter power back up.

"Shit!" I slapped my hand against the mesa's red wall, my eyes on the lip far above me, and traveled.

I was in the open. There was no cover on the bare rock. Sand blasted me, getting into my eyes, mouth, and nose, but I could make out the Blackhawk rising into the air, its nose pointed away from me. It swung back out over the desert in a wide arc that took it over the four bodies, then continued on its course.

Shoko was beside me a moment later, using her hand to block the sun as the helicopter shrunk into the distance. "I would like to say how cool that machine is, but ..."

I looked around, trying to remember where we'd seen the men. When I found the spot, I squatted to get a better look. I could still see indentations of elbows, of boot toes dug into the sand, and two small holes where the bipod had rested. There were no spent cartridges, no other sign that anyone had ever been here and there was definitely no residual energy of an Evil One.

"The undertakers wish to cross over," Shoko said, startling me. "I told them it is safe now."

I looked up at her. "You're really getting good at that."

She smiled at me, but it faded quickly as she lowered her head.

A moment later, the earth's energy flexed and several people appeared not far from the bodies. One was a Miko.

We traveled down to meet them.

A cloud of flies had already settled on the bodies. It smelled horrible and I wanted to feel sick, to throw up as Mack had in Scotland, but all I felt was anger, a seething fury so powerful I struggled to contain it.

"Their shots were true." Shoko pointed to the hole in the forehead of one girl. I couldn't even remember her name. I saw no other bullet holes, no injuries. The other girls were the same: one shot each.

I looked back toward the mesa, maybe six hundred yards away. Was that an easy shot for a sniper? I'd have to ask Jason.

"What are you thinking, Junya?"

"Why would men kill them? Those were soldiers, active duty." I was pretty sure you couldn't rent a Blackhawk.

Shoko followed my gaze to the top of the bluff. "More importantly, how did these soldiers know our Gatekeepers would be here?"

I pointed to the black dust, or what was left of it.

"They must've been working with the Evil Ones." An image of Sergeant Jackson entered my mind, and I began to wonder.

———

By the time we returned to Izumo, a large group had gathered on the shrine grounds. A few Elders stood at the front. Gatekeepers and others who were probably family members stood behind. These were the first deaths in weeks.

As the undertakers arrived with the dead girls, the Kannushi approached us.

"They are not invincible, I see." There was no judgment in his words.

"They were ambushed," I said through gritted teeth. "They didn't have a chance."

"It was inevitable," Chiyoko said, striding toward us. "Our girls are without their senses over there. It is unnatural."

"They were killed by men," I said. "Not Evil Ones."

That caused a stir.

"How did these men know the Gatekeepers would be there?"

"The Evil Ones know the times and locations as well as we do," the Kannushi said. "It seems they have shared that knowledge."

A burst of energy shook the air and a Special Forces team materialized in the compound, discernible even in their Gatekeeper uniforms by the silver bracelets on their wrists. They had six bodies with them: A Controller, a young Gatekeeper, and four girls wearing Western clothing—another Special Forces team.

"Oh no, no, no …"

The women's heads stayed bowed as we approached. They looked dirty and exhausted, their clothes splattered with red blood.

Shoko knelt in front of them. "What happened?"

A girl named Mizuki cleared her throat.

"When the Controller opened the gateway, a beast was waiting and leaped through," Mizuki said. "Her Gatekeeper escort fought it and called for help. This team," she indicated the dead girls on the ground, "was the closest when the call came in. The Gatekeeper escort had defeated the beast by the time they arrived, but not before it killed the Controller and one escort Gatekeeper." Mizuki pointed toward the younger Gatekeeper in a green uniform, then nodded toward the other four bodies. "This team then crossed over, as there were two more Evil Ones waiting."

"And?" Shoko asked gently.

"My team arrived moments later," Mizuki said. "When we looked across, there were five men with guns dressed in tan clothing, wearing many things on their bodies." She moved her hands to indicate their chests and waists. "And they killed these honorable Gatekeepers with guns."

Mizuki lowered her head and started to sob.

Shoko gently pulled back a blanket. It was Mekie, the girl who'd shot the arrow through the orange in the warehouse. Her clothes— a brand name T-shirt under a short jean jacket—were soaked in blood. There were six ragged holes in her torso. Hana, the Gatekeeper who'd helped me in Córdoba, was also dead.

The anger swelled within me, then something snapped. "This is bullshit!"

Shoko spun toward me. "Stop!" she whispered. "Your energy is filled with darkness."

"Tell me where they are!"

The Gatekeeper looked up at me. "They lie under the desert sun. All of them beheaded and left for the vultures!"

I sucked in a deep breath, felt some of the anger drain out of me. "Good," I whispered.

Shoko grabbed Sakura's arm. "Call our forces." She was closer to panic than I'd ever seen her. "No more teams must cross over!"

The Kannushi squatted beside a Controller who knelt beside her fallen comrade. "How many other gateways open today?" he asked her quietly.

The Controller looked up, tear tracks on her dusty face.

"None that we are required to open," she said. "However, there are many that open automatically."

The Kannushi nodded, then glanced toward the top of the shrine. He looked uneasy.

"There is something amiss," he said.

My gaze followed his. He was right: the energy flowing from the shrine felt different. The gods were restless.

"Chiyoko," the Kannushi said. "Are we prepared for more attacks?"

"We already have patrols at each gateway, as always," she said. "We are prepared."

Shoko heaved a heavy sigh. "Thank the gods," she whispered, mostly to herself, I think. "I cannot take much more of this."

I was about to reply when bells rang out and a horn started wailing like an air-raid siren.

The Kannushi spun toward the shrine.

Evil Ones have breached the Gates! Beasts are attacking villages. Many are dying.

"Multiple gateways are breached!" Chiyoko yelled.

"Where?!" someone yelled.

"Everywhere!"

CHAPTER
32

CHIYOKO HUDDLED WITH HER SIX COMMANDERS. More Gatekeepers arrived every second, running in from all directions, some in uniforms, most not, but all armed. As they assembled into groups, their commanders shouted orders, dividing their groups into sections, calling out destinations.

Rina ran toward us, weaving her way between the other Gatekeepers. She yelled something I couldn't hear, and a second later Shoko spun toward me.

"We are ordered to the Bay!" She checked her weapons.

"What Bay?" I asked as Rina tossed me a bokuto.

"Those who fed us the first time you crossed."

A growing chorus of voices cut her off. At first there was only loud shouting, then I heard it.

"We cannot travel!"

My heart dropped.

More yelling, more screaming—the cry was going up everywhere. Dozens of Gatekeepers knelt on the ground, staring blankly at each other, their disbelief quickly changing to panic.

The Kannushi fell to his knees at the base of the staircase.

"Oh gods of Izumo, creators of Japan and all things under heaven!" he cried. "Please hear me! Your servants need your energy!"

I strained to listen, even sent out some of my own energy, but there was no response. The gods were silent.

"What if we all hold hands?" Yukie said. "Maybe that will help."

A group nearby heard her. They dropped to the ground and slammed their joined hands into the earth. For a long moment, nothing happened. Then they slowly faded until they were gone.

A command went out to all the Gatekeepers. Shoko grabbed my hand and her apprentices', and several agonizing moments later we arrived outside the village by the Bay, greeted by screams of terror and agony.

We didn't get far before we came across a body. An elderly man, already beginning to rot from the poisonous jaws that had severed his torso.

I looked around, trying to take it all in. "How'd it get in here?"

"That does not matter right now!" Shoko bolted past me, headed for the village.

I followed and saw six Gatekeepers, three of them down and one dead. There were more bodies here, some of them very small.

Shoko skidded to a stop. "Oh gods!"

I weaved around her, running straight for two Gatekeepers fending off an Evil One. It moved slowly, bleeding heavily from several deep wounds. The girls were bleeding too, but not from bites. Not yet, anyway.

"Joining center!" I yelled as I dove between them, coming face to face with the biggest lizard I'd ever seen.

It lunged and knock down the Gatekeeper beside me. She screamed as claws ripped into her body. I slammed my bokuto into its head. Black blood spewed out, but the Evil Ones kept coming, driving me backward while I hit it again and again.

"Die, you stinking son of Bartholomew!" I hauled in a deep

breath, forced out my energy, and swung the bokuto with all my might into its head. The bokuto snapped and the beast let out a horrible scream, then collapsed to the ground, disappearing into a smoky cloud of ash.

I twisted around, blasting out energy, and looked for my next target.

"We need a Miko!" I yelled. Off to my left, Kyoko and Rina had a small beast down and dying. "A lot of them!"

"There are none available!" Shoko shouted from where she gutted a lizard.

More cries came from behind a large hut. A child. I grabbed the katana from the injured Gatekeeper near me—she didn't look like she needed it anymore. When I rounded the corner of the hut, I found another lizard with its back to me, tail swishing back and forth like a cat.

A small boy darted left, trying to escape, but the lizard cut him off. It made a strange sound. Laughing, maybe?

I ran forward, one foot on its tail, the other on its back. My overhead strike slammed the lizard's jaws shut, but the katana barely cut it. The lizard thrashed and twisted, throwing me off. I managed to stay upright and slashed at it again. Nothing. These suckers had tough skin.

The lizard let out horrible roar as a spear plunged deep into its side. As it spun toward the new threat, it swatted me off my feet with a swing of its tail.

"Leave my son alone!" It was the village chief. He tugged on the spear, desperate to pull it out and stab the beast again.

I flipped my blade and again with an exhale of energy, slammed the katana's blunt edge into the lizard's head. With an ugly crunch, its skull cracked open. Shoko's katana sliced deep into its throat.

We all stood back, gasping for breath. A moment later, nothing remained but a pile of black dust and pools of black blood.

The chief grabbed his son and squeezed him into a hug. Then he looked over the boy's shoulder.

"How did this happen?!"

I struggled to get a breath in. "I don't know."

"Are there more?!"

Shoko shook her head. "Not here."

"Where?" I said, turning toward her. She was a mess of dirt, black blood, and sweat.

She squinted, as if hearing a message.

"Apprentices, we must go!"

—

The next place was worse. We were the first to arrive. More than a dozen adults lay sprawled on the ground of a small desert town, their bodies torn apart. A group of kids screamed in terror as they huddled against an adobe wall, cornered by three lizards.

"No!" I screamed. My rage—and my energy—blasted out of me with such force I fell backward.

The wall behind the kids exploded, sending them flying backward and away from the lizards. Shoko dropped to her knees. Her katana skidded away as she clutched at her head.

With an ungodly roar, I sprinted toward the lizards and started beating on them with the katana. They weren't frozen, not even slowed, but it didn't matter. I slashed eyes, arteries, and tendons, and the first two turned to dust.

"Junya! I need my katana!"

Shoko was on her butt, backpedaling and unarmed, a lizard hovering over her. I dove between them as it lunged toward her, and its jaws closed on my leg.

I screamed in agony as its teeth sank deep into my muscle. Shoko squirmed under me as the lizard dragged me backward, shaking me like a rag doll, its teeth buried to the bone.

Poison pumped into me, scorching through my veins like fire. Half-blind from the pain, I saw only the beast's yellow silted eyes staring into mine. I reached toward it, my hands curled like talons. Then everything went black.

—

The lizard shook me, bringing pain like a thousand razors.

"Junya! Junya! Wake up, please!"

I pried open an eye. It wasn't the lizard. It was Shoko and she looked terrified. In the background came screams, an endless wail of fear and pain. I squeezed my fists and energy surged through my body and into my leg. The pain eased, and I struggled onto an elbow. We were still in the desert town. Children knelt beside their parents' bodies while a man who looked like a shaman worked on the survivors.

More Gatekeepers had arrived while I was out, some still in their leisure kimonos. A few sat with the kids while others searched the houses for any remaining lizards.

Shoko looked ashen and smelled of vomit. She stared at me with pure horror.

"Where is the lizard?" I said.

"You ... you ripped its throat out," Shoko whispered. "You were like ... the devil himself."

I looked at my hands. Thick black blood and little slimy pieces of something still clung to my fingers.

I threw up.

—

By the time we returned to the shrine compound at Izumo, I felt more dead than alive—until I saw all the bodies.

Dozens of dead Gatekeepers lay on bamboo stretchers. Red blankets had been thrown over each of them, but their faces were uncovered. Some were as young as thirteen. Nearby, a few Miko worked on the injured, helped by several of our Special Forces and Nene. Those who'd been bitten lay off to one side with family gathered around them. Everyone knew they had no chance.

I glanced at Shoko. She had her eyes squeezed shut, her teeth clamped tight, her small hands balled into fists.

"Shoko!" someone called.

"Tomi!" Shoko rushed over to her mother. "What happened?"

Tomi looked flustered. "There was no one guarding the gateways. They are gone!"

Shoko's mouth dropped open. "Gone?"

"Yes, gone!" It was Chiyoko.

I struggled to get closer to them.

"The Gatekeepers ... they were taken?" Shoko said.

Chiyoko glared at Shoko, her anger sharp enough to cut. Then she looked at me, first at my face, then down at my leg. Her face went white.

"You—"

Feeling energy and anger, I turned. It was the Grand Elder.

"More than thirty Evil Ones crossed over today!" he shouted at no one in particular. "Thirty!" The veins in his neck looked ready to burst. "They wandered across and no one stood in their way!" He stopped in front of Chiyoko. "Where were your Gatekeepers?!"

Chiyoko's mouth opened then snapped shut again as she struggled for control. "They deserted their posts," she said. "They traveled away and are no longer in this world."

The Kannushi swept out his arm, taking in rows of bodies. "Grand Elder," he said. "So many Gatekeepers are dead! Never before—"

"Civilians died too!" the Grand Elder yelled in response. "Whole villages! Such a massacre has never occurred here!"

I looked up at the shrine and listened. I felt anxiety, a troubled energy that floated out from the shrine like dark mist.

"Elders," Shoko said, bowing low. "I will regroup our teams. We will—"

"It is over," the Kannushi said. "There is nothing left to do but bury the dead." Then, like Chiyoko, he looked at my leg. He shook his head slowly as his anger rose.

"Why do you live," he said, sounding disgusted, "while they must die?"

I looked past him at the dead and dying. "I don't know …"

A great booming sound ripped through the air, making my insides shudder. The Grand Elder slammed his staff into the fourth step of the Grand Staircase a dozen more times.

"As of this moment, no one crosses over!" He looked up toward the shrine. "In the name of all the gods of Izumo, no one shall disobey this command!"

A long, dense silence fell, not broken by the call of a bird or even the breeze.

Chiyoko broke it. She pointed a shaking finger at Shoko.

"This is your fault!" She spun and pointed to the dead Gatekeepers. "They have paid for your arrogance with their lives!"

"No …" Shoko sunk to her hands and knees.

I walked up beside Shoko, instantly angry. "No! They're dead because *your* goddamn Gatekeepers abandoned their posts!" I yelled at her. "That's got nothing to do with Shoko!"

Chiyoko turned toward me. "Did you not assure the Elders that *regular* Gatekeepers were no longer needed?" Her voice dripped with venom. "That girls could go and live *normal lives*? Do you think they did not hear this?"

I stood there seething, my fist clenched, but she was right. I had said that, and I'd believed it.

"I have stood firm against the other Elders in my opposition to this new force!" Chiyoko yelled. "Because if one is not *special*, the only other option is second rate! You let them bring back foreign ways and objects, and they created envy and rivalry where none had ever existed!" She pointed at Shoko, who still had her face pressed in the dirt. "And where were you while all this was happening?"

"Where was *she*?!" I yelled at Chiyoko. "Where the hell were *you*?! You *opposed* it, then did what? You sat back and watched it happen? Who commands the Gatekeepers, Shoko or you?!"

Chiyoko's chest heaved. She looked like she might hit me and believe me, I was ready.

The Grand Elder approached us. "You must also blame me,

Chiyoko," he said. "I sanctioned this."

"I too am responsible," said the Kannushi. "I gave the order."

Shoko jerked upright. "No!" Her voice was surprisingly strong. "I will not let you carry this disgrace. It is mine to bear alone!"

The Grand Elder glanced at Chiyoko, then looked down at Shoko with deep concern etched into his already deep wrinkles.

"No, not alone." Chiyoko cleared her throat, the anger draining out of her. "I am the commander. I will accept full responsibility." She closed her eyes for a long moment before continuing. "However, you will be held accountable for your part in this." She looked down at Shoko, and when she spoke, she didn't sound angry anymore, just exhausted, and somewhat sad. "You are relieved of your duties. Now go."

Shoko backed away, still on her knees, her face still lowered. I stepped toward her, but a firm hand on my arm stopped me.

"Return to your world and stay there," the Grand Elder said. When I hesitated, he thumped his staff against the ground. "It is not a request. Go!"

Then he and the Kannushi walked away, leaving me alone with Chiyoko. Behind us, someone shouted for more bandages.

I squatted to travel away.

"Junya, wait." It was Chiyoko.

I glared up at her. "What, *grandma*?"

She hesitated. "I still believe my Gatekeepers abandoned their posts because of your Special Forces," she said quietly. "But why have they not returned? They would be back by now if they could."

"Meaning?"

"Meaning the Evil Leader planned this well."

I rolled my eyes. "Ya think?"

She turned to look toward the bodies. "The Kannushi is wrong. This is not over until we know where the missing Gatekeepers are. There may be far more bodies to bury than these."

"They're your Gatekeepers, so find them."

She met my gaze. "I cannot," she said quietly. "But you can. On your side, or somewhere else."

"Somewhere like Zion, you mean? Because I'm evil?"

"Stop your childish self-pity!" She lifted her chin and regained her composure. "This is bigger than you, or any of us! I do not care if you are truly Junya *the pure* or the darkest of evil, only you can find my Gatekeepers and bring them home." She stared at me for a long moment then said, "You are their only hope."

I looked into her eyes. They were identical to Okaasan's, and mine.

"If you cannot bring yourself to do it for me, or even these wayward girls, then do it for Shoko."

"Like you care about Shoko."

She released a deep sigh. "I know Shoko far better than she or you could ever imagine," she said. "I have observed her for years, and unless those girls come back alive, I fear she will destroy herself and her future."

CHAPTER

33

I ARRIVED IN OUR ZEN GARDEN, tired and covered in blood, and sat down on the bench, my head in my hands. I knew Chiyoko was right, about Shoko at least. She'd take the blame for the dead *and* the missing, if I let her. But how could I find the girls? I didn't even know how many were missing, let alone where they might be.

But I knew someone who might.

I still had Mr. Müller's thin metal business card. He answered on the third ring.

"Your little war is turning into quite the bloodbath."

"And we won," I said through clenched teeth. "We killed every goddamn lizard you sent."

"And how many of yours did they get first? Several dozen?"

"Bartholomew will never get in, ever!"

Mr. Müller laughed. "He already did."

"Not unless he was disguised as a dead lizard."

"Well, you'd know better than me, I'm sure," he said. "Of course, my employer would have happily overrun Izumo, but having it destroyed from within is so much more satisfying."

Something dropped into the pit of my stomach. "What do you mean?"

"Gatekeepers turning on one another, the rise of ego and envy, the Elders losing control, loyal warriors turning their backs on thousands of years of tradition." He made a sound that could've been a chuckle. "Actually, I think you might have done more damage than he ever could have."

I closed my eyes. He was just trying to get under my skin. "Where are the missing Gatekeepers? Do you have them?"

"*I* do not have them," he said. "I'm a businessman. I have nothing to do with the more ... *hands-on* aspects of my employer's concerns."

"Gee, you mean you actually have some morals?" I said. "Tell me, where do you draw the line? You won't kidnap someone but you'll gun them down in the desert?"

He took a moment to reply. "Killing in battle is one thing," he said. "This situation is somewhat different."

I clenched my fists. "They better not be dead!"

"Not yet. My employer is currently occupied with business, but once he has a moment, he'll take your little Gatekeepers from their concrete box and bring them back to Zion. And I'm afraid he won't tolerate any heroic rescues this time."

My anger began to build. "Your *employer* is a psycho pedophile creep."

"Then perhaps you shouldn't have dropped them in our laps," he said with a touch of annoyance. "Two of them strolled into the soba-noodle restaurant where my men were eating lunch. Wearing their Gatekeeper uniforms! Who could pass up such an opportunity?"

"I want them back!"

"That is out of my hands, I'm afraid."

I focused all my energy into the phone. "Tell me where they are!"

There was a loud crackle and I pulled the phone away from my ear. Had I fried it? It looked okay—no smoke. I put it back to my ear in time to hear Mr. Müller's reply.

"You honestly believe I could tell you, even if I wanted to?" There was a long pause. "However, this whole affair is very distressing." His tone surprised me. He didn't sound upset, exactly, but he did sound worried.

"Don't you need a heart to feel distressed?"

"Shall I hang up now?"

That got my attention. "No, please don't …"

"Good. Now, is it safe to assume I am your only lead in this search?"

I sighed. He had me and we both knew it. "Yes."

"And you want to save the girls and be a hero once again?"

"I just want them back, alive and well."

"How noble." He chuckled. "Then perhaps we can come to an understanding."

"Like what?"

His voice dropped, so low I had the cram the phone against my ear to hear him.

"Do you realize my employer was actually worried?" he said. "You and those Gatekeepers, working on this side. Your ideas are unprecedented."

"He was worried?"

"And that is no small thing, believe me," he said. "His counterattacks were rushed. He had to call in favors. Even his considerable power can't explain away the death of active-duty US soldiers on American soil. People are talking." He cleared his throat. "You are already a powerful young man, one who is not afraid to pursue unorthodox ideas." He paused. "Such as confiscating dead people's offshore accounts."

My head drooped. "You gotta be kidding me …"

"It was an immature, but ultimately practical move. I respect that type of thinking."

"What's the 'understanding', or do you really mean that now I *owe* you?"

He cleared his throat again. "I won't think of it as a debt. All I ask is that when you reach a position of power, you remember this conversation. I am not your enemy and perhaps one day, I can be of service to you."

"Fine," I said. "Now are you going to tell me where they are?"

"I cannot *tell you*," he said. "But I can repeat what you obviously missed earlier."

"What?"

"I said the girls 'walked into a soba-noodle restaurant.'" he said, speaking slowly. "And I said, 'concrete box.' Now it's time for you to prove how resourceful you are."

The line went dead.

I threw the phone on the ground. Soba-noodle restaurant? There were noodle shops all over Japan, all over the goddamn world!

And what the hell did he mean by a concrete box?

—

Dad and Okaasan came running into the living room from different directions when I slammed the glass door so hard the entire wall shook. I stood there in my dirty boots on the spotless floor and glared at them. I could only imagine what Dad was thinking. This was the second time he'd seen me covered in black blood.

He stared at me for a long moment, then turned to Okaasan. "Are you going to try and keep this a secret too?"

Okaasan closed her eyes.

"No," she finally said. "I've pretty much had it with all the lies."

I looked at her, startled.

"Were you bitten again?" she asked, coming toward me. The panic she'd had last time wasn't there.

I looked down at my leg. The teeth holes in my torn jeans were obvious. "Yeah, but ..."

When Okaasan ripped my pant leg, she and Dad gasped, and so did I, but for a different reason. The marks from the teeth were still there, but they were already closed. They might not even leave a scar.

"They used the potion on you?" Okaasan said.

"No … I just used my energy to stop the pain." I looked at her. "Do you think I did that?"

She scratched her earlobe. "I don't think we've even begun to understand your energy."

"He … his energy can heal a …?" Dad looked closer. "What the hell bit you, a shark?"

"Tell me what happened," Okaasan said.

I looked over her shoulder at my dad. He wanted truth—we all did—and I didn't have time for bullshit.

"There was a massacre," I said. "Dozens of civilians and Gatekeepers are dead. Maybe even hundreds."

Okaasan stared at me in utter disbelief. "How?"

I told her while she cleaned the blood off my leg. What had happened to the Special Forces, the villagers, and the Gatekeepers, and what Chiyoko had said to Shoko. I finished with the missing girls.

To my surprise, the last part shocked her the most.

"They deserted?"

I heaved a heavy sigh. "I don't want to believe it was because they felt useless," I said. "Maybe they were lured away."

She made a face. "What could lure a Gatekeeper away from her duties?"

I was down to my boxer shorts by now, my ruined jeans in a pile beside me. I remembered what Shoko had said.

"Look around," I said, indicating our house. "Weren't you blown away the first time you saw all this? For god's sake, you still thank the washing machine every time you use it!"

She looked at the stainless-steel scissors in her hand. "I suppose, if they were given the chance."

"There's a lot of jealously and rivalry now," I said, "with girls crossing over and bringing back new stuff."

"Jealousy?" Okaasan looked surprised. "That isn't something that exists there."

"Well, it does now."

My dad, who'd stayed remarkably quiet the entire time, cleared his throat. "Where do you think the girls are?"

"How the hell should I know?"

"If they haven't returned, it's because they can't," Okaasan said.

I nodded. "That's what your mom said."

She smiled sadly at that. "When they crossed over before, do you know where they usually went?"

I thought about that. "Everything I'd seen, the clothes and books and stuff, were all Japanese. They probably got them from the shops in Izumo City."

"Okay, so they like to stay close to home, where the countryside looks familiar," Okaasan said. "I was like that too."

"That narrows things down," Dad said.

Okaasan looked up at him. "It's still a huge area."

I thought about Mr. Müller's hint. "Where's the best place for soba noodles in Japan?"

"Izumo, of course," Dad said. "Besides the Grand Shrine, soba is what they're famous for."

I nodded slowly. "Then they're in Izumo City somewhere."

"You know that for sure?" Okaasan asked me.

"It makes sense," I said, rerunning my conversation with Mr. Müller. "And he said something about them being in a concrete box." I looked up at dad. "So, some kind of concrete building."

"Okay, that's something," Okaasan said. "But we'll need to search the whole town, which won't be easy."

"Misako," Dad said. "Get your family to help."

Okaasan's expression sagged. "My ... my family?"

He scowled at her. "Give me a break. Call the Satos. If anyone can do this, they can."

"Dad's right," I said. "Do it."

When Okaasan still hesitated, he asked, "Is Lin on good terms with her family? Better than you, I mean?"

She nodded slowly. "Lin's blood, I'm adopted. I'll ask her to call."

Dad nodded. "They can help until we get there."

"*We?*"

"No more secrets, Misako."

Okaasan stood up. "You will *not* be going with us. You can't … not the way we're getting there."

He gave her a sad smile. "And how is it you get around, magic powder?"

Okaasan laid her hand on his chest. "There are some things you can never know, Robert," she said. "Leave it alone and our life goes on as usual."

He pulled back. "Our life hasn't been usual in a damn long time." He pointed at her. "You and I are like strangers. After all these years, why won't you trust me?"

Okaasan glanced at me. I knew she was thinking about her assignment, the one to marry Dad.

"It's time, Mom," I said. "Life will be way easier if he knows."

She looked back at him. "We'll talk about this once we get the girls back, okay?"

"You'll tell me everything?"

She nodded. "I will tell you the truth," she said. "And it will either make us stronger … or destroy us."

"Well at least we'll have a fifty-fifty chance."

—

When I came out of my room a few minutes later, Dad had gone to his shop. His energy was really strong and negative. Okaasan was in the living room getting her stuff ready.

I studied her face. "Are you okay?"

"It'll be weird seeing my family, but there's no one better for this sort of thing."

"I'm talking about Dad."

She looked up, expressionless. "It's fine."

"No, it's not. I know how worried you were about this."

"And like I said, I'm tired of living this lie. It's been a burden ever since you found out. Now it's become impossible."

"And what if it doesn't go well?"

"Then that's our destiny." She shrugged. "What else can I do? I've put a wall between us, and every day the wall gets thicker."

"He knows way more than he lets on," I said. "Maybe it won't be so hard."

"The more he knows, the more he knows how much I've lied to him."

I rolled my eyes. "Then he could've asked, right? He suspected the Satos were ninja, but he never brought it up."

She waved a hand at me. "Arguing won't solve this," she said. "I talked to Lin. We're meeting her in your grandpa's backyard, near Mr. Sugimoto's cottage. Can you get us there?"

I nodded. I could already see it in my mind. "Do you think your family will help us?"

"We're going to meet with them, but I'm sure they will."

"I hear they don't work for free."

"Then you can use the sergeant's money to pay them."

I looked at the ceiling and shook my head, exasperated. "Does *everybody* know about that?"

She straightened up. "Pretty much," she said. "Now let's go."

CHAPTER
34

"MY BROTHER SAID TO MEET AT the ramen shop," Lin said as Okaasan and I walked out from behind the garden shed beside Mr. Sugimoto's cottage. "He already has people out scouting possible places."

Okaasan smiled. "The little ramen shop near the moat?"

Lin nodded. "Been a while, huh?"

"Yeah …"

Lin blew out her breath. "So ah, we're really doing this *traveling* thing?"

I glanced at Okaasan.

"We have to," she said. "There's no time to waste."

Lin nodded. "Junya, your mom told me you'd need a visual." She opened her tablet. "This is a satellite view of the shop."

"Zoom in, please."

She did. "And here's the street view. Does that help?"

I closed my eyes and concentrated. No energy, I reminded myself. Just listen.

A moment later, things began to take shape, but it never got clear, not like usual. Something was wrong.

I opened my eyes. "Can I see that again?"

I tried again. This time I put a bit of energy into it, and an image began to appear.

"Junya?"

"Be quiet ... please." Now the image was clearer than usual, almost like when Sakura took me across. It was a good spot, private and quiet.

I pointed to the map. "We'll arrive in that small parking area." I knelt on the cool grass and took Lin's hand but I froze as emotions suddenly overcame me. She didn't notice because her mind was elsewhere, but the feel of her hand reminded me of Shoko.

Okaasan knelt beside us and put her hand on my bare arm.

"Don't explain anything, just go."

I managed a smile. "Okay, here we go." I slapped my palm against the grass and forced some energy into it, and as the world began to spin and blur, Lin let out a muted scream. But again, things didn't feel normal. I squeezed out more energy. Okaasan started to whimper, and it turned into a full-on scream by the time the spinning and blurriness vanished.

The lot was dark and empty, as I'd hoped.

Poor Lin had her head between her knees, her hands over her ears. I patted her back and let some energy flow into her.

"Just breathe," I said. "You'll be fine in a minute."

"Do you usually use energy like that?" Okaasan asked, squinting as if she had a headache. "It was like you were overriding the Mother Earth."

"I used more than usual," I said, avoiding her gaze. "I think carrying both of you was too much." But I knew that wasn't it. The energy of the earth felt weaker.

"It didn't feel good," she said. "It was so dark."

"Is that why you screamed?"

Okaasan looked confused. "I didn't scream."

I stared at her for a long moment. If it wasn't Okaasan or Lin, who was it?

—

The street Lin led us to—I'd call it an alley—was deep in shade and barely wide enough for a car to drive. Small restaurants and bars lined both sides. A few older women bowed as we passed, inviting us to visit their restaurants. Outside a bar, a big gruff-looking guy offered me a *conversation* with one of his hostesses.

"They really do only talk and listen to you," Lin said as we passed, sounding like her usual self again. "If you want sex, a prostitute costs a lot less."

"Men pay to *talk* to a girl?"

"There are a lot of lonely people in Japan." Lin stopped in front of a small ramen shop. "This is the place."

I felt uneasy, a slight tingling in my neck. "Are you sure your family is on our side?"

"Their side is whichever one pays the fees," Lin said over her shoulder. "But I'm family."

"I'll stay outside," Okaasan said, then she leaned against the wall of the shop.

As I followed Lin inside, I felt like I'd pushed through the swinging doors of a Wild West saloon. A man of about forty and a teenage girl looked up. The man behind the counter, and a woman who was probably his wife, froze. Two other men in their early twenties watched us from a table off to the side. Though they looked completely natural, their energy betrayed them.

"Did your mother teach you our ways?" the man said, sizing me up. He was a tough-looking, serious guy with small eyes.

I nodded. "Plus quite a bit more."

He nodded, then stood and bowed, not deeply, but deeper than he needed to considering our ages.

"I have great respect for Misako."

I bowed back. "She speaks highly of you as well." Actually, I had no idea what Okaasan thought of this guy.

"Lin," the man regarded Lin, who'd stayed by the door. "It's been a while since you visited your family."

"Hello Toshio," Lin replied, sounding less than pleased to see him. "My assignment keeps me away more than I'd prefer."

"Yes, so busy playing fiancé." His tone was unpleasant, and so was his energy. "You've certainly gone above and beyond the call of duty."

Her gaze flicked toward me, then settled on him. She looked ready to reply when the girl sitting beside Toshio, as if she couldn't stand it anymore, jumped up and ran to Lin and gave her the biggest un-Japanese hug I'd ever seen.

"Yuko." Lin embraced her. "You've become a beautiful woman while I've been away!"

"We don't have much time, Toshio." I was getting anxious.

"Okay, okay." Toshio indicated the seat across from him. "If these men are in Izumo City, we'll know, but an operation this big, this fast ..." He looked apologetic. "... will be rather expensive, especially if we need to dispose of bodies."

I blinked, taken aback by his directness. "Uh ... okay. I can pay."

Suddenly, Toshio's eyes widened, and he jerked to his feet. "Honorable Misako!" He bowed so low his head nearly hit the table.

Okaasan stood in the doorway, coolly surveying the room. She had her katana and wakizashi strapped to her belt now, and it occurred to me how much she looked like her mother. Worthy to be the Grand Gatekeeper of Izumo.

She returned his bow with a nod. "Do you need a bag of silver to assist the gods?"

"The gods are irrelevant, and useless," he said, his respectful tone suddenly gone. "Earthquakes, disease, starvation, and war still kill millions every year, whether we worship them or not." His voice faltered. "Where were the gods when my daughter died of cancer last year?"

We all stared at him, silent, as he regained his composure.

He cleared his throat. "But I do believe in Gatekeepers," he said. "After all, it's only been one hour since Lin's call and here you are."

"You can't disregard the gods," Lin said. "Without them, there would be no Gatekeepers."

He looked at her. "Maybe, but the gods don't pay, and neither does anyone else from Izumo, so I'm done with them."

Okaasan's expression turned cold. "You're *done*?"

He nodded to her, then looked back at Lin. "Which also means the Thompson assignment is over."

Lin looked shocked. "Does the entire family feel this way?"

"The old folks don't like it but it's not their decision to make. I lead the family now."

Lin nodded slowly. "I hadn't heard."

"Old Sugimoto, the gardener, knows," Toshio said, a slight smile on his thin lips. "Didn't he tell you?"

Lin shook her head.

"He's decided to keep working for the Chairman," he said. "It's about time he retired, so I allowed it."

"You *allowed* it?" she said, eyebrows raised. "Perhaps you forget who Sugimoto is."

His face took on an ugly expression. "We'll talk about that later."

He turned to me. "Don't take any of this personally," he said. "You should feel relieved we're not around spying on you. Of course, I'll always give you the family discount, because of your mother."

"That's very ... kind of you." I gave my head a mental shake. "Can we get moving on this?"

"I'll take your word as a deposit." He sat back down and spread out a map. "So, you think they're somewhere in Izumo-Taisha?"

"Yeah, but they plan to move them soon."

"Their captors would need special transportation," Okaasan said. "Like a steel shipping container because the Evil Ones can't *travel* them."

"Can Bartholomew?" I asked her.

"I'm not sure." She looked uneasy at the idea. "Maybe."

Toshio turned to the two guys at the table. "Akio, Koji, get people out searching—now!"

"*Searching* for what?" one of them said. His casual reply surprised me, considering Toshio was supposedly the new boss.

"Shipping containers!" Toshio glared at them. "They're not exactly common around here."

Okaasan moved away from the doorway, but the two young men took another way out, leaving silently through the back of the shop. When I turned back, Toshio was studying me.

"Bartholomew is a unique name," he said. "Do you mean the billionaire from Geneva?"

I nodded. "He's a lot more than that. How do you know about him?"

He shrugged, a bit too casually. "It's our business to know people."

I looked him in the eye. "Bartholomew is the enemy of Izumo."

"And an enemy of the gods," Okaasan said from her place near the door, her voice cold as ice.

Toshio hesitated just a bit too long. "I'll remember that if he ever comes calling." He held my gaze for a moment longer, then went back to his map. "This will be a difficult task," he said. "There are a lot of buildings in town."

"We're looking for a concrete building, one they can't escape from," I said. "That should narrow it down."

"Half the buildings in Japan are concrete," he said with a laugh. "Maybe because the only buildings left standing in Hiroshima were concrete. So, there must be a—"

His phone rang.

He said something, but it was cryptic and made no sense to me. Okaasan seemed to understand, though.

"Thank you, Toshio," she said when he hung up.

He nodded. "We have everyone out searching." He stood up. "I have a car parked on the next street. Let's get going."

"Take Lin," Okaasan said. "Junya and I will make our own way there." Then her brow furrowed, and she looked toward the door. "Someone has arrived."

I was on my way out the door. I'd already sensed them.

Yukie and Sakura, both dressed in Gatekeeper uniforms, stood in the alley, their weapons in full view.

"Why are you here?" I said. "You're breaking the Grand Elder's decree by crossing."

"My master has been discredited and shamed," Sakura said. "It would be an honor to suffer beside her."

I appreciated the sentiment, but it still sounded stupid. "What about you?" I said to Yukie.

"I could not let Sakura come alone." I'd never seen her look this unhappy before. "We decided after Córdoba that we would never be alone over here, and that is a promise I will not break."

I let out a deep sigh. "Okay, but we still have no idea where—"

"We do," Sakura said. "A young one escaped."

—

We traveled to a farm about five miles outside the Izumo City limits. Sakura led us to a low hill where we could overlook the property, though we were still quite far away. The sky was cloudless, with a partial moon that bathed everything in silver light.

Toshio and Lin pulled up in a dark blue BMW about a half an hour after we got there. Through the binoculars Toshio passed to me, I saw the 'concrete box', a pre-war concrete garage with a sloping rusted tin roof and an equally rusted metal roll-up door. It was one of several outbuildings but was by far the largest. A dozen cars could fit in there, easily. A large old traditional-style house stood closer to the road. There were several vans parked on the gravel driveway beside it.

I tapped Okaasan's arm. "What's with the trees?" A row of tall thick pine trees lined one side of the property. I'd noticed several similar rows of trees on other properties scattered across the flat valley.

"They're obviously to block the wind." She rolled her eyes. "Or do you think people here just like tall hedges on the west side of their houses?"

"I don't think it's that obvious."

She glanced at Toshio. "When will more of the family arrive?"

He looked at his watch. "Five minutes."

With a bit of time to spare, I went to talk to Lin. She was over by the BMW, looking unhappy, but she forced a smile as I approached.

"So," I said, trying to keep my expression neutral. "What are you going to do now that your assignment is over?"

"You get right to the point, don't you?"

"We don't really have time for a long chat."

She glanced past me toward Toshio. "I don't have a choice."

"What if you refuse?"

"I might refuse certain assignments, but I cannot refuse to be a part of my family." She looked down at her hands and touched her engagement ring. "I feel like I've been living in a dream." A single tear rolled down her face.

"You can't just leave us."

Before she could respond, Okaasan called to me.

A van traveling on the road near the house slowed briefly, then moved on. Maybe a rabbit had crossed the road.

"Another team is here," Toshio said, nodding toward the van.

"I didn't see anyone."

"For god's sake, Junya," Okaasan said. "They're ninja!"

"There's another team in the field behind the garage," Toshio pointed. "The others will be in the trees in a few minutes. How do you want to play this?"

I looked at Okaasan, then Lin, who was now squatting beside us.

"The ninja would be the most useful attacking the house, from all sides," Okaasan said. "It looks like the garage only has one entrance besides the roll-up door. Gatekeepers are very experienced with direct frontal attacks."

I took Okaasan's hand. "Let's look inside the garage."

"Look?" she said.

"Yeah, Sakura can do this mind-travel thing," I said. "It's way better than what I can do." Then I looked at Sakura and frowned. "Does it work on this side too?"

She took my hand. "We shall find out."

She closed her eyes. A long moment later, we were inside the garage, but the view wasn't clear. It looked cloudy, like a bad cable connection.

"It does not work," Sakura said, struggling. "I cannot hold this."

I let go of her hand. "I'll try it on my own," I said. "Yukie, you come with me."

"Ah," Sakura said. "Without your weight, the image is clear."

"Remarkable," Okaasan said, sounding far away.

After Yukie took my hand, I focused, and we were back inside the garage, seeing everything in my usual thermal vision.

"This is very odd," Yukie said. "But very cool!"

It was bigger inside than I'd imagined, like a small school gym but with a lower ceiling. Overhead, a dozen bright orange-red lights—thermal hot—made me squint. Against the far wall, about two dozen human shapes sat on the floor, their bare skin showing yellow and green, their clothing light and dark blues. Five human shapes lay off to the side.

"Shit," I muttered. "Some are dead!"

"Maybe they are only hurt." Yukie sounded worried. "Or asleep."

The shapes were cold, a dark blue that blended into the cool concrete floor. "I don't think so."

"Look!" Yukie pointed.

Two Evil Ones, wearing their usual long black coats, sat on chairs with their backs against the garage door, MP5s pointed at the girls, fingers on the triggers. Three others stood near the wall, close to the side door, the only other exit. Those three held compact machine pistols, like an Uzi. Unlike the girls, they gave off little warmth.

There was a couple dozen feet between them and the Gatekeepers, giving them plenty of time to react if the girls tried to make a move. I guessed that was what had happened to the five on the floor.

"Let's go," I said to Yukie, but somehow, I couldn't.

I turned. An Evil One was looking at me. *Right* at me.

I opened my eyes and we were back with the others, but the image of that Evil One stayed with me. Did they know we were coming?

"Three of my people are already inside the house," Toshio said. "There are several men in there, over a dozen."

Okaasan nodded. "A Gatekeeper should attack the guards leaning against the garage door," she said. "From the outside."

Sakura held up her hand. "I will do that."

"Okay, then Junya, Yukie, and I will take care of the others from inside." Okaasan looked at me. "Let's—"

An Evil One pushed open the side door and strode toward the main house. Halfway to his destination, he stopped dead and spun in a slow circle, his weapon up.

"Take him out," Okaasan said, "and attack the house—now!"

CHAPTER
35

TOSHIO HIT THE "SEND" BUTTON ON his phone and a few seconds later, the man in black fell to the ground. Then black shapes raced toward the house from all sides.

Okaasan slid her katana from its sheath and handed it to me. "I'll use the wakizashi."

Sakura slapped her palm on the ground and disappeared. Lin and Toshio gasped. We hadn't vanished when we looked into the garage.

I grabbed Okaasan and Yukie's hands, then we traveled in.

Sakura's blade stabbed through the rusty garage door with a bang, making the whole thing rattle. The two Evil Ones spun off their chairs, their rifles coming up, but the katana disappeared. A second later the blade smashed through the door again, almost the whole length of it, swinging horizontally like a baseball bat, slicing easily through the rusty steel. It hit an Evil One and sliced his chest wide open, while Okaasan sank her blade into the second one. He emptied his gun through the door as he fell.

Sakura!

"Junya!" It was Yukie. Our targets were moving, one toward the door, his machine pistol up and firing. I dove for the ground as the other one swung his gun toward us. I landed hard and slid as bullets ricocheted off the floor close by. Flying concrete chips stung as they hit my face and arms.

I rolled and held out my palm as the gun spat fire again.

Everything froze.

Yukie was caught in full stride, her katana pointed at the chest of the Evil One closest to her. I rolled two more times toward the Evil One near the door.

I ignored the bullets that drifted slowly through the air past me. He'd missed me.

I released my energy.

An Uzi clattered to the floor as Yukie drove her blade through the Evil One. She let out a shout of victory as he fell. My katana arced upward, taking my target by surprise, and sliced through his belly. He hit the ground beside me, showering me in black blood and dust. His Uzi hit the floor, barrel still smoking. Then I was back on my feet.

I kicked the side door and it smashed open, tearing off its hinges. Gunfire came from the main house: automatic weapons. There were screams and grunts as bullets and blades found flesh. I ignored it. I was looking for Sakura.

She rushed around the corner toward me and I pulled her into the garage as someone ran toward us from the house.

Toshio stood silhouetted in the doorway a moment later. "All those in the house are dead, and several are … *gone*."

I cringed. "Right, I should've mentioned that."

He nodded. "Yes, you should have."

"Did you … are your guys okay?"

"Two were shot but will live." He looked indifferent. "Not bad considering the situation."

"Nice work, Toshio."

He gave me a wry smile. "You get what you pay for."

"Junya!" It was Okaasan. She was on her knees, leaning over someone on the ground. I ran over and dropped to my knees.

It was Yukie.

Blood poured from her torso, soaking her uniform and pooling underneath her.

"Oh shit!" I blasted my energy out.

We need a Miko!

I put my hands over her and forced my energy into her. Her eyes widened for a moment and she looked into mine.

"Did we ... save them?" she whispered.

"Yes." My head bobbed up and down. "We did it, Yukie."

She smiled. "Cool ..."

I felt a burst of energy as someone traveled in, but it wasn't a Miko. It was Nene. She carried two modern First Responder's cases with her, Thompson Security logos on the sides.

That was fast, and unexpected.

"Chiyoko sent me," Nene said to no one in particular. She looked down at Yukie, then at me. She looked scared.

I was sweating from the exertion of keeping my energy on Yukie, trying to hold back her blood and her pain.

"Please help her," I said through gritted teeth.

Nene knelt and pulled Yukie's uniform top away from her skin. Nene didn't react, but I nearly threw up. Her chest and stomach looked like raw meat. I didn't need to look inside her as I had with Nene when she was hurt. Everything was already exposed. Blood bubbled up from a hole in her chest.

Nene looked at me. "Barrymore-sensei taught me much," she whispered. "This is bad, very bad. Far beyond my training."

Yukie choked up blood.

"Hang in there, Yukie." Tears leaked out of my eyes. "Do what you can!"

Nene pulled a large dressing from the pack and applied it to Yukie's chest. "Have to stop the sucking," she muttered. She unwrapped another large bandage and tried to make it cover Yukie's open stomach, but it wasn't nearly big enough. She added another one. "Infection ..." She grabbed an intravenous bag, passed it to Okaasan, then began to search for a vein.

I tried to blink away my tears. "What's that?"

"Antibiotics," Nene whispered as she taped the needle in place. "But there is too much damage, Junya."

Yukie let out a sigh and I felt her energy slipping away.

"Please, Nene," I whispered, my tears unstoppable now. "Do something!"

She had her fingers on Yukie's neck, feeling for her pulse. After a long moment, she sat back on her heels and shook her head.

"Please!"

She hesitated, then pulled a blue bottle from her bag, the same healing liquid Himiko had used on her. When she poured half the contents over Yukie's torso, there was a hissing sound.

The wounds began to close.

"Yes!" But my voice was barely audible. The effort of holding my energy on Yukie had drained me.

Okaasan put her hand on my shoulder.

"Junya," she whispered. "It is only healing the outside."

I looked up at her. "But it's working."

But it wasn't. "You need to let go," Okaasan said.

Yukie's eyes were cloudy. I realized I felt no energy coming from her, none at all.

I released the last of my energy and fell backward onto the cement floor.

—

I was outside when I opened my eyes, a sky full of stars above me. It took me a minute to figure out where I was, but reality came crashing back soon enough.

A girl was explaining what had happened.

The Evil Ones had taken the Gatekeepers by surprise, right in Izumo, two or three girls at a time. A van drove up, and the girls were sprayed with something hot, probably pepper spray, and dragged into the van. The Evil Ones rounded them all up within a few hours.

"How did the others die?" Okaasan asked.

"They tried to fight," said another young voice, filled with anger. "The Evil Ones made an example out of them!"

"And the young one who escaped?"

"She jumped out of the van and traveled directly across," Sakura said. "She marked the place before trying to return to Izumo. I wanted to come here—alone—to tell you." She started to cry. "But Yukie would not let me leave without her."

I stared up at the sky and tuned out the voices. I couldn't listen anymore.

Yukie ...

I rolled up onto my elbow when the old garage door rattled up. The rescued Gatekeepers were carrying their dead onto the yard. Near the house, several bodies were being loaded into a white van. I guess there'd been men in the house as well as Evil Ones.

Okaasan knelt beside me. "Can you stand?"

I tried but didn't make it. Okaasan grabbed me by the arm and pulled me to my feet.

"You used a lot of energy on Yukie," she said, her voice soft. "It felt beautiful, by the way."

"It didn't save her."

"Nothing could save her, Junya. Not even the best emergency doctors in the world." She put her hand on my shoulder. "You did everything you could."

"Misako!" Sakura came running over. "They cannot travel!"

I flinched. "Have they tried together?"

Sakura's head bobbed. "Even with their combined energy, six Gatekeepers cannot travel a body away, or even themselves."

The Gatekeepers looked up at me. "Please help us," one said. "Your energy is strong."

I looked inside myself. Did I have enough? I knelt, or maybe fell, and put my hand on the arm of a young, dead Gatekeeper. Her face looked peaceful, but her skin was cold. I squeezed my eyes shut, both to build my power and to cut off my tears. I tried to build energy, but nothing happened. I thought of the gods, of Izumo, of Shoko.

Still nothing.

"I can't."

From far in the distance came the sound of sirens.

"Do you think they're coming here?" It was Lin.

"I don't think we can chance it," Okaasan said. "Can Toshio get the girls out of here?"

"The jerk's already long gone," Lin said, with a contemptuous snort.

I looked around. There were more than two dozen Gatekeepers here, plus the dead, with no way to get home.

"Please," an injured Gatekeeper whispered. "Please help us, Junya."

I licked my lips and looked up at Okaasan. "I've got nothing left."

She looked past me at the Gatekeepers and the muscles of her jaw tightened. "Summon the power of the gods and try again!"

They tried, and I could feel their energy, but was too weak.

"Damn you all!" she yelled with sudden force. "You had no problem getting yourselves here and now—"

"Okaasan."

She looked down at me.

"There's only one way I can do this," I said. "I need to use *His* power."

Her eyes widened. "No Junya, you cannot do that to yourself!"

The sirens were definitely coming this way.

"Do you have a better idea?"

She bit her lip as she surveyed the chaotic scene in the yard. "We'll deal with it somehow …"

Sakura called out to me. "Junya, what will we do?!"

I looked up at Okaasan as desperation began to fill me. "There's no other choice."

She turned to look at me, tears in her eyes. "No Junya, you can't."

I shook my head. "No, you have to say I should do it, because I'm going to hurt them." I knew that for sure. I sucked in a breath. "And *He's* going to know ..."

She put her hand to her mouth. "Oh, Junya," she cried as she knelt beside me. "I will help you fight his evil until the day I die." Then she gave me a short nod. "Yes, there is no other choice. Do it, now!"

I looked for Yukie. She wasn't far away, surrounded by Gatekeepers. The ones who deserted their post, who abandoned their homes, who let men and women and children die.

I felt Bartholomew rise in me as I crawled over and knelt beside Yukie.

"Those treacherous little bitches killed you," I whispered to her. "It's their fault you're dead!"

I heard a gasp from behind me but ignored it. My anger started to build, deep down, dark and getting stronger by the second. As the energy made its way up, I thought of Shoko, the things Chiyoko had said to her, the way she looked when I left.

You can make Chiyoko pay for that.

The energy grew larger, and darker.

Yes, do it! Use my power!

I leaned over and kissed Yukie on the forehead. Then, I put my hand on her shoulder and closed my eyes.

"Put your hands on her!" I growled at the Gatekeepers. I didn't open my eyes to see if they did or not. I just pushed the energy from my belly and into my hands.

My hands dropped to the dirt as Yukie disappeared. The other Gatekeepers went too, and it took a long time before their screams faded away.

"Oh my god, Junya!" Okaasan cried. "Oh god, oh god, oh god, I'm so sorry!"

Isn't it great?!

I did it again with the second group, and the third. Everyone

311

around me stared in horror as I sent them away, screaming, until only Lin, Okaasan and I were alone in the yard.

I fell to the ground, into the arms of the Mother Earth, and sobbed.

"Get up, Junya." Okaasan put her hands on my shoulders. The sirens sounded close now, just blocks away. "We need to go."

"Not like those girls, I hope," Lin said, clearly frightened.

"No ..." I felt darkness still coiled around me like a heavy chain. "I won't do that to you. I'll never ..."

"How will we get out of here then?"

"We can try hiding," Okaasan said, looking around.

Lin looked down at me. "Can he even walk? If not, we're done for."

"No!" I grabbed Okaasan's leg. "You can travel us home."

"Me?" She looked shocked. "It's forbidden."

"Goddamn you!" I yelled. "After all this, you can't break one fucking twenty-year-old decree?!"

She stared at me a long moment, then rolled onto her knees and took Lin's hand and mine.

"Mother Earth," she whispered. "Please forgive me and take us home."

CHAPTER
36

I'D NEVER FELT SO EXHAUSTED IN my life, physically or mentally, and I spent the next few days either in bed or sprawled on the sofa. When I was awake, all I could do was think about what had happened. When I closed my eyes to sleep, all I saw was Yukie's dying face.

Okaasan wasn't doing a great job of keeping herself together either. She'd seen firsthand the power of evil in her son, and she had a husband who'd just found out she'd been lying to him for years. So, when she wasn't watching me, or cooking, she cleaned the house. I'd never seen it so spotless, and that was saying something.

She and dad were talking, but I don't think it was going well. Dad was taking a lot of long walks alone in the evening, and sometimes when Okaasan was in the bedroom alone, I heard her crying.

"If you think about it," Mack said the first time I ventured out about a week later, "you two really should've told your dad everything right after you got bitten the first time."

We'd met up at the pizza shop not far from his house. Now we were sitting in a booth near the back, waiting for two larges to show up.

"He's got a lot to be mad about," Mack continued when I offered no comment. "Maybe not so much the before stuff, because it's ancient history, but definitely since and it's just gonna get worse." Mack shook his head. "I mean, from a dinner point of view, this sucks. Your house is *really* uncomfortable these days."

I looked down at my hands. "Now I know how my mom felt when I started questioning her. What to tell and what to keep secret."

"You knew our friendship could go either way. That worked out okay, right?"

"Yeah, but I wasn't keeping the secret from you for twenty years, either."

Our pizza arrived. I grabbed the ham and pineapple first. The 'everything' pizza would have to wait.

"Think things are back to normal over there?" Mack asked around a mouthful of pizza.

I put down the slice and stared at him. "How could it be?"

He shrugged. "The way Shoko talks, I thought Gatekeepers died in battle all the time. It's awful, but it's nothing new, right?"

"Yeah but being invaded is." I sucked in a deep breath to calm down. "And Shoko's life won't be going back to normal anytime soon. She looked awful the day I left, and that was before Yukie died. Plus, I have no idea what state the Gatekeepers were in when they arrived back there. For all I know, I infected them with evil, or killed them all."

Mack took a long swig of pop and emptied the tall glass. I waited for the usual burp, but it never came.

"How did all this happen?" he said.

"I don't know," I said, the pizza forgotten. "But it's pretty damn obvious that Bartholomew's plan worked. Killing all those shamans made the gods and everyone in Izumo weaker." I thought about that. "Maybe it affected the Gatekeepers more than we thought and made their morals drop or something."

"What did that Müller guy say?"

I shrugged. "He said I'd done more damage than Bartholomew ever could, which is bullshit." A few people looked our way so I lowered my voice. "I worked my ass off to keep him *out* of Izumo."

Mack looked thoughtful. No, he looked suspicious.

"That's true," he said, frowning. "But you changed a lot of things in the process."

I nodded. "It had to be done."

"Did it?"

I looked up from my slice. "What?"

He wiped his face with a napkin. "Why did girls start crossing over and buying stuff, and getting jealous and rebelling against their leaders?" When I didn't answer, he said, "Because you made it all right to wear modern clothes and cross over, to break rules, even to disobey the Elders. Heck, you made it *cool*." He shrugged. "It sounds like you actually screwed up their society pretty bad."

I glared at him. "You've got to be kidding me."

"Nope. Sounds like you and Shoko broke just about every rule they've got."

I stared at him. "But the Elders allowed it."

"Sounds more like they looked the other way."

"So, you're saying this is all my fault?" I didn't even try to hide how annoyed I was getting. "That I did this for Bartholomew, to help him destroy the place?"

"No," he said carefully. "I'm just saying the changes you made *created* the environment for all that stuff to happen."

An icy silence followed.

That familiar anger started to grow in my gut. "I can't believe you'd say that."

His eyes narrowed. "Don't you *dare* get pissed off at me," he said. "If you can't see this yourself …" He threw his half-eaten piece of pizza back onto the plate. "You changed things, bro, and change isn't always good."

I stared at the silver band still around my wrist. I'd told the girls they were *special*. I told them they could do things regular Gatekeepers couldn't do. And don't *special* people get special privileges? They could cross when they wanted. I encouraged them to buy things ...

I realized I was having trouble breathing.

"But," I said, "I didn't mean ..." I looked up at Mack and had to fight back tears. "Shit, you're right. I screwed everything up. I destroyed Izumo, just like Bartholomew wanted!" I had to grab the edge of the table to steady myself. "Do you know how many people died because of this ... because of me?" I started to stand up. "I've got to—"

Mack grabbed my arm and yanked me back into the seat. "Whoa, buddy. Take a deep breath before you puke or something."

I collapsed back into the chair.

"Did you use energy on anyone, force them to obey you?"

I shook my head. That I knew for sure.

"Then listen to me," he said, sounding an awful lot like a big brother might. "There's no way you took out an entire civilization singlehandedly, okay? You may have set a bad example, but every one of them, from the youngest Gatekeeper right up to the Grand Elders, made their own choices." He let go of me. "You already told me the Elders took the blame, so I'm not letting you carry the guilt for all this."

"But Shoko is."

"Well, she shouldn't either."

———

Okaasan looked up from the table when I walked into the kitchen, still wearing my shoes, and carrying an almost full box of pizza. She looked about as sad as I'd ever seen her, and her energy was worse.

"Where have you been?" She glanced at my feet but didn't comment, even though wearing shoes inside a Japanese home was a major sin.

I tossed the pizza box onto the counter. "I helped destroy their whole world."

She looked confused but didn't reply.

I took a deep breath. "I let the Evil Ones get inside," I said, while holding onto my emotions as best as I could.

At her incredulous expression, I told her what both Mr. Müller and Mack had said.

She thought about that for a while, then said, "Mack's a very smart young man, and a good friend."

"Why, because he said I caused the *environment* that caused their society to implode, or because it's not only my fault?"

"Both." She motioned me to sit. "The Elders supported your plan."

I dropped into the chair. "Yeah, so that can lessen my guilt about the Special Forces who were killed, but what about all the villagers and Gatekeepers who died during the invasion?" I pointed at my chest. "That was my fault."

She sat back and frowned at me. "I thought that happened because those Gatekeepers deserted their posts."

"They deserted because of me!"

She looked shocked. "What do you mean?"

"I told them they weren't needed anymore," and I reexplained what had happened that day. "You see?" I said when I was done. "I *am* responsible!"

She crossed her arms on her chest. "Just because you said that they could be replaced with the Special Forces does not justify deserting their posts to cross over and go shopping!" She ended the sentence at a high volume.

I ran my fingers through my hair and leaned forward onto my elbows. "I don't know what to believe anymore."

"It may seem orchestrated, but I'd say it's more like the Butterfly Effect."

I screwed up my face. "You know about the Butterfly Effect?"

She nodded. "A bunch of little random events occur over time that end up causing a ..."

"Massacre?"

She nodded. "But in the moment, when each of those random events occur, no one can positively say whether it's good or bad. You can't predict how one small action will change the future. You and Shoko had no bad intentions. You and everyone else did what they thought was best at the time."

"Yeah, maybe, but what if it *was* all planned and Bartholomew used me to make this happen?"

"How could he do that?"

"You saw his evil energy first hand! Look how I traveled those Gatekeepers away. They could be dead for all we know!" I jumped to my feet and slammed my fist into my chest. "I have Bartholomew's blood! He's inside me and he could've used me to do all that!"

She didn't react, other than to motion for me to sit. When I didn't, she pointed to the chair. "Sit!"

I sat.

"You've had energy inside you all your life, pure energy, that was awakened by Shoko. But at the same time, you also had dark energy. She felt it, and I felt it. What makes you think this is Bartholomew's power?"

"Because I hear his voice in here." I tapped my head. "He encourages me to use his power. That never happened until after he bit me. I may've had some 'dark energy' but I sure as hell couldn't do what I can now."

"Yes, but when you travelled those Gatekeepers away, you chose to use the power. Bartholomew didn't force you."

"Chose?" I glared at her across the table. "I used his power because I had to!"

Her expression hardened. "Don't give Bartholomew so much damn credit!"

I stared at her, mouth gaped.

She lay her hands flat on the table, as if to calm herself. "What I mean is," she said quietly. "You're a loving boy who can heal a little girl if you choose. And yes, you traveled those Gatekeepers away with a power that still scares the hell out of me, but *you* summoned the power. You chose to bring it up and that means you control the evil, not the other way around. So, own it and *you* decide whether it's good or bad, and what you're going to do with it."

CHAPTER
37

I STARTED TOWARD MY BEDROOM with the pizza box, mulling over what Okaasan had said, but I changed course when I heard dad's table saw. His energy wasn't hard to miss either. It was as negative as Okaasan's, so I altered course and trudged toward the workshop.

Dad turned off the saw when he noticed me at the door.

"Hey," he shouted, probably because of his earplugs. His energy dropped a few notches lower, but he forced a smile as he pulled the earplugs out. "How's it going, buddy?"

"I've been better." I stepped inside and dropped the pizza box on a work bench.

He brushed some sawdust off his sleeves. "You've had a rough week," he said. "It's good to see you up and about."

"I needed to get out of here for a while."

His forced smile drained away. "Yeah ... I'm sorry it's been like this. Your mother and I are trying to talk, but once you find out someone's been lying to you—for years—it's kind of hard to believe any of the new things she's saying. Especially when what she's telling me now is this … fantasy story."

I leaned against the bench. "I've been lying too so I guess we'll have to deal with that one day too."

"Maybe, but you're a teenager so I'd be surprised if you never lied to me, but she's my life-partner, my soulmate, and she been hiding this other life from me for years!" His energy was rising fast. "It's … it's like she's had an affair or something. God, for all I know she has and—"

"Okay, stop. Just stop it." I ran a hand over my face. "If you keep going on like this, you're going to screw everything up."

"Everything *is* screwed up!" He pointed a finger at me. "And don't you dare act all wise and cocky about this. You're overstepping your boundary, big time."

I turned to face him. "First," I said quietly, "this is my family and I'd rather we stayed together as one, and second, your domestic issues kinda pale compared to everything else that's happening. A fourteen-year-old girl died in my arms the other day."

He looked down. "Right. Your mom told me about that …"

"Yeah." I waved the subject away. "So, what has mom told you about her old life?"

He let out a weak laugh, a release of nervous energy I suppose. "Like I said, it's like fantasy—unbelievable. Parallel worlds and some ancient Izumo shrine. Women warriors protecting gods and fighting evil. It's some of the craziest stuff I've ever heard."

"It's all true, dad."

He bent to brush some sawdust off his jeans, maybe to delay having to respond. When he looked up he said, "If it *is* true—and I'm not ready to admit that it might be—it would explain a few things about her. A lot of things actually, but seriously? This was her life, and yours now too?"

"At least now you know why she and I practice *deadly* fighting techniques."

"But this is dangerous!" he said. "I can't sit by knowing you and your mom are out there fighting. Look at the way you came home the other day. You could get killed, just like that teenage girl!"

"It's no different than being married to a police officer or having a son in the army. And I have a bit of an advantage when it comes to injuries."

He rubbed the stubble on his cheeks. "Maybe …"

"Look dad, she wasn't lying to you," I said. "She just didn't tell you about a past life she thought she'd left behind. It just wasn't necessary to tell you … until recently." I gave myself a mental pat on the back. I really had come a long way since I accused her of lying when she first told me all this stuff.

He closed his eyes. "So … everyone's got a past, a few skeletons in the closet? That's how this should work?"

"I guess so."

He gave me a sad smile. "No, it's not that easy. You two have a secret life. How do you think that makes me feel?"

I shrugged. "I don't know … We just have a mother-son relationship of martial combat," I said. "And we have a father-son relationship with renovating houses and stuff. It is what it is. We weren't out there conspiring against you. Hell, up until last summer, I didn't know anything about this either. Then I yanked poor mom back into it."

We were silent for a while. I couldn't imagine what was going through his mind.

"When did all this begin?" he said after a while. "I mean, when did you figure everything out about your mom?"

"The night Grandpa's men chased me."

"Because of Shoko too?"

I nodded, didn't trust myself to speak.

"Shoko's a Gatekeeper, like your mom is … was?"

"Yeah," I said. "She's the reason I was allowed into that world."

His energy brightened a bit. "You've been there, to this *other side* then?"

I nodded. "Crazy, huh?"

He smiled, ever so slightly. "What's it like? Your mom and I haven't talked much about … anything good."

So, I told him the good parts first: about the tall shrine, the amazing buildings, the skill of their woodworkers, and the village, the Gatekeepers and Elders, and the peace I'd once found there.

"But it's also a rigid, totalitarian society," I said. "The Elders control everything, even who marries who. And a lot of stuff they do seemed dumb, so I tried to change a few things." Then I gave him a summary of what had happened, right up to the kidnapping of the girls. "I may've wrecked the place, just like Bartholomew wanted."

"Wait, what? Bartholomew's involved in this?" He sounded somewhere between shocked and angry. "Who exactly are these men who are trying to destroy their society?"

I hesitated. "Bartholomew's *underlings*." I didn't want to call them men. "Didn't … didn't Mom tell you that?"

His eyes widened as a slow realization began to settle in. I started to speak, but he held up his hand. "Give me a minute here." He sank down onto his stool.

He sat there for so long that I opened the pizza box and managed to finish two slices before he looked up at me.

"This is all connected, isn't it?" he said. "My dad … it started with him out in the desert with that gold, and Bartholomew." His scowl deepened. "And then your mom *coincidentally* comes to live in Matsue and ends up marrying me. What the hell?" He stood up. "I don't like how this comes back to me!"

I closed my eyes and swallowed the lump in my throat. Obviously, Mom hadn't told him about her assignment to marry him either.

"It's a coincidence," I said. "You went to Japan of your own free will, right?"

He nodded, but his energy was starting to spike. "Yes, but—"

"No, you said it yourself. Matsue's not that big and she was practically your neighbor. She saw you and fell in love. Don't read more into it." I thought about throwing some energy at him, to persuade him, but thought better of it. He needed to come to peace with this on his own.

He looked me in the eye. "Why are you lying for her?"

I stared back. This wasn't my story to tell, but I had to say something. If they were going to stay together, he needed the whole story.

"Do you have any idea how scared Mom is of losing you over this?"

"She should be!" he yelled. "How many lies do I need to accept? People who love each other don't lie to each other, ever!"

I raised my eyebrows. "Really? Remember the time you took me into that bar with the strippers, when I was fourteen? You told her we were *delayed* at the lumber store and you swore me to secrecy." I thought about that for a second. "Jeez, you made me lie to mom."

His face twitched. "They weren't strippers, and besides, I didn't know it was a bar when we walked in."

"Well, they sure weren't wearing much, and we didn't leave once you did figure it out," I said, hands on hips. "Then there was the whole 'broken surfboard' incident. You never told her I could've died when I hit those rocks. No, the board fell off the truck and broke, right?" I frowned at him. "You made me lie to her about that too."

He scowled at me. "James—"

"And how about that girl you dated at Harvard? Shelley *What's-her-name*? Does Mom have any idea you two still—"

He held up his hands. "Okay, fine. I lie too but there's no comparison here. I want to know why I'm married to a Gatekeeper!"

I sat down on a box. "Look, she should be telling you this, okay? But before you go all squirrely, there's stuff you need to know so I'm going to tell you, straight out, for your own good."

His hands went to hips. "My own good?"

I sucked in a breath. "I'd kinda like to keep our family together, remember?"

I took his silence as a green light.

"Mom was assigned to watch you in Matsue, but that was after she'd moved in with the Satos. She wasn't there as a Gatekeeper, more like an exchange student." He was about to interrupt, but I shushed him. "It was a casual thing, just see what you were up to, because the Elders couldn't figure why you were there. From their point of view, you coming to Matsue was pretty damn suspicious."

He looked confused by that. "Why?"

"Because of grandpa and his connection to Bartholomew."

"What did that have to do with me?"

"Nothing, but they didn't know that," I said. "After a while, the Elders decided you weren't a threat to them. Mom was commanded to return to Izumo, but you two were already dating by then."

He didn't look very happy.

"But guess what?" I said. "She refused to return because she was *so* in love with you." I let that sink in for a moment. "And in Izumo, the punishment for disobeying a command is death."

His brow wrinkled in concentration. "She was willing to die ... to be with me?"

"Apparently." I leaned toward him. "Now, here's the most important part." I took a moment to think of the right words. "Her mother—my grandmother—comes from a very powerful family and is the Commander of the Gatekeepers, which was a problem for the Elders. How could they execute her daughter?"

"That would be hard, I guess."

"Right. But if they didn't do anything, that would set a bad precedent."

He nodded.

"So, grandpa happens to be a colleague of Bartholomew, who's one of their biggest threats. Why not give mom a command she would obey, and order her to marry you? Then she could keep an eye on you in case you 'turned evil.'" I used my fingers as the quotation marks.

He was squinting at me. "So ... she's here to spy on me?"

"It was politics!" I threw up my hands. "The Elders got to save face by pretending it was an assignment, so mom wasn't being disobedient, and Izumo didn't have a rebellious and very dangerous young Gatekeeper to hunt down and try to kill. Oh, and it made the said dangerous young Gatekeeper pretty damn happy too." I leaned back and crossed my arms on my chest.

He scowled for a while then finally said, "Okay, but I can't help feeling like my entire life was orchestrated, right back to when my father got involved with Bartholomew." He closed his eyes and I felt his anger bubbling just below the surface, but there was confusion too. "None of this would've happened if my father didn't—"

"Then you wouldn't have met Mom and I wouldn't be sitting here."

That took the wind out of him. Dad believed in destiny.

"And Grandpa didn't know what he was getting himself into when he approached Bartholomew about the gold. Sure, he was greedy and became power-hungry, but you can't blame all of this on him." I thought for a moment. "Actually, you might even need to thank him."

He made a face. "How do you figure that?"

"Well, if grandpa wasn't rich, do you think you would've been able to travel to Japan and meet mom?"

He rubbed his face with his hands. "Argg, this is so complicated."

It became more intriguing when I had another thought. "I guess I better not complicate things by adding Bartholomew to this equation."

"Please don't." He looked at the floor. "I was so scared of Bartholomew when I was a kid. He was so creepy." He seemed to shudder at the memory. "I hope to god you never meet him."

I cringed. Should we go there now too? Well, why not? Then there would be no secrets left to hide. "Ah, it's too late for that," I said.

His head came up. "Did your grandfather—"

"No, Bartholomew found me, and I'm tired of keeping my shirt on every time you're around."

He looked confused. "What do you mean?"

"Remember last summer, when I came home covered in that black stuff and with the huge cut in my leg?"

His eyes narrowed. His mind was working, and I helped him.

"Bartholomew did that to me."

Dad's eyes widened, and his hands balled into fists. "What?! Why the hell—"

Then I grabbed the hem of my t-shirt. "He did this too." And I pulled it over my head and let him see the ugly scars from Bartholomew's teeth on my chest and arm.

"Oh my god!"

I let him stare at it for a long moment, then gently pushed him back.

"Please, talk to mom." I said as I pulled my shirt back down. "But you need to approach her with an open mind. This isn't about you and mom, or me. Hundreds, probably thousands of people for hundreds of years have been part of this. She thought she got out. She made a life with you, but somehow, I got pulled in and took her with me. This isn't something she should have to apology for." I let a few seconds go by. "And really, you have to take some responsibility for part of this too."

That caught him off-guard. "How?"

"You told mom to train me, so she wouldn't leave you, remember?"

He covered his face with his hands again. "Oh no ... please."

"Yup, who can say what's good or bad."

"This is ... I don't know what this is." He looked at me. "Where are we at now?"

I shrugged. "Depends on how you deal with this," I said as I moved towards the door. "I've been thinking all this is really bad, but I'm not sure anymore either. But I'm glad you did it though, even if it was for the wrong reason."

"Did what?"

"Allowing mom to train me. If you hadn't, I'd be dead right now because Bartholomew would've found me anyway."

He nodded slowly. "That would be bad."

I stopped at the door. "And all of a sudden, I'm thinking of one really good thing about all that's happened."

I think he was too flustered to try guessing.

"Mom trained me well, and if I really carry Bartholomew's blood inside me, then I'm uniquely qualified to stop him."

CHAPTER

38

I TRAVELED TO IZUMO, BUT NOT RIGHT to the shrine. I needed time to think, to cleanse my heart of darkness, and hopefully build the pure energy I'd need. So, I arrived in the little meadow where I'd come the first time I crossed alone, transported by the gods themselves.

Everything looked the same—the mountains, the carpet of beautiful wildflowers at my feet, the clear air—and when I stood up, the shrine was only few miles away, standing high above the trees.

What was missing was energy radiating from the shrine. There was none.

I reached out with all my senses. There had to be something. Maybe I was just missing it. But the only thing that carried on the breeze was a sense of emptiness ... and sadness.

A shiver started in the back of my neck and I glanced around. Had I traveled to Zion by accident? Were there beasts waiting in the trees around me? I shook off the feeling. No, I was in Izumo, and soon I would see Shoko. If I could just see her, I knew everything would feel better.

I started toward the shrine.

Unlike the first time, I didn't stop to enjoy the views or pick berries. I hurried forward, my speed increasing as my anxiety grew until I broke out of the trees about a half hour later. Then I stopped. This was the meadow where I'd seen my first Gatekeepers, Tomi and two apprentices. I'd used my energy to stop her attack. And it was here that we felt the message from the gods, carried by the breeze like a song, telling them I belonged here.

I wished I could get a message like that today.

Far across the meadow, Shoko's straw-roofed house sat in the shade. Taro was outside working on something, maybe piling firewood. There was no sign of anyone else. I started to walk through the knee-high grass toward the shrine.

Gatekeepers crowded the main compound, all apprentices, all armed and in their traditional uniforms. It was quite the sight—there must've been more than a hundred there—but my gaze kept dropping to the dirt beneath their sandals. All I could see were bodies, row after row of lifeless faces.

I had to stop. "I'm so sorry," I whispered. I closed my eyes, but that only made the images clearer.

"Junya?"

When I opened my eyes, Sakura stood in front of me, dressed in civilian clothing.

"How did you get here?" she said.

"I traveled," I said. "With my own energy." I forced a smiled. It was good to see her. "I really needed to know if there'd been any more attacks."

"Any gateways due to open are heavily guarded by full-ranking Gatekeepers. The apprentices wait here as reinforcements and go only if called."

I watched them standing stoically in formation. "Did everyone make it back here okay after I ... traveled them?"

She studied my face for a moment. "The living stayed that way," she said. "Although some needed many days to recover."

I shoved my hands in my pockets. "I guess that's good."

"No!" she said, startling me with her sudden anger. "They deserved worse. Those girls deserted their posts, the worse transgression imaginable. These deaths are on their hands alone!"

Of course, I still didn't see it that way. "I gave them a reason ... the temptation to cross."

"*Temptation* does not absolve them from the consequences of their selfish choices," she said, sounding far older than her fourteen years. Then her face twisted in anger. "I wish I never came to help you save them!" Her hands had balled into fists. "Yukie would still be alive! She died because of them too!"

Oh Jeez. I hadn't considered Yukie's place in all this.

"Are you ... how are you doing?" I asked her, "with Yukie ..."

"*Doing?*" She stared at me for a long moment. "Do you mean, how do I feel now that Yukie, my sister, is dead?"

I swallowed. "Yeah ..."

"I came to help Shoko," she said. "I did not mind dying for her, but Yukie came because of me!" She began to cry.

I reached out and touched her arm. "She died honorably." I said, and I think I finally understood what that meant.

Sakura nodded as she rubbed her eyes. "Yes," she whispered. "With great honor."

I wiped my cheek with my sleeve. "Has anyone been punished?" Besides Shoko, though I didn't say that out loud.

"The Elders' first priority was to bury our dead, but the tribunals will begin soon." She turned to look at the apprentices. "Some good has come of this, at least. We have all been reminded of why we are here, and why we have the rules that we do."

"Did you get in trouble for crossing over to help?"

She shook her head. "I was praised for my contribution ... but I have taken on dishonor once again." A touch of color came to her cheeks. "Shoko is my one true master and I will serve no other. I am masterless once again."

"What do you mean? What happened to Shoko?"

Sakura avoided eye contact. "She is … she resigned."

Oh Shoko, what have you done?

———

I walked to the bottom of the long staircase and knelt on the gravel below the first step. It was such a long way to the top, and I wondered again why the gods' energy had touched me that night.

"You said I belonged," I said, looking at the humble building far above me. "But look what's happened to your world. Look what's happened to you." I let out a deep sigh. "Why did you choose me?"

No energy flowed down and no message came. The only sound was the crunch of feet on the gravel behind me.

"We seldom understand why the gods call to us or forsake us." The Grand Elder's voice was unmistakable. I sensed other movement and turned. Full-ranking Gatekeepers were gathering around him, at least eight so far.

"You have returned despite my command," he said with a sigh. "Why does that not surprise me?"

Still on my knees, I acknowledged him with a low bow.

He sat on the second step and looked down at me. "It is a sad time in Izumo," he said. "So many young lives lost and futures ruined."

"It's horrible," I whispered. "I'm so sorry this happened."

We stayed silent for a few minutes.

"When shamans began dying in great numbers and incursions increased," he said in a quiet, relaxed voice, "we did not appreciate the effect these killings would have on the gods. It was significant and thus needed investigating, but what could we do? Then, young Shoko reminded us of your ability to sense evil and suggested that you could help, working from your side. We were skeptical of course. First that you even would help, or that we would want your help. It was decided a test was needed to demonstrate your abilities, and your loyalties so it was *suggested* to Shoko that she could bring you to

Chichén Itzá."

I frowned. "That was your idea?"

He nodded. "Many Mayans still worship their gods, so the opening of their gateway is always a significant event. We knew Cebrián, their high priest, was dead and his replacement inexperienced. If the Evil Ones wanted to make more trouble, that was the place to expect it."

"Did Shoko know all this?"

He shook his head slowly. "Her knowing could have changed the outcome."

I sat back on my heels. "So, you sent Shoko and her apprentices into danger, unprepared?"

Now he looked at me, eyebrows raised slightly. "Is Shoko ever unprepared?" he said, looking faintly amused. "But I had a Miko ready, just in case *you* were injured."

"But it turned out I was useful."

"You responded with great power, leadership, and loyalty," he said. "We wondered if perhaps your ability to detect Evil Ones was the reason the gods favored you ... because there must be some reason."

I looked up the stairs. Yes, maybe that was the reason.

He turned to look up the stairs, following my gaze. "A boy bred of purity and infected by evil. You truly are a curiosity."

"I know that I carry Bartholomew's blood inside me and so, maybe I am evil." I looked at the ground. "But ... I hope I didn't cause all this."

He chuckled. "You overestimate your importance." He looked away, in the direction of the ocean. "I have never said you were evil, or that you brought evil here. However, too many changes at once, and exposure to outside temptations, caused unprecedented damage to the Gatekeeper legacy."

"Everyone was so eager for me to find a solution," I whispered. "Our tactics worked for a while."

"Many shamans were saved, I believe. However, for Izumo, the good appears quite diminished when compared to the lives lost. And as you can feel, our gods are silent. But the death of the shamans did not do this. We did it to ourselves." He let out a deep breath, as if dispelling some built-up energy. When he spoke again, he sounded tired. "There will be a formal tribunal, and all those who chose to succumb to the temptations of your world must answer for their weaknesses. As a leader, I accept a large portion of the responsibility, as does Chiyoko. She let ego guide her thoughts and actions, just as my pride allowed you to continue with your plan when it was obvious things were spiraling out of control. And as for young Shoko," he chuckled softly. "She owns a piece of my heart. I also let that misguide me."

What the heck did that mean?

"What's the punishment for the girls who deserted?"

"That will be decided."

"I hope it's not a death sentence." Even after all they'd done, I didn't want that.

A short silence ensued, as if he was considering his reply. "All events in life are a lesson," he finally said. "And the worst are the best teachers. They were assigned to bury the dead, both their comrades and the citizens. From this, they will truly understand the consequences of failing in their devotion to the gods. Further punishment can wait." He fell silent for a moment. "However, I do wonder if the weakening of the gods somehow led to the decline in ethics and discipline amongst the Gatekeepers."

I looked up at him. That was interesting.

"For now though," he continued, "it is a time of deep reflection for all of Izumo."

I looked up at him. "And is Shoko 'deeply reflecting' on what Chiyoko said to her?"

He regarded me. "Chiyoko has since apologized for her outburst, though that did little to lessen Shoko's remorse. Out of all of us, she feels the most responsible." He looked thoughtful. "It is unfortunate, although admirable and honorable, that she carries this weight alone. She had a bright future ahead of her."

I squeezed my eyes shut as anger swelled in the pit of my stomach. "You can't allow that to happen!"

"Calm your energy, boy!" He glared at me until my energy lessened. "She chose to punish herself, and that is not something you or I can change. The more blame others take, the more she retreats into herself."

"You could start by refusing to accept her resignation."

He grunted. "Resignation is a decision, not a question." He stood up and gestured to the Gatekeepers and they formed a half circle around him. When he pointed his staff toward me, I half expected a lightning bolt to come out.

"On behalf of the Elders and the Gatekeepers of Izumo Oyashiro, I thank you for returning our young ones," he said. "I realize you took on a heavy burden to do so, another measure of darkness."

I nodded. I wanted to say it was worth it, but honestly, I wasn't so sure anymore.

"I have no malice against you," he said, his staff now pointing right at my chest. "But you do not belong here. You must understand this by now."

He turned and walked away with the Gatekeepers following close behind him, leaving me alone at the foot of the stairs with my head in my hands while the sun set over the Sea of Japan.

─

It was after dark when Shoko came to find me. Like Sakura, she wore civilian clothing, and was unarmed. She also looked exhausted.

I stood and held out my hands. "Shoko!"

"Hello Junya. I have missed you." Her voice lacked any enthusiasm and she dropped onto the bottom step with a thump, leaving my hands to fall to my sides.

I sat down beside her and tried to think of what to say but before I could, she spoke.

"Thank you for rescuing the girls."

"Oh yeah …" There was a lump in my throat I couldn't swallow. "I'm so sorry about Yukie."

She let out a deep sigh. "Ah Yukie, we buried her where the sun will shine on her all day, just as she shined on us."

"That's … nice." I needed to take a few breaths before I could continue. "I saw Sakura earlier. Do you know she resigned too?"

Shoko grunted. "And proved yet again what a stupid girl she is."

"She's very loyal though."

She looked at me, unhappy. "Why are you here?"

I licked my lips, a bit taken aback. "I've been worried about you, and … I wanted to see you."

"You only worry about your own desires."

That stung. "I sent dozens of Gatekeepers back here and I haven't heard anything. I wanted to at least know if they were still alive," I said, more than a little angry. "And you can't blame me for wanting to know how you were. You … you're important to me."

Her dark eyes met mine. "I am not the girl you once knew. I am nothing now."

"No, you aren't, Shoko, and you shouldn't have resigned," I said. "I'm more to blame than you. I was a bad influence—"

"And I brought you here."

"Only because the Elders told you to," I said. "And I heard Chiyoko apologized to you, and the Grand Elder says what happened was everyone's fault. You don't need to take all the blame for this."

"And does this make you feel better?" When I hesitated, she continued. "Many Gatekeepers under my command died because of my negligence. I should have been here, providing leadership, not lying in bed with you and living like a goddess. Regardless of words spoken or blame accepted, no one can be held accountable but me."

I poked my chest. "I'm the one who distracted you. I'll take the blame for that too."

"You cannot!" She hit the step with her fist. "You can return to a life of leisure and eventually put all this out of your mind, but I live here. I violated the laws of Izumo—*my* land—and even worse, I violated my principles. For that, I must pay penance."

"Do you think I'll ever forget the look on Yukie's face as she died, back while I'm living my *life of leisure?*"

She closed her eyes. "I am sorry, Junya," she said after a long moment. "I should not have said that."

I let out a sigh. "Anyhow, I came because I wanted to see you, but it's not the only reason."

She turned to me with the slightest bit of curiosity in her eyes. "Why else?"

"So many people, both here and in my world, are fighting and dying for one reason: Bartholomew. It's like he has a personal vendetta against Izumo and the gods. We need to end this, once and for all."

"There will always be others like him."

"Maybe, but he has a real personal interest in me." I tapped my head, like I'd done with Okaasan. "I can hear him whenever I use his energy."

Shoko looked shocked. "You can hear him?"

"Yeah and I want to get him out of my head," I said, growing agitated. "He isn't going to stop, no matter what tactics we try. I have friends here now." I looked toward the training compound where the dead had laid. "And I've lost too many because of him." Then I looked at her. "And I don't want to lose you. He came too damn close last time."

"You do not sound like the Junya I know," she said quietly. "What has changed?"

"Do you remember the night we raided Walter's penthouse suite, on the top of that building?"

She nodded.

"Later when we went for pizza, you said I should cut Walter down. Not just for what he'd already done, but for what he might do, and I wouldn't do it."

"I remember," she said. "I wanted so desperately to be with you, yet we argued. It was sad."

Desperately? I had no idea.

"Well, if I'd listened to you, a lot of people wouldn't have gotten hurt … Okaasan and Mack, and you wouldn't have been captured by Bartholomew's men."

"Perhaps, but then you would have killed another human being," she said. "And you could not live with yourself for that. Nor would I respect you the way I did."

"He needs to die, deserves to die. It's the only way to stop this from happening again."

"No one can kill Bartholomew."

"How do you know that?"

She hesitated. "Because that is just—"

I held up my hand. "If you plan on saying, 'that's just the way it is', don't bother. I bet no one here has ever tried."

She frowned. "I … No, we are Gatekeepers and as I told Jason-sensei, we don't assassinate, we defend."

"Yeah, well I'm not a Gatekeeper and I'm going to stop him."

She grabbed my arm. "You plan to fight him? Junya, you cannot—"

"Why not? Everyone was right, I do have his energy inside me and apparently, it's really strong." I smiled in the dark, my mind now made up. "I plan to use it against him and stop this, one way or the other."

"No …" She stared into the darkness, the only sound her labored breathing. Finally, she turned to me. "Perhaps … perhaps you can defeat him. Others will still exist, but … maybe you could rid yourself of his evil blood, once and for all."

I hadn't thought of that.

"He will not be alone though," she said, sounding more like herself. "It will be like last time, perhaps worse."

"I guess I'll find out." I touched her hand. "I'll send a message to you when it's done."

She jumped up. "You will *not* face Bartholomew without me!"

God, how I wanted her help, but ... "You can't, Shoko. You're not allowed to travel across, and you're not even a Gatekeeper anymore."

"That is true." Then after a slight hesitation, she smiled mischievously. "So, I am no longer bound by their strict rules of engagement. I can fight and kill any way and anywhere I chose."

I was stunned. "Wow ... I don't know ..."

"We will cut him down together," she said. "Even if I need to return to Zion to do it."

"We're not going to Zion!"

"Thank the gods for that." She wiped her forehead with the back of her hand. "But how will we find him in your world?" she asked. "No one knows where he lives."

"I don't know where he is right now, but there's a G7 Summit, a meeting of the most powerful world leaders, in San Francisco next week. I guarantee he'll be there."

CHAPTER
39

HIGH CONCRETE BARRIERS TOPPED WITH RAZOR wire surrounded the hotel and convention complex. Outside, thousands of shouting protesters faced hundreds of police in riot gear and there'd already been clashes and dozens of arrests. Shoko and I were in the crowd but at the edge. We didn't really fit in since I was in dress pants, a shirt and blazer, and she wore her school uniform. Everyone else seemed to be wearing black.

"I thought your people chose their leaders," Shoko said we surveyed the chaotic scene. "Why are they so angry? And why do their leaders hide behind soldiers and walls?"

"A lot of people think there's a worldwide conspiracy," I said. "They believe world leaders are taking too much control, making decisions that are best for the rich at the expense of the people and the environment."

She looked up at me. "Is that true?"

I paused, though I didn't really need to think about it. "Yes. Bartholomew and my Grandpa and a bunch of others like them are part of it. That's the reason he's here today."

Her brows furrowed. "But those men are not the chosen leaders of the people."

"No, but they tell the leaders what to do," I said. "They have way more power than any president or prime minister."

"How can that be? That is like the Grand Elder having a leader above him."

"Basically," I said. "Do you know that one percent of the people in this world control about the same amount of money as the other ninety-nine percent combined?"

She thought about that for a minute. "So ... if there were one hundred people and one apple, one person gets half and the other ninety-nine share the other half?"

I nodded, impressed.

"Are you part of this one percent?" she said.

I looked around at the angry crowd. "I suppose indirectly ... but let's not tell them that."

She stared into my eyes. "Then you are far more powerful than any of us believed you to be. You could effect change in ways that few others could."

I didn't know how I felt about that. "I guess so."

The crowd suddenly surged forward, taking us with them. I fought against it, literally at one point, sending two men in balaclavas to the ground who were blocking our escape.

"Is there no other way to reach him?" Shoko asked as I pulled her through the crowd.

"Meetings like this are the easiest way to find him." I had to shout so she'd hear me. "I'm using the same strategy the Evil Ones used. Why search when we know he'll be here?"

"At least we do not need to go to Zion," she said. "I believe I have a better chance of surviving here." She looked at the police again. "They are far easier to kill than beasts."

"Yeah, but we only kill Evil Ones, okay? These guys are just doing their job, trying to keep the peace."

"The soldiers in the desert were also just doing their jobs."

"Yeah, but their job is to kill so they expect they'll have casualties too."

We finally broke free of the crowd and found a spot to stand where we could see the entrances.

Shoko looked toward the hotel tower. "Where will we travel to?"

"Traveling gives off too much energy." I'd already thought this through. "I want to surprise him."

"You think he would sense you with all this *noise*?"

"I'm not taking any chances." Then I touched her arm. "Are you okay here, with the noise, I mean?"

"I have been fine since the day you ... awakened me."

I smiled. "We haven't done that in a while."

She gazed at the tower. "So how will we get in then?" she said, as if she hadn't heard my comment. "I hope you do not expect me to climb that."

"With these." I held up two access passes, complete with our pictures, listing us as part of the Thompson Group delegation. "We need to go in like regular people so our passes are valid throughout the building." I pointed at the first security checkpoint. As I'd hoped, private security guards manned it. Police officers were beyond them, ready to respond if needed but they weren't paying much attention. They seemed far more concerned with the crowds outside the gates.

"I'll use a little bit of energy on them, just enough to control them. Bartholomew shouldn't be able to sense that." I smiled at her, feeling quite pleased with myself. I pushed her gently toward the full-body scanner. "You go first. Walk inside and do what they tell you."

The scanner operator's eyebrows came together when she stepped inside. Shoko had a short dagger strapped to the small of her back.

I focused my energy on the operator. *It's only jewelry. Nothing to worry about.*

Another guard waited with a handheld metal detector, ready to scan Shoko as she stepped out.

The operator waved her through. "She's clean."

The other guard looked unconvinced. Maybe he'd seen the green LEDs switch to red as she walked out so I focused my energy on him.

Let her pass, she's clean.

I may have used too much because Shoko's shoulders twitched and the guard squinted, like he was staring at the sun. When he recovered, he blinked at Shoko with an odd expression on his face.

"Carry on, miss," he muttered.

Perfect. Then it was my turn. I was carrying her wakizashi. It was a shorter version than her usual one with a lower profile handle, but it still bulged out the back of her blazer so I offered to carry it alongside the short bokuto I already had strapped to my back. I also carried a large metal pen in my shirt pocket as a decoy.

I looked at the operator as I entered the machine.

Ignore me too. I forgot to take a pen out of my pocket. Then I focused on the waiting guard. *You let me go too.*

But I'd barely stepped into the machine when the operator yelled. "He's got something under his jacket!"

A police officer behind the guard pulled his gun. What the hell was wrong? I looked at the operator, then the guard, and finally down the barrel of the officer's gun. He had it leveled at me.

My eyes locked on Shoko as another officer moved closer, his gun drawn, but still pointed at the ground. "It's ... it's probably my pen," I muttered. I was suddenly sweating.

"Hands away from your body. Do it now!" The first officer ordered as he moved past the nervous guard.

My head jerked back toward the operator.

Tell them to stand down, it's just a pen!

Instead of saying anything, the operator's eyes rolled back into his head and he slumped over the machine. From the corner of my eye, I saw Shoko grab her head.

Shit, too much energy!

More guns came out of holsters. An officer leaned over the

operator and gave his shoulders a shake. "You okay, buddy?"

I turned back toward the others, tried to control the panic growing inside. I thought we were done for when someone started to giggle.

It was Shoko.

She pointed at the operator. "He wet his pants!" She had her hand over her mouth in perfect Japanese-girl fashion.

The operator slowly straightened up, looking embarrassed as hell. *It is a big pen. Tell them, it's just my pen and you're scared of guns.*

His eyes met mine, his confusion obvious. "I ... I made a mistake ... he only has a pen. It's really big and I thought ..." Then he looked at the officers. "I hate guns, I'm sorry. I thought you were going to shoot him."

I blew out my breath.

The cop motioned me with his finger. "Let's see the pen." When I handed it to him, he laughed. "That is a big pen." He unscrewed it and looked inside.

"Yeah, I ... it writes really well though." I felt like smacking myself. That sounded really stupid.

The officer behind him rolled his eyes. "Stand down, guys," he said, then he jerked his thumb toward me. "I'm surprised he didn't piss *his* pants."

I let out a nervous laugh, which I didn't have to fake at all. If my bladder were full, I may have.

The officers holstered their guns. "Next time," the officer said as he handed back the pen, "Don't bring *anything* in."

I nodded, breathing too hard to answer.

"Now get out of here."

We hurried away from the security post.

"Nice move back there," I said to Shoko when we were out of earshot.

"I always need to rescue you." She sounded annoyed. "And with all the energy you used, I am sure every Evil One in this building knows we are here."

—

The main meetings took place in a medium-sized conference room surrounded by layers of security. We didn't have a chance to get near there, but I was pretty sure Bartholomew pulled the strings from backstage anyhow. The only problem was finding where that was.

Shoko and I walked for over an hour, from one meeting room to the next. Some rooms we could walk right up to the doors or even inside. Those were for aides or lower-level meetings. The largest conference room in the complex was a buzz of activity. International media had that room, and it was a mess of wires, computers, and general mayhem. And while we went through more checkpoints, manned by security officers, there were no more searches. Our passes were good enough.

Everywhere we went, the air sizzled with negativity, enough that it would've knocked me down only a few months ago. I didn't sense any Evil Ones though.

Shoko and I finally sat down on a leather sofa near the hotel lobby. My feet were sore from walking. I wasn't used to the dress shoes.

This was starting to feel impossible. "He must be upstairs somewhere, in a suite or something," I said as I rested my head against the back of the sofa. "But I'm pretty sure the presidential suite's already taken."

Shoko smoothed her short skirt against her legs. "I thought Bartholomew was more powerful than a president."

I laughed. "Yeah, you'd think if anyone has the best room here, it'd be him." Then I sat up straight. "Maybe he even owns this hotel." I pulled out my phone. "I'll see if I can find out."

While I called Mr. Barrymore, Shoko stood up, stretched, then wandered off to look around the lobby. About five minutes later, Barrymore had succeeded in tracing ownership through five corporations before hitting a roadblock.

"I'll need my people to dig deeper," he said. "That could take a few hours."

"Never mind," I said, disappointed. "I can't wait that long." As we said our good-byes, Shoko sat back down beside me.

"He is probably on the thirty-first floor," she said.

I looked at the map I'd picked up earlier at the front desk. "There is no thirty-first floor."

"The boy over there in the cute hat says there is," she said. Then she lowered her voice. "It is a secret."

"But he told you?"

Shoko gave me a smile that nearly melted my heart.

"Ah, right," I said with a roll of my eyes. "Boys are so easy to manipulate."

"It is *so* true."

"And did the cute boy tell you how we get there?"

"I only said his hat was cute," she said. "He said there is a private *elevator*, whatever that is."

I smiled. "It's a way to travel—move—to the top of a building."

She slowly nodded, obviously thinking about that. "Okay, the boy said the elevator travels from a place called *loading dock*. It is hidden, and most employees do not know it exists. He was proud to tell me that."

"I wonder where the loading dock is."

"Near the kitchens, of course."

I looked up, startled. "Lin!"

Her white teeth sparkled between perfectly painted red lips as she smiled, though she didn't look happy.

"Mr. Barrymore just called me on the secure line," she said as she steered us away from some police officers. "He told me what you'd asked, but I hung up on him. God only knows how many intelligence agencies are listening right now." She lowered her voice. "I happen to know The Committee owns this hotel chain, but you'd have to dig about ten layers deep to find that out."

I stared at her. "So, Grandpa—"

"And therefore you too." She moved closer and lowered her voice. "Why do you need to know?"

"Because I think Bartholomew's on the thirty-first floor."

Her hand went to her mouth. "How do you know about ...?" She glanced around. "What are you up to?"

I glanced at the cops behind her then lowered my voice. "We're going to have a little chat with him."

Shoko looked confused. "I thought we were going to try to kill him."

"What?!" Lin waved her hand in a random swing. "There are more cops and media here than any place on earth right now!"

"But they're not watching a floor that doesn't exist."

"I know where his house is in Geneva," she whispered. "You don't need to confront him here! And from what I've heard, you shouldn't go near him at all."

"I'm not giving him time to think up ways to kill any more Gatekeepers," I said. "You mentioned the loading dock was near the kitchen?"

She poked her index finger into my chest. "I'm not helping you," she hissed at me. "You'll get killed or caught, and either way you'll ruin your grandfather."

I looked down at her hand, the nail still pressed against my shirt. "Is that really what you're worried about?"

"What does that mean?"

"Toshio said your assignment is over so ..."

"So what? Nothing has changed."

"Then where's your engagement ring?"

She looked at her hand, startled. "I ... I must have left it in my condo."

"What a coincidence."

"You think this is easy for me?" There was something in her voice: anger, fear ... something. "Don't do this, not here, not now." She was clearly shaken. "Please, Junya."

I hesitated. The stream was sending me a message—a warning.

Shoko touched my arm. "That's enough, Junya," she said quietly. "Save your anger for he who deserves it." Then she looked up at Lin.

"Honorable Lin, Bartholomew dies today."

I took a deep breath, then another. "I'm sorry, Lin." Then I looked her in the eye. "Don't get involved. We'll find our own way."

Lin closed her eyes for a moment. She was worried about something, but it wasn't me.

"Those passes won't get you anywhere near it," she said with a tone of resignation. "I can take you as far as the loading dock. After that, you're on your own."

"As in, you wouldn't help us if we really needed it?"

"As in there'll be nothing I can do for you."

She led us through the main kitchen, striding like she owned the place, which I suppose she indirectly did, if she actually married Grandpa. When we reached a store room down the hall from the kitchens, she stopped.

"You'll find a set of double doors just through here." She pointed to the far end of the large room. "The loading dock is right through them, but it'll be under guard for sure. The private elevator is behind the door with the 'Restricted Access' sign."

I frowned. "How do you know all this?"

"Because I've been up there," she said. "I'm warning you, this won't turn out well for any of us."

I forced a smile. "Especially not for Bartholomew."

"You're not invincible and you have no idea what's waiting up there for you."

"I owe it to the Gatekeepers to try."

She shook her head sadly then looked at Shoko. "Try and talk him out of this." Then she walked away.

I stood staring after her, but she didn't look back.

"Lin is a warrior," Shoko said. "Her attitude toward this is odd."

Yes, something didn't add up, but there was no time to think about it now. I handed Shoko a balaclava. "There will be security cameras—magic eyes—out there." I slipped my balaclava on as we walked through the store room. "And I'd rather not end up on the evening news."

Through the crack in the double swing doors, I could make out three uniformed security guards standing together, watching a worker move a stack of tomato boxes. They looked like the minimum-wage type.

Over by the door marked 'Restricted Access,' two men in black suits stood with their backs against the wall. They had their long hair tied back in ponytails, white access cards around their necks along with their ID passes, and bulges under their jackets. I didn't need the pain in my shoulder to tell me they were Evil Ones.

And they looked bored.

"Perfect," I whispered to Shoko as I pulled out her wakizashi to give to her. "Ignore the other guards. We go straight at—"

"Hold it right there!"

We both spun and found ourselves face to face with a very large security guard.

Shoko fired a kick into his bulging gut that sent him backward into a stack of produce boxes. He hit them, still upright and bounced back, surprised and winded. His arms came up in defense, but Shoko was too close, and too fast. She kicked his left thigh above the knee, then spun under his arms, taking his right pinky finger with her. His leg gave out but his body instinctively followed Shoko as he tried to keep his finger from breaking, but she was still spinning, and I heard his finger snap a half-second before her rising right foot connected with his head.

Shoko stepped back and watched him crumble to the concrete floor. She glanced at me then studied him for a moment longer, waiting for a reaction. There wasn't any.

"I hope you didn't kill him."

"Should I?"

"No! Now let's go."

We burst through the double doors together and sprinted toward the Evil Ones. They must've heard the commotion because they were alert but we covered the twenty feet before they could draw their weapons. I went between the Evil One's raising hands, slammed my left hand into his throat and drove him back against the steel doors. I drove my right fist under his ribcage, once, twice, then smashed an elbow into his jaw for good measure.

Shoko finished her sprint in midair and her heel hit her target mid-chest with a flying kick. I heard the sickening crunch as he hit the wall, eyes bulging. He was beginning to slide down the wall when she spun in the air and drove a knee into his head. As she landed, her wakizashi flashed out and she stabbed him in the chest. The point punched out between his shoulder blades and dented the steel door.

My guy grabbed my hair and yanked while his other hand struggled against my hand on his throat. I drove my fist into the side of his head then grabbed his ears and yanked his face down into my raising knee. As his head popped back up, black blood pouring from his crushed nose, I jumped back and spun. My shoe caught him in the side of the neck. His eyes rolled back, and he started to fall but I grabbed his collar and shoved him toward the access card-reader. With my free hand, I swiped his access card against the reader. There was a beep, the light turned green, the lock clicked, and we fell backward through the doorway and landed hard on the concrete floor.

I rolled away from the unconscious Evil One and looked around. The room was about ten feet square with concrete with walls. A security camera on the far wall pointed at the elevator door.

I ran back out to the loading dock. The uniformed guards were freaking out, screaming and yelling. Shoko turned to face them, her sword extended, dripping black blood, and the yelling dropped to whimpers.

I picked up the guns that lay on the ground—two MP5s—and slung them over my shoulders then grabbed the back of the other Evil One's collar and dragged him toward the doorway. He was limp, bleeding like crazy and then … he was gone. I fell on my butt as he turned to dust.

Shoko backed up to the doorway, her sword still pointed at the guards and the delivery guy.

"What about them?" she asked me as I stood up and dusted my pants off.

In response, I pulled her toward me and wrapped my arm around her head, covering her ears. Then I looked to the guards and the delivery guy and I let my energy go.

"You didn't see us or any fighting here, understand?"

All four of them nodded like zombies. I knew the security cameras would tell a different story, but there was nothing I could do about that.

"The second this door closes, go back to what you were doing before we showed up. You didn't see anything unusual. Got it?"

Again, zombie nods.

Then I pulled Shoko into the room and closed the door. I grabbed her face with both hands so I could see into her eyes, the only thing that showed through her mask. "Are you okay?"

Her hands reached up to cover mine. "You did not use much energy. At least it did not feel like it."

I wanted to kiss her and started to raise her mask when the elevator bonged, causing us both to turn. The LED readout said the elevator was on the thirtieth floor, but it had started to descend. The stream—and the growing throbbing in my shoulder—told me the elevator wouldn't be empty when it arrived.

I noticed the security camera again, staring down at us with its unblinking red eye. I unslung one of the MP5s and threw it up at the camera. The camera didn't break off its mount, but it twisted towards the blank concrete wall. The MP5 clattered to the floor beside the Evil One. He was still unconscious.

Shoko must've read my mind. She walked toward the Evil One, her wakizashi raised. I took a firm grip on the other MP5 and silently thanked Jason for the training. As Shoko's sword whistled through the air, arcing toward the Evil One's neck, I flipped the safety off and pointed the MP5 at the elevator doors.

CHAPTER
40

THE ELEVATOR DOORS SLID OPEN, REVEALING white marble tile and wood paneling. I moved my finger to the trigger. Shoko took a slow step forward, her wakizashi ready for a quick thrust.

The elevator was empty.

I took a tentative step forward and peeked inside. Nothing. So why was my shoulder killing me?

Shoko looked at me, puzzled. "What do you sense?" she whispered.

Through gritted teeth, I tapped my shoulder. She nodded.

"Do you actually have a plan?"

I shook my head. "Not even the *what ifs*."

"The biggest *what if* is if we cannot travel away."

I nodded. Bartholomew was up there, waiting, and I was pretty damn sure he knew we were coming.

We stepped inside, the doors slid closed and the elevator began to rise, even though I hadn't pressed a button. A moment later, Shoko put a hand against her stomach, as though she might throw up. It wasn't moving that fast, but—

I lunged and slammed her against the wall as the marble floor exploded, right where she'd been standing. Bullet holes stitched across the floor and sprayed our legs with shrapnel. I aimed the MP5 at the floor, then swung it toward the ceiling and pulled the trigger. The sound was deafening, both the shots and Shoko's scream. I struggled to hold the gun as it jerked in my hands, sending bullets everywhere above me. A few seconds later, it clicked—empty.

My ears were ringing.

Shoko crouched in the corner, hands over her ears, staring at me with huge eyes. She pointed at an unbroken part of the white marble floor. Black blood dripped onto the tiles, one big plop after another. Then it stopped and the pain in my shoulder eased.

"They were only aiming at me," she whispered.

Seeing Shoko's legs bleeding from a dozen or more cuts from the marble shrapnel, I felt my anger, and guilt, rise. My long pants had saved me.

When the elevator passed the sixteenth floor, I pointed to the corner by the buttons. "Stand there and get ready." Then I listened, and the stream carried messages to me.

"Two more Evil Ones are waiting ... a bunch of people too."

"Can you sense Bartholomew?" she said.

I shook my head as I watched the numbers pass twenty-five, then I raised my palms and faced the door. "This better work ..."

The doors slid open.

Two Evil Ones waited, same black suits as the guys downstairs, with MP5s aimed at us.

I exhaled as a blossom of fire expanded from the muzzles. Bullets—a burst of three from each gun—drifted out. I laughed as I strolled toward them. They'd be dead before the bullets reached the elevator ...

"No!" I jumped back and grabbed Shoko around the waist and spun back into the lobby. I stumbled and we fell onto the marble floor. Her weight knocked the wind out of me and my energy released. Gunfire roared, and the bullets punched through the back wall of the elevator, right where Shoko had been.

The echo of the shots hung in the air and it took a moment before the Evil Ones processed the change, but they noticed us as I squirmed out from under Shoko. Gun barrels swung toward us.

"Shit!" I lunged to my feet. I hadn't protected Shoko at all.

I made it to the closest one and shoved the gun barrel up as I plowed into him. He was big—I'm not—and he didn't move far. The other one raised his gun and aimed, though not at me. I reached for him as I fell, trying to knock the gun off target.

"Shoko!"

She flew past me—literally—midway through a cartwheel, her feet a blur as they smashed into the Evil One's face. As he staggered back against the wall, Shoko drew her wakizashi.

A hand grabbed my hair and yanked. A second later, something thumped into my head and I saw stars. As I went down, I heard the familiar whistle of a blade slicing through air.

Someone slapped my face. It was Shoko.

"Ouch!" I moaned. "I'm conscious. Jeez."

"I did not know that." She yanked on my arm. "Get up. He is here."

"Are you—"

He laughed, the slow, creaky cackle of an elderly man.

Shoko and I exchanged looks, then burst through the doorway together, sending the doors swinging into the walls with a loud bang.

Bartholomew stood in a large, opulent room, near the floor-to-ceiling windows. He looked frailer than I remembered, his shoulders slightly stooped. A dozen people, each with a laptop and wearing a communication headset, sat in high-back leather chairs at the large boardroom table. They stared at us, wide-eyed. Two Asian women dressed in cocktail dresses—one near the bar, the other seated on the sofa—looked surprised, but they seemed more composed than the others.

I felt nothing particularly dark from any of them, just the usual negative energy I'd come to expect from adults. And, of course, fear.

I glanced at Shoko. We still wore the masks, and her wakizashi dripped a steady stream of black blood onto the lush carpet.

"What an entrance," Bartholomew said in a wheezing voice.

A man at the far end of the table stood up. "Ah ... sir?"

"David." Bartholomew motioned to the people seated at the table. "Take everyone to our other boardroom and continue working. You *will not* remember any of this, only my instructions. Continue with them. Do you understand?"

I felt his energy and realized he could control minds too. Or maybe that's why I could.

The group at the table stood and gathered their things while keeping a wary eye on us, their fear palpable. The two women didn't move.

"Take the stairs," one of them said to the group.

"You two also leave," Shoko said from beside me. "Or today you will taste this blade. I have no mercy for traitors."

The old man sat down. "They won't fight unless I tell them to," he said, his breath labored. "Now take off those stupid masks."

I yanked mine off. "Hello Bartholomew."

He regarded us. "James and the Fallen Gatekeeper," he said. "Such a nice young couple. Too bad you won't live happily ever after."

I moved closer to the windows while Shoko stayed where she was, watching the other two.

My anger grew the more I looked at him. "We'll see about that."

He started to laugh, which turned into a cascade of coughing. "You're still as arrogant and stupid as ever." Then he leaned back and studied me, starting at my feet, and worked his way up until our eyes met.

"I've lost a lot of underlings because of you," he said. "And a garage full of young meat."

"*Meat?*"

He smirked. "How's your shoulder? I can't imagine how much it must hurt but," he glanced at Shoko. "I bet she loves the scar."

"Your blood hasn't changed me."

"But you *have* changed," he said to me. "Much more than I imagined you would. You're confident and powerful, influencing stodgy Elders and impressionable Gatekeepers alike." He slapped the table, startling me. "And I absolutely love what you did to Izumo, and what you're doing with her." He made a crude motion with his fingers.

"You disgust me!" Shoko said, spitting the words out like venom. "If the gods would curse you—"

He pursed his lips and puffed out a breath, like he was blowing out a candle. Shoko dropped to the floor.

"They won't, because they *can't*." He shook his head. "You Gatekeepers die, day after day, year after year, for a bunch of useless, powerless gods. What a waste."

"You know nothing about the gods!" Shoko yelled, still on the floor.

"Why don't you leave them alone?" I said as I moved closer to him. "Don't you have enough lives here to destroy?"

He coughed again. "I don't *like* those archaic gods," he said after he wiped his mouth. "They've occupied that perfect world for centuries, allowing only those they think are *good enough* to go there." He turned his head slightly in Shoko's direction. "But not for much longer. They are weakening."

Shoko squinted up at him from her knees. "Our gods and their worshipers remain strong!" she shouted. "You achieved nothing with your campaign of murder!"

He coughed. Or laughed. I couldn't tell anymore.

"Shut up," he said to her. "Do you think I don't know what's happening there? It may take ten years, or a few hundred years, but they *will* wither. There are too many rules, too many boring ceremonies. And for the people on this side, there's no evidence the gods even exist. Hell, even you Gatekeepers crumbled at the first taste of a little material pleasure and freedom." He grinned at me.

"They couldn't wait to get out of Izumo."

If Shoko could kill with just a look …

"Yeah, and you snatched them up to use as *meat* for your lizards," I said as I drew my bokuto. "You're so … disgusting."

He raised his eyebrows as he regarded the bokuto. "And what do you plan to do with that?"

"This thing kills lizards," I said as I gave it a spin. "Perhaps you remember?"

"Do you intend to become an executioner now? A murderer?" He laughed, sounding younger than a moment before. "And you say my blood hasn't changed you!"

I faltered and the bokuto drooped to the floor. I didn't like the sound of that.

"Seriously?" He sighed with disappointment. "This was just getting interesting." He crossed his arms and glared at me. "Come on, hit me with the damn thing. I'm a helpless old man. I can't change into my other form here. It's the perfect opportunity!"

"I'm … I'm not like you."

"No, you're a loser. So much potential but you have no *will*, and no balls."

"I do not need balls!" Shoko started toward him, her wakizashi held out straight.

Bartholomew rose off his chair as if pulled by a cable. Energy radiated out from him, encircling me, spinning and swirling like a tornado. Shoko flew backwards, out of my sight as pain blasted into my shoulder and I dropped to the floor, screaming in agony. It was worse than the time he'd sunk his teeth into me. The pain sucked the very life from my soul.

"You pathetic, useless half-breed," he snarled. "You carry my energy, my power, but you reject it. Why? Because of her, or the stupid gods?" His eyes bore into mine. "Why?! Why would you reject this?"

I looked up at him through squinted eyes. "I don't … want your power." I sucked in a breath as pain shot through me again.

"Don't … need it."

"You're a hypocrite! It's okay when it's *useful* or when you're desperate. Like when you want to fight harder or travel little Gatekeepers away! Otherwise it's *Evil*, right?" His growing anger made the pain in my shoulder worse and I cried out.

He came closer. "The only reason you—and her and those Gatekeepers—are even still alive is because of my blood! And you'll use it later to make this pain stop, won't you?"

I lay there panting, and wishing I couldn't hear him, because it was the truth.

He squatted beside me, so close I could see every wrinkle on his elderly face. "You call me evil, but did I kill you, or her, in Zion? I could've let you fall," he said. "And my underlings don't beat their youngsters half to death in training, and I don't kill my own as punishment. But your mother faced a death sentence. Why? Because she *didn't want to go home*?! And they sentenced you to death because you survived in my *evil* world and rescued her, and you heard the gods speak." He let a few seconds go by then asked: "You consider that *good*?"

I squinted into his eyes. How could he know all this?

"Do not listen to him, Junya!"

He glanced over his shoulder at Shoko. "Why not?" Then he turned back at me. "Because she only wants you to hear her version of the *truth*." He narrowed his eyes as he looked at me. "Well, it's decision time. Do you want my power or not? You can't have it both ways."

When I didn't answer, his scowl deepened. "Well, screw you." His voice was full of contempt. "I'm taking it away."

Maybe he already had because I couldn't move, not even enough to raise my head. It felt like ten lead x-ray blankets had dropped over me.

"Get up!" Shoko yelled from across the room. "The power inside you is not Bartholomew's, or the gods. It is yours and you are more powerful than him!"

His eyes changed to yellow slits and his tongue forked as he lunged to his feet.

"I should've killed you in Zion," he hissed. He threw up his palms and the force of his energy knocked her over the sofa, arms flailing, into the opposite wall. She dropped to the floor and lay still.

"Shoko!" I struggled against the weight and got my hands under me. Using every bit of energy I could muster, I started to crawl toward her. I only made it a few feet before he grabbed my collar and threw me across the room like I weighed nothing. I hit the wall not far from Shoko.

He stopped about ten feet away, palms up and shook his head in disgust. "You're a fool. She doesn't even love you anymore."

We both turned to look at Shoko. She still lay where she'd landed but her eyes were open, watching Bartholomew. They were emotionless, as if she knew death was coming and accepted it.

He pointed his hand at her and I felt his energy build ...

I let out a primal scream that split the air like cracking ice, then pulled myself up the wall. Energy surged up inside me, faster, stronger than ever before, but different. I grabbed the energy like it was a two-thousand-pound barbell and flung it straight at Bartholomew.

The world shifted into slow motion. The windows seemed to bend outward as if made of plastic as he lifted off his feet. He glided across the room, flew past Shoko's crumpled form, past the frozen women at the bar, over the boardroom table and into the far wall.

He slid down the broken drywall onto his butt and sat there looking dazed and shocked. After a long moment, he looked up at me and smirked. "Yes, you're more than willing to use it." Then he stood up.

I stumbled toward him. "I'm not using your power!" I yelled. "Shoko's right, this is my power!"

He laughed, sounding a lot like the younger man I'd met in Zion. "Really?" His yellow eyes held mine as he flexed his hands. "Let's see how strong you really are then."

He still looked like an old man, but his energy was more powerful than anything I'd ever felt. His hands were up, palms forward, pumping like pistons. Each energy blast lifted me and sent me backward, tumbling over furniture, fighting to stay upright until I hit the far wall near the elevator.

He closed in, his energy smashing into me like waves—an endless onslaught—that slammed me into the wall, again and again. I had my hands up, palms out, trying to protect myself, but I was helpless to stop him. I struggled to breathe, and I felt like I was in the ocean, trapped near the shore, being sucked out, then thrown back by the waves—drowning.

The ocean...

Did you fight the waves? No, if you wanted to survive, you had to relax and go with them.

I let his energy flow over me, then past me, and it lost its strength. Once free of it, my own energy began to build, and he faltered as it surged out of me.

I straightened, and we held each other in place like two opposing magnets, palms out, forcing energy back and forth, gaining ground then losing it, but he advanced more than me and slowly closed the gap. I was weakening. There was no way I could keep this up.

He made one final push and we were face to face. His grin told me he knew he'd won. He reached for my throat.

I'm not sure why my body choose to react the way it did. Years of training I guess.

I punched him in the face.

His head snapped back and he went down hard, his energy dropping with him. I stared at him, heaving to pull in a breath, as he lay there clutching his face. When he finally looked up, he seemed more surprised than hurt even thought his nose was a crumpled mess.

I must've let my energy drop too because Shoko let out a loud groan.

Bartholomew started to sit up, but I didn't give him a chance. I staggered forward and kicked him. Nothing fancy—I couldn't manage anything better—just a clumsy roundhouse kick to the head. He cried out and fell back. I went to my knees from the exertion. I had nothing left.

Then Shoko was beside me, wakizashi in hand. A line of blood ran down her face and onto her shirt, but she was in better shape than me. She was upright.

"What did you do to him?"

"I ... I just punched him."

His energy spiked, and he growled. "I wasn't even going to kill you but now—"

Shoko lunged forward, her blade arcing towards his torso. He rolled away, but the blade still cut deep into his arm and he howled in pain, sounding more like an animal than a human.

I sensed them coming.

"Shoko!" We'd forgotten about the women!

One drew a knife from under her skirt while the other pulled a long pin from her hair. Both weapons flew—the blade toward me, the pin at Shoko—with the women following close behind, new blades already in hand.

I didn't have time to react, but somehow Shoko did. She batted the weapons off course with her wakizashi, then continued the spin, and let them run into the arc of her blade. With one slash, she slit both their throats—nearly decapitating them.

I rolled out of the way as they slid to the ground beside me, blood pouring from their necks—red blood.

I leaned back against the upturned sofa. My arm hurt like hell.

Bartholomew groaned. He'd rolled onto his back, his gaze locked on Shoko, and her sword. She stood over him, looking as beat up and disheveled as the day I found her in Zion, chained to the rocks with Bartholomew ready to kill her. This time, it was her looking down at him.

"No ..." he whispered. "Don't let her kill me ... not like this ..." His wide eyes met mine and I saw genuine fear.

I frowned at him. "Who better than a ... Gatekeeper?" I said, teeth gritted against the pain.

"She's not just a Gatekeeper! If she kills this body, I—"

Shoko slammed the wakizashi straight down into his chest so hard it sunk into the floor beneath him. Then she stepped back and stared down at him, the wakizashi still upright in his body.

His energy, already weak, faded away and he looked about as dead as any other body I'd ever seen, except ...

"He does not bleed," Shoko said as she struggled to pull her blade free. "Neither his arm or his face."

"Doesn't everything bleed?"

"Gods do not," she said, looking at me now. "But they do not die either." She tapped Bartholomew's body with her shoe. "And he is definitely dead."

"Why doesn't he disappear?"

"I have no idea."

CHAPTER
41

CONSIDERING WHAT HAD JUST HAPPENED, there wasn't that much damage. The windows hadn't blown out as I'd thought. There were only the two broken doors, an overturned sofa, a few scattered office chairs, and some dents in the walls—well, some big holes actually.

And three dead bodies.

"How's your head?" I asked Shoko. "You hit that wall pretty damn hard."

"It hurts," she said as she rubbed the back of her head. "And I am sure that tomorrow I will feel worse." Then she gave me the slightest smile, barely enough to turn the corners of her mouth. "Thank you for asking."

Then she touched my shoulder. "Your arm is bleeding," she said. "I am sorry. I thought I stopped the knife."

Shoko pointed her sword at one of the women and slit her sleeve, then used the cloth to tie around my arm. I studied the women as she worked.

Thigh holsters and hair pins?

"They're kunoichi—ninja?" I whispered. "Here?"

Shoko looked at me. "They are traitors."

It was too much of a coincidence. "They must work for Toshio."

Shoko grunted in agreement. "Perhaps that explains Lin's odd behavior," she said. "Perhaps she knew they were here."

I covered my face with my hands. I was completely exhausted, and I didn't want to consider that possibility. Not now, not ever.

I struggled to my knees. "We better get out of here."

She sheathed her wakizashi then pointed to the table. "It is real wood, I think."

I touched it, then nodded in agreement. Even under all the coats of stain and lacquer, the Mother Earth's warmth still flowed within the thick oak planks. I took Shoko's hand and we both laid our palms flat on the surface.

"Mother Earth, please take us to my house."

Nothing happened.

I looked at Shoko. "What's wrong?"

"You are not providing any energy," she said, her voice strained. "And I am weakened. I cannot carry both of us. We will try again, the proper way this time."

We knelt and gave thanks to the Mother Earth for allowing us to travel. Then we tried again.

Still nothing.

Shoko looked at me. "Where is all the power you possessed just moments ago?"

"Maybe … maybe Bartholomew really was the source of my power after all." I looked over to where his body still lay. "And it died with him."

She shook her head. "No …" she said, but she didn't argue further.

I struggled to my feet. "We need to find another way out of here." I knew Jason was at the summit as part of Grandpa's security team, but he was on the other side of the complex when I called him.

"Do you know where the private elevator is, the one that leads to the thirty-first floor conference room?"

There was a long pause. Long enough that I started to wonder if the call had dropped.

"Yes," he finally replied. "It was part of my job orientation."

"Can ... can you meet us there? We need a pick up—an evac— right away." I don't know how much blood I'd lost but I was having trouble focusing.

Another pause. "Okay. Give me ten minutes," he said. "I'll be driving a black SUV." To his credit, he didn't ask why.

"Do you sense anything?" Shoko asked as I hit the down button on the private elevator.

I shook my head. No messages came from the stream—at all— and that worried me. I couldn't calm the pain in my shoulder either.

Jason had the driver's side window open so I heard him swear as the SUV jerked to a stop outside the non-descript metal door that led from the private elevator lobby to the underground parking lot. I could barely stand and the blood from my shoulder wound had overwhelmed the bandage Shoko had applied upstairs. She didn't look much better.

We stayed within the shadows of the doorway as Jason jumped out.

"Stay there," he said as he hurried to the rear hatch of the truck. I was expecting a first aid kit to emerge, but he hauled out a blanket instead. He didn't say anything else, just tossed the blanket over Shoko and me, opened the rear door of the SUV and hustled us inside. He'd obviously done this before.

"I assume we aren't going to the hospital?" he said over his shoulder as he climbed into the driver's seat.

"My house," I muttered. "My mom ... she's good at this stuff."

"I'll bet."

"She has a blue bottle of the potion now as well," Shoko whispered to me. At my questioning stare, she shrugged. "I thought it would be useful one day."

"Keep down and under the blanket while I drive out of here," he said as we emerged into the sunlight. A few minutes later, once we cleared the last of the barricades, and were stopped at a traffic light, Jason turned in his seat. He studied us, his face expressing more annoyance than concern.

"Mind telling me what the hell's going on?" he said. "And how do you know about the thirty-first floor suite? When Barrymore showed me your grandfather's properties, he made it seem like its existence was a big secret. I even had to sign a non-disclosure agreement."

"Yeah well, I'm the heir, right?" My eyes met his in the mirror. "Do you know who was using it?"

"I assume it's that Müller guy, or his boss," he said. "I saw those black-haired bodyguards covering the entrances earlier today."

"So, none of our people will be going up there?" I could only hope.

Jason waited about two blocks before he answered. "If they do, what will they find?"

I leaned back into the seat and closed my eyes. Every jolt of the vehicle made my shoulder throb.

"Do yourself a favor and make sure it isn't you who goes," I said. "And you probably should clean the blood off these seats after you drop us off."

"Great …"

—

"Mom?" I called from the front door. Jason stood with us, supporting most of my weight. Shoko stood to one side,

"Mrs. Thompson?" Jason's voice was far louder than my weak attempt.

My dad arrived first and when he first saw me, his expression reminded me of the time when I'd made this same entrance, after I'd been bit by Bartholomew. He recovered quickly though.

"Misako!" He yelled. Then to me he said, "I'll get the first aid kit."

"That's probably—"

"Junya, Shoko!" Okaasan burst into the foyer. "I've been worried sick! Lin called and said you were going after Bartholomew."

"He is dead," Shoko said.

"Oh, jeez," Jason muttered. "I don't want to hear this."

Okaasan's eyes widened. "How?"

"Junya fought him and I finished him with my wakizashi," Shoko said. Then she looked up at me. "Junya carries no blood on his hands for this."

I frowned. Was she taking credit or accepting the blame?

"You *killed* an old man in your grandfather's hotel and I helped you get away ...?!" Jason wiped his face with his hand. "During a G7 summit ..."

"He did not bleed when I stabbed him," Shoko said to Okaasan.

Okaasan's brows came together. "No blood? What was he then?"

Something was bothering me, and it wasn't a lack of blood. "It was too easy," I said. "I mean, I just punched him in the face."

Shoko scowled at me. "Easy? You could have knocked the gods of Izumo off their perch with the energy you used before that."

"You can't be serious, Shoko," Okaasan said. "Evil energy can never match—"

"It was not evil energy, or even pure that he used," Shoko said, turning to look at Okaasan. "It was Junya's own, neither one nor the other."

She was wrong, though. The energy felt different, but I had no doubt it was Bartholomew's. Somehow, I'd used it against him—and won. But was it gone now?

"And you're sure he's dead?"

"I have seen many dead bodies, as have you," Shoko said. "He was dead."

Jason muttered something I couldn't hear as he lowered me onto a bench. I winced in pain as I looked up at him.

"Thanks Jason," I said. "You saved the day, man."

He nodded slowly, probably wishing he hadn't answered his phone.

"Consider this a Black Op," I said. "It never happened, and you were never here."

He backed toward the door. "Oh, I won't say a damn word." He pointed a finger at me. "But one day, you have a lot of explaining to do."

"It was weird," I said after Jason closed the door behind himself. "Bartholomew was scared—terrified. He begged me to stop Shoko from killing him."

"What's so weird about that?" Okaasan asked. "No one wants to die."

"No, I mean he didn't want *Shoko* to kill him. He made it sound like she was different somehow." I looked at Shoko, but she just shrugged.

A short silence ensued before Okaasan said, "I hope the Elders know what all this means."

"Ah, the Elders." Shoko didn't look happy. "I must face them in disgrace ... again."

Okaasan put her hand on Shoko's arm. "Don't you think killing Bartholomew will make up for you crossing without permission?"

She shook her head. "It will just reveal to everyone that I broke a decree again."

"Ah, I hate to interrupt our little chat, but I'm bleeding all over the floor here ..."

"I think you'll be a hero, Shoko," Okaasan said as if she didn't hear me. "After I deal with him," she tilted her head toward me, "I'll help you get cleaned up and find something you can wear. You can't return to Izumo looking like that."

Dad came back into the foyer carrying two large first aid bags. Mack was with him, a thin coat of sawdust on his shirt and hair.

"I brought everything." Dad put them down and started to open them but Okaasan stopped him.

"I just need the little blue bottle." She pointed to it, then smiled at him. "I think you'll be amazed when you see this."

"Damn," Mack muttered as he came over to me and inspected

my bloodied shirt. "Bartholomew again?"

"Not this time. Ninjas. Knife wound."

Shoko sat down on the bench beside me. "I tried to stop it," she said in a low voice. "But I was too slow."

Despite the pain, I laughed. "Slow? You took out those two ninjas pretty damn fast. That was more important."

"Still …"

"Ninjas were there?" Okaasan asked as she knelt in front of us.

"Yeah … two Kunoichi," I said through gritted teeth.

Her eyes net mine. "Toshio's?"

I nodded. "I think so."

I cringed and closed my eyes as she poured some of the liquid onto a white cloth. I knew this would hurt.

Shoko sucked in a quick breath and I opened my eyes. Okaasan was dabbing the cuts on Shoko's face.

"Seriously?" I grumbled.

"Hush," Okaasan said to me. "We don't want Shoko having scars on her face. Your body's already a mess. One more scar won't make a difference." Then she went to work on Shoko's legs.

My dad and Mack stared in astonishment as the cuts closed. Okaasan kept dabbing until there wasn't a trace of the wounds.

Finally, she turned her attention to me. Dad had tears in his eyes as he watched my wound heal to a pink scar. As soon as Okaasan finished with me, he pulled her toward him.

"I'm sorry, Misako," he said. "I was overwhelmed, I still am, but … I'm just in awe of you. I always knew you were someone special, I just … please, let me into yours and Junya's life."

"Oh Robert, I'm so sorry…"

After they finished hugging and kissing and basically grossing me out, Dad gave me big hug. The first one we'd had in a long time.

When he finally let go, he wiped a sleeve across his face. "I'm so glad you're okay." he said quietly. "It's going to be hard getting used to this."

"I'm hoping this is the last time."

"I hope so too." Then he turned to Shoko. "Thank you for looking after Junya. It makes me feel better knowing you were with him."

She bowed. "You are welcome, sir."

Mom took Shoko away to fix her up and dad carried the unused first aid kits away, leaving me alone with Mack. We walked to the sofa and sank into the soft cushions. I let out a deep sigh. It was good to relax.

"Me too," he said after we'd sat there a while.

I looked at him. "Huh?"

"I'm glad you're okay too," he said with a serious expression on his face. "But do you honestly think this is over?"

"You mean with me, or the fight against the Evil Ones?"

Mack took a while to answer. "I think you can get out if you want to," he said. "With Bartholomew dead, you lost your personal 'mortal enemy'." He emphasized that with air quotes. "But all those Evil Ones are still out there, maybe leaderless, and Shoko and the Gatekeepers will still need to defend Izumo."

I nodded. "I'm starting to wonder if we even made a difference. Besides killing Bartholomew, what did we really change?"

"You saved some shamans. That counts a lot." He started to say something then just sat there looking thoughtful.

"What?"

"I've been thinking a lot about those Druids, you know? They said I should seek out my heritage, and I'm curious. They're still fighting the Evil Ones. Maybe I have a place in that." He looked a bit embarrassed. "I didn't tell you, but I've been talking to that William McLeod guy, in Scotland. He keeps saying I should come . . ."

That surprised me. "That's really cool, Mack. You gonna go?"

He snorted. "Like I can afford to. I'm struggling just to build my college fund."

I smiled at him. "You're going bro. I'll pay."

"I'm not taking your money," he said. "I don't think it's good for our friendship if I owe you."

I thought about that for a minute then stood up. "You want a cola?"

He nodded and followed me to the kitchen. I tossed him a pop and grabbed one for myself. After he took a sip, I said, "It's just like that."

He swallowed then looked at me. "What?"

"You want a pop and I've got a lot of it." I said. "More that I could ever drink myself." I leaned against the counter. "You've been with me through everything—especially all this crap. And you've never failed me, never once resented me because of my grandpa, never changed when everyone else did. You deserve something good and there's nothing that would make me happier than to help you do this."

He took another chug and I swear his eyes were a little glassy. "I dunno …"

"We can plan it together if you want."

"I'd be stupid to say no, right?"

"You'd be brilliant to say yes."

We walked back into the living room to find Dad and Okaasan talking quietly. Shoko stood by the window, looking out at the Zen garden. Her ripped and blood-stained clothes were gone, replaced by one of Okaasan's kimonos. She looked beautiful, and I walked over and told her so.

She smiled, the first good one I'd seen in a while. "Thank you."

"Now that you look presentable, you two should go tell the Elders," Okaasan said. "It might help if Junya is with you."

I turned to Shoko and her expression confirmed what I already knew.

"I shouldn't go there right now."

Okaasan seemed disappointed. "Well, let's have dinner together before she has to go. Bartholomew is gone. You're both safe. That's worth celebrating."

Mack followed her into the kitchen. "I'll help, Mrs. T."

After they left the room, I reached to take Shoko in my arms and she let me, neither accepting nor resisting.

"Your first dinner here," I said. "It's about time, huh?"

When she didn't respond, I gently lifted her chin. "Are you okay?" I searched her eyes.

"It has been wearisome, these past few weeks," she said, pulling away now. "We need to talk."

I waved a hand. "Why don't we just relax on the sofa? Or, we could go to my room—"

"I said we needed to *talk*." She looked quite serious. "But not here."

I studied her face. "We can figure stuff out later, Shoko. It's been a crazy day."

"Please, Junya, it must be now."

"Oh … okay." I popped my head into the kitchen. "We'll be back in a bit, okay?"

Okaasan nodded. "Take your time. Dinner won't be ready for a while."

I walked back to Shoko. "So, where to?"

She held out her hand. "I believe I have enough energy to travel now."

CHAPTER
42

WE COULD'VE GONE ANYWHERE I suppose, but Shoko traveled us to the park bench near Grandpa's house where she and I had first met, all those months ago. It was dark now, the sky overcast, with the only light coming from the old-fashioned streetlamps. We sat down on the bench, side by side, but for some reason the distance felt immeasurable.

"I remember when I first saw you there." She pointed at Grandpa's carriage house. "You were not much to look at."

I laughed. "Gee, thanks!"

She smiled, still looking across the street. "You have changed into a powerful man since then."

"Yeah, I guess." I glanced at her. "We've both changed a lot."

"Yes … in many ways." She looked around. "I like it here."

"Do you mean *here*?" I pointed at the ground. "… or this world in general?"

"Here, where I first saw you, and awakened you."

"So … that's why you wanted to come here?"

She nodded. "This is the most appropriate place to say good-bye."

I looked at her. "We can say good-bye after dinner."

"That is not what I mean."

My stomach tightened. "We'll still find a way to be together, Shoko." I was trying to reassure myself as much as her. "After the Elders hear about this, I guarantee they'll let us cross."

"That does not matter," she said. "Whatever existed between us is dead."

"I ... what do you mean?"

"The feelings I had for you are gone."

I felt like I was drowning. I couldn't breathe. "What ... why?" My voice shook and my chest started to hurt. "I mean ... you're kidding, right?"

She didn't react, just shifted her gaze to her feet.

"Love isn't ... something that just dies."

"Do you think I decided this today?" she said in a quiet voice. "My life and world have changed, and I have a long and trying path ahead of me. You cannot be part of that."

"You don't have to punish yourself," I said, beginning to feel desperate. "Even the Grand Elder doesn't think you need to. I love you and I want to be with you."

"As your girlfriend?"

I nodded.

"You would wish for us to make love every day and I will cook your breakfast? Perhaps we can walk arm in arm down the street, like *normal* people?"

"You say that like it's impossible. That *is* what our life could be like, you know."

She let out a sigh. "Do you remember when I said love makes us weak?"

I nodded. How could I forget?

"When I first said it, I did not truly understand," she said. "But I have learned that love is an amazingly powerful thing. I now believe that when the Elders of old forbid us to have relations with boys, it was not just because of pregnancy. It is because love consumes us and distracts us. Our thoughts are on the one we love instead of our duties, and that can kill us … or others."

I tried to interrupt, but she held up a hand.

"I loved you before we had sex, but I could still maintain my responsibilities without distractions," she said. "And I did not have sex because I loved you. I was curious. What was this thing my body craved to do?" She smiled. "But I did not expect how it would change me inside. My heart became so close to yours. I had this … this fountain of joy inside me I could not harness. When we lay together, when we talked and walked and laughed together, it was always wonderful. And through the intensity of our passion, I received the gift of my senses, which made this place, with you, all the more wonderful. I did not want to ever lose you."

"So why can't we be together?"

She closed her eyes. "After all our time together, you still do not understand me."

"You just spent the last five minutes telling me how great we are together." That desperate feeling was getting worse, ripping through me and leaving nothing behind.

"Do you even know what is most important to me?" she said.

I hesitated.

"It is duty, Junya. Duty before anything else." Her disappointment was clear in her tone. "And I grossly neglected my duty. Do you not understand? I lost my way!"

She started to cry and I slid over and held her.

"I prepared all my life to be a leader," she said between sobs. "I faced that ogre and never looked back. I had more at sixteen than most Gatekeepers will ever achieve in a lifetime." Her body shuddered as she sobbed harder. "And I squandered it, along with dozens of young lives. If it were not another great dishonor to add to my growing list, I would kill myself!"

I nearly fell off the bench. "Are you serious?"

She pulled away. "Instead I will start again, at the very bottom, and if the gods and Elders allow it, I will work my way back up. But this time I will be faithful and unwavering in my devotion to the gods."

"But no one's asking you to give everything up and start again," I said. "You told me you're the greatest Gatekeeper since my Okaasan. The Elders need you. Everything will be back to normal in no time, you'll see. You don't need to give up your life."

She wiped her nose and looked at me with curiosity. "Are you concerned about me, or do you hold hope that we will be together again, like Edward longed for Tomi?"

"Tomi regretted leaving him every day of her life!" I realized I was shouting. "And now you're doing the same thing, for nothing!"

"You consider dozens of dead Gatekeepers and civilians nothing?"

"Leaving me won't bring them back!" I glared at her. "You can sacrifice yourself, but do you think anyone will give a shit?" I grabbed my head, trying to maintain control. "Think of yourself, your future!"

"It is time to begin thinking about others instead of myself."

I jumped to my feet, astonishment quickly giving way to anger. "That's the stupidest thing I've ever heard!"

"Is it?" Her eyes narrowed. "To me, there is no greater achievement."

"We killed Bartholomew! What more can you possibly do?"

She stood up. "It is time for me to go ... Thank you for all you did for Izumo, and for me."

I grabbed her arm. "If you do this, I'll come there and—"

"And what?" She shoved my hand away. "Rescue me from my *terrible* circumstances? Well, you cannot because I have asked the Grand Elder to ban you from Izumo forever! If you come, you will be sent back, or ..."

My anger dropped through my stomach. "You ... how could you do that?"

"The only power I have left in Izumo is the love of my great-grandfather—the Grand Elder. I begged him to make a decree, revoking your access to my side."

I tried to catch my breath as her words sunk in. She'd cut ties to everything with determination and unwavering decisiveness, two of the very qualities I loved most about her.

"Please, Junya." Her bottom lip began to quiver. "I cannot do this anymore … it hurts too much."

My anger was almost gone, replaced by a deep pain.

"Don't do this to yourself … to us … to me."

"Please, just let me go."

"What about my evil energy?" I was practically pleading now. "Who's going to keep me from going bad?"

She offered the faintest smile. "You will."

I stared at her. "So, this is it?"

She nodded as she backed away, watching me as if she was afraid I might try to grab her.

"Goodbye, Junya."

And then she walked away, across the circular lawn of the Crescent and down the hill, looking straight ahead, never back, and though I watched until she disappeared and listened with all my strength, I never felt her travel away. Maybe it was better that way, to watch her fade into the distance without a hint of magic.

She was just an ordinary girl walking away from a boy.

GLOSSARY OF JAPANESE WORDS

- Bokuto - The bokutō 木刀 is a Japanese wooden sword used for training. It is usually the size and shape of a *katana*, but is sometimes shaped like other swords, such as the *wakizashi* and *tantō*. Sometimes called A *bokken* (木 剣 , *bok(u)*, "wood", and *ken*, "sword") in the west.

- Iaijutsu (居合術), a combative quick-draw sword techniques. This art of drawing the Japanese sword, katana, is one of the Japanese *koryū* martial art disciplines in the education of the classical warrior (bushi)

- Izumo - Izumo-taisha (出雲大社 *Izumo Grand Shrine*, also Izumo Ōyashiro) is one of the most ancient and important Shinto shrines in Japan.

- Kannushi (神主 *god master*, originally pronounced *kamunushi*), also called shinshoku (神 職) *kannushi* were intermediaries between *kami* and could transmit their will to common humans. A *kannushi* was a man capable of miracles or a holy man who, because of his practice of purificatory rites, was capable to work as a medium for a *kami*, but later the term evolved to being synonymous with *shinshoku*, that is, a man who works at a shrine and holds religious ceremonies there.

- Katana - Historically, katana (刀) were one of the traditionally made Japanese swords (日 本 刀 *nihontō)* that were worn by the samurai class of feudal Japan, also commonly referred to as a "samurai sword".

- Kenjutsu or Kendo - Kenjutsu (剣術) is the umbrella term for all (*koryū*) schools of Japanese swordsmanship, in particular those that predate the Meiji Restoration. The modern styles of kendo and iaido that were established the 20th century included modern form of kenjutsu in their curriculum too. Kenjutsu, which originated with the samurai class of feudal Japan, means "the method, or technique, of the sword." This is opposed to kendo, which means "the way of the sword".

- Kunoichi (Japanese: (く ノ 一) is a modern term for a female ninja or practitioner of ninjutsu (ninpo). The most accepted interpretation amongst the Japanese of Kunoichi is: *ku* (く) meaning "nine"; *no* (ノ) meaning "plus" and *ichi* (一) meaning "one". "Nine-plus-One" is supposedly referring to orifices in the human body. Males have nine while females have one extra.

- Matsue, Japan - Matsue (松江市 *Matsue-shi*) is a city in Japan, located in Shimane Prefecture of the Chūgoku region of the main island of Honshu. It is the capital city of Shimane Prefecture.

- Miko - A miko (巫女) is a Shinto term in Japan, indicating a shrine (jinja) maiden or a supplementary priestess who was once likely seen as a shaman but in modern Japanese culture is understood to be an institutionalized role in daily shrine life, trained to perform tasks, ranging from sacred cleansing to performing the Kagura, a sacred dance.

- Ninja or shinobi - A *ninja* (忍者) or *shinobi* (忍び) was a covert agent or mercenary in feudal Japan. The functions of the ninja included espionage, sabotage, infiltration, and assassination, and open combat in certain situations. Their covert methods of waging war contrasted the ninja with the samurai, who observed strict rules about honor and combat. The *shinobi* proper, a specially trained group of spies and mercenaries, appeared in the Sengoku or "warring states" period, in the 15th century, but antecedents may have existed in the 14th century, and possibly even in the 12th century (Heian or early Kamakura era).

- Okaasan - *Mother* (おかあさん *Okaasan)*

- Shimane Prefecture, Japan - Shimane Prefecture (島根県 *Shimane-ken)* is a prefecture of Japan located in the Chūgoku region on the main Honshu Island. The capital is Matsue. It is the second least populous prefecture in Japan, after its eastern neighbor Tottori. The prefecture has an area elongated from east to west facing the Chūgoku Mountain Range on the south side and to the Sea of Japan on the north side. It is divided into the Izumo Region in the East, the Iwami Region in the West and the Oki Region, a small group of islands off the northern coast. Most of the cities are near the shoreline of the Sea of Japan. Izumo Taisha in Izumo City is one of the oldest Shinto shrines in Japan.

- Wakizashi - The wakizashi (Kanji: 脇差 Hiragana: わきざし) meaning "side inserted sword" is one of the traditionally made Japanese swords worn by the samurai class in feudal Japan.

(Explanations from Wikipedia)

ABOUT THE AUTHOR

C.R. Fladmark lives in a small historic town in the Pacific Northwest and travels often to Japan where he researches his novels among the ancient sites in Shimane Prefecture. To learn more, visit www.crfladmark.com or find him on Facebook at www.facebook.com/crfladmark